“Entertaining [illegible] d
satisfies you o [illegible]



*Author of Mental Eye-roglyphics*

"Dejohn is a brand new kind of writer. He doesn't bore you with dumb trimmings. He takes you right to the good stuff."

Alexy F.
*Entertainer*

"The Return of SF is crazy action packed fun. When I read it, it was like watching a great action movie."

Troy Simms
*Actor*

"If you like Scarface, you'll love The Return of SF."

Jeff C.
*Diehard Scarface fan*

"The last one hundred pages contains more action than any book I've ever read. Dejohn keep on writing bro'."

Radical-One
*Rapper*

"THE Return OF SF is a thriller, romance, mystery type of book. But simply put it is a masterpiece."

Jan Thomas
*Suspense writer*

"The best book I've read in over ten years. Dejohn is a great storyteller."

Genevieve Watson
*Activist*

"After you've read THE RETURN OF SF tell a friend about it. They will owe you big time."

Jose Soto
*Current Books Review Newsletter*

"This book is everything I heard about and more. It's a masterpiece. Thank you Dejohn."

Tom Brown
*Librarian*

"The action makes The Return OF SF a great book. And when you add the hot romances it takes the story to the Epic level."

Cindy E.
*Freelance Romance Writer*

# The Return
# Of
# SF

---

**A Novel**
**By Dejohn**

**Published by**

***Dejohn Enterprises***

*Designed by*

SunRASon **Production** Company

**Visit us online at**

**WWW.SUNRASON.COM**

**WWW.THERETURNOFSF.COM**

*Published by*

***Dejohn Enterprises***

P.O. Box 2058
Peekskill, NY 10566
**Email Feedback to: dejohnenterprise@aol.com**
**www.dejohnenterprises.com**

*Consultation & Design By*

*SunRASon Prod. Co.*

*P.O. Box 2020*
*Canal St. Station*
*New York, NY 10013*
*Ph.: (718) 444-7464*
**WWW.SUNRASON.COM**
***Email: info@sunrason.com***


*Design and layout by Tehut-Nine & Heru Ptah*
*Cover Design by Tehut-Nine*
*Cover Art by Leslie Boamah*



*ISBN: **0-9677644-8-3***

*Published 2003.*

*Printed in the United States of America*

# Chapter 1

It was Wednesday afternoon and the twins had just gotten out of school for the day. As usual they went to Carmen and Gabrielle's house. Wednesday was the only day that the twins didn't have soccer practice. But more importantly the sisters' parents were never home on that day. They both had late shifts on Wednesday nights, the father worked as a cook and the mother worked in a factory. If the nuns ever found out that the boys were alone with the girls instead of soccer practice, they would be punished severely. But this routine had been going on for the past three months and there were no signs of them getting caught.

Carmen was Alejandro's girlfriend. She was Alejandro's height, but was about 10 pounds heavier. The fifteen-year old girl had bright red curly hair that she loved to twirl with her fingers. Carmen was quite loud and often flirted with boys and sometimes even grown men. Folks often marveled about her because she had a baby face and the body of a woman. It was this combination that Alejandro found irresistible and he vowed that Carmen would be his first sexual partner.

Four-weeks later, Carmen and Alejandro had sex for the first time, Alejandro was a virgin. It was a great experience for Alejandro and sex was something that he enjoyed doing-a lot. In a short time, Alejandro had become quite the ladies man and Carmen became one of many that Alejandro was seeing in that way.

Alejandro wasn't Carmen's only boyfriend either. She was deeply involved with Mario, a twenty-seven year old policeman. Mario was also married.

Gabrielle was a thin girl with long jet-black hair that went down to her waist. She had Bambi brown eyes and was thirteen years old-just like the twins. Unlike her sister, Gabrielle was very quiet and shy. The only time Gabrielle became talkative was around Roberto. He made her laugh a lot and she treasured his company. In the three months that Roberto had been coming to the house, they had only kissed twice. The first time was just last week. She was at first afraid to talk to Roberto because her mother always told her that boys just wanted to use girls for sex. According to their mother, sex was a great sin if you did it without being married.

That never stopped Carmen from doing it. In fact Carmen and Alejandro had sex in her parent's bedroom every Wednesday. They would coax Gabrielle and Roberto into going outside to play and then go at it.

Sometimes Gabriel and Roberto would play tag or hide and seek. Other times they would sit on a pile of rocks and just talk. They spoke about what it must feel like to be rich and the different things they would buy for their families and each other. At first, Roberto didn't like Gabrielle, but the more time he spent around her, the more he missed her when she wasn't around. He could talk to her about anything, even things he couldn't discuss with his brother. When Gabrielle was with him, he didn't have to be concerned about being macho like he did with his brother. Roberto knew, even at thirteen, that he had found someone very special and he didn't want to ever let her go.

*****

"There he is," the angry leader growled. "Let's get him!"

Before Roberto could react, he found himself surrounded by three of the toughest teens in the neighborhood. At first Roberto thought about trying to out run them, but then he realized that would have been useless. He had just spent the past four hours playing soccer in the blazing Cuban heat.

"Maybe, I can reason with them," he thought. It was not like he had any other options left.

"I don't have a problem with you," Roberto said gently. "Why are you bothering me?"

"Well, we have a problem with you!" the leader shouted. "We are tired of you and your brother acting like you are better than us."

"Yeah," another agreed. "The nuns give you everything you want. You get good clothes and eat three times a day when we're lucky to eat once."

"And another thing," the leader continued. "Just cause you speak English, doesn't mean you're better than us."

"All of this is stupid," Roberto voiced boldly. "We don't think we're better than you."

"You better not," a short stocky boy grunted. "We've got something for your ass."

"First of all, the clothes my brother and I wear are nothing but hand-me downs." Roberto explained. "And even though we do eat three times a day, we work for every meal we get. Everyday at five o'clock in the morning, we do chores around the house and on the farm. I eat breakfast at around seven."

Roberto could feel himself becoming more nervous as he tried to convince his adversaries of his point of view. In a last attempt to win them over, Roberto chirped, "And if any of you want a good meal, you're welcome to come to our house anytime."

Some of the angry expressions changed after Roberto extended a friendly invitation to them. However, one of the boys was anxious to see a fight and wouldn't settle for anything less.

"Well, we still don't like you," the tallest teen replied. "And today we will get our revenge."

Roberto braced himself for the hardest fight of his life. Out of the corner of his eye, he saw a punch coming to his face but it was too late to react. It caught him square on the lip and blood squirted everywhere. As he tried to recover, the tallest kid took a swing. Roberto quickly took two steps backwards and slightly bobbed his head. The boy missed him by an inch. Roberto responded with a blow that sent the tall kid retreating. He then perfectly positioned himself to throw another jab when the leader of the group tackled him to the ground.

Roberto didn't know whether he hit the hard pavement first and then felt the kicks from the gang members or if everything happened in reverse. On one hand it all seemed to happen quickly but on the other hand the scene appeared to be going in slow motion. Roberto could feel the anger mounting with each hit he absorbed. His legs, chest, and stomach were throbbing with pain. It was as if the three teens were playing soccer and he was the ball. After what seemed like forever, Roberto heard a loud cry in the distance.

Alejandro had just come from playing a sport of his own-girls. As he walked down the hill, he noticed three local bullies preying on another victim. To his surprise, he realized that the target of the group's wrath was Roberto. Without warning, Alejandro flew into a blind rage and charged towards the group wildly swinging his hands and feet.

First, Alejandro kicked the shortest boy in the center of his back. He then wheeled himself around and punched the tallest kid in the throat. Both of the injured boys fell to the ground. Next, Alejandro faced the leader of the pack. By now, the boy had concluded that he was no match for Alejandro and was ready to declare defeat. Alejandro's adrenaline was pumping so strongly that he failed to hear the boy's apology and was only focused on beating him to a pulp. He picked up a branch that had fallen from a nearby oak tree and swung it at the boy with all of his might. Just as the boy raised his hands in a futile attempt to protect himself, the powerful blow came crashing down on the boy's shoulder blade.

For a normal person that would have surely been enough, but not for Alejandro. With the next several blows, he tried to break the boy's legs, then every rib. It was as if a master surgeon was performing some sick operation. Alejandro decided that one more blow to the head would be enough but then someone yelled.

"Alejandro, what did you do?" yelled Roberto.

"I beat the living shit out this guy, that's what I did!"

"Oh God, I think you really hurt him!"

"So what?" Alejandro snapped. "They were trying to hurt you."

"That doesn't make it right," Roberto said tearfully. "Alejandro thanks for saving my butt, but let's go home. I'm not feeling too good."

The boys picked up their books and headed home, leaving the bloodied teen alone once more in the all too familiar mean streets of Cuba.

*****

"Hello, I am Constable Alvarez and I'm looking for Sister Catherine."

Law officials always contacted Sister Catherine when any of the children got into trouble. She was the head Nun and had run the facility for the past twelve years. They saw Sister Catherine as a strict disciplinarian who commanded respect, but her bark was often bigger than her bite. Sister Catherine's life revolved around the children's home and she couldn't imagine doing anything else with her days. There seemed to be an endless supply of children that required her assistance and her only regret was the lack of funding that prevented the home from taking in more little ones. The Cuban government provided almost no assistance and as far as the U.S. Government was concerned, Cuba didn't even exist, since America had no diplomatic ties with them. Sister Catherine descended from the upstairs room when she heard his voice.

"Mr. Alvarez, what brings you to this side of town?" Sister Catherine asked urgently. "I hope it is not bad news,"

"It's about the twins."

"Have they been picking apples from the neighbors backyard again? If they have, I will definitely speak to them when they get in."

"I wish it were that simple" Alvarez sighed. "It seems that the twins got into a fight with some boys near the park."

Sister Catherine held her breath to prepare herself for the remainder of Constable Alvarez's story.

"One of the boys who was fighting yesterday is still in a coma."

“One of the boys who was fighting yesterday is still in a coma.”

“Are you sure the twins were involved in this?”

“Yes, we are very sure.” Alvarez explained. “We have a few eyewitnesses and one even says he saw one of the twins beat the boy with a lead pipe.”

“Well, I wouldn’t jump to any conclusions until I heard their side of the story,” Sister Catherine insisted. “This just doesn’t sound like them, especially Roberto.”

“I agree with you. That’s why I want to talk to them to find out their version of yesterday’s events.”

A dead silence covered the room.

“Sister Catherine, I’ll be honest with you. Things really don’t look good. Before I leave here tonight, I need to find out which of your boys put that kid into the hospital. It isn’t fair for both of the boys to be punished.”

“Punished?” Sister Catherine cried. Tears streamed down her face. The thought of losing either of the boys was almost too painful for her to hear.

“Sister Catherine, I’ve known you for over ten years; I get no pleasure from doing this.” Alvarez’s said in a shaking voice.“Personally, I think you do a find job with these kids, but on occasion, one is bound to turn out bad.”

“Well Mr. Alvarez the boys are not here right now and I am not expecting them for at least another twenty minutes.”

“Under normal circumstances, I would return at a later time, but right now I better wait for them.”

Sister Catherine escorted Constable Alvarez to the living room. After placing his briefcase securely under the large mahogany coffee table, Constable Alvarez sat uncomfortably on the couch. Sister Catherine let her body fall back into an overstuffed armchair. As the minutes passed, they both became more anxious. Sister Catherine held onto the cross that was draped around her neck as she prayed quietly. “Dear God, please let there be a good explanation for all of this. When the boys come home, let them convince Constable Alvarez that this was all a big mistake.”

*****

At five o'clock, the twins ran up the hill returning from soccer practice. As they approached the house, they became alarmed when they spotted the police car in front of the house.

"Something isn't right," Alejandro whispered.

"How do you know?" Roberto nervously replied.

"Just call it instincts." Alejandro's instincts were almost always right on target.

"Hello boys come on in," Constable Alvarez called out from the front window in a stern voice. The boys reluctantly entered the house and waited for the roof to cave in. Sister Catherine looked worried but her voice was extremely calm.

"Boys this is Constable Alvarez from Headquarters; he's just here to ask you a few questions. Yesterday there was an incident near the school yard and a young boy was seriously injured."

The twins, firmly planted in the hallway, shook their head in agreement as they were forced to relive the terrible incident that had happened the day before.

"I told the Constable that you could not have been involved, but that if you knew who was involved, you would help him as much as possible."

"Which one of you boys is Roberto?" Alvarez interrupted.

"I am."

"I heard the boys really worked you over. Is that true?"

Roberto looked at Alejandro for assistance but there was none. He began moving his mouth but he was at a lost for words.

"Were you around the park yesterday about four thirty?"

"Yes I was there," Roberto finally answered. "I was alone, though."

"Look Roberto, I need a straight answer. Did you have anything to do with what happened yesterday?"

"Yes," Roberto voiced in a wavering tone. "It was all my fault, I did it!"

"No Roberto, stop lying it was all my fault," Alejandro interrupted.

Sister Catherine's face was overcome by grief. She couldn't believe what she was hearing. One of her worst nightmares was becoming a reality. Her greatest fear was that she would lose one of her kids to the harsh streets. Sister Catherine was also greatly disappointed because she always believed that if any of the children had a chance to make it in this tough world it would be

Alejandro and Roberto-they were extremely smart and looked out for each other. It was her belief in their success that caused her to be harder on them than any of the other kids. "What will happen to my beautiful boys?" Sister Catherine wondered.

"If you are going to tell the story, tell them everything." Alejandro explained. "Roberto was walking back from soccer practice when three boys jumped him. They punched and kicked him all over his body."

Roberto was beginning to feel relieved; Alejandro was once again coming to his rescue.

"You can still see the marks on his face, that should prove what happened," Alejandro continued. "Well, I showed up a few minutes after they began attacking Roberto and tried to break everything up. Those three guys are always jumping other kids in the neighborhood. Just ask one of those punks, I'm sure they'll tell you what happened."

"That's exactly my problem. We have only been able to talk to one of the boys, since we haven't been able to locate the second one."

"What about the third kid?"

"He is in a coma right now and things aren't looking good for him," Alvarez stated sadly. He then stood upright as if to remind himself about the reason for his visit. "Boys, which one of you beat him with a lead pipe?"

"Neither one of us did," Alejandro replied.

"Well, one of you better come clean," Alvarez grunted sternly. "We're determined to get down to the bottom of this matter."

Alejandro and Roberto remained silent as they stood bravely in their respective positions. Constable Alvarez figured the two boys needed time to think about the consequences of their actions, so he decided to give them a few days to clear their heads.

"You will definitely be hearing from me in the near future, do you understand that?" The two boys nodded in agreement.

"Sister, I am sorry that I had to come here with such bad news but I promise you that the boys will be treated fairly no matter what comes of this."

After Constable Alvarez left, a dark gloom overshadowed the brightly-lit house. Sister Catherine and the twins stood still consumed in their own private thoughts. Sister Catherine believed that this incident would put the boys in danger and thought of ways she could help them. Roberto was confident that once the police got all of the facts, they would realize it was self-defense and this whole ordeal would soon be behind them. Alejandro concluded that no matter what happened, he would never depart from his only family member, Roberto.

*****

Unable to sleep that night, Sister Catherine decided to talk to the Captain of the police department. In her opinion, the whole incident was being blown way out of proportion. She hoped that once she sat down with the Captain to explain that the boys were just trying to protect themselves from harm, he would certainly understand and allow the boys to go on with their lives. "As punishment, I'll even tell him that I'll force the boys to stay inside for the entire summer," Sister Catherine mumbled.

As she got into her old blue van, Sister Catherine knew the task before her wouldn't be easy, but she had to make a case on the boy's behalf. "Even the most stubborn people can be reasoned with," Sister Catherine thought. "I'll get through to the captain, I have no choice."

"Sister Catherine, what brings you to Police Headquarter?" Constable Alvarez asked.

"I am here to talk to the Captain about the case involving my twins. Is he in?"

"Sister, the Captain is a very buys man. He only takes people by appointment."

"I know Constable, but this is important."

At first, Alvarez intended to escort Sister Catherine to the door, but when he looked into her tearful eyes, he could not deny her request. "Okay Sister, I can't make any promises but I'll tell him that you are here."

"Thank you so very much." Sister Catherine cried. "May God continue to bless you."

Mr. Alvarez walked swiftly into the Captain's office. Sister Catherine heard mumbling but was unable to make out the words.

When Alvarez returned, he motioned her to a nearby room. It was scarcely furnished and Sister Catherine remained standing to avoid soiling her coat. It was clear that the room hadn't been cleaned in years. Moments later, the Captain entered, closing the door behind him.

"Sister Catherine please sit down." With both arms outstretched the Captain motioned to the chair in front of the desk. Sister Catherine reluctantly complied.

"Sister, I am going to get right to the point. What we have here is very serious, I have all kinds of superiors very upset about this and they were even in an uproar when I told them how your boys were involved in this situation."

"I know, but..." Sister Catherine stammered.

"You do a find job for the people in the village and they highly respect you." Suddenly the Captain shifted gears to appeal to Sister Catherine's religious sentiments. "For God's sake, you must convince the boys to tell us which one is responsible for putting the boy in a coma."

"I asked that question before they went to bed last night and they didn't tell me any more information than they told Constable Alvarez."

"Well that's too bad because if they won't tell us which one, we will have to take both of the boys from your home."

"I don't understand. What exactly do you mean Captain?"

"The bottom line is, whomever was responsible will have to be taken out of your home and put in the House of Detention for Wayward Youths,' the Captain uttered bluntly. "If the boys won't cooperate, they both go."

"Captain, let's be rational about this," Sister Catherine said calmly. "Regardless of which boy struck the kid in the hospital, you must believe he is not really a bad boy. It was in self-defense."

"That's their version of the story."

"Captain, neither of the boys could survive in a place like that. The twins are not street kids, they were brought up in a decent God-fearing home." Sister Catherine explained. "I have heard many bad things about that group home. Even if the boys could survive, they would become hardened criminals by the time they got out. Is there anything that I can do to prevent such a drastic measure?" Sister Catherine pleaded.

"I'm sorry, it's completely out of my hands. Sister, you have four days to find out which one is responsible," the Captain ordered. "If we still don't have a definitive answer by then, we'll take both of the boys and charge them with assault."

Sister Catherine gathered her strength and arose from the dusty chair. She brushed herself clean with her hands and buttoned her coat. It seemed that her effort to sway the Captain was useless.

"Good luck with your investigation," Sister Catherine struggled.

"And good luck to you Sister Catherine." The Captain began shuffling the papers that he brought in the office. "It may not look like it, but I really hope everything works out for you."

"So do I," Sister Catherine said softly. "So do I."

*****

"I wonder what the guys are doing now?" Gabrielle asked.

"They are probably still practicing that dumb soccer." Carmen complained. "That's where they spend most of their time."

"Soccer isn't dumb," Gabrielle argued. "In fact when Roberto makes it big, he's going to take me away from all of this." In that instant, Gabrielle jumped off the bed and began spinning around in a circle as she envisioned herself in a long wedding gown.

"Give me a break."

"You'll see, one day Roberto and I will be together forever."

"Gabrielle, you're such a dreamer." At this time, Carmen was transforming herself into one of the sex symbols she saw in the latest teen magazines. With her short skirt, high heels, and dramatized make-up, she was ready for her hot date.

"Carmen, where are you going looking like that?"

"I'm just going out for some fun. Don't worry, I'll be back before Mama gets home from work."

"If you want me to cover for you, tell me the truth," Gabrielle ordered.

"If not, I can always tell Papa that you wandered out by yourself looking like one of those tramps in the village."

Gabrielle was gleaming with a victorious smile on her face.

"Okay, okay I am just going downtown to see Mario. We're just going out to eat."

"Didn't you stop seeing him once you found out that he was married with three kids?"

"I did, but he says he wants to talk to me abut something very important," Carmen mouthed excitedly. "Maybe he is going to leave his wife for me."

"What abut Alejandro?"

"What about him? I like Alejandro very much and we have a lot of things in common. But Alejandro is still a boy,' Carmen insisted.

"I need a man. What could Alejandro possibly do for me now?"

"A lot more than a married man can do for you!"

"You still have a lot to learn about life, Gabrielle."

Carmen sprayed herself with perfume and then fanned it in the direction of her little sister. She gave Gabrielle a sly wink and dashed out of the door to see her married lover.

*****

It was Thursday afternoon and the twins had just come home from school. Ever since the incident, Sister Catherine told them they could not play soccer until everything was resolved. As the boys prepared to go upstairs to their room, Sister Catherine motioned them to join her in the living room.

"Boys I have never kept anything from you before and I don't plan to start now." Sister Catherine voiced wearily. "Earlier today I visited the Captain of police in an effort to save you boys from a terrible situation."

The boys could tell by Sister Catherine's face that a better solution had not been reached.

"After pleading with him, the Captain admitted that the matter was out of his hands and that there was nothing he could do."

"So what does that mean?"

"Well Roberto, whoever is responsible for putting the boy in a coma will be taken to the Detention Center for Wayward Youths."

"But that is not fair," Roberto debated. "They attacked us first, we didn't start anything."

"I know, I explained that very same thing to the Captain, but he said we must abide by the law. According to the law, one of you must be punished."

"Well nobody knows which one of us actually did this, so maybe it's best if we never tell." Alejandro suggested.

"That would not work. We have until Tuesday morning to tell him the truth. If we don't tell him by then, he will arrest you both."

"Sister Catherine, I did it," Roberto confessed.

"Not you, Roberto. I thought it must have been Alejandro," Sister Catherine shrieked.

"Sister, please don't believe him. I hit the kid over the head with the tree branch." Alejandro insisted. "I should be punished."

"No he didn't, it was me," Roberto charged.

"This is not getting us anywhere. I want both of you boys to go upstairs and think this whole thing over." Sister Catherine ordered.

"Listen to me good, I will not allow them to take both of you from me. So think about who really did this and tell me after dinner."

As sister Catherine watched the twins stumble up the steps, she knew the stubborn boys probably would continue to protect each other even after dinner. Although, she suspected that Alejandro was the real culprit and believed she could force him to take the blame, she wasn't convinced that was the best alternative. What if she was wrong? If Alejandro was taken away, Roberto would always hold her responsible for separating them and she couldn't live with that.

All of her life, Sister Catherine helped everyone else with their problems and had been quite skilled at coming up with answers. But now she was stumped. She knew there had to be a solution, but in God's name-what?

*****

Shortly after dinner, the twins drifted off to sleep in their bedrooms. Downstairs sister Catherine was dressed in street clothes trying to think of everything she would need for her late adventure.

"Sister Catherine, where are you going?" Sister Maria quizzed. "You shouldn't go anywhere alone at this hour."

Sister Maria was seventy years old and had been a member of the facility for nearly four decades. She lived in Cuba all of her life and had never even ventured outside of the tiny village where she grew up. Sister Maria distrusted the outside world and this anxiety only heightened her concern for Sister Catherine. She began nervously pacing the floor and wringing her hands. The thought of anything happening to Sister Catherine was overwhelming.

"Sister Catherine, please don't go out there."

"Don't worry, I'll be fine. I'm just going to get some help for the twins."

"It will be much safer in the morning. Can't this wait until then?"

"No, it really can't. You see sister, the person that I need to find is only around at night," Sister Catherine stated convincingly.

"Well, if you must go now, then take me with you," Sister Maria said as she raced over to the closet and began searching for her coat.

"I can't do that. I don't want to scare him off or cause too much attention by bringing someone else along."

"Sister Catherine, just what kind of business are you getting yourself into?"

Sister Catherine shrugged her shoulders and let out a sigh.

"Believe me, you don't want to know," she reluctantly responded.

"Just be very careful!" Sister Maria warned. "Be wary of everyone you meet."

Sister Catherine bent down and kissed the elderly woman on her wrinkled forehead. "I'll be just fine."

After driving for more than two hours, Sister Catherine was beginning to get discouraged. She had explored all the seedy bars in town and still Pedro Mendez was no where to be found. Sister Catherine believed he was the only person that could help her and the twins. He had connections in every part of Cuba imaginable. Whenever anyone needed the impossible, they would turn to Pedro Mendez. He dealt with guns, drugs, women, or anything of value that a person would spend good money to acquire.

Sister Catherine decided that "La Habituela" would be her last stop for the night. Once inside, she asked the bartender if he knew of a Pedro Mendez.

"I don't know him" he replied.

Sister Catherine looked him straight in his small bloodshot eyes and strongly believed that he was lying. This was exactly the type of joint Pedro Mendez would call home. Overcome by tiredness and despair, Sister Catherine plopped her purse on the counter and hoisted herself on the tall bar stool.

"May I buy you a drink?" a gruff voice asked. Sister Catherine twirled her chair around in the direction of the startling words. She found the sight of the drunken man nearly repulsive. Apparently, he hadn't groomed himself in at least a week and his stench was so strong it made her nauseous.

"No, I don't need a drink," Sister Catherine answered abruptly. "But, I do need to speak to Pedro Mendez."

"What kind of bizzness do ya have with him?"

"I'm here to discuss personal business with him. Do you know where I can reach him now?"

"I know where he is, but I can't discuss that with you in this place. Cum' wit me outside and I'll give you the scoop on Pedro."

"Outside!" Sister Catherine stammered. "Why do we have to leave here?"

"Look lady, do you want Pedro Mendez or not?"

"Yes, I definitely do,' Sister Catherine replied. "But can you at least tell me your name."

"Yeah, yeah, whatever. I'm Juan Martinez."

"I'm Sister Catherine."

"Sister?" Juan asked excitedly. "Oh this is going to be fun."

A weird sensation suddenly filled Sister Catherine's fingers and toes. Her heartbeat began to pick up speed. Sister Catherine didn't quite trust this stranger, but he seemed to be her only lead to Pedro Mendez. What other choice did she have?

Once outside the bar, Juan offered another excuse: "There are too many people on the streets, I just don't feel comfortable talking here. Ya know Pedro is a very secretive man. He'd be real upset with me if anyone overheard me talking to you about him. I have another idea."

Juan then assured Sister Catherine that his apartment would be a much better place to chat. "It's only around the corner from here,' Juan explained. "Then I'll be able to tell you everything you want to know about Pedro Mendez, I promise."

The two of them walked hurriedly down the dark street. As they approached a four-story building, Sister Catherine tried to carve a precise picture of the short rugged stranger in her brain. One of his legs appeared shorter than the other one, yet he seemed to get around surprisingly well. She also tried anxiously to get a sense of her surroundings but she couldn't see much because the street lamps in the area were all broken.

Ahead of them was a dimly lit corridor. They walked briskly down the hallway into the last residence. The paint on the walls was badly chipped and the apartment had a musty smell. Juan seemed somewhat uneasy as Sister Catherine closely watched his every move.

"Please have a seat, Sister."

Sister Catherine looked around trying to decide whether to take a seat on the dusty couch or on the edge of the bed. Neither seemed appealing, but there weren't too many choices in the tiny one-room space.

"I think I'll stand," Sister Catherine finally responded. "I don't plan to be here too long."

"Suit yourself," Juan shrugged as he walked over to the stack of boxes that were on the floor. He opened the top one and pulled out two cups. He then opened another and grabbed a bottle of red wine. With the glasses in one hand and the bottle in the other, he made his way to the stereo on the other side of the room. He placed the glasses on the top of the record player and filled each glass. He then pressed a few buttons, flicked a few switches, and Donna Summer's "Love to Love You Baby" filled the air.

"Excuse me Juan, but we've been here about ten minutes and you still haven't told me where I can find Mr. Mendez," Sister Catherine stated impatiently. "Do you know where he is or not?"

"Let me explain something to you. People contact Pedro through me, so unless you tell me what you want, I cant' help you," Pedro voiced nonchalantly. "Besides, what's our hurry?"

Sister Catherine was confused about what to do next. This man obviously didn't now how to get in contact with Mr. Mendez but now she was faced with trying to get out of his apartment without upsetting him too much. The alcohol was beginning to get the best of Juan and it became clear that he wanted the company of a woman and never intended to help her find Pedro Mendez.

"Juan I must be leaving now."

"But why, the fun didn't even start yet?" Juan asked with a devilish grin. As he moved closer to her, Sister Catherine cringed as she smelled the cheap liquor on his breath become more apparent.

"Juan, this has been along night for me, I can't stay another minute."

"You're not going anywhere," Juan insisted as he began playing with Sister Catherine's wavy hair. At first, he looked at her with what seemed to be admiration. Moments later, his feelings changed to pure lust.

"You know you really are a beautiful woman," Juan smiled sheepishly. "Has anyone ever told you that?"

"Well Juan, you know I'm a nun," Sister Catherine interrupted.

Juan immediately swung his arms and hands around Sister Catherine's waist. He then grabbed her close to him and began groping her buttocks through her trench coat.

"Oh shit! You are a fucking nun," Juan laughed. "It's been along time since I've had a virgin."

Sister Catherine struggled to release his grip but it was no use.

"I beg you," Sister Catherine cried. "Please don't do this!"

Unable to push him away from her, Juan tore open Sister Catherine's blouse and threw her on the bed. The middle-aged nun stood frozen with fear as she waited for the inevitable to happen next.

*****

"Roberto are you asleep?" Alejandro whispered.

"No I am wide awake. How long have you been up?"

"For about an hour. I was just lying here thinking everything over in my head. I have decided to tell the police that I was the one who hurt that kid."

"No Alejandro you can't do that. They will certainly separate us for sure." Roberto insisted.

"Aren't you afraid of that detention center? I hear it's pretty rough in there." Roberto asked in a worried tone.

"Don't worry about me, I can take care of myself. Between the two of us, I am a much better fighter than you are." Alejandro said proudly.

"Plus, they'll probably just make me spend the summer in that place, it'll be like going to camp or something. And remember it isn't that far away, you and Sister Catherine can visit me as often as you like."

"Well, you may be right Alejandro but let's talk about this in the morning."

"Good night Roberto."

"Good night Alejandro."

Neither one of the twins got much sleep that night. The thought of the two of them being separated was very discomforting. Each one realized that they needed the other more than they had ever imagined.

*****

Sister Catherine lay down helplessly on the bed as Juan nervously fumbled with the zipper of his pants. The faces of his numerous sex partners shifted through his head.

"Yeah, this will be the best pussy I've ever had," Juan boasted. Sister Catherine's purity wildly excited him. "You betta believe I'll do you right, Sis."

As he managed to pull loose the threads that were caught in his zipper, Juan let a sigh of relief. "Finally," he belted out loud. He then dropped his pants around his ankles and began stroking his semi hard penis.

Sister Catherine held her breath and tightly closed her eyes whispering a silent prayer. At that moment, Sister Catherine heard a loud noise. The front door burst open and a tall man in his early forties entered. He was wearing a black leather jacket with matching boots. His jet-black ponytail hung neatly past his shoulders and his nails were perfectly manicured.

When he realized what was taking place, a look of disgust crept across his face. Although, he took a few seconds to speak, his stance communicated the intensity of his anger. The temples on the sides of his head were throbbing and one of the veins in his neck pierced boldly through his skin.

"Juan, what the hell do you think you're doing?" he growled.

"Are you out of your fucking mind?"

A crazed Juan spun around flinging the knife he had snatched from under his mattress. He wondered who would try to interrupt his moment of passion, but when he recognized the face of the angry voice he dropped his weapon immediately. Even in his savage frenzy, Juan knew he was no match for Pedro Mendez.

"I am very sorry Mr. Mendez." Juan stammered as he pulled up his pants. "I had no idea it was you."

By this time, Sister Catherine had become so overwhelmed with fear that she nearly passed out. Her limbs were numb and her vision was fading to black until she heard the voice of her rescuer. When she realized her nightmare was about to come to an end, she snapped out of her daze and sprung to her feet. She then gathered up what was left of her blouse and covered herself.

"Mr. Mendez this is Sister Catherine. She has been looking for you the entire night," Juan offered in an attempt to change the subject.

"I know, I know, I have been very busy. The bartender around the corner told me that she left with you." Pedro Mendez mouthed in an annoyed voice.

"I knew she couldn't possibly be safe with you."

"It is not what you think. I guess I had too much to drink and we both got carried away."

"Shut up Juan! Enough with your lies, do you think I'm stupid?" Pedro grabbed Juan by the collar and lifted him above the ground. He then tossed Juan into the stereo system and watched the set-up crumble like a poorly stacked deck of cards.

"I know, I know, I have been very busy. The bartender around the corner told me that she left with you." Pedro Mendez mouthed in an annoyed voice.

"I knew she couldn't possibly be safe with you."

"It is not what you think. I guess I had too much to drink and we both got carried away."

"Shut up Juan! Enough with your lies, do you think I'm stupid?" Pedro grabbed Juan by the collar and lifted him above the ground. He then tossed Juan into the stereo system and watched the set-up crumble like a poorly stacked deck of cards.

"Sister, get yourself together and let's leave this place. The odor in here is enough to kill somebody."

Juan hoped that he'd felt the last of Pedro's wrath but he was wrong.

"You have exactly 24 hours to leave town," Mendez said calmly.

"If you're still around here by tomorrow, I'll be sure to introduce you to some friends of mine."

"Friends?"

"Yes, they'd be more than happy to take care of the guy who tried to rape a nun," Pedro winked. "Do you get me?"

Juan definitely understood that Pedro would have him killed if he stuck around. Although Juan didn't have a clue where he could relocate in only 24 hours, but he knew he had to move fast. Pedro Mendez always kept his word.

"I'll be gone by tomorrow," Juan voiced humbly. "I promise."

"Sister, please excuse Juan's behavior," Pedro expressed apologetically.

"Please know that whether he stays in this town or not, you've definitely seen the last of him."

*****

During the walk back to "La Habituela," Pedro attempted to find out the nature of Sister Catherine's visit. "What on earth would bring you to a place like this?"

"Mr. Mendez, I need help and they say you can almost do anything."

Yes, I can–if a person wants drugs, guns, or a twenty-five inch TV set. But what could I possibly get for a Nun?"

"Mr. Mendez it's not what you can get for me, it's more about what you can do for me."

As the two walked down the street, Sister Catherine told her tale from the very beginning, starting with how she had become the twin's legal guardian after their mother died in a car accident. An uncle was the only relative that she knew about, but he suffered from polio and was in no condition to raise two young boys. Some time ago, she'd heard that their father was still living in Miami, Florida but she didn't even know if the father knew the boys existed.

"Mr. Mendez, I need you the help me find their father,' Sister Catherine voiced quietly.

"I want to send them to Miami. That's the only way I know to keep them out of the detention center."

"Sister Catherine I don't know if this is enough information to go on, but I will try my best. Miami is a very large city and we don't even know if their father still lives there."

"I have faith in you. I know I am asking a lot but I would appreciate it if you can find this information out as quickly as possible," Sister Catherine pleaded.

"This is really urgent. If it wasn't I wouldn't be out here at this time of the night."

"Okay Sister I understand, but let me go over this one more time. Their father is named Alejandro Sanchez, right."

"That's right," she answered.

"As far as you know, Alejandro moved to Miami to be closer to his mother and younger sister." Mendez repeated.

"That's all that I now," Sister Catherine smiled.

"If anybody can find him, I know you can."

Sister Catherine hugged Mendez tightly before she hopped into her van. Mr. Mendez knocked on the window and whispered,

"Sister, do me a favor. Stay home, I have your address and as soon as I get the info, you'll be the first one to know about it."

With that, Mr. Mendez returned himself to the night. Now behind schedule, he knew he had to work faster to make up for lost time.

# Chapter 2

It was Saturday afternoon, Sister Catherine had just cleared off the dining room table, with the help of Sister Elise and Sister Anita. She was on her way upstairs when she heard a knock at the door.

"Hello Sister Catherine, how are you?" Constable Alvarez greeted. "I hope I did not catch you at a bad time."

"No, we've just finished having lunch. Would you care to have some?"

"No thank you. As you might have guessed, this isn't a social visit. Where are the boys?"

"In the backyard playing." Sister Catherine answered reluctantly. "Is there something wrong?"

"Are you sure the twins are back there?"

"Of course," Sister Catherine reassured. "Constable, is there another problem?"

"I am sorry that I've only been coming here with bad news but this is my job." He answered hesitantly.

"What is it?"

"Luis Cruz, the boy that was in the coma, died four hours ago. I didn't want to tell you the bad news over the phone, so I thought I would come over to you in person."

"Oh no, how could this have happened? I prayed for him day and night. May GOD bless his soul." Sister Catherine cried aloud.

"Now what?"

"The Captain wanted me to bring in the boy who did this in today so he could be charged with murder." The Constable looked down at the floor in search of better news.

"I told him that I promised that you had until Tuesday morning to bring in the guilty party, he said I could keep my word."

"How long do you think he would spend behind bars?" Sister Anita asked in a concerned tone.

"We are talking at least fifteen years," Constable Alvarez shook his head and kissed Sister Catherine on the cheek. "I must go now. The only thing I can tell you to do now is enjoy this last weekend that you and the boys have together."

After he left, Sister Catherine called in her assistant Sister Maria. She told her the bad news and asked her to gather all of the Nuns in the church for an emergency meeting.

"We have to do a lot of praying today," Sister Catherine ordered.

"There was a life that was lost and two other lives that we are desperately trying to save."

*****

"It can't be true. Fifteen years is such a long time," Roberto thought to himself in the kitchen. Apparently, Sister Catherine and Constable Alvarez were not alone when they discussed the boys' fate. Roberto came inside to get a glass of water when he overheard the entire conversation. He then darted back outside to share the terrible news with his brother.

"Alejandro! Alejandro!" Roberto called out.

"Yes Roberto, what is it?"

"Mr. Alvarez stopped by the house with some bad news."

"What did he want?" Alejandro asked impatiently.

"Luis died."

"Oh no," Alejandro cried. "What does that mean for us?"

"Well, Mr. Alvarez says they'd give one of us at least fifteen years."

"I can't do fifteen years," Alejandro insisted.

"What else can we do?" Roberto asked helplessly.

Alejandro stood still and watched the tears build-up in Roberto's eyes. Just as he was about to admit that they really had no choice, an idea popped into his head.

"Roberto," Alejandro comforted. "We could leave this place. You know, skip town."

"Alejandro, what are you saying?"

"I'm saying, we could run away."

"Run away?" Roberto asked in a confused voice. "Where would we go?"

"I don't know where we'd go, but we sure as hell can't stay here." Alejandro proclaimed.

"Alejandro, what about Sister Catherine and the rest of the nuns?"

"What about them?" Alejandro snapped. "We wouldn't be much good to them in jail, would we?"

"But, won't you miss them?"

"Of course, I will. I'll tell you what," Alejandro assured.

"As soon as we find a safe place we'll start making plans to see them again. Maybe, Sister Catherine can come live with us."

"Maybe," Roberto sadly responded. Now the tears that had been building up in his eyes were streaming down his face. He couldn't believe this was happening. He really enjoyed living with Sister Catherine and he knew he would miss her deeply.

"What about Carmen and Gabrielle?" Roberto asked. This question was one that he'd already answered in his heart. He knew he'd also be losing his best friend in a very short time.

"We'll say good bye to them," Alejandro replied. "Let's see if we can get away for a few minutes."

No adults were in sight. Sister Catherine had called all of the nuns inside the chapel for a special prayer meeting.

"Perfect," Alejandro whispered.

"Now is our chance."

The twins raced to Carmen and Gabrielle's house to bid them farewell.

"Alejandro, what are you two doing here?" Carmen asked.

"We came to say good bye."

"Good bye?" The girls asked.

"Yes Carmen, it seems we've gotten ourselves into some serious trouble and we have to leave town."

Gabrielle looked at Roberto in hopes that he would disprove Alejandro's story. As she studied Roberto's face, she knew Alejandro was telling the truth.

"No you can't go!" Gabrielle screamed.

"We have no choice, we have to go."

"If we stay, they are going to lock me up for a long time." Alejandro explained. "You see, I was the one who put that kid in the hospital and now he's dead."

"On the news they said they weren't sure who was responsible for the attack," Carmen explained. "What if neither one of you confess to it? Then what will they do?"

"They will lock both of us up and I can't see that happening to Roberto. This whole thing is my fault. If I didn't have such a bad temper, none of us would be in this predicament."

"Look Alejandro, you have to stop blaming yourself for what happened. It's nobody's fault. If you didn't come to help me out, I probably wouldn't be here right now."

"Roberto, why can't Alejandro go alone?"

"Gabrielle, you know I can't do that. Alejandro is my only family. We need each other."

"I can't let you leave now." Gabrielle insisted.

"Why not?"

"I have fallen in love with you Roberto and I don't want to see you go." Gabrielle sobbed as she collapsed into Roberto's arms.

"I have a solution," Carmen interjected.

"What is it?" Alejandro asked.

"Take us with you," Carmen said triumphantly. "That way, we'll all be together."

"You girls can't do that, what about school?" Roberto asked.

"There is nothing here for us that is important, we can go to school wherever we go," Carmen explained. "It's just that simple."

Gabrielle was now more worried than ever. She had never done anything to get her parents upset with her and although she know she would miss Roberto, she didn't know if she was ready to leave home. If she left with the boys, her parents would probably never forgive her. Was her newfound love worth being disowned by her parents?

"So Sis, what do you think of my idea?" Carmen asked excitedly.

With all eyes focusing on her, Gabrielle breathed in deeply and replied: "Sure, I want to go with you guys."

"Way to go Gabrielle!" Carmen cheered.

"I hope you gals realize that it's not going to be all fun and games. We have very little money and don't have a clue where we'll end up," Alejandro said frankly.

"That's okay, just as long as we're together, that's the only thing that really matters," Carmen voiced in a hushed tone.

"Okay, it's all settled. We will come here in two days at seven o'clock in the morning to pick you up. Bring only the things that you need. We don't want to be tied down by too much of your girl stuff," Alejandro ordered.

"Don't worry, we will be ready. Now come over here and give me a nice, long, wet, kiss," Carmen coaxed.

As the two wildly kissed, Roberto took Gabrielle's hand and gently placed it by his lips.

"Roberto, I hope everything turns out okay."

"Don't worry Gabrielle, I love you too and I won't ever let anything bad happen to you. You mean too much to me," Roberto promised.

Roberto then gently cupped Gabrielle's face in his hands and softly kissed her on the lips. He had seen a popular Mexican actor do this move in the movies.

"Roberto look what time it is. If Sister Catherine realizes that we're still outside, she'll kill us," Alejandro called out.

For the first time in his life, Roberto wasn't concerned about what would happen to him. He only wanted to stay with his Gabrielle.

"Roberto you better go, I'll see you later," Gabrielle whispered.

The boys began to run from the girls' house down the hill. Roberto looked back and waved at his special friend.

"Love you!" Roberto shouted.

"Love you more," Gabrielle responded. She blew Roberto a kiss and smiled when he pretended to catch it.

"I'll be waiting for you."

*****

"After sneaking off of the premises last night, you better believe we'll all be keeping our eyes on you two. Now that you've finished breakfast, clear off the table and do the dishes," Sister Catherine instructed. "That should keep you out of trouble for at least an hour."

While the twins were busy handling their chores, Sister Catherine thought it would be the perfect opportunity to prepare for Sunday morning services. During her brisk walk towards the church, Sister Catherine noticed the forming clouds. "I hope this isn't a sign of more bad things to come," she thought.

Suddenly, someone grabbed her from behind. Sister Catherine prepared to scream as the person covered her mouth.

"Relax," a soothing voice whispered. "It's me, Pedro Mendez."

"What are you doing here?"

"I told you as soon as I found out anything, I would let you know. Well, here I am."

"Mr. Mendez," Sister Catherine said as she let out a sigh of relief.

"What have you found out for me?"

"What's this Mr. Mendez stuff' Just call me Pedro." Mendez insisted as his friendly grin instantly switched to a frown.

"I am sorry to tell you that I have some very bad news for you."

"What is it?" Sister Catherine asked shivering.

"The boys father did move to Miami, but he was recently killed."

"Oh no," Sister Catherine gasped. She grabbed Mr. Mendez by the arm and looked to the heavens for a sign of what to do next. She tried to speak but was at a lost for words. In her mind, she believed finding the children's father was her only option.

"Sister, please don't look so sad. I didn't say that was the only news I had for you, did I?"

Sister Catherine, afraid to receive more disappointing news, braced herself for the new information. "What do you mean?"

"As I said, the father died but the children's grandmother is still alive and well. I even managed to get her address."

Tears began to swell in Sister Catherine's eyes. This was the miracle that she needed to save the boys. She held her hands open waiting for Pedro to give her the vital piece of paper. When he handed it to her, she held it close to her heart.

"Well sister, you got all of the info that you wanted so I better be going. You see, it's not good for me to be around a place like this. I may cause the whole place to come tumbling down." Pedro laughed.

"Mr. Mendez, please don't leave. I have another enormous favor to ask you."

"Let me guess."

"I need help in getting the boys to Miami," Sister Catherine interjected.

"They have to leave by tomorrow."

"I knew you were going to ask me to help you with that. So, I've already looked into that for you," Pedro smiled triumphantly. "But, it's going to cost you a lot of money."

"Don't worry Mr. Mendez. I'll give you everything I own if it means saving the boys."

Pedro Mendez handed Sister Catherine a business card of a cargo company, a dollar amount was scribbled on the back.

"Sister, have the boys and the money ready by tomorrow morning at eight o'clock," Mr. Mendez ordered. "This is the best I can do right now."

"Oh, Pedro, how can I ever thank you?" Sister Catherine asked tearfully.

"You don't know how much this means to me." Sister Catherine gripped Pedro's hand tightly and shook it graciously. She then looked to the heavens with a smile on her face and the reassurance that somehow God had made finding a solution possible.

*****

It was early Monday, the twins were in their rooms packing clothes and gathering momentous. By now, they were convinced that they were doing the right thing but they were still filled with a great deal of sadness. The place where they'd spent the last six years of their lives would soon become a distant memory and they knew how much they would miss all of the people that crossed their paths.

They would miss the sisters most of all. Each nun had their own personality and had taught them a great deal. Sister Maria was more like the grandmother they never had. Whenever Sister Catherine would put them on punishment, it was Sister Maria who slipped them cookies and milk or some of her homemade cake. Sister Anita taught them how to master their soccer game. Even Sister Elise, who at first didn't like them, grew to care about them. Roberto and Alejandro always felt lucky to grow up in the midst of the nuns, it was like living in a house with all of your favorite aunts.

"Alejandro I am really going to miss this place," Roberto cried.

"You aren't the only one," Alejandro said solemnly. "Let's just hurry up and finish packing."

"I am going as fast as I can but I'm still tired. A smile emerged on Roberto's face. "Alejandro what do you think the girls are doing right now. Do you think they're up?"

"No, they are probably still asleep. You know how it is with girls, they always wait until the last minute to get ready." Alejandro's girl bashing speech was interrupted by a knock at the door.

"Come in."

"Boys I have something very important to talk to you about," Sister Catherine stammered nervously.

"It has to do with the case."

"Is it good news?" Roberto asked excitedly.

"No, I'm afraid not. It's about..." Sister Catherine suddenly noticed that the boys room looked unusually bare.

"Roberto, what happened to your shoes in the corner? Alejandro, where is the stuffed bear that you sleep with for good luck?"

"It's in that old plastic bag in the corner," Alejandro quickly responded.

Sister Catherine then caught a glimpse of the duffel bag Roberto had stuffed under his bed.

"Boys are you planning to run away?"

"Yes, we are. Please don't try to stop us. We've decided that we will not be broken up," Alejandro voiced boldly.

"Don't worry Alejandro," Sister Catherine said soothingly. I am on your side. I have already arranged for both of you to be smuggled across the Cuban boarder into America in just two hours."

"Where are we going to live? We don't know anyone in America." Roberto questioned.

"Don't you think we'd have a better chance if we stayed here in Cuba?"

"Of course not. Boys, I have been able to track down your grandmother in Miami. I've already sent word to her and she is anxiously awaiting your arrival."

At first Roberto was thrilled, then he remembered Gabrielle. Sister Catherine didn't know of their plans to runaway with their girlfriends.

"Sister we can't go to America," Roberto insisted. "We have to stay in Cuba."

"Buy why?" Asked Sister Catherine.

"We have already agreed to take Carmen and Gabrielle with us. They will be waiting for us at seven o'clock."

"Don't be ridiculous! You boys are going to Miami whether you like it or not," Sister Catherine charged. Then she realized that adolescents in love could be a very serious matter and opted for a more compassionate approach. "Roberto, why would you want to drag those girls into this mess?"

"We care a lot about them."

"If you really care about them, you'll let them stay here to finish school and be with their families. Taking the girls with you would be a very selfish act, don't you want what's best for them?"

"Sister, I agree with you. They should stay here where it's safe and not tag along with me and Roberto."

Roberto gave Alejandro a sharp look.

"How could he give in so easily?" Roberto thought…"This trip will take me far away from the girl I love."

"Can we at least tell them good-bye?" Roberto pleaded.

"No Roberto, there isn't enough time. It is already six o'clock and the man will be here in one hour to pick you up," Sister Catherine contended. Roberto sat on his bed and yearned for his new found love.

"She's right Roberto, we have to do what's best for us." Alejandro turned to Sister Catherine and gave her a nod of approval.

"What is our next step?" Alejandro asked enthusiastically.

"Be patient Alejandro, so much has happened in such a short time. Mr. Mendez will be here to pick you boys up shortly and I'm sure he has everything under control. In the meantime, let's finish packing and get you boys ready for your long trip to America."

*****

At seven thirty there was still no sign of Mr. Mendez. Sister Catherine began pacing around the living room wondering how everything was going on his end. "What if he was unable to organize things on such short notice?" Sister Catherine thought.

"What if the police found out about our plan?"

Without warning, there was a loud knock at the door. Sister Catherine breathed a sigh of relief as she opened it. "Good morning Mr. Mendez. I was beginning to get worried."

"It took day and night to get everything in order. A lot of people are involved in this and it wasn't easy getting this arranged."

"Mr. Mendez, I really appreciate all of the trouble. Thank you so much."

"Sister, don't thank me yet, the boys still haven't made it out of Cuba." Mr. Mendez warned. "Are they ready to leave?"

"Yes sir. Boys, come here." Alejandro and Roberto raced from the living room into the hallway. Their hearts beat furiously, because of their anxiety. "Mr. Mendez, this is Roberto and this is Alejandro."

"Wow! I didn't know that they were identical twins. You can't tell them apart."

"I know, I have raised them for the last six years and sometimes I still get confused," Sister Catherine laughed. She then turned and focused her attention on the boys realizing the time for their departure was drawing closer. "Boys go grab your stuff."

The boys picked up their bags and the hearty lunch that Sister Catherine had packed for them. As the twins walked towards the door, Roberto turned around and grabbed Sister Catherine tightly. He hugged her waist tightly and buried his face in her long house dress. Sister Catherine tried to maintain her composure but when she saw how afraid the boys were she thought her heart would break. "Can I come with you?" She asked Mr. Mendez anxiously.

"I just want to make sure the boys get off okay."

At first, Mr. Mendez intended to refuse Sister Catherine's request. The whole process had already taken too much of his time and he was also concerned about her safety, but something told him to bring her along.

"Normally I would say no, but for you, I will make an exception."

Before stepping outside the boys took one last look around the house. Alejandro thought of all the memories that he had and was leaving behind. He also focused on all of the damages to the house that he had caused. The dent in the hallway wall, the chip on the banister, and the cracked window were all due from Alejandro's various accidents. By now, tears were streaming down his cheeks.

"This is it," Roberto quivered.

"We'll be far away from here, real soon."

"We sure will," Alejandro whispered.

A car with tinted windows waited for them in the driveway. When the boys noticed their mode of transportation their mood was instantly boosted. The only time they saw a car like that was on the rare occasion they went to the movies.

"I want the window," Alejandro hollered.

"Me too," Roberto called out.

"Boys, there are enough windows for everyone," Mr. Mendez assured. "Just hop in."

During the drive, Mr. Mendez tried to provide Sister Catherine and the boys with as much details as he could. First, the boys would take a boat to the Dominican Republic. Then the boys would stowaway on another ship that would drop them into Texas. From there, the boys would be transported by car to Miami. Mr. Mendez's companion, Armando, would escort them on most of the trip.

"Well, we're here." Mr. Mendez stated calmly. Sister Catherine wondered why the dock was still secluded even though it was already 9 o'clock in the morning. She looked around in search of answers when she got a glimpse of a sign marked

"Caution - This area is closed to the public."

Now, Sister Catherine wondered if coming to the pier to see the boys off was a wise decision. It seemed she was becoming even more worried. As much as she tried to stay strong for them, she was dying inside. Sister Catherine felt as if she was losing her own children and didn't know if she would ever see them again.

"Now you boys better make me proud of you when you get to America," Sister Catherine said as she hugged the boys tightly. "Boys somehow I will get word to you when we can see each other again. It would be too dangerous for you to contact me from America, so please don't call or write."

The boys reluctantly agreed. By this time, Mr. Mendez was becoming impatient. "Come on boys, let's get you on the boat," Mr. Mendez ordered.

The boys had every intention of following Mr. Mendez's orders but they could barely see where they were going; the tears were clouding their eyes. Alejandro, who rarely displayed his feelings, was even having a difficult time maintaining his composure. Just as the boys were nearly out of Sister Catherine's sight, Roberto turned around to wave one last goodbye. That was more than Sister Catherine could take, she gathered up her last bit of energy and ran towards them.

"Did you think I'd let you boys leave without one last hug"? Sister Catherine whispered.

At this point they all openly cried in each other's arms. Roberto's face was buried in Sister Catherine's bosom while a weeping Alejandro had fallen to his knees and grabbed Sister Catherine's legs. Pedro Mendez and his companion turned their backs to give the three a little privacy.

"Boys, I don't know if I've ever told you that I love you, but I truly do. You mean so much to me. I don't know what I am going to do without you two." Sister Catherine wiped away Roberto's tears with her hands.

"Just make sure that you take good care of each other and listen to your Grandmother in Miami."

"We will," the two said simultaneously.

"Armando, make sure you take good care of my boys for me," Sister Catherine said as she patted him on the shoulder.

"Don't worry I will Sister, this isn't the first time I've taken the trip," Armando confidently answered.

"It'll be a piece of cake."

"Okay boys you better get out of here before I break down crying again."

"Sister don't worry we will both make you proud of us," Roberto assured.

"Boys, remember to pray day and night," Sister Catherine called out as she clutched her rosary. "Put God first in everything you do. No matter what, put God first!"

*****

It was well after 9 o'clock. Roberto and Alejandro had promised to pick up the girls at 7 o'clock sharp. They now realized, that the twins had probably left them behind and were gone for good. Both girls sobbed uncontrollably in their room but Gabrielle was especially devastated. For the first time in her young life, she finally understood how people felt when they suffered from a broken heart. "Life is so unfair!" Gabrielle screamed. "I've finally found someone I truly love and now he is forced to leave. I don't know if I'll ever see him again."

Carmen was also visibly shaken by the recent turn of events. Although Alejandro wasn't her only boyfriend, she had finally realized that Alejandro was more than just a sex-partner. For the most part, he accepted her unconditionally. Her wild ways and blemished reputation didn't seem to bother him. She also appreciated his tendency to live life on the edge.

"Why are you crying, Carmen?" "I thought you didn't care about Alejandro," Gabrielle accused.

"Look Gabrielle, you are not the only person who can get upset after losing the one you love," Carmen said defensively.

"Give me a break, Carmen. By next week, you will already have at least two other boys to take his place. But for me, I will never love anybody the way that I love Roberto. He is the best thing that ever happened to me," Gabrielle cried as she collapsed on her bed.

"I know how much you loved Roberto, but in losing Alejandro, I have probably lost more than you have."

Gabrielle sprung from her bed and looked at her sister.

"Carmen, what are you talking about?"

"Remember when I went out to dinner with Mario?" Carmen asked. Gabrielle nodded.

"Well, he told me that he had an operation after the birth of his last kid."

"So what does that have to do with Alejandro?" Gabrielle asked sarcastically.

"So, Mario can't have any more babies."

"I still don't get it Carmen."

"Gabrielle, I am pregnant. If Mario can't make babies then it must be Alejandro's," Carmen cried.

Gabrielle was speechless. She now understood Carmen's tears. She jumped off the bed and did the only thing that a sister could do. She hugged Carmen closely. For the next several hours, the two sisters rocked themselves back and forth, realizing they would probably mourn this loss-forever.

# Chapter 3

It was a beautiful warm summer day in Miami, Florida. Some people strolled down the streets wearing the latest fashions. Others spent their time at the beach, soaking up the sun so they could get the perfect tan. The children played in the water or spent the afternoon building sandcastles. A popular weatherman described the day as 'picture perfect.'

Not everyone was able to enjoy the fun times that the city had to offer. A lady sat motionless on the edge of the bed as she stared out of the window. Nurse Mitchell watched this ritual daily and couldn't understand how a person could be so still for such long periods of time. On the other hand, Nurse Mitchell was still somewhat relieved knowing how much this patient had improved since she had first arrived at the facility.

Two years ago, Candice entered the Smith's Mental Facility after she was diagnosed as a manic-depressive. Later, she was believed to suffer from paranoid schizophrenia. Before doctors could treat her many mental issues, they first had to address her drug habit. Candice had been using a wide assortment of uppers and downers for several years. She was a cokehead and an alcoholic. The doctors concluded that her body suffered from a severe case of drug overload. Her real name was later learned to be Cynthia Hancock.

Detoxification treatment was supposed to be the first step to a long road to recovery but Cynthia had a bad reaction to the process. There were times when the doctors believed she wouldn't make it. When she arrived, she weighed ninety pounds on her 5'5" frame, during her treatment she lost even more weight. Cynthia's cheeks were completely sunken in and her legs looked like two baseball bats. Cynthia was no more than a walking skeleton.

*****

He had just spent one year in the Bolivian jail and his lawyers continued to work around the clock in hopes of getting him out on some type of technicality. They were the best attorneys money could buy, but the politics surrounding the situation made an appeal almost impossible. A lot of powerful Americans were committed to keeping this man behind bars. No matter how much influence this man had, the pressure from the U.S. Government made his efforts useless.

Prison life wasn't as bad as many chose to believe. Although this brand new facility lacked many of the amenities that a man of his caliber would have received if he were in the United States, like a swimming pool and tennis court, he still received more benefits than most of the Cuban middle class. He enjoyed being secluded from the rest of the prison population and remained confined to the quietest part of the prison. He even had his own private security team, headed up by Rafael. He was an extremely devoted employee who volunteered to accompany his boss to jail so he could protect him.

His isolation may have even saved his life. Bolivian prisons were notorious for gangs. It was nearly impossible to leave there alive if you failed to join one. For this prisoner, gangs were the last thing on his mind.

By now, the man practiced a daily routine. First, he started his day by talking to his wife over the phone or reading one of the letters that she wrote to him often. He then submerged himself in a book from the prison library. Reading was his favorite pass time and he absorbed anything he could get his hands on. The books he chose were on various topics, everything from history to gourmet cooking. Visiting hours was always busy for him, especially on Tuesday afternoons. At this time, one of the lieutenants from his multi-million dollar cartel would drop by to update him on the latest news surrounding the drug business. He'd end his day with a late movie and a midnight snack. Then the ritual would start all over again.

It was Saturday night and the man was reading a book on economics when two guards approached his cell.

"Excuse me Sir, I am sorry but we have to move you tonight," one of the guards explained.

"Our orders are straight from the top."

"Why on earth do you have to move me to another cell?" the man asked angrily.

"I don't know. We were only told to move you to another cell," the guard answered nervously.

"Get me the Warden. I want to talk to him personally, right now!"

"I am sorry, Sir. He's not here and he won't be back until tomorrow."

"Okay, I'm not going to continue a conversation with you two idiots, let's go."

"Where are you taking him?" Rafael called out. "I will go with him."

"You can't go with him, but don't worry, we'll take care of everything. We've got him a room in section two."

"What do you mean you'll take care of everything?" Rafael yelled. "Why are you taking him to section two?"

Rafael was beginning to worry about this new move. Although, Rafael generally controlled the joint, section two was one of the few areas that he could not influence because it was run by a rival gang. Section two mainly consisted of lowlife muggers and junkies. They couldn't be trusted and always looked for trouble.

"Rafael, don't worry about me," the man called back. "It will only be for a day. When the Warden gets back tomorrow, I'm sure he will straighten out this whole mess."

Contrary to the man's brave exterior, he was really very worried about the change in scenery. He wondered whether he was in the midst of a set-up or if the U.S. government wanted to get him in a place where they could get a better look at him. Whatever the case, he was sure he'd have the answers to his questions soon enough.

# Chapter 4

The place was immaculate. Everything was in its proper place in the paisley pink apartment. The double bed stood boldly across from the plain couch covered with a floral sheet. Nurse Mitchell tried to make the room look and feel as cozy as possible after she heard the psychologist declaring that an improved environment would help Cynthia's recovery.

It was now noon. That meant it was time for Cynthia's afternoon walk. Normally, the assistants would take patients for their walks, but Nurse Mitchell insisted on taking Cynthia for a tour of the grounds during her own lunch break.

"Come on Miss Hancock, it's time to visit the garden."

In a trance-like state, Cynthia would rise from her bed and mechanically walk towards the garden. To Nurse Mitchell, that was a great improvement. It meant she understood some of the things that were being communicated to her. She also stopped wetting the bed. Although sometimes, just like a little child, you had to remind her to go to the bathroom or blow her nose.

"Look at all of the pretty flowers Cynthia. They really have grown a lot in the past month." Nurse Mitchell tried to get Cynthia to notice her surroundings but her efforts seemed fruitless.

Nurse Mitchell thoroughly enjoyed escorting Cynthia on her walks. To an outsider, it may have appeared that she was just wasting her time on an invalid, but Nurse Mitchell was committed to Cynthia's recovery. As long as she showed the slightest sign of life, Nurse Mitchell promised to stay by her side.

She took her fingers and gently moved Cynthia's hair from her eyes.

"Cynthia," Nurse Mitchell whispered. "It's time for you to snap out of this trance you're in. The doctors say there is nothing physically wrong with you. It's really a lot more fun out here in the real world, if you come see for yourself."

Cynthia continued to stare blankly.

"Even though you're not responding, I know you hear me," Nurse Mitchell whispered. "I know you do."

As they headed back towards her room, Nurse Mitchell bent down to pick out some flowers for the vase in Cynthia's room. She grabbed several yellow daisies, stood up and took Cynthia's hand. Suddenly, Cynthia bent down to pick out two more flowers. She then handed them to Nurse Mitchell. At first, the stunned nurse had no reaction, then she broke out into a big smile. Even if the doctors failed to notice, Nurse Mitchell knew in her heart that her special patient was showing improvement.

"The flowers were definitely a good sign," Nurse Mitchell thought. "I wonder what Cynthia will do next."

*****

It's been more than two years since Roberto and Alejandro moved in with their grandmother in Miami. Now on their sixteenth birthday, the two decided to do something daring to signify their initiation into manhood. Alejandro recommended that they trek downtown to get identical tattoos, Roberto reluctantly agreed.

"Maybe we shouldn't do this," Roberto suggested. "You know if Mama' ever found out, she would kill us."

"Well she's not gonna find out. And even if she does, it will be too late."

As they got off the bus to walk to the tattoo parlor, Roberto thought if Alejandro could hear how loudly his heart was beating. Not only was he worried about the pain rumored to accompany getting a tattoo; he wasn't too crazy about the stigma that was associated with guys that got tattoos. After all, he dreamed of being a successful attorney. He didn't want to do anything to tarnish his dream.

Alejandro's heart was also racing, but it wasn't due to fear. He was thinking about the number of girls he could attract because of the tattoo. A few months ago, his girlfriend dumped him for another guy that had a small tattoo on his arm. Alejandro was not only planning to get a tattoo, but one that was twice the size of the competition. Unfortunately, Alejandro failed to realize that the tattoo had little to do with his ex-girlfriend's departure, she was merely fed up with Alejandro never having any money to spend on her.

"Only two more blocks, I can still back out," Roberto considered. He knew that Alejandro would never have the nerve to go through with it if he backed out.

"I hope you're not thinking about changing your mind," Alejandro said loudly. "We both worked extra hours at the supermarket so we could have this done. Besides, you gave me your word."

Alejandro was certainly pulling out all of the ammunition for this feat. Roberto knew he had to go through with it even though he was having second thoughts. Since they didn't have a father around and their grandmother spent so much time devoting herself to Church. The twins made a pact that they would never break a promise that they had made to each other. No matter how much Roberto respected his Mama', Alejandro came first.

With one block to go, the boys ran into a familiar face. "Hello, Mrs. Gonzalez."

"Hello boys, how is your grandma?"

"She is fine," Alejandro replied impatiently, he prayed Mrs. Gonzalez wouldn't be as long-winded as usual.

"That is good to hear. Boys what are you doing in this area on a school day?"

"We are going to the tattoo parlor," Roberto blurted out.

"A tattoo parlor?" Mrs. Gonzalez asked sharply.

"Yes, we are going to get some art supplies for a big school project," Alejandro quickly responded.

"Why is she so fucking nosy?" Alejandro murmured. Roberto elbowed Alejandro in the ribs.

"Well we gotta go, see you in church on Sunday, Mrs. Gonzalez. We will tell Grandma that we saw you." Alejandro and Roberto continued their stroll towards the parlor and sent friendly farewell waves back to their fellow church member.

"Playing the piano in the Church doesn't give her the right to meddle in everybody's business. She should spend more of her time trying to get her son off of drugs and keeping her daughter from selling her ass for a measly ten bucks," Alejandro laughed.

"Wow, that was a close one," Roberto sighed.

"With no help from you. Why do you have to be so fucking honest all of the time?"

"I guess it's just in my nature." As the two approached the parlor, Roberto peaked inside and was almost sure he had found another excuse.

"Boy, it looks a little crowded inside, maybe we should come back on another day," Roberto offered.

"Are you crazy? Roberto, we have a two o'clock appointment. I'm not leaving here without my tattoo."

"An appointment for a dive like this, you've gotta be kidding me?" Roberto cringed.

"Look, just to make sure you don't back out on me, you will go first." Alejandro insisted. The boys sat shifting in their seats for hours. Roberto wondered what he had gotten himself into. Somehow, he knew there would be consequences but a promise was a promise.

*****

Nurse Mitchell was just about to finish another double shift. The weary nurse used her remaining minutes to check all of her patients one last time.

Nurse Mitchell, a heavy set African American woman, sent herself back to school to become a nurse after her husband left her to raise four kids. Too proud to get on welfare, Nurse Mitchell often worked two or three jobs to support her family. She'd promised herself that after she was settled in her new career, she would take some time to focus on her own needs, especially since she spent the majority of her adult life caring for her husband and children. Now that all of her kids were grown and successful in their own professions, she often thought back to her promise.

"But, who would take care of my patients while I'm away,' she pondered.

Nurse Mitchell raced over to Cynthia's room after hearing a loud commotion. Apparently, the patient was in another one of her frenzies. The crazed Cynthia, screaming at the top of her lungs, was throwing and kicking anything in her reach. Nurse Mitchell ran over to the bed and gently shook her awake. Cynthia continued to swing her arms wildly, even striking Nurse Mitchell in the nose. Finally, the rage passed.

Cynthia's fury was triggered by another nightmare featuring her abusive father. He molested her regularly from the time Cynthia was ten until she was fifteen. It all started with him touching her in the wrong places. Then as she got older, actual sex.

Cynthia's mother was no help at all. To Cynthia's surprise, her mother appeared totally oblivious to the situation or if she did know, she didn't seem to care. One thing was becoming clear, she knew she had to leave home and go somewhere very different. So, this girl from a small town in Baltimore left home and traveled throughout the country before settling in Miami.

Nurse Mitchell slowly rocked a weeping Cynthia in her arms and had already decided to do this the whole night to make Cynthia feel better. "Don't worry child, Nurse Mitchell is here and I won't let nobody bother you anymore." she whispered.

"You can always count on me."

*****

"Okay kid it's your turn." the big burly tattoo artist roared.

As Alejandro got into the chair, he became instantly charged with energy. Now, he and his brother would again be identical once he received his tattoo. "Did it hurt much?" Alejandro asked.

"It sure did, but you'll get used to it."

Alejandro reminded the guy that the tattoo had to be exactly like the one that Roberto had, “Otherwise, it will ruin everything."

The man went through the same motions that he did with Roberto. First he rubbed Alejandro’s shoulder with an alcohol pad. Then he picked up the loaded needle to do the outline. For a minute he hesitated, he wasn't sure if he had cleaned his utensils or not.

“What's the difference?" he thought. “I've got a long line of people waiting."

“Alejandro, Roberto! What is going on in here?" a familiar voice called out. Roberto and Alejandro turned to see their little grandmother angrily pointing her finger at them. “Alejandro get down from that chair.”

“But he'll be finished soon, mama.” Alejandro responded anxiously. “Besides Roberto already has one.”

“Excuse me Sir, did you know that both of these boys are minors?” she asked.

“Look lady, I don't want any problems. They both told me that they were eighteen,” the man asserted.

“How was I supposed to know the difference?”

“Did you at least check for identification?" she asked.

“This place is so busy that half of the time a person don't have time to check for that type of stuff. And anyway, most of these kids have fake ID's."

“Boys let's go. We will talk about this at home." Mama' Sanchez ordered. “Let's go, Alejandro!"

The boys knew it was gonna be a long ride back home. As embarrassed as Alejandro was about the scene at the parlor, part of him wanted to giggle. “Mama’ is a feisty old woman," he thought.

“How on earth could you do something like that to your bodies?" Mama' Sanchez asked the boys.

“It's almost sacrilegious to do that to yourselves."

“Mama' it's only a tattoo." Alejandro said.

“Roberto how could you get a tattoo? You look like a common thug. Did Alejandro convince you to do it?”

“No he didn't.” Roberto lied. Anytime the twins went against her wishes, Mama' Sanchez always assumed that Alejandro was to blame. Although Alejandro was more the mischievous brother, Roberto would always come to his defense.

“We both wanted to get one."

"Mama' since Roberto already has his tattoo. Can I go back to get my shoulder done?" Alejandro injected.

"Of course not, didn't you hear anything I've just said? Alejandro you must promise me that you won't ever go back there." Mama' pleaded.

Alejandro had never seen Mama' so upset. He had no choice but to agree and wait a few years longer.

"Boys I am really disappointed in both of you. Go to your room and stay there until I call you for dinner." Mama' ordered.

After the boys went to their room, Mama' Sanchez went to her own bedroom and closed the door. She sat down on her squeaky bed and began bawling. As she wiped her face with the bottom of her dress, she wondered if this was the beginning of a bad future for her twins. She tried her best to raise the boys in a good God-fearing home but this act of defiance was not a good sign. She knew this was a crucial time for the boys and she hadn't figured out which direction her boys would choose to go. What she did notice, was how much they resembled their father Alex and that was what scared her the most. So, she continued crying to herself, partly due to her grandsons but mostly because this incident reminded her of Alex and Karina, the two children that she'd lost to the streets.

The boys continued to exchange guilty stares across the room. Since their bedroom was located next to their grandmother's room, they could hear her crying and knew that they were the cause of her despair. They felt terrible. For the past two and a half years, the only thing that she asked was that they did well in school and stayed out of trouble-and they couldn't even do that right. This was only the second time they'd ever heard her cry. The first time was when the boys arrived from Cuba. She was so happy to see them that she crumbled to the floor and wept for nearly fifteen minutes. Even though those were tears of joy, the boys were so shaken by her display of emotion that they vowed that they would never cause her to cry again. Now, they listened quietly at the sounds of their grandmother's pain.

*****

It was a restless night for the man. He kept one eye closed and one eye open the entire night. In his unfamiliar surroundings, he didn't know what to expect. Fortunately, the guard kept his promise and provided the man with his own locked cell. Even still the man remained skeptical. If they were really concerned about my safety they wouldn't have brought me here in the first place, the man complained.

"Sir, it's time for you to take your shower." the guard calmly stated.

"That's okay, I'll stay in my cell today."

"Sir, don't worry. We've arranged for you to take a shower by yourself. And as far as your meals are concerned, we'll have someone bring them directly to your cell. After this, there won't be any need for you to leave your cell today."

"Maybe today won't be that bad after all," the man thought confidently. In any case, the idea of not taking a shower repulsed him. Ever since he entered prison, he had become transformed into a clean freak. Everything around him had to be germ-free, especially himself. He never shook anyone's hand and always had the impulse to constantly wash his own.

The man was escorted to the showers by two guards that he'd never seen before. One of them handed him a white towel and a new bar of soap, just as the man requested.

When the man entered the shower room, he scoped the place to see if he was alone. He didn't see anyone else. As usual he was amazed at the vast size of the shower area and always feared someone would be hiding in some secret compartment.

Like all prisons, the water was never hot enough and the man shivered as the water hit his back. He rubbed the soap in every crevice of his body and breathed a sigh of relief as he watched the dirt drift down the drain. When he finished rinsing the lather from his body, he stepped away from the spray of water to dry himself off. He walked passed the other stalls and reached for the doorknob to make his exit when he heard the latch click, it was now locked. His sixth sense was now telling him that he was not alone. He quickly whirled his body around in the opposite direction and found himself face to face with one of the bullies from section two.

"Who the hell are you?" the man demanded. "And how'd you get in here?"

"I am Gustavo Silva," the muscular dark-haired man proudly raved. "I run things in this part of the prison."

"I don't care what you do," the man argued. "Do you have any idea who I am?"

"Of course, I do. Why in the fuck else do you think I am in here?" As he spat out his last word, the two hundred and fifty-pound goon flashed an army knife.

"Who's paying you to do this? I will pay you twice the amount," the fearful prisoner bargained. "You have my word."

"I can't do that." Gustavo said laughing aloud.

"You know what's so fucking funny, the guy that's paying me said you'd probably make me another offer. But listen to me you piece of shit, I hate people like you. You think that you can buy anything that you want. But you can't buy Gustavo Silva. Money means nothing to me. I'll be spending the rest of my life in this hell hole."

As Gustavo approached he swung the knife wildly and drew first blood from his opponent's arm. The man retreated further into the shower area and Gustavo again lunged at him with the knife. "Look, let's make this real simple," Gustavo offered. "Don't try to escape, there's no way out."

The man threw a swift kick to Gustavo's right hand and watched the weapon land on the floor.

"This is going to be even more fun that I had thought," Gustavo cheered. "You're a dead man."

Gustavo stooped over and charged at the man much like an angry animal in a bullfight, knocking him to the ground. He then scooped up his victim and flung him to the ground. The man sprouted up into his best fighting stance. Though the man is accustomed to the finer things in life, fighting isn't completely foreign to him, especially since his childhood days were spent in the streets of Bolivia. He quickly tried to consider which strategies would shift the battle in his favor. He would not be an easy victim. Even if Gustavo were able to snuff him out, at least he would have died putting up a good fight.

Gustavo hit the man soundly on the jaw. This sent him reeling backwards. The man tried to land a combination of his own but it was wildly short. The man's follow through hit Gustavo in the midsection but the punches appeared to have no affect.

Gustavo continued to attack the man's previously unblemished olive skin, one punch at a time. Gustavo then picked up the man and launched him into the mirror, causing glass to splatter throughout the shower area.

Give up already!' Gustavo shouted.

The man was on his back nearly lifeless on a mound of glass. Gustavo moved toward him wondering where he would send forth the final blow. "Is this the way it's going to end for me?" the man pondered. "With all of my fancy planes, cars, and ritzy parties, who would have thought that I'd be killed in a prison shower by some gorilla?"

Gustavo picked up his adversary and placed him squarely on his feet. He then hurled several blows to the man's stomach. The victim again collapsed to the ground as he looked up at the huffing Gustavo. "Why is he getting tired?' the man wondered. "I'm the one getting my ass kicked."

Gustavo then bent down to deliver a final whack when the man spotted an opportunity for revenge. With all of his remaining energy, he gave Gustavo a sharp kick to the knee. Gustavo collapsed faster than a ton of unbalanced bricks. As the man watched Gustavo clench his busted kneecap, he gained new confidence and began dancing around him with his fists in combat mode. For the next several minutes, the man kicked his former intimidator in the head and side of the body. The weary Gustavo, now screaming in pain from his busted eardrum and cracked ribs, felt completely defenseless. The man walked over to the area where he'd once laid helpless and picked up a large piece of glass. He grabbed Gustavo from behind by the hair and held the sharp edge by his throat.

"Motherfucker, before I kill you, I want you to tell me who put you up to this?"

"Fuck you man, I'm not telling you shit." Gustavo said as he gagged on his own blood. "Go to hell!"

The man snatched back Gustavo's head to expose the veins in his neck. He then sliced deeply into Gustavo's neck and watched him shiver on the ground like a chicken that just got his head cut off.

The man began to bang furiously on the shower door. The guards, anxiously awaiting Gustavo's signal, opened the door immediately. To their surprise, the man stood before them covered with blood, as Gustavo was on the shower floor, dead.

# Chapter 5

“Alejandro stop we shouldn't be doing this!" Cathy warned.

“Listen Cathy, since I love you and you love me, there is nothing wrong with us doing this," an anxious Alejandro asserted.

“But I really haven't known you long enough to do it yet."

“That really shouldn't matter. I feel like I've known you a long time.”

At this point, Alejandro was consumed with lust and had one thing on his mind. He didn't care that he was in a strange girl's bedroom miles away from his grandmother's house. His only concern was figuring out how he could have sex with the long blond hair, blue-eyed girl. He had never been with a white girl before, and he always wondered what it would be like.

“Alejandro, what if my parents come home now? If we get caught, they'd kill me,” she wined.

“Cathy you told me earlier that they won't get back from church for another two hours. We have plenty of time to spend together, please don't worry," Alejandro said soothingly as he positioned himself on top of her. He slowly guided his hand up her thigh. The further his hand rose, the more passionate their kisses became. Alejandro then started to kiss all over Cathy's neck, he then began alternating between licking and nibbling behind her ear.

At this point Cathy didn't care if her parents were on their way home or not. Her whole body suddenly felt like it was on fire. Alejandro's body also was playing tricks on him. His hands were practically trembling in anticipation of what was going to happen next.

Alejandro slowly removed Cathy's panties and watched her shiver with excitement. He then placed his hand over her pussy. It felt wet and warm. He knew she was just as ready for him as he was for her. He dropped his shorts in record time.

"Alejandro please go slow," Cathy said worriedly. 'I've only done this three other times."

As he slowly entered, he let out a little sigh of relief. It had been a long drought in between conquests and Alejandro was proud that he never beat his meat for satisfaction. Alejandro rocked back and forth on top of Cathy. At first she cautioned Alejandro not to go too deep but **as** the moments passed she began to get used to his size. Cathy took a deep breath and started to spread her legs out further to give him an even better angle.

"Cathy honey we're home. I hope you are feeling better," Cathy's mother yelled from the living room downstairs.

"Oh my God," Cathy whispered. "My parents are home. What are we going to do?"

Alejandro could not believe his luck. Just when he was going to come, her parents arrived from church. Apparently, they had decided to come back early to check on Cathy. Driven by his sexual urge, Alejandro stroked inside of Cathy a few more times until she pulled away.

"Alejandro hurry up and get dress," Cathy frantically implored. "You've got to get out of here."

"Cathy where did I put my shoes?'

In a mad rush, Cathy hopped in her pajamas and raced downstairs. She knew she had to make it downstairs before her parents came upstairs to check on her.

"So honey, how are you feeling?" Cathy's mother asked.

"I am feeling much better," Cathy responded.

"Are you sure? You look awfully flushed," her dad remarked. "Did you get enough rest?"

"Look honey go upstairs and get ready for dinner. After your father and I get out of these clothes, I am going to make you a nice hot meal." Cathy's mother kissed her on the forehead and gave her a big hug.

"Some of your mother's home cooking should fix you right up."

Cathy returned her mother's comment with a friendly smile and then dashed back upstairs to a very indifferent Alejandro. He had already decided that if he got caught he would just blow it off. He stayed in Cathy's bedroom for another twenty minutes until the coast was clear. He then ran out of the back door like a bat out of hell. As he sprinted down the street he realized how close he actually came to getting caught by her parents. He knew he had to be much more careful in the future. "Next Sunday I'll go straight for sex," Alejandro thought. "I can always talk to Cathy at school."

*****

Some hours later, the man sat on a prison hospital bed and was examined by a nurse.

"You're pretty bruised up," the nurse commented as she tended to the various cuts and bruises that covered the man's body. "Luck was certainly on your side."

"I don't believe in luck," the man murmured. "It just wasn't my time to go."

"You can believe what you want, but most folks that have received wounds as serious as yours are in intensive care."

"I see."

"Okay sir, now that everything is pretty clean, I'll have the surgeon come to sew you up," the nurse said as she looked over the wounds for the last time. "You'll need about fifteen stitches to close the gash in your scalp and another ten for your hand."

As the man sat in the hospital room, he thought back to the day's events. He was also surprised that the two guards who came to the shower door took him to the infirmary rather than kill him themselves. What the man didn't know is that the guards were under strict orders to escort him to the shower area-nothing more, nothing less. One of them for a moment did think about shooting the man but he wasn't comfortable making the decision, especially since his boss hadn't specifically requested him to snuff the man out.

The warden barged through the door with his two aides at his sides.

"In God's name, what happened here?" the warden queried. "I need answers."

The man slowly turned around in his chair and looked menacingly at the warden.

"You know what the hell happened here! Don't you dare play me for a fool!"

"Excuse me nurse, can you leave us alone for a while? I will call you back, when we are finished," the warden then turned to his accompanying aids. "Fellas you can wait outside too."

The nurse carefully removed the bloody bandages that were on the counter. She then took off her plastic gloves and tossed them in the trash as she escorted the assistants outside.

"I don't know what you're talking about. Every since you arrived, I've given you every possible thing that I could," the Warden insisted. "How can you turn on me?"

"Well, it appears that I've overstayed my welcome because somebody tried to kill me in the shower earlier today."

"No kidding?" the warden asked as he paced from one side of the room to the other. "Do you think it was a gang hit?"

"Why would they do that? Since I've been here they have been kissing my ass hoping that I would take care of them once they got on the outside."

"Well do you think Gustavo acted alone? He would have had a bigger name for himself if he'd killed you," the Warden suggested.

"You son of a bitch. Stop fucking around with me. You know who was responsible for this entire shit," the man charged. "If not, you better believe I'll find out who's behind all of this."

There was a knock on the door. It was one of the Warden's aides. "Sir, they've just found the assistant Warden hung in the supervisor's locker room."

"What?" the warden gasped. An intense silence fell on the room. The warden refocused his attention back on the man.

"You see Sir, I guess he was guilty of this whole thing and he knew there would be hell to pay when I got my hands on him," the Warden explained.

"Listen Warden, I can't prove that you had anything to do with what happened today. But since you are in charge of this place, I am personally gonna hold you responsible. You see I sent out the word. If anything happens to me while I'm in here, not only will I have you taken out, but your wife and kids will be killed as well. I'll even go after your parents and siblings. By the time my men get finished you won't have a fucking relative left on this continent!" the man exclaimed. "Did you get that?"

There was a frozen white look across the Warden's face. He knew the man very well and was convinced that he was not bluffing. The Warden looked deep into the man's cold eyes and believed that he was playing with the devil. Regardless of his personal feelings toward this prisoner, the Warden knew that this special VIP had to be protected at all costs, even if he had to guard him with a shotgun while the man slept.

*****

Roberto and Alejandro were at the table enjoying dinner like always, with Mama' Sanchez at the head of the table. She'd cooked one of their favorite meals-"arroz con pollo". Even though they'd had chicken and rice dishes at least a thousand times, no one cooked it as well as their grandmother.

"Mama' you put too much food on my plate again." Roberto smiled as he rubbed his stuffed belly. "You're not trying to make me into a little Santa Clause are you?"

"Look Roberto, you are a growing young man. You need to eat a lot of food to keep going," Mama' Sanchez cheerfully responded.

"You don't see me complaining," Alejandro interjected. 'I love it when Mama' packs my plate."

"I know you do. You are always hungry because you're just so greedy," Roberto snapped.

"After dinner I made a special dessert for you boys," Mama Sanchez said smiling widely. She loved cooking dinner for the boys and appreciated the flood of compliments she'd receive after they'd tasted her food. It was like spending time with Alex and Karina all over again. "I have a special treat for my very special grandsons."

"Mama', can I ask you something?"

"Sure Alejandro, you can ask your grandmother anything you want." Mama' Sanchez said as she placed her hands on Alejandro's shoulders. "What is it?"

"Well um, it's about our father." Alejandro stammered. "Me and Roberto have some more questions."

At first, Mama' Sanchez was startled by Alejandro's request but then she quickly regained her composure. Every since the boys arrived, she had been preparing herself for this conversation. In other discussions about her son, she remained very vague and refused to go into any detail.

"Okay boys, after supper we'll go into the living room and I will tell you everything I know about your father," Mama' Sanchez yielded. "I promise."

As soon as the boys scooped up the last grain of rice, Mama' Sanchez cleared the table and headed straight for her favorite Velvet green chair. The boys found a soft spot on the couch.

"Like I've already told you boys, me and your aunt Karina came to America in 1975. We left your father back in Cuba because he was heavily involved in politics," Mama' Sanchez began. "He was in a movement to free the people from Castro's communist rule."

"How long did he stay over there after you and our aunt came here?" Roberto quizzed.

"My goodness, he must have stayed over there for another five years. During that time, your father was a well-respected man in the community. His deeds helped a lot of people."

"So why did he finally leave?" Alejandro interrupted.

"It became too dangerous for him to stay over there. He had to leave and that was around the same time that the United States government opened up their borders for Cuban political prisoners."

"What did he do once he came over here?"

"Roberto, he basically did the same things here that he did back home. He started a program to help the poor Cubans in Miami. Your father was a very strong, proud man. He would have done so much more with his life had he not been assassinated."

"Why would anyone want to kill him?"

"Because Alejandro, your father got too powerful for his own good. One Sunday afternoon, your father and Karina were gunned down in Alex's car. It was a complete ambush. Although it was never proven, many people still believe that Castro was responsible for your father's death."

Roberto and Alejandro sat completely still. It was the first time they'd ever been provided with a vivid picture of their father and they wanted to inhale every word their grandmother uttered.

"Castro never forgave your father for going up against him all of those years," she continued. "That's why he had him killed."

"So Mama', Papa was really a hero.' Roberto cheered.

Mama' Sanchez was so caught up in weaving her tale that she'd forgotten her audience. As she looked into the wishful eyes of her two grandsons, she wondered if she should retract her story and tell them the truth. Alex Sanchez was the furthest thing from a hero but she knew if the boys knew the real reason for their father's death they'd be crushed. "Yes your father was a hero." Mama Sanchez recited as she looked away from the boys. "But Alejandro and Roberto, you can not tell anyone that you are his sons. Your father still has many jealous enemies who would love to hurt his children. So promise me you won't tell a soul."

Like so many times before, the boys agreed to keep another promise to their very dear grandmother.

*****

July fourth was a favorite time of year for the patients at the Institute. The staff planned to repeat their annual fireworks display and the patients acted just like kids on Christmas morning, they were full of reckless energy.

The head doctor decided to exclude Cynthia from the festivities. He believed she wouldn't be interested in a celebration and didn't feel it was worth moving her from one location to another. "Anyway, she probably won't even notice the fireworks," he confided to one of the nurses. "Why bother?"

The doctor was wrong. Cynthia sat in her room looking out the window at the joyful scene. She admired the bright colors that seemed to fill the heavens. She even clapped her hands when the rockets shot right into the floating stars. She enjoyed herself thoroughly until the constant sounds of firecrackers reminded her of a place that she didn't want to visit.

*"Candice, you hold the gun like this." Alex Sanchez ordered.*

*"You hold the gun your way and I will hold it mine." Candice insisted.*

*"Okay, but if you shoot yourself in the foot, I don't want to hear shit about it."*

*Alex and Candice were in the backyard of their massive estate. On one side was an Olympic size swimming pool with a small bathhouse behind it. On the opposite side of the yard was a beautiful garden filled with exotic plants.*

*The two battled verbally as Alex attempted to show Candice how to shoot a gun. "You never know when you'll have to protect yourself, so take this shooting real serious."*

*"Yeah, yeah, Alex. You've already told me that, I heard you the last time."*

*At first, Candice had no desire to learn how to shoot a gun, but after a few weeks of practicing, she started to enjoy it. Eventually, Alex taught her how to master many different kinds of weapons. In a short period of time, she could hit targets better than he could. At this point, the shooting lessons ended. Alex wasn't about to give her, the confidence to one-day shoot him. As far as he was concerned, anything was possible during one of their wild arguments.*

*****

As Mama' Sanchez cleaned up around the house, she wondered how only two boys could make such a mess in such a short period of time. She dusted off the furniture in the living room and caught a glimpse of an angelic picture of her Karina. Although that photo had remained in the same spot for many years, today it bothered Mama' Sanchez more than usual. She collapsed into the chair thinking about what she could have done differently to save her.

Karina was so young and so beautiful. She had her whole life ahead of her, but had it suddenly taken away because of her brother's evil deeds.

Next to Karina's photo was a picture of the twins. They were the only thing that kept her going in this crazy, sometimes cruel world. She laughed aloud when she thought about how two people who looked so similar could have such different personalities. Roberto was very giving and enjoyed helping people with their problems. He made friends very easily and was well liked by his peers. Alejandro, on the other hand was more of a loner. He was more secretive than his brother and had very few friends. Mama' Sanchez believed that Alejandro felt Roberto was the only friend he would ever need.

She knew she had done the right thing by lying to Roberto and Alejandro about their father. What other choice did she have? They would have been upset if she told them the truth about him. Every boy who never had a chance to meet his father dreams of him as a great athlete or leader. How could she take that image away from the twins? What purpose would it have served if they knew that their father was a notorious drug dealer?

All of a sudden there was a hand on her shoulder that caused her to jump from her seat.

"Mama' why did you get so startled?" Roberto asked in a concerned voice. "Didn't you hear me come in from outside?"

"No, I guess I didn't," Mama' Sanchez admitted. She was so busy thinking about the past, she was oblivious to everything around her.

Now that Roberto was home, Mama' Sanchez anxiously waited for Alejandro's arrival. Her home was never complete without both of her grandsons. As different as the twins were, she couldn't help but to love them both equally.

# Chapter 6

*"Candice move your ass. We're gonna be late for the fuckin' wedding.' Alex Sanchez growled. 'You know, I no like that shit. It's disrespectful to the fuckin' couple if we're late."*

*"I don't even want to go to the wedding, so if you don't want to wait for me, just leave." Candice yelled from upstairs.*

*"How the fuck would it look if my own wife didn't go with me to the wedding?"*

*There was no answer.*

*"I'll tell you. It would look fucked up. So hurry up and move your ass."*

*Candice leisurely walked down the stairs leading to the living room. She was wearing a simple but very expensive yellow dress by one of the best designers in Miami. It was made from fine silk, imported directly from India. The dress had a scoop neck, capped sleeves and fell about two inches above her ankles.*

*"Why the fuck are you wearing that dress? You know I hate yellow. You look like an undernourished banana. Why don't you wear that white dress that I like?"*

*"Alex you stupid bastard. The bride is the only one who is supposed to be in white," Candice snapped back. 'Don't you know anything?"*

*"Fuck tradition, Oscar works for me. I'm paying for the wedding so my wife can wear whatever the fuck I want her to wear."*

*"Alex I am not changing, so let's go. Do you have the directions to the church?"*

*"I don't need directions. I know Miami like the back of my fuckin' hand. In fact, I know a short cut to the church."*

*The not so happy couple made their way out of the house and into the royal blue Mercedes. In spite of Alex's prior speech about how well he knew Miami, he was of little help that day. Not only were they stuck in traffic for an hour, they were lost because of Alex's so-called short cut.*

*"What the fuck are you looking at me like that for?" Alex barked.*

*"Because we are lost and the wedding started over an hour ago."*

*"Fuck the wedding. I didn't want to go there anyway."*

*"So, just take us home then."*

*"Shut the fuck up," Alex said angrily as he searched the road for landmarks. 'I would take us home, only I don't know where the hell we are."*

*He was definitely on the wrong side of Miami. Somehow he managed to come across a desolate location, near a bunch of factories and a construction site. He came to a road that he thought would lead him to a familiar territory only to find it was a dead end. Three strange men, that seemed to emerge from nowhere, approached the car. Their overwhelming stench and slurred speech indicated that they had drunk too much cheap liquor. Alex thought they were going to beg for money and was taken by surprise when one of the men pulled out a .38 caliber revolver.*

*"Get out of the damn car." he yelled. "You do what we say and nobody gets hurt."*

*"Who the fuck do you think you're talking to mother fucker?"*

*"Alex let's just get out the car and give it to them," Candice said calmly.*

*"Look my man, I think you better listen to the little lady before you wind up with a cap in your ass."*

*"Fuck you and fuck her to. I'm not gonna give you my new car that I just had custom made," Alex argued. "If you want it so fuckin' bad then shoot me."*

*Candice opened the passenger door and slowly got out the car.*

*"You guys really don't know who the fuck you are dealing with, do you?" Alex said as he propped his feet on the dash and shifted his seat in a more comfortable position. The three thugs began to think Alex was crazy.*

*"Hey man, we just want the car," the shortest guy offered. "We don't want to kill anybody."*

*Candice, in her three-inch heels, began stumbling across the gravel road towards a distant tree. Alex noticed how high the split was along the side of Candice's dress and became angry when he realized the three car -jackers also noticed. Candice strategically dropped her pocketbook to the ground and then stooped slowly to retrieve it. This action gave the men all the thigh and underwear they could handle.*

*Alex knew it was his turn to act. He discreetly pressed a secret panel on the side of the door to acquire a 9mm. glock gun right in his hand. Without moving his upper body, Alex quickly raised his weapon and shot the gunman directly in the forehead. One of his buddies stood frozen in fear, while the other started to run.*

*Alex shot the human statue twice in the chest, killing him instantly. He then motioned for Candice to get back in the car, so he could catch the last guy.*

*"You've already done enough, Alex. Let's find our way back home," Candice wined. "I'm exhausted."*

*Alex began to ease his foot off of the gas. "You know Candice, all of this fuckin' shootin' has gotten me real horny."*

*"Well Alex, just be real quiet in the bathroom when we get home. I'm going back to bed."*

*"Fuckin' bitch," Alex spat. "I don't know why I flatter you anyway." Alex accelerated once again leaving the bloody scene way behind them.*

*****

It was seven o'clock in the evening. The orderlies David and Lewis were making their rounds, collecting the dinner trays and throwing out the garbage in each of the patients' rooms. They tried to finish their last job as quickly as possible because they had tickets to see Miami Sound Machine. The group had this really sexy lead singer named Gloria Estefan. Lewis always thought that she was good enough to leave the group, while David thought she would never be as successful.

David and Lewis loved their jobs. They even liked the patients, except Cynthia Hancock. She gave them the creeps. Whenever either of them went into her room she always stayed still. One day David intentionally dropped a tray on the ground to get her attention, but she didn't flinch. Whenever it was time to clean her room, they were in and out.

"She looks just as lively as she usually does," David said sarcastically as he stood in Cynthia's doorway. "What a life."

"Just go in there and get the tray and let's get outta here. The show is gonna start in two hours and we still have to pick up the girls," Lewis whispered.

Cynthia had just finished eating and was staring motionless out of the window. She would remain like that for the next several hours.

"She is such a waste. Why don't one of these doctor's just give her a needle and put her out of her misery? It's obvious that she's practically a vegetable. There's nothing going on upstairs and there never will be," David concluded.

The orderlies left to clean the next room. Like so many other people at the Institute, they also failed to realize that while Cynthia's body remained inactive her mind was very much alert, constantly racing, and thinking about the past. If people only knew.

# Chapter 7

"Five fucking years of my life I spent locked up in jail, like some caged animal," the man thought to himself.

For the last few years, the man missed seeing his three children grow-up. He wasn't able to attend their birthday parties, graduations, or other festivities. He wasn't around to teach them how to swim or ride a bike. He also wished he could be a better husband to his loving wife, who wrote him adoring letters nearly every day, while he was in jail.

His pride prevented him from letting his wife and kids see him locked up and he wondered if things would be the same after so much time had passed. Although his wife repeatedly pledged her love for him, the man could not be convinced. So, he arranged for his wife to be monitored by the Assassin.

Her every move was closely watched. It was understood that if she were ever unfaithful, she would be killed immediately. Of course, the Assassin needed to have proof from love letters, pictures, or video clips. Once the man was convinced of the affair, her and her lover would be bumped-off. There was only one condition, not in front of the kids. After all, he was a family man.

The prisoner's biggest regret while in jail was not being able to attend his mother's funeral. The love they had between them was extra special. He would never get over missing her final days. Now that he was finally being released, his first stop on this dreary February day would be to pay his respects to his mother.

Before the man left his prison cell for the last time, he looked back at the place where so much of his time had been spent and became very angry. His cell was better than the cells that the other inmates had. It was furnished with the best pieces that the prison guards could scrape up and the floor was spotless. Even with those things, it still felt like prison and the man saw it as the place that kept him from reaching his dreams. He felt so cheated. Many people engaged in crime and his punishment seemed so unfair. He knew he could never get back those years and vowed to make up the lost time to his waiting family.

"I'll make all of my days count," the man said as he shook the hand of the warden that came to bid him farewell.

"Warden, keep everything," the man insisted. "The TV, the VCR, the books, the clothes, paintings, everything."

"Are you sure?" the Warden anxiously inquired.

"I don't want anything that will remind me of this place. Don't worry," he continued. "I'll still take care of your children's education, even after I'm released."

The man instantly returned to his former self as he entered his black bulletproof limousine, surrounded by accompanying armored cars. He directed the driver to the first stop, the cemetery.

After the man and his entourage vanished down the highway, the warden let out a large sigh of relief. He was glad to see his most famous inmate leave. The past three and a half years since the attack had been like hell for the warden, but he knew it could've been much worse. There weren't too many people still alive after trying to betray the notorious Sergio Fernandez. He considered himself lucky.

"Victor, my only good, trusted friend. It feels good to be out," a teary-eyed Fernandez confessed. They had just left the jail and Fernandez was trying hard to put the memories behind him.

"It's good to have you back, Mr. Fernandez," Victor responded as he shook Fernandez's hand firmly.

"Well, you know I'm not completely back in the swing of things but I will be shortly."

"Of course you will."

"Those bastards tried to destroy me, but they could not! First, they tried to charge me with murder but I won. Then they tried to get me on twenty-three other charges that I don't even recall and I still beat them. Can you believe they finally got me for tax evasion?" Fernandez said with a menacing snarl on his face.

Victor worked for Fernandez for many years. He knew his boss's moods and this was not a good one.

Many people in the organization only knew Victor as "The Assassin." He wore dark shades and rarely spoke to anyone other than Fernandez. Victor was greatly feared and that's just the way Fernandez wanted it. Victor was like his own personal pit-bull and Fernandez didn't want anyone to get too friendly with him, just in case he needed him to attack.

Victor always admired Fernandez for being such a shrewd and cold businessman but in listening to his boss, Victor realized that Fernandez had become more dangerous than ever before.

"Heaven help anyone that tries to get in his way," Victor thought.

"Victor, did you bring the roses?" Fernandez asked as the limos made their way through the cemetery.

"Here they are, Mr. Fernandez," Victor replied as he handed his boss the overstuffed bouquet.

Fernandez stepped out of the limo and walked straight to the cemetery plot that was reserved for the Fernandez family. His mother's tombstone was next to his father's. Fernandez remembered the location of his family plot. The Fernandez tombstones were extremely large and elegantly decorated, they stood out like sore thumbs among the others. Fernandez gently knelt down on one knee and placed the flowers on his mother's grave. As he glanced over at his father's tombstone, he shed a tear when he was unable to recall any fond memories.

Fernandez was only ten-year's old when his father was killed in 1952. Papa' Fernandez was a coal mine-worker just like his father. He was one of the leaders that organized the coal miners' revolt against the rich barons and wealthy landowners. This was later known in Bolivia as the April Revolution. Many good men died in the battle, including Mr. Fernandez's father. Miner's unions were born out of this historical event but unfortunately things soon returned to the way they were before.

With no one supporting the family, Fernandez dropped out of school and continued the family tradition of working in Bolivia's coalmines often working long, hard hours. In Bolivia, there were no laws governing child labor, so even though Fernandez was just ten years old, he worked alongside men four times his age. The job eventually took its toll on little Sergio Fernandez and he developed a bad case of bronchitis. His boss fired him. Rather than hang around and become another mouth that his mother couldn't afford to feed, Fernandez ran away from home to live on the streets.

Now at his mother's grave, Fernandez happily recalled the day when he returned home years later-a strong, successful man. He showered his mother with expensive gifts but she often rejected the lavish jewelry and fine clothes. She was a simple lady, content with being able to retire from the cocoa fields.

Mr. Fernandez, feeling that he had visited long enough, kissed the heads of both tombstones. Now he could close a very important chapter in his life and start a new one with a clear conscience.

*****

At some hidden location in Bolivia, a secret meeting with the board took place. Ironically, it was only considered secret by the people involved in the gathering. Everyone knew that Fernandez and his people would hold a meeting upon his release, even the police. But who could touch the Fernandez Cartel? Nobody who wanted to live.

Though it was once based on violence and intimidation, the Fernandez Cartel was now run like a Fortune 500 company. It no longer had one leader that made all of the decisions, but had a formal board of directors. Top positions included a president, vice president, treasurer, secretary of defense, and four members-at - large who ran various profit centers.

Carlos Zanducci, the organization's president, was the number two men and had full control in Fernandez's absence. He kept the books and was Fernandez closest aide. To most of the people, Carlos would be considered a nerd. He had thick-rimmed glasses and wore a bow tie with his cheap polyester suits. It also wasn't uncommon for him to mix plaids and stripes. He definitely didn't have the physical appeal of the other Cartel members but his accounting abilities were phenomenal and Fernandez valued him dearly.

Jorge Arias was the Vice President. He was considered a good man to have on the board since Jorge would be loyal to anyone who was in charge, no matter who was in control at the time. His only weakness was that sometimes he drank too much, but the Cartel accepted this fault because he always kept everyone laughing.

The treasurer, Luis Gomez, had a title that didn't mean much since Carlos Zanducci kept the books. Luis was really an informant, he reported anything that took place behind Carlos' back and that was often.

Ramon Zapata was the Secretary of Defense. He was a former General in the Bolivian Army and many believed that he still helped run the Army, even to this day. His specialty was keeping the Cartel out of trouble and if someone needed to disappear, Ramon would make it possible. A man from the old school, Ramon didn't take shit from anyone. Even Carlos knew not to push him too far.

In the five years that Fernandez was in jail, the Cartel flourished. The enterprises generated more money than ever before and Carlos Zanducci also shared more of the profits with them than Fernandez ever had. Over time, Carlos won the respect of each board member as they continued to benefit from the increased profit margin. Now with a financial wizard leading the way, decisions were based on money and the board appreciated this method.

Carlos Zanducci, a man in his late fifties, already had a head full of gray hair. Although he continued to renew his membership to the country's most elite sports club, he rarely exercised, that explained his pot belly. He was also very soft spoken and hated confrontation, but he definitely knew how to defend himself when it was required. He certainly wouldn't have been able to run the world's largest drug organization and keep Mr. Fernandez in the dark by being a wimp.

*****

It was early spring and both of her boys were doing just fine. Alejandro and Roberto were attending a community college and working at a restaurant as waiters. Mama' Sanchez promised herself that she would not lose the twins to the streets the way She'd lost Karina and Alex. She still blamed herself for both of their deaths. "Maybe they weren't given enough morals growing up to resist the temptations of street life," she wondered.

Without the twins, she didn't know what she would have done with herself. For two long years, the thought of suicide was a constant companion. If not for her devotion to God, she would have done it long ago. But now because of the twins, it was like God had given her a second chance to contribute something positive to the world. What more could she ask for?

There was a knock at the door. Mama' Sanchez wondered who it was because she knew the twins wouldn't be home for another thirty minutes. There also would have been no need to knock since they both had keys to the apartment. For some strange reason, she had the feeling that danger was lurking behind the door and something told her not to open it. Mama' Sanchez felt that if she did, her life would never again be the same.

"Hola, I am Hector Ramirez. Are you Mrs. Sanchez?"

"Yes I am. Can I help you?"

"You don't know me but I was a good friend of your son, Alex Sanchez," the stranger said proudly. "Can I please come in?"

Mama' Sanchez made no motion to invite Mr. Ramirez inside. Although most folks knew her for her warm hospitality, she somehow sensed that this man was up to no good. He seemed evil.

Hector stood about 5 feet 9 inches tall, with an average build. His hair was slicked back in some kind of 1920's gangster style and his brown suit was also outdated. It was only two thirty in the afternoon but you could already smell the cheap liquor on his breath.

"First, Mrs. Sanchez, I would like to offer my deepest regret for your loss. I know it has been almost seven years since his death but there isn't a day that goes by that I don't think about your son," Hector sobbed.

"Thank you, Mr. Ramirez."

"Alex always told me that if anything was to happen to him, he wanted me to check up on his mother, to make sure that everything was fine."

Hectors' words were so outrageous he could barely keep a straight face. Not only did Alex never say those things, but Alex barely knew Hector was alive. Hector Ramirez was a lower-level drug dealer in Alex's operation and Alex rarely had contact with the little guys. Sure Hector was up and coming, and even showed a little promise, but so did many others.

Hector knew that Alex's days were numbered because Alex had crossed too many people. It was only a matter of time before his enemies caught up with him. So, one Mother's Day when Hector offered to drive Alex to Mrs. Sanchez's apartment building for a private celebration, Hector took mental notes of his surrounding. Although it took Hector a long time to remember exactly where Mama' Sanchez lived, Hector believed the time spent was well worth it.

Hector suspected that Alex had left his mother a small fortune when he died but after taking a peak at the apartment, he couldn't understand where all of the money went. Mama' Sanchez's living quarters consisted of second-hand furniture and a small television set. Yet, Hector was convinced that Mama' Sanchez had hidden the money for safekeeping. "I'll just have to find it," Hector thought.

"Well, everything is fine. I am just a simple lady who is trying to lead a simple life, Mr. Ramirez. No more surprise visits, please. In fact, I would appreciate it if you never came to my apartment again. I never liked the crowd Alex hung out with," Mama' Sanchez voiced.

As Hector walked out of the apartment as penniless as he was before, he reasoned that Mama' Sanchez must have been waiting for the heat to cool down from the government. "That Mrs. Sanchez is one smart lady," Hector thought. "Now I know where he got his brains."

*****

It had been over a week since Fernandez was released from prison. Tonight, he was scheduled to make his first public appearance. The acting President of the Council, Carlos Zanducci, had planned a big gala in Fernandez's honor. Fernandez's mansion was filled with the best champagne and food money could buy. Everybody who was anybody was expected to attend. There were so many requests for invitations that many people had to be turned away. This event was basically reserved for politicians, bankers, celebrities, and Fernandez's long time friends.

Mr. Fernandez caught a glimpse of himself in the rear-view mirror as he sat comfortably in the back of the limo. "It's been a long time since I've been in a tux," he thought.

His escort for the evening was Eva Santos. Whenever Mr. Fernandez required a companion for an event, he brought her with him. His wife never attended his business outings because she hated to get dressed up and had trouble making small talk with people she didn't know. Eva Santos, an elegant lady in her early thirties, fit in very well with Fernandez's colleagues. She was also an excellent bodyguard. As one of the few women to excel in martial arts and in various weaponry, Eva had developed very sharp defensive skills. There was one more thing about Eva Santos-she was deeply in love with Fernandez.

Eva knew in her heart that if she had to, she would give her own life to protect him. As she sat across from her boss, she considered sharing her feelings with him at the gathering but then opted against it, fearing that she would ruin the friendship they already shared.

Seated beside Fernandez were his trusted bodyguards, Jorge Marta and Nelson Listos. Driving the limo was the always reliable and dangerous Victor.

“Pardon me, Mr. Fernandez, but you don't look very pleasant tonight," Jorge Marta suggested.

“No, Jorge, I'm very happy. From what was told to me, most of my admirers have already arrived at the gala and I am looking forward to seeing them. I guess I just want to get tonight over with and return to running the organization again."

“You look very nice Eva,” Nelson complimented.

“Yes, I have to agree. You do look lovely in that long black dress," Fernandez winked.

“If only he could notice how I feel about him," Eva thought.

"Well thanks for the compliments but remember to be on your toes tonight guys. Not everyone there will be happy to see Mr. Fernandez," she advised.

That's what Fernandez admired about Eva, she always had business on her mind.

"Here we are, Mr. Fernandez," Victor called out as the limo pulled up to the front of the mansion.

Victor stepped out of the limo first. He then opened the side doors to allow Nelson and Jorge to exit next. After waiting for the signal, Fernandez emerged looking well rested and very relaxed. He resembled a man who had just come back from a long vacation rather than a man who had just spent the last five years incarcerated. He reached back and offered his hand to Eva. As she took his hand she smiled to herself thinking, "This is the way it's suppose to be. Sergio and me, side by side."

A swarm of people descended from the steps of the mansion to the limousine. Carlos Zanducci led the pack. As soon as Carlos reached Fernandez, he gave him a big hug. "Sergio, it's so good to see you. I would have come by the house, but I was told you were not seeing anyone."

"Yes, Carlos, that is true," Fernandez answered as he began smoothing out the wrinkles that were ingrained by Carlo's bear hug. "I wanted to catch up on some personal things, you can understand that, can't you?"

"But of course." Carlos then turned to Eva and kissed her on the hand, saying, "My, my, my. Eva you're looking as wonderful as ever."

Thank you, Carlos. You're looking quite dapper yourself."

"Come on, Sergio, there are hundreds of people waiting for you inside," Carlos said as he pointed toward the house. He then began clearing a path as Fernandez walked through the crowds like a hero returning from battle. Fernandez couldn't believe the amount of people in attendance.

"All of them want to catch a glimpse of the great man that started this organization," he whispered to Eva. Although he was excited about the attention, he wasn't convinced that it was fitting. It had been a long time since he'd been around this type of hoopla and he was beginning to feel a bit uneasy. They could barely make it into the house. It seemed that everyone had a tale to tell, a bone to pick, an ax to grind, or some type of special request. Eva noticed this, and asked Carlos Zanducci if there was a place where they could catch their breath. They had been smiling and shaking hands with people for the past hour.

"Sergio let's go to my den. You can have some privacy there," Carlos offered.

Once inside, Fernandez let out a sigh of relief. While he appreciated the support, he didn't like having that many people in his personal space. Moments later, vice president Jorge Arias also entered the den.

"Sergio, you look great!" Arias exclaimed. Everyone agreed in unison and then the gang started with their own private celebration. After forty minutes drinking and reminiscing, there was a knock at the door.

"Come on in!" Carlos hollered now feeling a little tipsy from the alcohol.

The attending bodyguards opened the door and a fragile elderly looking man in his early eighties entered. Mr. Fernandez was stunned as he nearly dropped his glass. He sprinted to his feet and dashed across the room to embrace his new visitor.

"Mr. Palomino how are you? It's been entirely too long since I have seen you last."

"Sergio, look at you, when are you going to put more weight on those skin and bones? You should come over to the house and let me make you some of my special home-cooked meals."

Fernandez broke out laughing. This was the same line Mr. Palomino had been saying for years. Fernandez had an enormous amount of respect for the elderly gentleman. On many occasions, Mr. Palomino provided Fernandez with valuable advice on how to run the organization and had mentored him in the earlier part of his career. He was also the only person that he bowed to, out of respect.

"Senior Palomino, please, have a seat. What are you up to these days?" Fernandez inquired as he pulled up a chair for his special guess, waiting for him to take a seat. He gently sat himself on the comfortable chair.

"Oh, Sergio. I've just been keeping my head above water." Mr. Palomino then dumped his accounting papers all over the coffee table.

"Senior Palomino, what's the problem?"

"I just can't keep the cops outta my ass. The more I make, the more they take."

"Has your joint been busted?" Carlos injected.

"You bet, those damn pigs are trying to take every penny I make."

"You're kidding me," Fernandez responded curiously.

"I wish I were kidding. A man can't even make an honest hustle these days."

"Carlos, help Senior Palomino out."

Carlos nodded. "Sergio, I'll take care of it."

"Thank you so much," Mr. Palomino said tearfully. "You don't know how much this means to me."

"Don't worry about it," Fernandez assured. "I owe you." After exchanging several stories of the good-old days.

The old man rose from his chair and began gathering his paperwork. "Look Sergio, it's getting late and I have to wake up early tomorrow to look over my garden. I'll be expecting a visit from you during the week," Mr. Palomino insisted.

"You bet. Now take care of yourself, Senior Palomino."

"You too, Sergio. And remember don't trust anybody. You hear me?" Mr. Palomino warned. "Things aren't always the way they seem."

"I hear you my good friend," Fernandez confirmed as he kissed the old man on the cheek and escorted him to the door. After Mr. Palomino's departure, he then returned his attention to his colleagues.

"I can tell by the reports that you have done a wonderful job while I was gone."

"Thank you, Sergio, but you left it in such fine shape. Running it was easy." Carlos said.

"There is only one thing that I am rather upset about."

"And what is that, Sergio?" Carlos asked with a worried look on his face.

"Your house is much bigger than mine. Now you've forced me to go out and buy a larger one for myself."

As the four of them burst into laughter, the notorious Ramon Zapata, Secretary of Defense entered the room.

"Everyone seems to be having such a good time in here, why wasn't I invited?"

“We're just talking about old times and the new changes in the organization,” Jorge responded.

“Oh so you've decided to tell him tonight?" Ramon asked curiously.

“No we haven't discussed anything yet,” Carlos answered as he glared at his uninformed coworker. It was clear that Carlos' mood had changed since Ramon's comment.

“Ramon, what are you talking about?" Fernandez interrupted. “What the hell was Carlos supposed to tell me?”

“Now everybody look, this is a celebration for Sergio, let's not discuss business tonight. We can save that for next Wednesday at the meeting downtown,” Carlos uttered nervously.

“If something important is going on, I want to know about it now not next week," Fernandez demanded.

“Fine," Ramon proceeded. “It's like this. Before you were released, the council took a vote and decided to keep it as it is. Carlos will remain as President.”

“Now we've all agreed that you would be well taken care of financially. We will provide you with practically anything that you want, money won't be a problem," Carlos said while seeking Fernandez approval.

“Carlos, you're a fool! Don't you remember that I'm the one who started all of this? You learned everything you know from me. I am still running the show here. You were just a figurehead until I returned. Now I am back and it is time for you to step down,” Fernandez growled while shooting a piercing stare in Carlos' direction.

“Sergio, you're not thinking clearly. For the past five years, the council was in charge while you were in jail, not you. Sure we sent someone to keep you abreast of the little things that happened in the organization, but that was only to make you happy. You don't realize it, but we are a multi-billion dollar operation. For us to explain everything to you would take months. You're from the old school where there was one boss who ran everything. That is no longer the case. Sergio, time has passed you by,” Ramon offered in an unconcerned tone. “Face it, your reign is over."

“Did everyone in the Council vote to have me step down?" Fernandez asked.

“It was a majority decision," Jorge answered solemnly.

"Since we already control every facet of the organization, it would be in your best interest to make this an easy transition." Ramon threatened. "We don't react too kindly to troublemakers."

"Look, I know there are a lot of things to think about. So while you're at home over the next few days, make a list of all the things you want and give them to us at Wednesday's meeting. I will personally take care of all your final demands myself," Carlos Zanducci pledged. The awkward silence that followed was interrupted by a startling knock at the door. "What is it?"

"There are still a lot of people waiting to see Mr. Fernandez," Luis Gomez said. "When will he be returning to his guests?"

"Well I don't want to keep them waiting," a suddenly upbeat Fernandez responded as he took Eva by the arm and headed towards the door. "There's no better time than the present."

"I am sorry, it is all for the best," Carlos assured.

"Yes, I know, Carlos, I know," Fernandez said while leaving the remaining men to continue their dialogue about the handling of his organization.

For the next hour, Sergio and Eva were crowded again by anxious guests. Now as the couple danced in the main ballroom, Fernandez seemed alarmingly calm.

"I do have to admit that you are handling things a lot better than I thought you would," Eva said smiling. "You appear to be incredibly level-headed."

"Why shouldn't I?"

"It's not everyday that a man is removed from the
Organization that he created. No one would blame you for being upset."

"And spoil a great evening like this? That wouldn't be a good move. I let them run the organization for five years, so I can certainly wait a few more days."

Eva Santos could only marvel at her companion. She didn't know if he could succeed in regaining control, but she knew he would die trying.

# Chapter 8

"How do you think we should handle Fernandez?" the Vice President Jorge inquired as he initiated the conversation. It was eleven o'clock on a Monday morning and the entire Cartel was scheduled for a meeting in their downtown offices. The top guns decided to get an early start and planned a private get-together before the general gathering. Carlos Zanducci, Jorge Arias, Luis Gomez, and Ramon Zapata briefed each other in the eighth floor conference room.

"What do you mean? What is there left to handle? We told him of the council's decision and that's that." Ramon answered abruptly.

"But do you think that we have anything to be worried about?" Carlos asked in a concerned voice.

"Not at all. Fernandez is a very intelligent man. He must realize that there is little else he could do to change things." Ramon said confidently. "It's a done deal."

"But Ramon, you don't know Fernandez like I know him. He never gives up on anything," Carlos Zanducci stated as he nervously tapped his pen on the conference room table.

"That was the old Fernandez. The one that's been in jail for the last five years has mellowed out since then."

"I do have to admit," Luis offered. "After the initial shock of it all, he pretty much seemed to settle into the idea as the night wore on at the party."

"I am just saying, don't be too sure. He still has some influence in Bolivia," Carlos warned.

"But who controls the soldiers in this organization, I do. So don't worry, if Fernandez becomes a problem I will deal with him." Ramon insisted.

"What's going on outside the window?" Jorge asked.

"They are painting the building," Luis answered proudly.

"This is our headquarters, it must look nice and modern."

"Just be sure that they are finished before Wednesday afternoon. I want everything to look perfect," Carlos insisted.

"Don't worry, they will," Jorge said.

"Carlos, you just worry too much. As for this thing with Fernandez, you knew we would have to deal with him some day. Now is that time, so we just have to make sure that everything keeps working out just like we planned it." Ramon lit up a cigar as he spoke.

"Fellas, it's time for the general meeting," Jorge announced.

"Let's head downstairs."

"Well, open the doors and let's get this over with," Ramon ordered. "I have places to go and people to see."

*****

Wednesday soon came. The Cartel headquarters was in a ten-story building located in downtown Bolivia. It was secluded from the rest of the commercial buildings in the area. Ramon ensured that no other structures were assembled within a one-mile radius. The main building was always heavily secured but today it was guarded like a fortress. Eight armed guards stood in the main entrance and there were at least eight more guards in the rear of the building. In addition, two sets of patrols containing six men each constantly walked around the perimeter and four guards were stationed on the roof. On the inside, more guards patrolled the lobby and adjoining hallways.

This definitely wasn't a typical day. For the most part, the building posed as a financial institution. Now it would serve as the setting for what many believed would be Fernandez resignation.

At 10:55, a black Lincoln Town car with tinted windows pulled in front of the building. Fernandez, always extraordinarily prompt, sat comfortably in the back seat as he watched the curious onlookers await his arrival. When the car came to a complete stop, out stepped the guest of honor wearing a very sheik gray suit. Eva Santos, also dressed rather extravagantly, followed. Moments later, Jorge Marta attempted to exit the car when Fernandez indicated that it wouldn't be necessary for him to get out. All eyes were upon Fernandez and Eva as they entered the heavily secured building.

The guards were in awe of him since most of them had never seen him in person. When several of the guards made eye contact with Mr. Fernandez, they didn't know whether to speak to him or bow in appreciation. Most just froze in place.

Members of the Cartel were already seated in the main conference room. Carlos was pacing near the window praying for a short and sweet resignation. Jorge, who was seated directly in front of the podium, nervously twitched in his chair. He still marveled at the results of the election since he'd cast the deciding vote.

“What would have happened if I had voted for Fernandez?" he wondered. “Well, it's too late now.”

Treasurer Luis Gomez, who had his fingers crossed in the creases of his pockets, also hoped that everything would go smoothly. Even though he truly believed that Carlos was the better man for the Presidency, he had a great deal of respect for Fernandez and wished they could continue their friendship. Ramon wasn't the least concerned about the meeting's outcome and was already lighting one of his victory cigars. Ever since Fernandez left for prison, Ramon had been planning his displacement and constantly did things to pull the organization away from Fernandez influence. Although some of Ramon's efforts were fruitless, he ultimately convinced the board to consider Carlos for a permanent presidency. Now he could use his influence to further manipulate Carlos until he chose to vie for the Presidency himself.

Carlos began to panic when he realized the men had not finished painting as Luis had promised.

"What in the hell are those guys still doing painting? I said, I wanted everything to be finished yesterday!" Carlos yelled out. Although Carlos rarely raised his voice, his nerves were starting to get the best of him.

"I'm sorry, but this whole process has taken them longer than they originally thought," Luis explained. "Believe me, most people probably haven't even noticed them."

"Well it's too late to change things now. Fernandez is on his way upstairs," Jorge Arias intervened. We will discuss this after the meeting."

Moments later, the charming couple entered the room. Carlos immediately raced across the plush carpet to greet them.

"Welcome, welcome Sergio, we're glad you made it." After shaking Fernandez hand firmly, Carlos lightly kissed Eva on her cheek. "It's always a pleasure to see you my fair lady."

As soon as Fernandez and Eva excused themselves to mingle with other Cartel members, Carlos' anxiety floated away. It seemed that Fernandez didn't bring the large entourage that many had anticipated. Now Carlos believed the meeting would run smoothly. As Fernandez walked deeper into the room, Carlos gestured for the Cartel to give his former boss a standing ovation. For the next two minutes, everyone stood applauding-except Ramon Zapata, of course. Carlos then escorted Fernandez and Eva to their seats. It was time for the meeting to begin.

"First I would like to thank Mr. Fernandez for making all of this possible," Carlos explained in his opening remarks. "If it wasn't for his vision, none of us would be seated in this room now. As many of you know, Mr. Fernandez started the organization more than twenty years ago. Through his leadership, the Fernandez Cartel is one of the most powerful Organizations in the world. Let's hear it again for the man of the hour!"

The Council responded with a roar of applause. Unfortunately, the more the men applauded, the angrier Fernandez got. To him, it seemed more like a wake than a meeting in his honor. "These guys can't think I'm this stupid," he murmured.

As the audience took their seats, Luis crept to the front of the room and motioned for one of the waiters to provide him with a microphone. First, he talked about the good times that he and Fernandez shared. Then he ordered the waiting staff to bring out glasses of champagne.

"All the best, my man," Luis spat out as he raised his glass high in the air. "We're going to miss you at the helm."

"Here, here," a voice called out in agreement. There was nothing but joy on the faces of the Council and they were very pleased with the way that they handled a very delicate situation. This was their chance to finally tie up all the loose ends that had been swaying in the winds since Fernandez imprisonment.

"I have another toast," Carlos said from the podium. "As the Council knows, I've already told Sergio that whatever in the world he wants, we will provide-no questions asked. Whether it be a new mansion, a plane, or small island. No amount of money could repay him for his hard work. So now I want everyone to stand so we can wish the great Sergio Fernandez continued success."

The men stood in unison and raised their glasses. "To the Great Sergio Fernandez," they chanted, "continued success!"

"Before we drink, there is something that I would like to say," Fernandez interrupted. "First, I want to congratulate Carlos Zanducci and the other members of the council for doing such a great job."

"That is not necessary, Sergio," Carlos said smilingly.

"No, Carlos, but it is. Secondly, after careful thought, I have finally figured out what I want most. I've decided to stay on as President of this organization."

There was nothing but a deafening silence in the room. Everyone stood still in complete shock. Until Fernandez announcement, it seemed that things were going perfectly.

"Sergio, the council agreed that you must step down," Carlos interceded. "We've already discussed this, you were voted out."

"So what, I never agreed to anything. No matter what anyone says, this is-and always will be-my organization," Fernandez shouted. "And that's final!"

"Sergio you must be losing your mind. We've been running the Organization without you for the last five years. We didn't need you then and we don't need you now. In fact, the Council controls everything and I know you don't want to go to war with us. You wouldn't stand a chance!" Ramon argued as he blew cigar smoke in the air.

"You see, that is where you are wrong, Ramon. I have already started a war against you!" Mr. Fernandez threw his champagne glass at the window. "I've already won."

As soon as Victor heard the champagne glass shatter, he and his two-hired hit men burst through the window. Their guns were already drawn and the men in the painting uniforms immediately got everyone's attention.

"Oh shit! It's the Assassin," Ramon called out as he went for his trusted .45 revolver.

Every one of the Council's men was armed, but only four attempted to go for their weapons. Ramon was the first to reach for his pistol. Although he knew it could one-day come to this, a battle between him and the notorious Assassin, the ex-general hoped that on that day, he would be in a more favorable position. The Assassin, with his trademark black sunglasses and sawed off shotgun under his arm, had all of his attention focused on the ex-General. Now Ramon, who had successfully retrieved his gun out of its holster, was preparing to take aim until the first shotgun blast hit him directly in his lower abdomen. As blood spewed wildly, Ramon crumbled to the floor as he struggled to cover the hole that now exposed his intestines. A second blast severed his right arm and parts of his shoulder. With the last of his energy, Ramon looked over at Fernandez seemingly to acknowledge his defeat.

The two guards standing outside of the meeting room burst through the door and were immediately met with a barrage of gunfire from Eva Santos.

Fernandez and Eva, now standing front and center with their guns drawn, wondered which traitor they should knock off next. As Eva aimed her weapon at the remaining members of the Council, Fernandez pointed his gun directly at Carlos.

In a calm voice, Fernandez mouthed his directions, "Carlos, first I want you to get on the portable radio and tell all of your men that everything is okay. They are not to come to this floor for any reason."

Carlos picked up the portable radio with his hands trembling wildly. "This is Carlos Zanducci. Everything is fine in the conference room. We've just been celebrating a little too loudly.

There is no reason to be concerned, everybody should continue manning their posts."

After following instructions, Carlos dropped the radio and began pleading for his life. "Sergio, I know what you're probably thinking but I never planned to take the Organization from you. We all got together and voted on this."

"But you never spoke with me about this!" Fernandez yelled.

"That's true but we all thought that running the Organization was the last thing you would want to do when you got out of prison," Carlos said desperately trying to convince Fernandez to spare his life. "After all, this stuff got you behind bars in the first place."

"Oh come on, you guys didn't even think I'd make it out of prison alive, did you?" Fernandez said sharply.

"Fernandez, what are you talking about?"

"You tried to have me killed while I was in jail. Don't stand there and lie to me about it!"

"I'm going to be perfectly honest with you. I heard about the attempt on your life after it happened. Ramon planned the whole thing."

"It's quite convenient for you to blame a dead man." Fernandez snapped.

"No that's the truth. I swear by it."

"Not only are you a coward, you're also a damn liar. I will enjoy killing you myself."

"After everything that I've done for this organization, how can you kill me like I'm some dog in the street? How brave is that?"

Fernandez looked around at the faces of the remaining members of the council. It wouldn't go over well with his staff if he just shot Carlos in cold blood. He decided on an alternative.

"Somebody get me a revolver?" he demanded.

A nearby waiter picked Ramon's revolver off of the floor.

"Now, take Carlos' gun from his waistband," Fernandez ordered. He handed his gun to Eva and took Ramon's revolver from the nervous waiter. Fernandez then began emptying bullets from the gun's barrel into his hand until one remained.

"Carlos, you and I are about to play a game of Russian Roulette," he laughed. "Let's get started."

"That's crazy, I won't do it."

"But Carlos, you have no choice. Victor come here. I am ordering you to shoot the man that doesn't pull the trigger on his turn."

Fernandez took his index finger and spun the barrel fiercely, "Carlos since you look a little scared I will go first."

An energized Fernandez put the gun to his head and pulled the trigger. There was a clicking sound, but no bullet was in the chamber. As he handed the gun to a trembling Carlos, he began to realize how much he had at stake, In spite of his efforts to help the Organization prosper, he would still lose it by causing his own death. Carlos quickly took the gun and pressed it against his temple. He pulled the trigger, the chamber was still empty.

"Now this is getting interesting," Fernandez smiled. This was the first time, in a long while he was feeling like his old self, powerful and dangerous. He took the gun and dried it on his shirt. It was damp from Carlos' sweaty palms. He then took the pistol for another spin as he looked directly into Eva Santos eyes. She couldn't believe this was happening. The man she'd loved for years, the man who had finally shown some type of affection towards her, was about to blow his brains out. Fernandez pulled the trigger. The gun clicked but no bullet was released. Eva let out a sigh that must have been heard by everyone in the room.

Carlos cautiously took the pistol while silently cursing under his breath. He even considered pointing the gun at Fernandez and firing three times. Of course, a move like that would have got him killed instantly and Carlos felt he had a better chance playing the game. A quick calculation reinforced Carlos' fear, that he had a one in three chance of being killed. He placed the gun to his temple once again as he looked up at the ceiling and prayed for another miracle. He slowly pulled the trigger, BOOM! The .45 caliber revolver went off like a cannon, spurting blood and brain matter all over the room.

Spectators were relieved that everything was finally over and Eva began breathing again. Fernandez was a little disappointed that the game had ended. Now that the President and Secretary of Defense were dead, Fernandez quickly scanned the room. He knew he couldn't afford to kill anyone else, he needed the staff to tell him what had transpired while he was away.

"Don't worry the rest of you can stay on. You are important members of this Organization and I do not hold you responsible for the actions of these two," he said pointing down to Ramon and Carlos. "Jorge, you will remain as Vice President. Treasurer Luis Gomez, you have just been promoted to Executive Treasurer." Fernandez laughed. As if on cue, the remaining men also laughed. Jorge Arias and Luis Gomez were grateful that they were spared and felt they owed him their lives. Suddenly, a message on Carlos' radio indicated that a group of policemen were surrounding the building. Fernandez ordered the guards to send the police upstairs immediately.

"What are we now going to do?" Jorge asked nervously. "Look at all of these dead bodies, what will we say?"

Fernandez looked at Eva and nodded his head. She quickly raised her gun striking each hit man twice in the chest, catching them completely off guard.

"Now, everyone let's all sit down calmly. When the police arrive, we'll tell them that two gunmen burst into our meeting and killed our fellow coworkers before we returned fire to defend ourselves," he said having thought out everything in his head days ago. "As far as we know, they must have been some outside group trying to take over."

"What if they don't believe us?" an anxious Council member inquired.

"They'll believe it because they don't have much of a choice. I am Sergio Fernandez and I am finally back!"

# Chapter 9

It was only yesterday since Mama' Sanchez had turned Hector away from her apartment. He didn't expect to be treated like a long lost son. But he certainly didn't know he would be treated like he was Al Capone either. Whatever the case, Hector was a man who could not easily be discouraged. He was like a roach. Just when you thought you got rid of him, he would always find a way to come back. Hector knew Mama Sanchez was hiding something he just couldn't figure out what it was. He vowed to find Alex's fortune even if he had to watch the house from across the street all week.

The twins had a day off from work and were going to the local park to play soccer. They were both considered very good players and the neighborhood kids would often argue to get them on their teams. Just one block away from the apartment, a middle-aged man approached them.

"Excuse me boys, do you have a minute?" Hector asked.

"Why?" Alejandro asked. "We're in a hurry."

"My name is Hector Ramirez. Are you related to Mrs. Sanchez?"

"Why do you know her?" Alejandro snapped.

"Well, I was a good friend of her son Alex Sanchez and I just wanted to know if she was at home."

The twins' eyes lit up. "What do you know about Alex Sanchez?"

"I know a lot about him? Why do you ask?"

"We're his sons. My name is Roberto and this is Alejandro."

"Ah, you guys must be identical, I can't tell you apart."

"Were you really friends with our father?" Roberto continued.

"I was one of his closest advisors," Hector lied. "Guys if you want, we can talk about him some other time. I know you said you were in a hurry and it looks like you're going to play football or something. I'll talk to you later."

"No don't leave yet," Roberto pleaded. "We can play soccer anytime. Mr. Ramirez would you please tell us all about our father?"

"Of course. Is there a place where we can have some privacy?"

"Right near the park," Alejandro suggested.

Once they got to the park, Hector described his visit to their grandmother's house from the day before. He told them that Mama Sanchez said she never wanted to see him again. Roberto and Alejandro listened in disbelief. That didn't sound like the grandmother they knew.

Hector then painted a picture of the twins' father. "Alex Sanchez was one of the biggest drug dealers that ever lived in Miami," he explained. "He was the meanest man in town and didn't give a damn about nobody. He lived in a big mansion on the hill, drove fancy cars and wore fine clothes. Everybody feared him because he ripped through these Miami streets like a fuckin' tornado."

"If our father was so powerful and feared, why was he killed?" Alejandro asked anxiously.

You see, Alejandro. That's the point right there. Your father became too powerful, so this big drug lord ordered a hit on him. One Sunday night, hundreds of men stormed your father's mansion and killed him," Hector said sadly.

"He didn't die in a car with his sister?" Roberto inquired.

"No way, they were both executed by some crazed drug lord because he thought Alex was going to start doing business without him."

"Why would our grandmother lie to us about him?" Roberto defended. "She said our father was a hero."

"I guess she didn't want you to know the truth. She's a church lady, maybe she didn't feel comfortable talking to you about all that kind of stuff," Hector replied.

"Do you know anything else about this drug lord, that you say had our father killed?" Alejandro quizzed.

"All I know is that he lives in Bolivia."

"Roberto I just knew Mama was hiding something from us," Alejandro said.

"Guys the only thing I don't understand is why didn't you live with your father? He certainly could have afforded to care for you."

"Mr. Ramirez, our father didn't know about us. Our mother never told him he had children," Roberto responded.

"Do you know if our father has any other children living here?" Alejandro intervened.

"I am not sure. I don't think so. But he was married at the time he was killed."

"To who?"

"To some gringa named Candice. I don't know her last name but I can find out for you. She's staying at some nut house here in Miami."

"Which one?"

"I'm not sure but I can get the information if you want it."

"Thanks a lot Mr. Ramirez you've been a big help," Roberto said shaking the stranger's hand firmly.

"Don't worry, call me anytime. Here's my number in case you need to get in touch with me. We have to get together in a couple of days so I can tell you more about your father," Hector offered strategically.

"Thanks."

"And remember if you ever needed anything, come to Hector Ramirez." I'll take good care of you."

*****

“I hope she’s still here.” Roberto said.

“I doubt it,” Alejandro said negatively. “She arrived here more than five years ago. She’s probably changed hospitals at least ten times since then.”

“Look, it won’t hurt to check for ourselves.”

“I still don’t know why we just didn’t call before we traveled all this way.”

“Like I already told you, they won’t give out that kind of information over the phone to complete strangers,” Roberto answered impatiently.

“We’re not strangers, she’s family,” Alejandro snickered. “We’re the sons she’s never had.”

Alejandro and Roberto cautiously approached the entrance to the Institute.

“Do you boys have a pre-approved pass to see someone here?” the security guard at the desk inquired.

“No we don’t, but we’ve come along way to see a relative,” Roberto answered.

“Obviously, this is your first visit,” the guard insisted as he shook his head and pointed his finger at the boys. “If you had been here before, you would already know that nobody sees anyone without a pre-approved pass given by one of the staff members. Understand?”

“So, there’s no way we can see her then,” a disappointed Alejandro confirmed.

“You got that right kid. Now you guys gotta leave now.”

They boys sulked deeply as they stood outside the entrance longing to see the mystery woman that Hector described to them. Roberto knew there had to be an alternative and he invited his brother to accompany him on a walk around the grounds. As they circled the building, the twins noticed a side door that appeared to be used only by the facility’s patients. Roberto smiled at Alejandro because he knew this was their way inside.

“Alejandro, I’m going to find Candice even if I have to search this whole hospital.”

"I’m with you, but maybe we should start with the second floor,” Alejandro suggested. “That way, we can duck the guards and the roaming staff.”

The upper level was quite different from the ground floor. It was divided into little apartments. The twins guessed that the answers to all of their questions were behind one of those wooden doors. As the twins turned one of the corners, they immediately bumped into a very large woman in a nurse's uniform.

"Who are you? What are you doing here?" Nurse Mitchell demanded.

"Hello, my name is Roberto and this is my brother Alejandro," he stammered nervously. "We're here to see Candice."

Nurse Mitchell looked suspiciously at the twins and abruptly stated, "there is nobody by the name of Candice at this Institute. Maybe you should try some place else.

Nurse Mitchell was accustomed to screening visitors for her patient. Ever since Cynthia's arrival, the facility had been swarmed with journalists who wanted exclusive information on one of the most notorious killings in American History. On some occasions, the government would send its agents in an attempt to seize some money that many believed Alex Sanchez hid in Swiss bank accounts. Over the years, they all tried to get past Nurse Mitchell, but most of their attempts failed. The few people that did sneak in to see Cynthia still were unable to obtain information. Cynthia hadn't spoken to anyone in over five years.

As the nurse stood opposite Cynthia's latest intruders, her curiosity heightened. These boys didn't fit the profile of Cynthia's former visitors. She was tempted to question them for more information but then decided it would only tip them off about Cynthia's whereabouts.

"Code Blue! Code Blue!" Yelled a nurse down the hallway.

"You boys wait right here. When I get back I will have security to escort you out," Nurse Mitchell ordered as she went huffing towards the commotion. The twins noticed how infuriated the nurse seemed by the recent alarm. It was just one more thing she had to add to the incredibly long list of tasks that were scheduled for the day. First, she had to deal with a suicide on the third floor. Then she had to handle a runaway on the first floor. The twins had just breached security and now there was another Code Blue, which meant someone was either dying or close to it. Although Nurse Mitchell loved her job dearly, she had been feeling overwhelmed ever since her promotion to head nurse and wondered if her new responsibilities were worth the money.

The emergency request came from a normally quiet wing of the Institute. As the alarms sounded, an army of nurses and psychiatrists went dashing down the hallway. Roberto and Alejandro decided to continue their search and began flipping through the files in a nearby cabinet draw.

"I know they must have a record of her somewhere," Roberto insisted as he checked the unattended records. Towards the end of the stack, Roberto noticed a Cynthia a/k/a Candice Hancock in room #317.

"This must be it," Roberto enthusiastically called out. He grabbed Alejandro's hand and the two scurried into the stairwell and raced up to the third floor.

"311, 313, 315, ah room 317" Roberto said happily as he extended his hand to turn the doorknob. He hoped this woman would answer the many questions he had about his father.

"What in the hell do you think you two are doing!" a very angry and winded Nurse Mitchell yelled. She looked intensely at both of the boys, and said, "This one better be good, or I am going to have you both arrested for trespassing."

*****

Later...

As Nurse Mitchell walked into the room, Cynthia Hancock remained motionless and continued staring at an old I Love Lucy episode. An outsider would have a hard time trying to figure out whether Cynthia even noticed if the TV was on or off, but Cynthia was very much aware and watching television gave her a chance to escape her unpleasant memories. Even though she was only in her early thirties, Cynthia had lived a life of a woman three times here age. It showed in her face and was imbedded deep in her soul. She often had that frozen cold look of a person who drank too much, partied entirely too long, and had too many bouts with life.

Even with Cynthia's difficulties, she had still come a long way compared to how she was when she first entered the Institute. Cynthia had put on some pounds and the sparkle in her eyes was slowly beginning to return.

"Cynthia, you got a letter this morning," Nurse Mitchell said excitedly. "I am going to leave it on the coffee table so you can read it."

Nurse Mitchell left the room. As usual, Cynthia waited until she was completely alone before she moved around her room. She slowly walked over to the table to examine the letter she'd received. It appeared strange. They only letters she ever received were from her mother and she didn't recognize the handwriting on the envelope. As she debated whether she would read the letter, without realizing it, she had already opened the envelope.

*Dear Ms. Hancock,*

*I know you don't know me, but my brother and I came to see you two weeks ago. You didn't speak to us but the nurse said that you probably understood everything we said. Since then, I've called your mother to try to get some advice about this whole situation but she got very angry. Instead of helping us she told me to never call again and then hung up. You see, Ms. Hancock, I know you were married to my father and I think there are a lot of things you could tell me about him. I would go to somebody else, but there really is nobody else. I am torn between what my grandmother tells me and the tales I've heard about him from one of his old buddies (so he says). If at all possible, please contact me soon. My address is on the envelope and my telephone number is 555-4170.*

*Sincerely yours,*
*Roberto Sanchez*

*P.S. Sorry to bother you.*

# Chapter 10

*"Frank, I need more of the purple pills," Candice raved. "Send them over, now!"*

*This was a typical conversation in the life Candice. After waking up in the early afternoon with the help of some uppers that laid on her night table, her first task was to phone her connection to remind him that she needed more "medicine." Lately, she had been increasing her doses because she was finding that they weren't as effective as they had been in the past. After confirming her order, she slammed the phone down and rolled out of her king size bed. Systematically, she dragged herself over to the mini bar across the room and poured a glass of her favorite champagne. This took the edge off of the uppers. Now Candice was now ready to start her day.*

*"Well look at this shit," Alex barked as he entered their bedroom. "Sleeping Beauty has finally woken the fuck up."*

*"Alex, don't fuck with me today, I'm really not in the mood," Candice snapped.*

*"Look, it's Saturday and we're going out tonight." Alex explained. "I'm telling you now because you always say I never give you enough time to get dressed. Today, you have five hours to get ready."*

*"Where are we going, Alex?"*

*"Don't worry about where we're going. It's a surprise."*

*"How in the hell am I going to know how to dress, if you won't tell me where we're going?"*

*"Don't worry you will look nice in whatever you put on." Alex then walked over and started to kiss Candice all over her face and neck. He then gently placed his hand under her robe and began gently pinching her breasts.*

*"Alex get off of me. It's too early for you to start that shit with me," Candice whined.*

*"Okay, but tonight when we get back in. I don't want to hear that I'm too tired shit," Alex complained as he headed towards the door. Candice, ignoring Alex's orders to get dressed, proceeded to lay back down on her unmade bed.*

*"Hey! Move your ass," Alex yelled. "You look like hell. Call the beautician to come over to do your hair."*

*"Alex, you don't look so hot yourself," Candice mumbled.*

*"And maybe she can bring over some kind of makeup artist. You're so fuckin' pale. You look like, what's that fuckin' cartoon character that I saw this morning? Oh yeah, fuckin' Casper the friendly ghost," Alex laughed.*

*"Alex go fuck yourself!"*

*"Candice, you're so fuckin' lady-like," Alex shot back. "I am going out on a few errands, I'll be back later. Be fuckin' dressed, on fuckin' time, please."*

*As he turned to leave the room again, Candice threw the empty champagne bottle at him. She was a little shocked that the bottle was empty, especially since she planned to have another drink. "They must be making the bottles a lot smaller these days," she thought. The bottle shattered in a million pieces after hitting the door.*

*"Missed him again!" a frustrated Candice screamed.*

*Finally, she had the whole house to herself, except for the maid, cook, and a couple of security guards. She hated the security guards they always seemed to be around, especially when she was getting dressed. Pancho and his friends stayed in the guest house. Their gardener and his family also lived on the property. "Hell, there are more people living here, than they're teenagers at a Menudo concert," she said.*

*Later, Candice tip-toed into Alex's private room. He spent the majority of his time in his home office and she also knew he kept his secret stash of coke in one of the drawers. As much as she tried to resist the temptation, she desperately craved another hit. At first, she was only planning to do two or three lines, but then decided to do two more when she realized she'd gotten the batch that Alex had starting mixing with the other stuff. Since she was going out tonight, she at least wanted to be in the right frame of mind, a couple of sniffs was just what she needed.*

*Candice called the hairdresser just as Alex had requested and the beauty entourage arrived with all of their essentials. The hairdresser was accompanied by a make-up artist and nail technician. Upon receiving Candice's call, all of them canceled the rest of their appointments. Nobody wanted to miss the trip to the mansion and the big tips that Candice handed out. They also couldn't resist an invitation to snort the best coke in town, for free.*

*At 9:20, Alex came storming through the front door. He was greeted by his maid Marina. He looked down at his watch to see how much time he had lost at his last pit stop. "I'm only twenty minutes late," he thought. "We can still make it on time."*

*"Marina, is Candice ready?" he asked.*

*"She should be Mr. Sanchez. The hairdresser left over an hour ago."*

*Alex walked into the bedroom and found Candice sprawled all over the bed face down.*

*"Come on Candice, don't do this to me, wake up. You're wrinkling the new clothes you just put on."*

*There was no movement.*

*"All right, move your ass. We gotta leave soon."*

*Still there was no movement.*

*Alex went over to the bed and started to shake Candice. He knew immediately that something was very wrong. As he turned Candice over, he was shocked by the dead look in her eyes and the saliva that was foaming from her mouth. It appeared that Candice had overdosed.*

*Later, as Alex paced back and forth in the corridor of the hospital's emergency room, his bodyguards reassured him that everything would be okay.*

*Hours later, the attending doctor emerged from surgery.*

*"Are you Mr. Sanchez?" the Doctor asked.*

*"Yes I am, and doctor, give it to me straight. Is my wife gonna be okay?"*

*"Well, she survived the surgery. We had to pump her stomach. It also appeared that she suffered a mild heart attack."*

*"Doc, get to the point, is she gonna make it?"*

*"We think she has a very good chance of surviving, but we're worried about the time she went by without a lot of oxygen. We don't know for sure, but she may have permanent brain damage."*

*Alex closed his eyes, and started to bang his hand repeatedly against the wall.*

*The doctor placed his hand on Alex's shoulder, "Mr. Sanchez, the only thing we can do is wait. You might as well go home, we'll know more in the morning."*

*"Doc, I go no fuckin' where until I know how my Candice is. I want to see her now and I don't want to hear any bullshit.."*

*Within minutes Alex was in the recovery room looking down at Candice. He had never seen a person so helpless. It seemed as if she was hooked up to every machine possible. Tubes were everywhere.*

*A single tear raced down Alex's face. "What a terrible way for Candice to spend her birthday," Alex thought. This certainly wasn't the surprise he had in mind.*

*****

Fernandez smiled widely as he looked out of his office window. Though he knew running the organization wouldn't be easy, he was glad that he was back on top. Victor entered the room and caught a glimpse of his gloating boss. "Mr. Fernandez, the board members are all here, they're waiting for you in the conference room."

"That's good, Victor. Everyone is here on time, now that's a sign of respect."

"I know you must love being in charge again."

"It feels great! From now on, I'll be running things a little bit differently."

"What do you have planned?"

"Victor, my friend, you will know soon enough, but now it's time for me to greet the board."

As Victor watched Fernandez rise from his plush executive chair and head towards the meeting room, he wondered what changes could possibly be in store for them. "Hopefully, these changes won't require any of my own personal talents," Victor thought. "They would not like that."

*****

*Dear Ms. Hancock,*

*Hello Ms. Hancock, how are you? This is Roberto writing you again. I hope everything is fine and you are getting better. I am writing again because you did not reply to my first letter. I was told that you received my letter and looked at it. Well that was over two weeks ago. I don't think it is fair how you won't share the information you have about my father with me. My brother and I risked getting locked up when we came to see you. The least you can do is contact me and tell me what I need to know.*

*Sincerely,*

*Roberto Sanchez*

*****

Roberto and Alejandro met up with Hector Ramirez a few blocks from home. The twins still had not confronted their grandmother with the new information regarding their father. They decided it would be best not to bring it up.

"Guys, I'm glad you both made it," Hector grinned. "I was looking forward to seeing you two."

"Hector it was no big deal," Alejandro shrugged. "Roberto and I have the day off."

As the boys got into the car, Roberto began to get a little nervous. "Where are we going to hang out?" Roberto stammered.

"Oh, we are going to the Westside of downtown Miami. They have this real cool bar where everybody likes to hang out," Hector said smoothly. "It's a real blast."

"We're underage," Roberto responded sharply. "They probably won't let us in."

"Don't worry, you are with me. You won't have any problems."

Once inside, the twins looked around excitedly. This was the first time they'd ever been in a bar and they couldn't believe it was filled with so many people even though it was only seven o'clock at night. Hector guided them to three comfortable seats at the bar.

"In the sixties, this was the first neighborhood where the Cubans came to live," Hector explained. "In fact, there were so many Cubans living here at one point they named this area little Havana."

The boys tried to focus on Hector's words but they were distracted by the movements of the crowd. On one side of the bar, men in their forties were drinking Corona beers. On the other side, up and coming hustlers and drug dealers were talking about the trade. And of course, lots and lots of women surrounded the big spenders. Some women were old enough to be grandmothers, pitifully trying to squeeze their sagging bodies into revealing dresses. Their counterparts, young girls that didn't look old enough to be out of Junior High School, struggled to walk in high heel shoes.

Although the place was a little on the sleazy side, it had a certain energy to it. Roberto was sure that Mama' Sanchez definitely wouldn't approve of it. Meanwhile Alejandro seemed drawn into the whole scene.

The waitress walked over to their table and gave them the run down of daily specials. “What are you handsome men gonna have to drink?”

Hector turned to his guests, “Well guys, pick your poison.”

“We'll have a couple of beers," Alejandro answered confidently.

"Make that three Coronas," Hector told the waitress.

As the three men talked and guzzled their drinks, Hector dropped one lie after another. First he spun tales about his childhood. Then he invented a partnership between he and Alex Sanchez. In the midst of another fabrication, Hector spotted one of his old flings.

“Boys hang out here for a while. I just saw this chick I used to go out with. If I play my cards right, maybe she'll let me tap that big ass of hers."

“Hector go for it. We'll be okay,” Alejandro assured. “This place is real cool.”

Alejandro and Roberto were identical twins. Their external parts looked exactly alike, yet it was times like this that their true differences were revealed. Alejandro was totally comfortable in this type of environment. On the other hand, Roberto was extremely nervous and couldn't wait to leave.

“Hey guys, can I join you for a drink?" a lanky stranger asked.

“Yeah it's okay, me and my brother Roberto are waiting for our friend to return."

“Are you guys from this part of Miami?"

“No we're not,” Roberto answered abruptly waiting for the unwanted guest to leave.

“Where were you guys born?"

“Cuba," Roberto quickly recited.

“What's with the questions? Are you planning to write our life stories or something?" a suddenly annoyed Alejandro interrupted.

“No, it's just that I noticed you two when you first walked in, it reminded me of the first time I entered a bar in my hometown in Cuba."

“What town are you from?" Roberto shot back.

"Varadero. Where are you from?"

"We are from Santiago de Cuba."

After Roberto answered, the man broke out into a wide grin. His suspicions were correct, these were the same twins who had run away from Cuba years earlier after the murder of a neighborhood teen. "I bet the authorities would love to catch these kids," he thought.

The stranger lied about being from Varadero. He lived in the same neighborhood from the twins and often saw them playing in the streets when they were younger. Although the twins had grown up a lot since he last saw them, he still recognized them. Now that he was sure that these were the boys that the Cuban authorities were looking for, he quickly toyed with ways to make some badly needed cash.

Alejandro looked at Roberto in amazement. Had he forgotten that they were on the run? Once again, Roberto was carefree with their information. Alejandro silently hoped his brother wouldn't get them in any trouble and assumed that maybe his loose lips were being caused by the beer. He guessed he couldn't help it. When the visitor spotted Hector walking back to the table, he took it as his cue to leave.

"By the way, my name is Juan," he said as he waved the boys goodbye.

"Hi I'm Roberto and this is my brother Alejandro," Roberto said as he extended his arm for a handshake.

"Nice meeting you, I'm sure we'll be in touch," Juan responded as he quickly disappeared into the crowd.

"Who was that?" Hector asked.

"Don't know, don't care," Alejandro responded.

"Hey guys are you ready to leave? Louise over there wants to get together and party. So I figured I would take you guys home now," Hector offered.

The threesome gathered their belonging and headed for the door. At that moment, Jimmy Acosta and his entourage were entering from a side entrance. Jimmy was one of the most powerful drug dealers in Miami. At twenty-nine, he had already acquired the presence and style of men much older. He helped control the cocaine trade in lower Miami and was the front man for a powerful drug operation. After receiving one-on-one training from the organization's top man in Bolivia, Jimmy returned to the same poor neighborhood where he grew up. There he was treated like a hero coming back from the war.

When Hector got a glimpse of Jimmy, he decided to reschedule his departure plans. “Listen guys, I gotta say hello to a buddy of mine.”

The twins remained at the doors and watched Hector walk over to the area where Jimmy was seated. A bodyguard immediately blocked Hector's path. “Just where are you going?" a gruff voiced questioned.

Jimmy looked over to the commotion and immediately recognized Hector. They knew each other from the days when Jimmy was a lookout for Hector. He cracked a smile and motioned for the bodyguard to let Hector through.

Back at the exit, Juan reappeared like a slithering snake as soon as Hector left. “I know who you are and why you left Cuba," he laughed. “I also know Sister Catherine really well."He, of course, left out the part about how he once tried to rape her.

“Back home, there is a big reward for information about you," Juan continued. “I really don't want to turn you in. But due to my financial situation, I have no choice. Unless you boys pay me five thousand dollars, I'm going to the local police and collect the reward money.”

Juan winked at the boys and raced out of the bar. The twins stood in shock as their hearts pounded with fear.

“I knew my luck was going to change," Hector said smiling as he returned from his visit.

“Why is that?" a very somber Roberto asked.

“Jimmy has finally decided to give me a job working for him," Hector said excitedly. “Fellas what's the matter? You both look like you just saw a ghost or something."

“No I think we just had a little too much to drink tonight," Alejandro answered.

As they drove to the house, Hector chattered endlessly about his new boss. “Tonight is just the beginning of much more to come."

The twins shook their heads in agreement as they looked intensely in each other's eyes. They were thinking the exact same thoughts and wondered what would happen next.

# Chapter 11

A very troubled Roberto walked aimlessly across the beach. Why was it that every time things appeared to be going so well, trouble always popped up? Just last week he didn't have a care in the world. Now he and Alejandro had to come up with five thousand dollars. If they didn't, Juan promised to go to the police to tell them everything about what happened in Cuba.

Roberto tried to convince himself that maybe the authorities over here would understand and that nothing would be done to them. Then he realized the truth. What happened in Cuba, was not a case of two boys stealing sweets from a candy store. He and Alejandro were two fugitives wanted for murder. Whether it was self-defense or not, in the long run it wouldn't matter.

Between the two of them, they could only come up with close to two thousand dollars. If Alejandro sold his beat up car, maybe a little more. Under no circumstances would they go to their grandmother. Although she would do her best to give them the remaining money, in all likelihood, it would probably take all of her life's savings. They just couldn't do that.

There was only one person they could ask for the money, Roberto thought. That was Hector Ramirez. Even though they had met him only recently, Roberto believed he would look out for them, especially since he was such a close family friend. Hector *did* say that they should come to him if they ever had any problems. Hector didn't look like he had a lot of money, but maybe he could loan them a few thousand dollars.

Now that Roberto had at least one alternative, he quickly turned around and started walking back to the house. He was anxious to get Alejandro's opinion. That was, if he could get a hold of him. Lately, it seemed that Alejandro was always into something and Roberto wondered what kind of trouble he was getting himself into now.

*****

"Would you like something to drink?' she asked.

"No thanks, I'm okay," Alejandro winked.

"Come on, just have one drink with me. I hate to drink alone."

"Okay Tina, I'll have one Rum and Coke." "That's good, I'll have one too."

As Tina slid off of her beige leather couch to get the drinks, Alejandro inhaled the extravagance of his hostess living room. He was impressed. Over the past six months he was able to conclude that Tina definitely had money, but he didn't know exactly how much.

Alejandro had met Tina and her girlfriends at the restaurant where he worked. Three times a month, the girls would meet over lunch to drink and talk about their problems-which always involved men. Tina, recently divorced, had been awarded the house and a nice monthly allowance from her husband. It wasn't until the past three months that Tina focused her attention on Alejandro. She made sure that whenever the gals met they sat in Alejandro's section.

Alejandro didn't mind at all. He loved it when the women eyed his body as he left their table. Last month Tina finally got the courage to give Alejandro her telephone number. Alejandro took the number knowing that one day he would use it. Today was that day.

"Alejandro, sorry I took so long but I had to take an important phone call."

"That's no problem, it just gave me a chance to check out your place."

"Well, how do you like it?"

"It's pretty cool."

Tina again made herself comfortable on the couch.

"Alejandro, move closer to me," Tina whispered. "You're too far away. Don't worry, I don't bite."

Alejandro refocused his attention on his date realizing that she had changed from her work clothes into a sexy piece of lingerie. He slowly advanced towards her and could feel the vibrations from her trembling body. She could barely control herself. Here was the kid that she'd been making passes at for the last four months sitting on her couch. For a second, Tina started to feel guilty and thought that she might be taking advantage of Alejandro. She then reasoned that she and Alejandro were actually closer in age than she initially thought. After all, even at thirty-five, she still had the body of a twenty year old. "Thank God for all that time I spent at the gym on the treadmill," she thought.

Tina was especially excited about being in the driver's seat. Hell, men have been having it their way for years. Why couldn't she try to even the score?

"Alejandro, it's a little warm in here. Let me help you take off your shirt?" Tina offered.

"That's cool; but first there's something I want you to do for me," Alejandro said seductively.

Alejandro stood up in front of Tina. He unzipped his pants and Slowly freed his penis. Tina grabbed Alejandro's cock with both hands and began to suck it ferociously. Before Alejandro lost control, he begged Tina to stop so that he could excite her.

"Thought you wanted to play with the big girls," Tina laughed.

Alejandro then proceeded to explore every part of her body. First, he kissed her passionately on the lips. Then he massaged her shoulders and allowed his fingers to crawl playfully around Tina's bosom. When he got to her right breast, he heard Tina moan deeply. "This must be the spot," he whispered as he kissed her nipples more intensely.

At this point, Tina knew that she was very wrong in her earlier judgment of Alejandro. When they first met, she assumed she would be doing all of the teaching. However, this encounter made her realize that Alejandro was no innocent little cub. He had her entire body on fire; she hadn't felt that way in years.

"Tina, you want my shirt off?" Alejandro teased.

Tina slightly dazed, just looked up at Alejandro's eyes as if she didn't understand the question. At that moment, Alejandro ripped his shirt wide open exposing his nicely chiseled chest. Tina instinctively reached up to grab it, but Alejandro grabbed her hands and placed them back over her head. He wanted to ensure she understood that he was in complete control. After some time of heavy kissing, Alejandro stood up on his knees on the couch. He then reached for her ankles, slowly pushing them back until her knees met her chest.

The bottom of Tina's sexy lingerie was a short white skirt. Now with her legs arched back, her thong bikini was immediately exposed. Alejandro quickly moved it to the side, revealing all of her hidden treasures. For a while, Alejandro seemed content repeatedly licking Tina's inner thighs and creeping up to the point where the first pubic hairs appeared. But the more Tina moaned, the more anxious Alejandro became. Suddenly, Alejandro entered her with his skilled tongue. Never in her life had Tina felt like this. Part of her was extremely vulnerable while her other half was totally consumed by lust. Wrapped in a web of mixed emotions, the only thing Tina could do at this point was to scream in ecstasy.

Minutes later, Tina begged Alejandro to stop, but he knew damn well that was the last thing that she wanted. Instead of halting the action, Alejandro opted to alter Tina's position. He helped her lift her ass about five inches off of the couch while she balanced herself on her knees. Although, she looked like some type of gymnast and felt a bit awkward, she was willing to try anything if Alejandro promised a reward. He continued a few more bouts of licking action as Tina jiggled wildly.

After countless orgasms, the couple were both consumed in mounds of sweat. Alejandro looked down at an exhausted Tina and removed his shorts. His manhood stood at complete attention.

"Are you ready to have some more fun?" Alejandro smiled.

Tina looked up at her stallion and knew it was going to be an incredibly long afternoon.

*****

In Washington, Jack Lloyd was busy at the computer terminal. Like always, he was scanning the various drug related murders or arrests in the major U.S. cities in hope of finding some new lead related to the Fernandez Cartel.

"Hey, Jack, are you about ready to call it quits for the night?" Bobby Coleman asked.

"Bobby, just give me fifteen more minutes and I'll be right with you."

"That's all right, Jack. We can hang out some other time. I know your fifteen more minutes will turn into two hours. Anyway, Virginia cooked my favorite dinner tonight, barbecue chicken with mashed potatoes. So, I'll see you tomorrow."

Bobby, anxious to depart, began gathering the items for his duffel bag when one of the newer agents walked in. "How long have you been a workaholic, Jack?

Before Jack could answer, Bobby threw in his two cents. "Chris, I have known Jack for the past ten years and he has always been like this," Bobby explained. "Let me tell you. Jack only knows one way to go and that's to floor it."

The three men laughed heartily at the remark. Bobby then gave his buddies the old high five and headed home.

Jack Lloyd was not a hard man to figure out. He had just turned thirty-four, had never been married, and had no children- at least that he knew of. His parents died at a relatively young age, within one year of each other. The only family that he did have was an older sister and a younger brother. His siblings often complained that they didn't get to see him as often as they would have liked and Jack promised himself that he would head for the west coast on his next vacation. Then he could check his brother and sister out as well as their children.

For the past 12 years, Jack served as a supervisor for the Drug Enforcement Agency (D.E.A.) and had been totally consumed with activity surrounding the Fernandez Cartel. Now that Fernandez was released, Jack's efforts to dismantle the organization were heightened. Although Fernandez resided in Bolivia, his ties in Florida remained strong. In fact, Jack believed that Fernandez was personally responsible for the famous massacre at Alex Sanchez's mansion back in 1983.

Even with all of the evidence that Jack had presented from his years of studying the Fernandez Cartel, he still couldn't get the government to put enough pressure on Bolivia to turn Fernandez over to the U.S. justice system. So Jack, now an obsessed men, felt he finally had the right team of guys to bring Fernandez down. His right hand man was Bobby Coleman and they had worked together for the past five years. Bobby was a security expert as well as Jack's best friend. He could get you in and out of most places with no problem, and claimed to "smell a booby trap a mile away."

Ken Izuka, a Japanese American, was a computer expert as well as a latent Prints expert. He could also provide you with information about any drug, whether it was organic or synthetic, or whatever else, it didn't matter. Ken knew about drugs dating back to biblical times.

Chris Rein and Tommy Jones were two of the newest additions to the agency. They both had roughly two years of experience and were itching for some real action. Chris and Tommy were under Jack's supervision for six months and were already getting bored with research stuff. At first glance, Chris could easily be mistaken for the typical beach bum with blond hair and broad shoulders but Chris' enemies knew that he was a martial arts expert who could kill you with one lethal strike. Tommy, on the other hand, resembled a misplaced Wall Street stockbroker. In the office among uniformed or casually dressed officers, Tommy stuck out like a sore thumb with his brunette hair, model looks, and sharp three-piece suits. No one would think that he was an ammunition buff that always carried at least three guns on him.

"What a team!" Jack thought to himself. He then looked at his watch and started to laugh. Just as Bobby had predicted, his extra fifteen minutes had certainly run into two hours. He picked up the phone to dial his friend Bobby hoping that the dinner invitation would still be open to him.

"Sure Jack, come on over. The food is still hot," Bobby said warmly.

"I hope Virginia won't get upset with you. It's kind of late and I know she has to work in the morning."

"Jack, if Virginia can get over my having a white man as my best man, I don't think she'll get upset with you for coming over so late." Bobby laughed.

As Jack Lloyd put on his coat he knew that he was a lucky man to have good friends like Bobby and Virginia. A home cooked meal beat a TV dinner any day of the week.

*****

*Dear Ms. Hancock,*

*This is Roberto writing you again. First I want to apologize for being upset with you in my previous letter. After I wrote it, I sat in my room many times and felt very ashamed. I was only thinking about what I wanted and not respecting your space. But don't worry, I won't bring up any unpleasant topics again.*

*The one time that I visited you, I couldn't help but notice the book on your desk. I later asked Nurse Mitchell if you had a special interest in flowers and she told me that you loved reading about them. What a nice coincidence. I love looking at flowers and am especially interested in different kinds of roses. Maybe one day I can come visit you again. Then we can have a nice conversation about flowers and plants. Or we can go to the very large garden that they have there and learn about plants and flowers at the Institute.*

*Well I again feel like I am taking up too much of your time. I hope that I did not intrude on your privacy. Take it easy. Perhaps our paths will cross some other day.*

*Sincerely yours,*
*Roberto Sanchez*

*PS: I finally figured out why the name Candice threw me. It just doesn't describe you. Your name should have been Violet because they are pretty to look at and are soft to touch.*

*****

Alejandro and Roberto were on their way to meet Hector Ramirez. Two days earlier, the twins told him of Juan's plans to blackmail them.

Hector gave them an address in a very dangerous part of Miami, so dangerous, that even the cops refused to patrol the area. There, Hector told him that he would figure out a way to help them with their problem.

“Well here is the address,” Alejandro remarked.

“Are you sure? The building looks condemned," his brother responded.

“Yes I am sure. Now let's go find apartment #4B."

After knocking several times on the apartment door there was still no answer. Roberto was beginning to feel relieved. Maybe if this was the wrong address, they would be leaving soon. Alejandro banged on the door again.

“Hold on a second.”

The twins recognized the voice, it was Hector. He opened the door and led the boys to the kitchen. To their surprise, Juan was tied to a chair in the center of the room.

“What's going on?" Roberto asked.

“This motherfucker's trying to kill me," Juan called out.

“Look boys, you wanted me to take care of the situation, so that's what I am trying to do," Hector said convincingly.

“I didn't want you to hurt him. I was thinking that you would loan us the money to pay him," Roberto appealed.

“I don't have that kind of money. And even if I did loan you the money to give to him, a junkie like Juan would be back in a week to threaten you all over again.”

“Hector, where are we?" Alejandro inquired.

“Juan's apartment,” Hector replied.

“And what are you doing over there on the stove?" Alejandro quizzed.

“I am making a special dose of heroin that Juan is going to shoot up," Hector grinned.

“I know you're not planning to kill him with it," Roberto naively suggested.

“Well, I'm not doing this to just give him a good high. I called you down here because I want you to shoot him up with the stuff."

“Oh no, I can't do that," Roberto said fearfully.

“This is the only way I know that you won't ever go to the police," Hector advised.

“Well, sorry, Hector. I can't take anybody's life,” Roberto confessed.

"Roberto, let's do this now. Everything is ready," Hector urged.

As Roberto looked down at a trembling Juan, he knew there was no way he could kill him. It just wouldn't be right.

"He may not be able to do it, but I can," Alejandro said bravely.

"What are you talking about? Are you crazy?" Roberto panicked. "That's murder."

"Roberto, he was willing to hurt us. So I say fuck him. Hector, let's do it!"

Hector hurriedly tied the elastic band around Juan's arm. Roberto couldn't believe what was happening. He felt so sorry for Juan that he was unable to hold back the tears that rolled down his cheek as he watched Juan plead for his life. When Roberto realized that his brother and Hector were actually going through with their plans, he dashed into the next room to avoid watching the whole scene. Alejandro grabbed the syringe and was instructed by Hector to find the largest vein possible on Hector's arm. Once he found it, Alejandro looked right into Juan's eyes and whispered, "Fuck you bastard."

Alejandro penetrated Juan's skin with the needle. Several minutes passed and Juan just continued to whine, "Roberto, call a fucking ambulance."

Suddenly, Juan's antics were transformed into a strange calmness. He was smiling and rocking from side to side in his chair. The room was so quiet that Roberto thought Alejandro and Hector had come to their senses and changed their minds. Roberto reentered the kitchen and found Juan rolling all over the kitchen floor, still tied to the chair, experiencing severe convulsions. He was foaming from his mouth until finally the violent convulsions came to a complete stop.

With the needle still in his arm, Juan was completely still on the cold tile floor. "Untie him," Hector ordered.

Alejandro took a knife out of the drawer and cut the rope that bound Juan to the chair. Hector then untied the remaining cord and stuffed the fibers in his pocket. After Alejandro spat on an already suffering Juan, the trio left the blackmailer to rot in his own kitchen. When the police found Juan days later, they assumed it was just another drug overdose.

# Chapter 12

Agents Jack Lloyd and Bobby Coleman headed from the airport straight to Miami's local D.E.A. headquarters.

"Jack, what in the hell are we doing in Miami in August? It's hot as hell down here," Bobby complained.

"You know I am doing my friend Ryan Heslin a favor. A couple of people from his team are on vacation so he asked me to help him out."

"Okay that explains you, but what do I have to do with this?"

"Bobby, you know I can't go anywhere without you. If I had come to Miami alone, you would have been the first one to get all over my back," Jack laughed.

"You got a point there. I guess you can't win with me. But listen, when we return to Washington I'm going on a vacation. I promised Virginia and the kids that I would take them to see her parents in North Carolina," Bobby said as he thought about how much he missed his wife. He then put on his glasses so that he could get a better view of the street signs. Lately, it had become increasingly difficult for him to see at night. “I am glad you drove us here and not me. This town is too confusing."

“Look Bobby, I only get around because I've spent a lot of time working in the area. That's another reason why Ryan wanted me to come."

“You mean he didn't want you for your winning personality," Bobby joked.

After the forty-five minute drive from the airport, Jack and Bobby arrived at Miami’s D.E.A. office for a ten o'clock debriefing meeting. Night meetings were rare but Jack wanted to get started as soon as possible. He looked forward to seeing his old partner again and always believed he and Ryan's escapades would make a great best seller. That Ryan was one wild dude.

Bobby couldn't wait until this project was finished. He had another mission of his own back at home. The way he figured it, he could be back in Washington by tomorrow afternoon-just in time for Virginia’s famous ribs.

In the elevator, Jack gave Bobby a harsh look of disapproval. “Jack don't say a damn word. I know I have put on a few pounds over the years, but I've earned them. I'm not as young as I used to be," Bobby argued.

"You know that is no excuse. We're both the same age and I weigh the same now as I did when I went into the academy."

“Sure, it's easy for you to say. You’re not married and you don't have to share cotton candy with your kids."

“I’m sorry I forgot, everyday after you get home from work, Virginia ties you down to the dinner table and forces you to stuff your face," Jack said sarcastically. “Bobby, you cram food into your mouth until you can't eat anymore."

“Okay Jack, you got me. Since you exercise daily, I will start working out with you on the first of the month."

“Bobby, this is the fifth of the month, why not start on Monday?"

“You know Jack, sometimes you can be a pain in the ass. Okay, we'll start on Monday."

Jack looked around the newly decorated office and noticed how much things changed since he'd left many years ago. “I guess with increased funding for the war on drugs, some of it eventually trickled down here," he thought.

"Well look at you, Jack!" Ryan yelled from across the room. "You're still in incredible shape."

"You don't look too bad yourself, Ryan."

"As for me, I jog two miles a day. I don't care if my house burns down, I have to get those two miles in," Ryan said as he began jogging in place. "Ryan this is my right hand man Bobby Coleman. He is the best security expert around and we're lucky to have him."

"How ya' doing Bobby?" Ryan shook Bobby's hand vigorously. "Come over here fellas, let me introduce you to the rest of the team."

"This is Gary, Earl, Samuel, and Ronnie. At the meeting, which is going to start in a half an hour, they'll tell you exactly what they do." Ryan pointed to a nearby table. "I know it's not much, but we've prepared a little spread for you."

While the team ate, Ryan and Jack caught up on old times. "So Ryan, are you still in Miami breaking hearts?"

"Breaking hearts?"

"Yeah man, you remember how it was. You'd love 'em and leave 'em until you'd run into another babe. Then the whole process would start all over again."

"No jack, I'm finished with that scene."

"You've got to be kidding."

"Jack, I've been married for a couple of months now. That wild shit is dead."

"I hear you man."

"It's nothing out there," Ryan explained. "Once you find the woman you love, there really is no reason to run the streets."

It hit Jack that Ryan was not the wild man he knew a few years ago. He was now a more mature version of his former self. Not only was Ryan recently married, his new wife was expecting their first child. Jack was happy for his friend and at the same time jealous.

"O.k. guys, this will be our fourth bust on a cocaine lab in the past month and a half," Ryan voiced as he geared himself up for tomorrow's business. "Our contact tells us that there will be some more action in another hot spot."

Ryan was the only person on the team that had direct contact with the DEA informant, Leo. He owed Ryan big time. Several years ago, Leo was sentenced to life in prison. As the story goes, the cops stormed in a recently robbed candy store and found Leo with a pocket full of money standing over the murdered store-owner. Leo claimed that his only crime was being in the wrong place at the wrong time. He said the store had already been robbed when he'd arrived and he was only trying to see if the Storeowner was still breathing. According to Leo's mother, she gave him $300 so that he could finish the rest of her Christmas shopping because she was too elderly to go out in the weather, Although Leo's story initially seemed fabricated, Ryan worked day and night to investigate Leo's claim and later proved his innocence. As far as Leo was concerned, his work as an informant was the only way he knew to repay Ryan. Besides, Leo was a big cop buff who enjoyed living around cloak and dagger stuff.

"We are going to a two story, art deco house near Washington Avenue and Tenth Street. The emergency Services branch of the Miami, Police Department will have our backs. They will handle the outer perimeter of the area to ensure no unauthorized persons enter the area while we're working. As usual, we're not going to tell them the exact location of the operation until the last minute. So please, don't let it slip out," Ryan urged.

"This is just a typical operation, boss."

"Samuel remember, there is no such thing as a typical operation, so I want everybody to stay alert and sharp. I want all of us to go home tonight."

The team headed downtown to one of the worse locations in Miami. They hoped to launch their bust at two in the morning. Ryan and Leo figured that would be the best time to catch the dealers off guard and maybe bring in a couple of the big guys.

At 1:45 a.m., they were two blocks away from the location. Everyone was set in place. Ryan decided that he would start the operation a little earlier than the group had originally anticipated. He was always afraid of someone, maybe even in the Police Department, tipping off the bad guys.

"You ready to rock and roll?" Ryan asked.

"You're in charge-let's do it," Jack cheered. "And don't worry about the back of the house, I'll have that covered."

The van door burst open and the entire team exploded to the outside of the targeted house. Gary and Earl carried the rammer, as they liked to call it, to the front of the house. The timing was perfect, all of the team members hit their assigned positions simultaneously. Ryan then kicked in the front door, knocking it clear off its hinges.

"D.E.A. don't nobody fucking move!" Ryan yelled as the first half of the team moved across the living room.

The men inside were unpleasantly surprised. On one side of the room there was a man half-asleep on the couch in front of a loud playing television set. On the other side, a teenager poked his head out of the bathroom to check out the commotion. When the drug dealer's employees finally realized that they were in the middle of a bust, it was too late for them to draw their weapons.

"Now I want the two of you to take your positions on the ground, face down. Stretch your arms out as far you can!" Ryan yelled. The rest of the team began moving upstairs.

"Please don't shoot us. We're lying down now and being very cooperative," said a very nervous man. "I was just watching a little TV."

"Bullshit!" Ryan yelled. "Gary, get their guns and I'll cover you."

As Gary approached the two men, a man suddenly appeared on the balcony upstairs with an uzi machine gun. Without warning, he proceeded to spray everyone on the first level until Jack stopped him in his tracks. From behind the kitchen door, Jack extended his arms firing both of his glock handguns at the lone gunman. When the smoke cleared, the attacker laid lifeless and Jack let out a sigh of relief. Ryan looked over at Jack and gave him that old familiar nod, "Thanks for saving my life, man."

The team vigorously searched the upstairs rooms until they came upon a large door with music blaring from the other side. Jack and Ryan paired up to force it open. When the door collapsed, the two agents entered the room with their guns drawn. They both looked anxiously around the room until smiles crept on their faces. They were directly opposite five masked naked women who were busy making crack. The music was so loud that they were oblivious to the shooting that had occurred only moments earlier.

After two-minutes, one of the women alerted her coworkers of the giggling DEA agents that had surrounded them. The women immediately dropped their masks, fell to their knees, and pleaded for their freedom.

"Do you believe this?" Jack asked.

“It looks like we hit pay dirt again," a smiling Ryan remarked.

“I don’t know, Ryan, this seems awfully strange," Jack whispered.

Bobby ran into the room to join them.

“How is it downstairs?" Jack asked.

“The downstairs area is completely secure," Bobby advised. “I was just going to check out this last room and then I'm all finished here."

“Did you talk to the people downstairs?" Ryan asked anxiously.

“Yeah, the conversation was pretty weird. The two gunmen said they'd only been with the organization for about two weeks. Why would they have two new kids running their main stash?"

Jack and Ryan shrugged their shoulders. Neither could explain Bobby's observations. The music was still blasting so Bobby went to turn the stereo off. He then noticed a vent behind the wall unit. It was also evident that the walls were newly plastered.

“Fellas, give me a hand with this wall unit," Bobby said.

“What do you think is behind it Jack, more drugs or guns?" Ryan asked.

“I don't know, but whatever it is, it better not move around too much, once we open this door." Jack positioned himself in a battle stance. “On the count of three, open it. One, two, three, now!”

In the center of the bare room was a badly beaten man tied to a chair. His bloodied hands and feet were bound together and his mouth was sealed shut with a strip of duck tape. His eyes were wide open but one of them was swollen and badly bruised as if it had suffered numerous blows. He had no reaction towards the three cops. In fact, he appeared to have no reaction to anything. Bobby cautiously walked to the nameless soul to check for a pulse.

“Who is this guy?”

“Bobby, it's Leo, my informant!" Ryan stammered.

“He's dead,” Bobby said as he removed his hands from the man's wrist. “I can't tell how long he's been in here but we're definitely too late."

“Bobby I don't like this shit at all," Jack raved. “Why the fuck would they do something like this?"

“Because they're scum, that's why,” Ryan answered angrily.

"You're right about that Ryan, but what I'm wondering is who did they think was going to find Leo," Jack said curiously. "This seems really strange."

"Ryan and Jack, I have the same fucked up feeling too," Bobby agreed as he looked down at his watch. "Jack, what time do you have?"

"It is 2:03."

Why?" Ryan asked.

Bobby looked closely at the clock ticking on the wall. "Do you guys hear that noise?" Bobby asked nervously.

"Yeah man, so what?"

"Well, if the clock is ticking why does it still say 1 o'clock?"

"Bobby, are you thinking what I'm thinking?"

"Ryan, Jack, it's a set-up!" Bobby shouted at the top of his lungs. "Let's get the hell outta here."

"There's a bomb inside the clock, get out!" Jack directed.

Everyone scrambled to clear the house including the remaining criminals. As the three agents searched for a way out, the nude women frantically raced downstairs to save their own lives and perhaps outrun the police. Time was of the essence, so Jack, Ryan, and Bobby decided they didn't have the time to run downstairs. They would now have to jump out of the window in the hallway. "We're almost outta here," Jack called out to his colleagues. "I think we're gonna make it."

Seconds later there was a large explosion that leveled the building. The second floor went crashing into the first. All of the people that could not escape the bomb's wrath were gone.

*****

*Dear Ms. Hancock,*

*How is the most beautiful violet in the garden doing today? Fine I hope. Recently, so much has happened in my life that I wouldn't know where to begin.*
*First of all, me and my brother Alejandro got ourselves into a sticky situation. Fortunately a family friend was able to help us out.*

*We are both doing well in school. Our jobs are okay, even though yesterday when I was at work, a lady named Tina pinched me when I walked past her in the restaurant. I asked Alejandro if he knew her and he said he didn't. I don't believe him. She probably got us confused because I hardly ever work during Alejandro's shift. I think she thought I was him.*

*Enough about me, I hope they are treating you nicely there. With Nurse Mitchell around, they probably have no other choice.*

*She seems to care so much about you. In fact, there are a lot of people who would love to see you fully recover, including me.*

*There are so many great things out there for you to see. Please give yourself another chance and don't be afraid to live again. I'm sorry. Here I go criticizing you again. Go at your own pace. There will be people that love you no matter when you decide to come around.*

*Sincerely yours,*
*Roberto Sanchez*

*****

Nurse Mitchell walked swiftly down the hallway to see her special patient. A nurse's aide called her on the phone to tell her that Cynthia was in her room throwing things. Nurse Mitchell silently prayed that she wasn't regressing, Cynthia had come such a long way.

When Nurse Mitchell walked into the room, Cynthia was recklessly throwing anything she could get her hands on across the room. "Are you having another one of your flashbacks?" Nurse Mitchell called out. "In a few moments, you'll be just fine."

She grabbed Cynthia tightly, hugged her closely, and began singing a lullaby. "Hush little baby, don't say a word Mama's gonna buy you a mocking bird."

At that point, Cynthia started crying uncontrollably.

"Don't worry, it's okay," Nurse Mitchell whispered. "I am here to take care of you."

"No, it's not okay," Cynthia shot back.

Nurse Mitchell immediately dropped her arms and pulled back. She looked at Cynthia's face wondering if the spell had actually been broken. This was the first time she'd heard the sound of Cynthia's voice and Nurse Mitchell was in complete shock.

"I have wasted so much of my life being locked up in this place. So much time in fact, that I don't even know how long I've been here."

"Don't worry yourself," Nurse Mitchell said soothingly. "I will tell you everything that you need to know. Let's just take one step at a time."

"No, I don't want to take it one step at a time. I want to know everything now," Cynthia demanded.

"Okay, I know I will probably get into trouble for doing this," Nurse Mitchell sighed. "First, let me contact your primary physician and tell him you've come back to us. Then, I'll tell you everything that I know about what's been going on with you."

"Thank you," Cynthia voiced anxiously. "Hurry back!"

Nurse Mitchell rushed down the long corridor to the nurses' station to make her important phone call. Though she rarely used it, she kept the doctor's pager number in her wallet in case of an emergency. When he returned her call, she was so excited she immediately blurted out the news of Cynthia's conversation in one breathe. She thought he would be just as excited as she was but her high spirits were soon extinguished. "Nurse Mitchell, you just keep on top of her physical health," he strongly advised. "Leave the storytelling to the hospital psychiatrist."

"Hospital psychiatrist?" Nurse Mitchell thought. "I know more about Cynthia than he does. If she wants to know what happened to her here, she should hear it from me."

Nurse Mitchell decided to take Cynthia for a walk in the garden. She was most calm in that environment and after hearing her life story, Cynthia would need to be in a comforting space. Nurse Mitchell told the tale the only way she knew how, from the beginning. She tried to leave nothing out. After almost two hours of talking and answering Cynthia's questions, Nurse Mitchell took a deep breath and just stared at her new miracle.

At first, Cynthia sat quietly trying to process everything she'd just heard, but soon she caught a glimpse of Nurse Mitchell's watchful eyes. "What is the matter?"

"It's just that for so long I prayed for the day when you would snap out of your trance and here it is. I am just so happy. This all seems like some kind of dream. I'm afraid that when I go to sleep, I will awake to find you as before." Nurse Mitchell said tearfully.

"You don't have to worry about that happening, I've got a lot of catching up to do. My main concern is getting out of this place," Cynthia assured.

Nurse Mitchell was impressed. Cynthia had more fire in her than she had envisioned.

"Cynthia, may I have one thing from you?" Nurse Mitchell asked calmly.

"What's that?" Cynthia smiled warmly.

"A hug."

"After all of the hugs you've given me through the years, of course."

As the women hugged in the middle of the garden, tears of joy ran down Nurse Mitchell's face. It certainly was a comforting space.

# Chapter 13

It had been two and a half months since the explosion at the crack lab and Jack Lloyd was still walking around in a fog. He'd survived the blast, only sustaining a couple of broken ribs. Ryan Heslin wasn't so lucky. At the last minute, Ryan opted to escape from the downstairs exit so that he could check on the other members of his team. He never made it because the bomb went off. Samuel Rodriguez was the only survivor from Ryan's team. The women who worked in the drug lab were also killed. Jack lost one of his best friends.

Although Jack's buddy, Bobby Coleman, survived the blast he broke his left leg in two places when he leaped out of the window. He was now back in Washington undergoing physical therapy.

None of Jack's people knew who was behind the setup, but they had their suspects. Solving this crime was at the top of their list.

Jack Lloyd needed a long vacation. He had been working one hundred hours a week trying to get to the bottom of the Miami incident. He couldn't get past the death of Ryan and his crew. At night, he would lay awake wondering why Ryan was taken and not him. Ryan was married and was only a couple of months away from parenthood. Now the kid would grow up without a father. Jack thought if it had been him instead, they could have a nice funeral and retire his number. No real people would have been hurt. But, since nothing could be done about the past, Jack convinced himself that the only way he could avenge his friend's death was by finding the people responsible and dealing with them in his own special way.

Most of Jack's investigation was done from Washington, until he'd gotten a phone call from a Mental Institute in Miami. Alex Sanchez's wife had completely recovered from her nervous breakdown and was going to be released tomorrow. When the D.E.A. first discovered that Cynthia was at the Institute, they asked the director to provide them with a full report of her progress. Now Jack found himself on the next plane back to Miami to talk to Alex's widow. At the very least, he hoped that she had some information about the gang battle that had happened years earlier, but wasn't very optimistic. He expected it to be a dead end but felt compelled to check out every lead.

When he got to the institute, the security guard escorted him directly to her room. The minute he knocked on the door, she opened it. Even though she wore only a simple T-shirt and a pair of Stonewashed jeans, Cynthia looked particularly fashionable. Jack was completely taken by surprise when his witness appeared at the door. She was more beautiful than he ever imagined.

“Hello, are you Mrs. Sanchez?"

“No I am not, my name in Cynthia Hancock, but Alex and I were married," Cynthia answered sharply.

“I am agent Jack Lloyd. Can I speak to you for a minute?"

“Do I have a choice?” Cynthia sarcastically replied.

“I don't think so,” Jack said sheepishly. “I am the lead investigator in the death of your husband and the others."

“Come inside, I am in a hurry so I hope this won't take too long. As you can see, I am packing my bags. I'm leaving this place today,” she smiled. “I spoke to someone on the phone last night and I told him I don't know anything. Nothing has changed.”

"Ms. Hancock I am aware of that, but I still wanted to talk to you. I figured we may be able to discover something important together," he said.

"O.K, let's get started." Cynthia said impatiently as she continued packing.

"How long were you two married?"

"A little over a year."

"Did you know that he was involved in drugs?"

"No, I thought he was an Avon salesman," Cynthia said. "Of course I knew what he did, but I never got involved with it."

"Did you know many of his associates?"

"Not really, I pretty much just kept to myself. His buddies weren't my kind of crowd."

Jack wondered, how a smart, gorgeous woman like Cynthia got involved with a piece of shit like Alex Sanchez. From what he knew about Alex, they seemed to make a very unusual pair. Despite finding it hard to focus on his line of questioning, Jack knew he had to be straight to the point with this witness.

"Look, Cynthia Hancock or Candice Sanchez or whatever you want to call yourself, I find it hard to believe that you have no idea who was behind your husband's death. You know if it wasn't for the fact that you went into the hospital, you probably would have been six feet under just like your husband."

"I am well aware of that Mr. Lloyd, but that still doesn't change the fact that I don't know anything," she firmly responded.

Cynthia just wouldn't budge. Jack decided to change his strategy. "Did I tell you that I went to the mansion to see the aftermath of that bloodshed?"

"No, you didn't."

"Let me tell you about it now. I've heard wild stories about Vietnam, but none of them could have topped what I saw at your place. There were bodies everywhere. Throats were slashed, brain matter was oozing out all over the place and the smell of blood was suffocating. We found the powerful Alex Sanchez face down. When the autopsy was performed, the medical examiner said Alex's body looked like Swiss cheese. Bullets had pierced nearly every exposed place on his body. To top it off, Alex had a large hole in his chest from a shotgun blast in his back."

"Are you finished Mr. Lloyd?" Cynthia sniffled. She was upset over what she'd just heard but she didn't want to give him the satisfaction of knowing he had gotten to her. "What a typical cop." she thought.

"Look I know you must have cared for Alex in some way. If you want to help me find his killers, here is my card," Jack offered.

"If I do remember anything you will be the first to know," Cynthia said sarcastically.

"By the way, where are you going to live?"

"I am going to stay with my mother in Baltimore for a little while. Do I need your permission to leave town?" she snapped.

"No, you don't, but maybe since I am based in Washington I can give you a call to check up on you from time to time."

"That won't be necessary. I am a big girl now and I can take care of myself. I know there must be someone else you can try to save," she said.

"That was unprofessional," Jack thought. He'd never flirted with someone that was directly involved in one of his cases before. But there was something about Cynthia Hancock that drew him. She was full of energy, style and danger; this made her very appealing to him.

"Well, you take it easy, Ms. Hancock. Remember, if you want to talk about anything at all, give me a call."

"Don't worry, Mr. Lloyd, I certainly will," Cynthia replied as she put the card in her pocket. She knew he was the last person on earth that she'd ever call.

There was another knock on the door. It was probably more of the staff popping in to say good-bye. Cynthia never realized how much they cared about her until it was time for her to leave.

She quickly opened the door and soon discovered that it wasn't one of the staff at all. Roberto and Alejandro stood across from her with bright smiles and flowers. Although she'd spoken to Roberto earlier in the week, and he said they'd try to make it there before she left, it was getting late and she didn't think she'd be there when they arrived.

"Fellas, come on in. I am glad to see you."

"We didn't want to miss the opportunity to say thank you for all the information you gave us about our father," Roberto said warmly. "We're going to miss you."

"It was the least that I could do. Everyone has a right to know their history."

"I still can't get over how well you look now compared to when we first saw you," Roberto smiled.

"I know what you mean, but maybe I was having a bad hair day or something."

The three of them laughed and Cynthia felt a certain connection to the twins. She believed they were a couple of good kids and had developed a special affection towards Roberto. They would often talk on the phone about almost anything.

"Well, I see that you are almost packed," Alejandro observed.

"Do you need help with anything else?" Roberto asked.

"No guys I am just about finished, but there is one last thing I want to talk to you about before I go," Cynthia said in a serious tone.

"And what is that?' Roberto wondered.

"You two are exposed to a lot of bad things in Miami. Please don't make the same mistakes that I've made and succumb to the street life. Stay in school, get a degree, take care of each other and your grandmother. And if you ever need me for anything, you have my telephone number and address in Baltimore."

"Don't worry about us, we'll be all right," Alejandro assured. "We've already survived a lot."

"I'll keep in touch with you Cynthia," Roberto said sadly. Even though he was happy about Cynthia's recovery, he wished that she'd selected a place closer to Miami.

"Make sure that you do, Roberto."

"Cynthia he will, he wouldn't want to make his beautiful stepmother mad at him," Alejandro teased as his brother poked him in the side with his elbow.

On the plane ride to Baltimore, Cynthia remembered the things Jack told her as he described the blood bath at the Mansion. She couldn't get the violent scene out of her mind. Alex wasn't the nicest guy in the world, but she didn't believe anyone deserved to die that way. Alex mainly acted the way he did because of his poor upbringing. His mother struggled everyday to make ends meet. While Cynthia knew poverty was no excuse, she could understand Alex's rage. There were also sides to Alex that people rarely got a chance to see, sometimes he was a kind, gentleman.

*****

*"Candice are you going to lay by the pool all day?" Alex asked.*

*"Alex, it's just eleven o'clock in the morning, what are you talking about?"*

*"Come on, sweetheart, get up, we need to be somewhere at one o'clock."*

*"You can go by yourself. I feel like relaxing today."*

*"You see, this is the kind of shit I'm talking about," Alex complained. "When I ask you to do something for me, very fuckin' nicely, you always say "no" That's why I fuckin' curse all the time. I think that it's the only time you fuckin' listen to me."*

*"No, you curse all of the time because those are the only English words you know how to use properly," Candice snapped back, she then put on her sunglasses, packed her towel and slowly walked towards the house.*

*"Property, damn right this is all my property. And if you don't like it, you can always leave," Alex yelled back.*

*At one o'clock, Alex and Candice entered their waiting car. Alex's security consisted of a car in front with three armed guards and a car behind them with three more armed guards. They drove about thirty miles before they came to a stand still.*

*"Why are we stopping at this park?" Candice asked as Alex grabbed her hand to help her out of the limo.*

*"Wait and see, it's a surprise for you," Alex said smiling widely.*

*"Well, you know I don't like surprises so you might as well tell me what it is now," Candice demanded.*

*"You always tell me that I'm no good. You say I never do anything worthy with my money. So, now I plan to do good things."*

*As they walked further in the park, Candice spotted a bunch of nine to twelve year olds getting ready to play softball. They wore shiny new uniforms and held sparkling equipment. Although the game hadn't started, the little umpires were already testing their whistles. It looked very organized.*

*"Alex, what is this?" Candice asked.*

*"I decided to buy the neighborhood kids some uniforms and put them in this baseball league," Alex answered proudly.*

*Candice was impressed. "Maybe, it's not too late for Alex to change," Candice thought. The two of them took a seat on the bleachers to enjoy the game.*

*"Honey, look on the back of the uniforms," Alex called out. "They're Alex's Tigers," Candice responded.*

*"That's me," Alex grinned.*

*"How did you come up with that name?" Candice asked.*

*"I was watching fuckin' TV one day and that cereal commercial came on advertising some shit. Then it hit me. Name them Alex's Tigers, they'll be GREAT!" Alex laughed.*

*"You're real original, Alex," Candice said as she leaned over to kiss her husband on the cheek.*

*"What was that for?" he asked.*

*"That was for nothing," she said.*

*The game went well, but Alex's Tigers lost. The final score was 8-3. Candice enjoyed herself tremendously and was hoarse from all of her cheering.*

*"Honey, wait here, I'll be right back," Alex said as he headed over to the team's umpire.*

*"My friend, do you know who I am?" Alex asked the man leaning on the fence drinking a cold soda.*

*"Yes, you are Mr. Sanchez," the umpire answered nervously.*

*"Well, I think you did a very lousy job today," Alex grumbled. "And let me tell you something, we have ten more games to play and we better win ten fuckin games."*

*"I did the best I could," the umpire answered swiftly. "We just need a little practice."*

*"Alex, what are you doing?" Candice interrupted.*

*"Just talking to the umpire," Alex replied.*

*Candice could tell by the fearful look on the umpire's face that it was no ordinary conversation.*

*"Alex, it's only a game. These kids are only here to have fun," Candice scolded.*

*"Honey, you are right." Alex then looked back at the umpire and said, "make that nine games."*

# Chapter 14

It was late in the afternoon and Hector Ramirez sat across the street from Mama' Sanchez's apartment while he devoured his sandwich. This had become a routine. Once or twice a week, Hector parked his car a couple blocks away from the apartment building, then hung around hoping to find a way to get to the old lady's money.

He had already figured out Mama' Sanchez's work schedule and also knew when the twins were out of the house at work or school. If Jimmy hadn't given him a job selling drugs, Hector probably would have already broken into the apartment to steal anything of value or find Alex Sanchez's money himself. But now, with the drug money coming in, Hector could be more patient. Besides, Hector knew that the twins were beginning to really trust him and believed they'd soon volunteer information about their father's money.

Hector, now in his late forties, was a bitter man. He had been in the drug business for almost thirty years, selling it or occasionally using it himself. He had nothing to show for all of the time he'd invested and thought that working for Jimmy would be his last opportunity to make it big. In the past, he'd come close to becoming the top dog and it seemed like yesterday that a half dozen kids were selling drugs for him. Yet, whenever Hector was on the verge of stardom, he would get arrested, spend time in jail, and have to start all over. Or worse, his own habit would get out of control and cause him to lose it all.

As Hector finished his sandwich and guzzled his last drop of beer, he concluded that he probably wasn't going to get any clues about the money today so he decided to leave. Even though Hector hadn't made any progress he still had a gut feeling that everything was going to change and that something good was going to come from out of that house. He just knew it.

*****

Roberto and Alejandro were clearing off the tables at the Restaurant when they heard a blast from an unfamiliar car horn.

"Who's that?" Roberto asked, startled by the loud noise.

Alejandro opened the door to get a closer look at the driver of the gold Lexus parked out front. "Hey, it's Hector," Alejandro called out excitedly.

"Amigos, what time are you getting off?" Hector yelled.

"In about ten minutes."

"Good, then I'll wait for you. We gotta talk."

Alejandro was very happy about Hector's surprise visit. Roberto, on the other hand, was overcome by anxiety. Ever since the incident with Juan, Roberto wasn't very fond of Hector. There was something about him he didn't trust.

As soon as the twins finished their shift they darted outside towards Hector's car.

"Come on guys get in," Hector commanded.

"Hector we haven't seen you around in a while. I thought you forgot about us," Alejandro whined.

"No fellas, it's just that I've been extremely busy. You know, doing a little bit of this and a little bit of that."

"We can tell, your care is dope," Alejandro said as he checked out Hector's new ride.

"And Alejandro, this is only the beginning. As you can see, I am back in business," Hector said smiling. "Jimmy gave me some start up money and a good selling location. I'll be back on top real soon."

"Isn't what you're doing dangerous?" Roberto asked, even though he knew Hector would deny it.

"No more dangerous than any other job out there. You always hear about cops and even teachers getting shot. And they don't make anything close to the kind of money that I make."

As Hector cruised down some of the busiest streets in Miami, Collins Avenue and Ocean Drive, Alejandro began to notice how much attention they were getting. "People respect you when you drive a car like this," Alejandro cheered.

"You guys are working too hard. Why don't you quit your jobs at the restaurant and start working for me? I'll teach you all there is to know about the business," Hector offered while he made a U-turn and began driving in the direction of the twin's house. "You guys are too smart to waste your time in a dump waiting on other people. You need to make some real money."

Hector parked the car in front of Mama' Sanchez's place and waited for the twins to respond.

"Well Hector, thanks for the offer. We'll think about it," Alejandro said as he and his brother got out of the car.

"Okay guys, you got my new number. Keep in touch," Hector winked before speeding down the quiet street.

"So what do you think?" Alejandro asked anxiously.

"You gotta be kidding me," Roberto argued as they entered the house. "Hector is bad news."

*****

As the men drove around town, they began to get a little impatient.

"Don't worry, this is a pretty good lead," Hector explained.

"It's been almost three weeks now, and he's done a helluva job ducking us," one of his partners complained.

The three men emerged from the car and raced upstairs to the fourth floor apartment.

"Damn, why don't these buildings ever have elevators that work?" Hector huffed. "Ring the buzzer."

"Who is it?" a child asked from behind the door.

"It's a friend of your father's. Is he home?"

"Dad, somebody is at the door to see you," the kid yelled.

When the men first arrived, they heard the children laughing and playing, now there was silence.

Hector knocked furiously on the door. Boom! Boom! Boom!

"Hey, Ricardo, what's going on? It's me and I have something very important to tell you."

There was still silence coming from the apartment. The men had just decided to knock down the door when they heard someone fidgeting with the locks.

"Hey Hector, what's going on?" a nervous Ricardo asked. He opened the door widely revealing the three kids that were in the living room watching television.

"Nothing much Ricardo, I was just a little worried about you since I haven't seen you in over three weeks," Hector commented calmly.

"I have been over here watching the kids while my ex is at work."

"Can I come in?" Hector asked.

"Sure Hector," Ricardo stammered, unsure of what to say next.

Hector tuned to his two companions. "Fellas, you can wait for me in the car. Ricardo and I have some catching up to do."

A serious Hector boldly entered the living room. Ricardo was suddenly concerned about his children's safety. "Go back in your bedrooms and finish playing Nintendo," Ricardo ordered. "Don't worry, I'll be there in a little while."

The two men sat on the couch facing each other.

"Ricardo what kind of shit are you trying to pull? Are you outta your..."

"I know I owe you some money but I will get it to you real soon," Ricardo quickly interrupted.

"Some money, nigga you owe us two thousand dollars. And the only reason we kept giving you crack was because you said you would give us your government check."

I know but something came up."

"Don't give me that shit that something came up. You tried to be slick. As soon as the check came, you split," Hector growled.

"Hector I promise you, I will get you the money."

"I know damn well I'm going to get my money or those kids are going to be fatherless."

Just then, Hector and Ricardo noticed a young woman standing across from them. "Excuse me daddy but Felix and Junior are thirsty. I'm going in the kitchen to get them something to drink. Do you or your friend want anything?" she asked.

"No Juanita, just hurry and go back in the room," Ricardo ordered.

"You know Ricardo, you have a very pretty daughter. How old is she, 17 or 18?" Hector asked.

"No, she's only fifteen years old," Ricardo quickly replied as he chewed on his bottom lip.

"Well, you know if you can't come up with the money. Maybe something can be worked out between me and your daughter. I think I'm in love," Hector teased.

"That won't be necessary, I will get you your money."

"You have three days to come up with the money or else."

"Hector be fair, where am I going to get that kind of money in only three days?"

"Looking around this apartment I see a lot of ways you could make some money. There's a nice TV. Over there is a VCR and that camera seems pretty special. You won't have a problem getting the money," Hector assured. "You have no choice."

"But Hector, these things aren't mine. It's all my ex-wife's stuff. I don't even live here. She just let me stay until I sorted out some stuff. She works two jobs to pay for all of this. Please don't ask me to take the things she's worked so hard for," Ricardo pleaded.

"I'm not asking you to do anything. But motherfucker you better have my money in three days. And don't bother running away from me again. I would hate to come here to check up on your daughter," Hector barked.

Hector got up from the couch and headed out the door. He felt no pity for Ricardo, not even for a minute.

Before Hector made it downstairs to his car, Ricardo was already upstairs gathering items to sell. He only had two hours before his wife would be arriving from work. He'd just tell her that they'd been robbed. The kids would soon be asleep so they couldn't dispute his story. He'd even given himself a bump on the head to make it look good. If Carla didn't believe his first tale, he'd planned to tell her the truth. Their children's lives were at stake, what choice did he have? He hoped that she'd forgive him, but if she didn't, he'd just do another one of his disappearing acts. After a year or so, the whole episode would be forgotten.

*****

"Roberto, come over here and help me clear the table. That last group of people made a big mess."

"Okay Alejandro, but let's hurry up. It's 7:50 and we both get off at eight o'clock."

"What are you doing tonight?" Alejandro quizzed.

"I am going to start that research paper for school. It's not due for a while, but I want to get a good head start. Then maybe I'll write Cynthia," Roberto answered smiling.

"You really got the hots for her, don't you? Alejandro teased.

"Don't be silly. I just find her interesting," Roberto defended.

"Anyway, what are you doing tonight?"

"I'm going out with this new girl I met a few days ago. Boy is she fine. And she's got hips and an ass that you would kill for," Alejandro bragged. "She'll be mine, tonight."

"Guys can I talk to you for a second?" the restaurant manager interrupted. He had just finished a heated conversation with one of his employees and was concerned that he would again be short staffed.

"Yeah, what's up? Alejandro asked.

"Marcus called in sick and I need one of you to replace him for the post dinner crowd," the manager calmly explained.

"You gotta be kiddin' me. This is the second time this week you're pulling this," Alejandro argued.

"There is nothing I can do about this. It's not my fault," the manager sighed.

"Well I'm sorry but we both have plans tonight."

"Guys, don't do this to me. I need one of you to cover for Marcus," the manager pleaded.

"That's okay Alejandro, I'll stay longer," Roberto volunteered.

"Thanks a lot Roberto, you really came through for me tonight," the manager said as he patted Roberto on the back. He then raced into the kitchen to tend to other problems.

"Roberto, I am tired of this shit. Why did you volunteer?" Alejandro asked.

"It won't be too bad, plus I can use the extra money," Roberto confessed.

"No, what we really need is a job where we won't have to put up with this shit. We need a gig that's paying some real money," Alejandro paused. "You know what I'm talking about."

"Yeah, I know what you're talking about, and I don't want to talk about it," Roberto demanded.

"Just do me a favor and think about it."

"Yeah, yeah, just get out of here before you wind up late for your next conquest," Roberto strongly advised as he prepared for the next shift.

"Alejandro is right about one thing, Roberto thought. "This bus boy stuff is for the birds."

# Chapter 15

"Honey, you better come inside and get something to eat. You've been working in the garden for hours," Betty Hancock called.

"Mom, I'll be inside in a little while. I just want to finish this last little bit," Cynthia responded.

"I just don't want you to over do it."

It had been three months since Cynthia left the Institute. By now she had developed a good daily routine. In the morning, she would wake up for an early jog. Then she would have a nice breakfast with her mother. After a bite to eat, she would spend the rest of her day fixing up the backyard. Betty Hancock hadn't done anything around the house since her husband died of a heart attack two years ago.

In the short time that Cynthia returned home, she'd made dramatic improvements. The gardening skills she learned at the Institute came in handy. This was Cynthia's first real hobby. She worked on the yard because it was something she truly enjoyed and it also gave her something to look forward to each day. The garden allowed her to totally relax. In it, she was free of criticism and could create on her own. Nurturing life into the world was also very therapeutic for her. It took her mind off of the terrible things that happened in her life.

Betty Hancock was so thrilled to have her daughter back that she had to battle the tendency to treat her like the fifteen-year old kid she was when she left home. Betty wanted to make sure that she didn't do anything to cause Cynthia to run away again even though that was the last thing on Cynthia's mind. Cynthia was very content at home. She enjoyed taking care of the garden and revisiting all of her old good books.

Anything was better than the life she'd left behind. The 1980s were a very chaotic time for her. Now in the beginning of 1990, she loved the calmness of her new pace. Who would have thought Cynthia would have found peace in suburban Baltimore? Surely, not her wild friends in Miami.

*****

Alejandro and Roberto were at the library doing research on some school papers. They had been at the library for two hours now, and were just beginning to put a dent in their project.

"Alejandro, let's hurry up and get ready to go home. We have to change for work," Roberto suggested.

Alejandro looked up wearily at Roberto, still tired from hanging out the night before, "Roberto I can't do this anymore."

"What are you talking about?"

"This is beginning to be too much for me. Going to school full-time and working forty hours a week. I'm tired of always feeling tied," Alejandro whined.

"You did it last semester and you wound up with a B+ average."

"Yeah I know, but I busted my ass to do it. I wish I could just go to school full time and not have to worry about working."

"I wish I could too but unless we find out that we're really Julio Iglesias long lost sons, it's not going to happen," Roberto joked as he playfully slapped his brother on the head with a few sheets of loose-leaf paper.

"We do have an alternative,"

"What's that?" Roberto naively asked as he stuffed his assignment in his book bag.

"I've been thinking about it for a long time. We could take Hector up on his offer and work for him." Alejandro wanted to further explain his comment but became cautious when he saw how outraged his brother had become. Roberto was so angry that his veins were throbbing in his neck. "Before you say anything hear me out. We could work for him, just for a little while. Then after we saved up some money, we could go back to school and never have to worry about a thing."

"What about going to jail? If we get caught selling drugs, that's exactly where we are going to end up," Roberto shouted.

"But, I've been talking to Hector all week long. He said we wouldn't have to sell drugs on the street. He could put us to work doing other stuff," Alejandro said soothingly. "Believe me, it's a cinch."

"I don't trust Hector. I don't like the idea and I'm not gonna do it," Roberto said firmly.

"Well, I told him that I would talk to you today and get back to him tonight."

"So, what are you gonna tell him?" Roberto asked.

"I'm gonna do it," Alejandro said firmly.

"That business is very dangerous, you can't trust anyone," Roberto warned.

"I know, that's why I figured we could both do it and watch each other's backs."

Roberto looked directly into Alejandro's eyes. "Alejandro you promise that we are only going to do this for a little while," Roberto insisted. "Then we're getting out."

"I promise, we will be back in school full time by next semester," Alejandro swore.

"Well, count me in too," Roberto reluctantly conceded. "But only for one semester."

"That's my bro!" Alejandro said as he hugged Roberto tightly. Somehow Roberto didn't believe things would be as easy as Alejandro thought. He only hoped that he was doing the right thing.

*****

"Damn, I can dress my ass off sometimes," Alejandro said as he admired himself in his bedroom mirror.

"Just hurry up Alejandro, we have to meet Hector in a few minutes," Roberto called.

"I know, don't worry. We'll be on time," Alejandro insisted.

"Where is this Disco Inferno?" Roberto asked.

"You must be kidding. Everybody knows about that club. It's one of the hottest spots in Miami. On a Saturday night it's almost impossible to get in. You've got to know somebody," Alejandro advised.

"So, why are we going?" a concerned Roberto asked.

"Relax, Hector will have no problem getting us in, we're his boys. Tonight is a special night. We're going to meet Hector's boss Jimmy. He likes to meet the new people in the organization."

"How do I look?" Roberto asked.

"Let me put it this way, you may have book smarts over me, but when it comes to fashion you haven't got a clue."

"What do you mean? My clothes match." Roberto defended. He was particularly proud of his new pin striped pants and matching suspenders.

"Yeah, but you don't look like you're going to a club. It looks like you're representing your school in a chess tournament. First of all, undo the first button on your shirt. Now throw on this jacket instead of the one you have on now," Alejandro ordered as he tossed Roberto a blazer and a pair of slacks. "You can try on this, but you better not get anything on them. They're brand new. I haven't even worn it yet.

An hour later, the twins were on their way to Hector's favorite hangout spot. At first, Roberto was really feeling uptight but Alejandro's excitement was starting to rub off on him. Alejandro even went on a shopping spree trying to find the right outfit to make the perfect first impression.

As Hector drove the twins to the club, he gave them some last minute instructions.

"Now remember guys, try to act real cool when we go inside. First, we'll get a table. Then, when Jimmy wants to see us, he'll send one of his guards over for us," Hector nervously recited.

"You got that?"

"Yeah, sure Hector," Alejandro answered smiling. "Are we gonna hang out with him all night?"

"I have no idea. We could talk for two minutes or an hour. But remember when we go over to his booth don't say a fuckin' word. Let me do all of the talking. This Jimmy is one dangerous dude. He could have you shot in the head if he takes a sudden dislike to you."

"I think you should do all the talking," Roberto agreed as he wondered how in the hell he'd gotten himself into this situation.

"That's the best idea I've heard all night."

Roberto, Alejandro, and Hector walked directly to the entrance, ahead of the huge line in front of the club. Instantly, they were stopped by a drag queen that was in charge of letting people into the exclusive club. "Fellas you have to go to the back of the line," she ordered. Behind the drag queen stood three bouncers who looked more like defensive linemen on a football team.

"We are with Jimmy Acosta's group," Hector proudly responded.

"In that case, welcome to Disco Inferno," she said while opening the velvet ropes. She then escorted them to the ticket window. Once they passed the bouncers, they could hear loud music escaping from inside. When they entered the club, the twins were very impressed. Disco Inferno was a large club with three floors. The first level, which had no chairs or tables, was called the pit. That was where the serious dancing took place. The second level was for VIP's only. The tables and chairs in that area was set-up so that you could overlook the pit. Most of the people on the second floor were regulars. They frequented the club at least twice a week. Although the second floor was reserved for special guests, two of the managers would often allow the drop dead gorgeous women from the first floor to enter. The third level was a highly restricted area. The majority of people in the club never got a glimpse of the third floor. Instead of tables and chairs, level three had cozy booths where the top guns either did drugs or conducted important business. Jimmy always stayed on level three. If he saw a girl that he liked dancing in the Pit, he would send one of his guards to bring her up to him. There was nothing like being in charge.

*****

Cynthia slowly opened the door to the house, trying not to disturb her mother. Lately, Cynthia had been going out more frequently but this time she was returning home later than usual. "Honey where have you been? It's almost two thirty in the morning?" Betty asked, startling Cynthia.

"Mom, why aren't you asleep yet?"

"It is hard for me to sleep when you are out in the streets with God only knows who," Betty cried. "By the way, who did you go out with tonight?"

"I caught a midnight show by myself," Cynthia answered.

"Cynthia, that can be very dangerous. Baltimore is not like it used to be. You should have went with someone."

"Well Mom, I really felt like being alone tonight. And right now I am going upstairs to take a shower and go to bed."

Walking slowly up the stairs, Cynthia turned around and asked, "Did I get any messages today?"

"There were two messages. The first was from your boss. She wants you to arrive at the flower shop an hour earlier in the morning. The second was from that guy that you've been ignoring for the last few weeks."

"The doctor?' Cynthia said.

"No, it was Jack Lloyd. Over the phone, he seems like such a nice man. Why don't you call him back?" Betty inquired.

"He does appear to be a nice guy. But just like most of the people I meet, we really don't have much in common."

"Well, you'll never know unless you talk to the man, Cynthia."

"Yeah Mom, I know," Cynthia said as she continued her walk upstairs to her room. "I'll return his calls-someday."

*****

"Hector do you know where we're going?" Roberto yelled as they made their way through the club.

"Of course I do. We're going to the third level. That's where Jimmy hangs out," Hector yelled back.

As the three made their way upstairs. They were engulfed by blinding disco lights and smoke. It seemed that all of the beautiful people were at Disco Inferno jamming to Madonna's latest hit "Vogue."

“We're finally here," Hector said as he escorted the boys into the lounge area. Normally, he would have been stopped by the club security, but Jimmy had already advised his personal security guard to let Hector inside.

“Now, what do we do?" Alejandro impatiently asked.

‘We just grab a seat, order a drink, and wait for Jimmy to call for us. Somebody will tell him that we're here."

Jimmy sat on the other side of the room. He was sitting with key members of his gang. Raul Martinez sat on Jimmy's far left. He was more like Jimmy's shadow. Wherever Jimmy went, Raul was there to protect him. Then there was the Gomez brothers' Carlos and Paco. They served as drivers and security for Jimmy. Raymond Diaz, a man in his early forties, sat on Jimmy's right. He was a big gang leader in the 70's and was still well respected and greatly feared by the young gangs. To Jimmy's far right was James Scott. He was a gringo in his mid thirties that everyone called the “chemist" because he set up drug labs for all of Jimmy's operations in Florida. Matilda sat comfortably on Jimmy's lap, she was Jimmy's main squeeze-for now.

With one wave of his hand, Jimmy summoned Paco to go get Hector. “Hey guys the boss is ready to see you now," Paco called.

As they walked, Hector reminded the twins to let him do all of the talking. It was obvious that Hector was quite nervous. His palms were sweaty and there was even noticeable perspiration on his face.

"Hector what's going on," Jimmy greeted.

“Nothing much, business is better than ever," Hector nervously responded.

“Who are your friends?”

“Jimmy, this is Alejandro and Roberto. Fellas, this is Mr. Jimmy Acosta, my boss," Hector proudly said.

“Guys, Hector has been telling me a lot of good things about you. He says that you're two smart cookies. If you stay loyal to me, you can wind up very successful,” Jimmy said calmly.

“And stay healthy,” Carlos Gomez added.

This was the first time that the twins really got a chance to check Jimmy out up close. He looked incredibly young and they couldn't believe he had so much influence. Jimmy controlled men more than twice his age.

"I want everybody but Raul to go away for a little while," Jimmy commanded. "I need to talk to Hector and his boys alone."

"I thought I could spend some time with you tonight," Matilda frowned.

"You will, but first I have to take care of some business'" Jimmy assured. "I'll be finished shortly, now ask one of the fellas to get you a drink."

Only Raul, Jimmy, Hector, and the twins remained. Jimmy then invited Hector and his guests to take the seats. "Hector first let me tell you that you are doing a helluva job with the territory I gave you. At first, I had my doubts, but you've proved me wrong," Jimmy admitted.

"Thanks Mr. Acosta, I've been working real hard to stay on top of things," Hector smiled.

"Fel las, where are you from?" Jimmy asked.

"We're from Cuba, Mr. Acosta," Roberto quickly replied.

"You know, Hector, I don't know if I'll like these two guys. I can't tell them apart," Jimmy laughed. 'Have you guys ever considered doing one of those gum commercials? Double your pleasure, double your fun."

Everyone except Alejandro laughed at Jimmy's little remark.

"It's easy to tell us apart Mr. Acosta," Alejandro interrupted.

"And how's that?" Jimmy asked.

"Roberto's the one that laughs at things that aren't even that funny," Alejandro said sharply. There was a long silent pause in the air.

"Jimmy, the kid didn't mean anything by what he just said," Hector explained in an effort to clean up the mess he thought Alejandro had made.

"Hector, don't ever call me Jimmy again. And as far as Alejandro goes, I like his balls. Just as long as he doesn't make a habit out of showing them off."

"I'm pretty sure he won't," Hector assured as he glared intensely at Alejandro.

"Hector, I am going to increase your supply. Do you think your area can handle it?" Jimmy asked.

"Mr. Acosta, for you we could handle any amount."

"Okay you will get an extra shipment on Wednesday's. Now, let me get back to my people. Guys take it easy and be careful," Jimmy warned.

An hour later, Hector and the twins were still at Disco Inferno but had been escorted to the second level immediately following their conversation with Jimmy.

“Alejandro, I still can't believe your attitude, you could have gotten all of us in a whole bunch of shit," Hector yelled.

“But I didn't, so just relax. In fact I think he likes us," Alejandro answered slyly.

“Me, he likes me. He don't know a damn thing about you two," Hector argued.

“Roberto, what are you staring at?" Alejandro asked.

“The girl at the bar. She keeps on looking over here,” Roberto said.

The one with the white mini dress?” Hector asked. “Yeah that's the one,” Roberto answered.

“Look leave that one alone. Her name is Rosa and she is nothing but trouble. She loves to float to anybody who has money," Hector advised.

“You must have her all wrong, Hector. She has such a sweet face, she looks like a little angel,” Roberto smiled.

\"Those are the types you have to watch out for. I like to mess around with women who look like tramps, because at least you know what you're getting," Hector said before downing another drink.

“Well I want to talk to her, what do you think?” Roberto asked.

“Hey, it's been such a long time since I saw you talking to a girl that I was starting to get a little worried about you," Alejandro laughed. “Go for it.”

“Wish me luck bro'." Roberto said as he hopped off the barstool.

Another hour passed, Roberto was chatting with his new friend and Hector was now snorting his fifth line of coke.

“Look at all the mommies," Hector rambled. “There are some bad asses in here."

“I know, I haven't made up my mind who I'm going home with tonight,” Alejandro smiled as he wondered out loud.

“Fuck it, why go home with one, why not two?” Hector snickered.

By now, most of the women in Disco Inferno had found out that Hector and the twins worked for Jimmy Acosta. They watched the way they carried themselves and admired how attentive the staff was to their every whim. Although Alejandro or Hector hadn't even spoken to any of the girls, they knew they wouldn't have any trouble scoring. Roberto, on the other hand, was focused on making a good impression on Rosa and had decided to drop his new friend home.

"Alejandro I'm outta here," Roberto said.

"Where are you going?" Alejandro asked.

"I am taking Rosa home then I'm going back to the apartment. Try not to make too much noise when you come in this time," Roberto warned.

"Just make sure you don't bust a nut too fast tonight," Alejandro taunted.

"Everyone is not like you," Roberto said sternly. "Rosa seems like a nice girl who just got caught up in a bad situation. I really like her."

"Yeah, whatever, just be careful out there," Alejandro warned.

In the cab ride over to Rosa's apartment, the young couple talked endlessly.

"You know, Roberto, you seem like such a nice guy. I have to be honest with you, I don't have the best reputation in the world. I have done some things in the past that I'm not too proud of," Rosa admitted.

"Trust me Rosa, everyone has skeletons in their closet," Roberto confided. "I don't really care about your past."

As the two got out of the cab, Roberto told the driver that he would be back downstairs shortly. He wanted to make sure that Rosa made it upstairs safely. Not only did she live in a bad Neighborhood, but her apartment was one of the worse ones on the block.

Rosa hesitated before unlocking the door. "Excuse the apartment, most of my furniture is very old."

"Don't worry I am used to looking at old furniture," Roberto smiled.

Once inside the apartment, Rosa turned on the lights. Although Roberto wasn't expecting much, he was still shocked by the way Rosa lived. The apartment was roach infested and one of the windows glass were broken out. Only a black plastic bag kept the air out. Roberto considered sitting on the couch but changed his mind when he noticed the mouse droppings on the pillow.

How could such a beautiful young girl live in these conditions?" Roberto thought. He felt really sorry for her.

"Look I have to go now, but I will call you later."

"I know why you are leaving so suddenly," Rosa said tearfully.

"What do you mean?" he said.

"You are too ashamed to be in this filthy apartment. I know your place doesn't have cracks in the ceiling or roaches but I am doing everything on my own and this is the best I can do right now," Rosa cried.

Roberto instinctively hugged Rosa to tell her that he didn't think badly of her. In fact, he even admired her independence. The hugging became more intense and before he knew it, she began to kiss him passionately on his lips. Rosa pressed her body up against Roberto's as tightly as she could. The tears still streamed from Rosa's eyes as Roberto continued to feverishly kiss her face. It felt so good to have Rosa in his arms, especially since it had been a long time since Roberto had been that close to anyone.

Rosa led Roberto into the bedroom where she immediately removed his pants. Breathing heavily, Roberto anxiously waited to see what would happen next. By now, the cab driver downstairs was repeatedly honking his horn but leaving was the furthest thing from Roberto's mind. It was time for lovemaking. Rosa dropped to her knees as she sucked and licked places that Roberto never imagined.

Roberto was on the verge of losing total control when Rosa pulled back. She stopped sucking Roberto's penis just as quickly as she had started but the session was far from over. She grabbed Roberto's hand and led him over to a chair that was in the corner of the room. She sat him down, removed her panties, and raised her mini dress to her waist. She looked directly into Roberto's eyes as she grabbed his stiff manhood and slowly lowered herself on him. They both let out a little sigh. With her feet planted firmly on the ground, she slowly bobbed up and down over and over again. She controlled the experience and her gentle movements determined how and when Roberto moaned. This went on for a while until Roberto flipped the script.

He placed both of his hands under her ass and gripped it tightly. Now, his strength dictated the encounter. This turned her on even more. Roberto felt better than he had ever felt in his life. He wanted to explode, but decided he wasn't ready for the feeling to end yet. Rosa screamed in ecstasy as she reached her climax. He gripped her closely to prevent her from wildly bouncing up and down but it was no use. Her contracting muscles were draining him. He soon followed her orgasm with one of his own, which resulted in an abundance of love juice that he squirted directly into her. She responded with another orgasm.

They remained in the same position, not moving at all, for several minutes. He continued to grip her rear end in his hand and was enjoying the moistness on his fingers. She held the back of his neck with her head cradled in his chest. With their last burst of energy, the couple took three short steps and collapsed on Rosa's bed. As they laid snug in each other's arms, Roberto hoped that Alejandro wouldn't be worried about him. There was no way he would make it back before morning.

# Chapter 16

ONE WEEK LATER

It was late Saturday night and Jimmy was going to check on one of his safe houses in downtown Miami. This was a place where most of the money collected from street drug sales was counted. It was called a safe house because few people knew the location. And even if they did, no one would dare confront the high security; they were mini fortresses.

Though Jimmy trusted the people that worked for him, he never trusted anyone totally. He believed money could make the most loyal employee dishonest, so he conducted random spot checks to keep his staff on their toes.

Within a few blocks of their destination, they ran into some unanticipated traffic. Worse yet, the entire neighborhood was flooded with cops. A police helicopter roved above with spotlights scanning the area; police cars were everywhere. The bright lights and heavy activity transformed this normally peaceful setting into a street festival.

“Raul let me out over here. I need to find out what's happening," Jimmy ordered.

“Wait a minute boss, I'll go with you," Carlos said as Jimmy got out of the car.

“No, that's all right. I can go by myself. I don't want to draw too much attention. I can fit right in with the rest of the crowd. You look like a fuckin' gangster.” Jimmy laughed as he slammed the car door.

Jimmy hurriedly penetrated the crowds and positioned himself across the street from one of his safe houses. His worst fear came true; the place had been raided. Everyone was handcuffed and escorted out of the house. “Damn!" he exclaimed. “There was over four million in there."

At the raided location, the police made their arrests and gathered evidence. “Who’s in charge?" Jack asked to no one in particular.

“I am," the gray haired Sergeant replied.

“Is there any way we can push back the crowds?" Jack asked.

“This area still isn't too well secured.” After his experience with the fatal blast, Jack had become fanatical about security.

“I'll try but it's going to be very difficult. The public believes they have a right to witness everything, even at the expense of their own safety,” the sergeant replied.

The men in handcuffs were quickly shifted from the house into the waiting police cars. Jack thought the process had gone pretty smoothly. He had seized millions of dollars, guns, and a little bit of recreational drugs. “The twelve guys will be doing some real time in prison," he thought.

Now everyone was tucked away and the squad was about to pull out, when Jack noticed something strange. Two of his men saw someone in the crowd that they recognized but couldn't place his face. “Hey Jack, doesn't that guy across the street look familiar?"

Jack looked more intensely into the crowd and noticed the very well dressed young man across the street. He looked familiar to him, so he decided to speak to the mysterious stranger himself. Since everything was pretty much taken care of at the house, Jack thought he should act on his hunch.

Jimmy looked away when the handcuffed men looked in his direction. Although he knew their only choice was to keep quiet, since everyone knew the penalty for snitching was death, he didn't want to tip off any of the surrounding cops. In spite of the scene, Jimmy remained relatively upbeat; after all, money laundering was the only real charge the cops had. He then noticed that one of the men in the blue DEA jackets had crossed the street and was headed in his direction. Jimmy figured it was time to leave at this point and began to walk swiftly down the crowded street. After a half a block, he looked over his shoulder and found the same agent following him.

Like a game that children play, the faster Jimmy walked, the faster Jack trailed. Then, what began as a walk turned into a full sprint. Jack was a block away from Jimmy but was gaining ground quickly. Now they were at least five blocks away from the police scene. Members of Jack's team were back at the safe house looking for him, they had no idea that Jack was involved in a high-speed foot chase. Jimmy's crew were also unaware of Jimmy's predicament and continued to wait for his return in the middle of a traffic jam.

*****

"Ah shit, it's Saturday night, I'm in my bad ass car and I got a pocket full of money. It doesn't get any better than this," Alejandro thought. "First I'll hit a couple of the local bars and check out the action there. Then I'll end it at the Club. Too bad Roberto didn't want to come along. But hey, he has his life and I have mine."

As Alejandro waited anxiously for the red light to change, he noticed one man chasing another in his rear view mirror.

"Somebody is in trouble. I guess that guy is about to get his ass seriously kicked," Alejandro laughed.

The man that was trying to escape his fate appeared to be getting very tired and began to slow down. The second man noticed this and took out a gun. "Wow this is better than the fuckin' movies," Alejandro cheered.

As two men got closer to the car, Alejandro realized that the man with the gun was a DEA agent and the men about to get caught was Jimmy Acosta. Without thinking, Alejandro stepped on the gas, shifted his gears in reverse and drove back to rescue his boss. "Jimmy hurry up and get in," Alejandro yelled.

Jimmy could not believe his luck. He didn't know who was driving the car but he also didn't care. He opened the passenger door and hopped in. Jimmy was so tired he could not even speak. It took him a few seconds to realize who had saved him from getting arrested.

"Damn!, damn!, damn!" Jack screamed as he watched his suspect get away. "I almost had him." Jack snatched his notepad out of his back pocket and jotted down part of Alejandro's license plate. He could only make out four of the six letters "R9801".

Hours later, Jack sat in front of a computer terminal at the DEA headquarters even more upset than he was before. He had picked Jimmy's photo out of a series of surveillance pictures of the Fernandez Cartel. Earlier, Jack thought the person he was chasing could have provided some information about the Cartel, it wasn't until now that he realized he'd almost captured a major player in the Fernandez Cartel.

"Fuck!" Jack exclaimed as he banged his fist on his desk. He was tired of just locking up the small guys. He wanted to nab a big fish, like Jimmy. Of course he really had nothing on him. The only thing Jimmy did was run away from a law enforcement agent, who did not have any charges on him to begin with. Yet, Jack was convinced that once he got Jimmy into his office everything would fall into place,

"Boss why don't you get some rest. You've been working on this for the past sixteen hours. Me and the rest of the fellas can take it over from here," Tommy offered. As one of the new jacks on the force, Tommy was anxious to prove himself to Jack. He hoped that Jack would give him the opportunity to handle this small task.

"Thanks, I'm going back to the hotel to take a nice hot bath. I'll be back here first thing in the morning."

Jack entered his hotel room still very pissed off about how the night ended. He ran his bath water and then collapsed on the bed. He rolled over and called his machine to see if anyone left any messages. There were two.

The first was his sister checking up on him.

"Hi Jack, this is your sister calling. You are never at home. Well, anyway I called just to see how you are doing and to remind you that you promised to visit me soon. Love ya big guy. Call me soon."

The second message made him smile.

"Hello Jack, this is Cynthia calling. How are you? I hope everything is fine. Maybe the next time you come to Baltimore we can go out for a couple of drinks. Talk to you later."

That was the best news Jack heard in months. Ever since he saw Cynthia, he couldn't get her out of his mind. After calling her so many times with no luck, Jack was considering giving up on her. Now, he might finally have a chance to get to know her. "I better act quickly before she gets cold feet and changes her mind," Jack thought.

Minutes later as he slowly lowered himself into the water, Jack recapped the day's events and concluded, "Today really wasn't that bad after all."

"Just hurry up and bring your asses over to the condo. I'll tell you everything once you get here," Jimmy barked at one of his men on the cell phone. It had been several hours since Jimmy's close encounter with the police but the men were still waiting for him to return to the car.

"Whew, that was a close one," Jimmy sighed as he dried himself off with the towel after just stepping out of the shower.

"Why was that guy chasing you anyway?" Alejandro asked.

"Maybe he was jealous of the way I was dressed." Jimmy laughed.

"Where were you running from?" Alejandro asked.

"I think that's enough with the questions," Jimmy replied while giving Alejandro a sharp look.

Alejandro realized that maybe he had over stepped his boundaries and began to feel uneasy. Maybe he had observed something that he wasn't suppose to see. In any case, he'd decided to leave before Jimmy's crew arrived.

"Well Jimmy, take it easy, I'm outta here," Alejandro said hurriedly.

"Wait a minute, I want to tell you something that I haven't told anybody in a long time. Thanks a lot. You really put your neck on the line saving my ass back there," Jimmy said as he extended his hand out. "I owe you big time."

"Forget about it. It was no big deal," Alejandro responded by gripping Jimmy's hand for a firm handshake.

"And that's the other thing. What happened tonight will be our little secret. I don't even want you to tell your twin brother, all right." Jimmy looked directly into his eyes.

"You got it." Alejandro replied.

At that moment, the intercom sounded and Jimmy instructed the doorman to send his men upstairs. Alejandro didn't get a chance to leave. For the next two hours, the crew discussed how much money they'd lost during the bust. Jimmy often excused himself to talk on the phone in his bedroom. He spoke in some type of secret code, just in case his telephone was being bugged. After one last phone call, Jimmy exited his room and told everyone to leave.

"Okay everybody grab your shit, It's time for us to go," Jimmy ordered.

"Where are we going now, it's almost two in the morning." Carlos asked.

"That's a dumb question. It's Saturday night, we're all going to Disco Inferno," Jimmy said.

"All of us?" Raul said as he looked in Alejandro's direction.

"Yes, all of us," Jimmy snapped back.

The club was really packed that night. As usual, it seemed that every cool guy and fine girl were in the house. Jimmy and his boys took their usual seats in the VIP section. The only difference was that Alejandro was now sitting next to him on his right side, a spot usually reserved for other members of the Fernandez Cartel. The drinks and the cocaine were flowing freely and Jimmy was relieved that he wouldn't have to spend the night in prison. The thought of losing all that money was the furthest thing from his mind and his last phone call reassured him that everything was under control. He was just told to be more careful next time.

Hector made his way over to their table. He was accompanied by his bodyguard and some chick he had been doing for the past two weeks.

"Mr. Acosta, how are you today?" Hector asked. Hector hoped Jimmy would ask him to join him, but that invitation never came.

"I'm doing good. My people are telling me that you are doing one helluva job for me," Jimmy commented. "I always like to hear stuff like that."

"Thanks again for giving me the chance to make this work," Hector brown-nosed. "We're really working hard for you."

"I know you are Hector, and we really appreciate it," Jimmy said graciously.

'Thanks again, Mr. Acosta."

At first, Hector was so busy sucking up to Jimmy that he hadn't noticed Alejandro sitting right next to Jimmy. It wasn't until he reached out to shake Jimmy's hand, that he caught a glimpse of Alejandro.

"Alejandro, what's up? I've been trying to get in touch with you all night. There's something that I want you to do for me, first thing in the morning," Hector ordered.

"That's not going to be possible, Hector," Jimmy said.

"Why not?" Hector asked.

"Alejandro and his brother don't work for you anymore. They both work directly for me starting tomorrow," Jimmy said as he winked at Alejandro.

All of the men at the table looked at Alejandro in shock. This move was totally unexpected. Even Alejandro was a bit surprised but he tried hard to play it cool.

"Okay, well good luck kid," Hector stammered. "Mr. Acosta, maybe I'll see you later on." Hector, still stunned from the news, nearly tripped over his feet as he and his entourage walked towards the staircase leading to the pit. He was suddenly feeling a little angry and needed some time to digest what he had just heard.

At Jimmy's table, the next two hours flew. At first, the fellas didn't like Alejandro but as they got to know him they started to think he was okay. He was still a little green but he was humble and respected his elders. A quality that most of the new punk ass kids lacked.

"Guys, I'll be right back. I'm going to take a leak," Alejandro announced.

"What the fuck are you doing, asking us for permission? Get the hell outta here," Jimmy joked as everyone laughed.

Alejandro walked hurriedly towards the men's room, all the beer he'd drank was starting to run right through him. Just as he approached the bathroom door, he heard a familiar voice.

"I have that motherfucka' wrapped around my little fuckin' finger," Rosa said as she held court around the bar. She was surrounded by three hustlers and one of her female friends.

"So, you think you turned him out?" a male voiced asked.

"Turned him out, that kid is totally whipped. He acted like he never got it so good." Rosa laughed as she recalled the night of passion between her and Roberto.

"Wait a minute, Rosa. I got some before, so don't sit here and act like you got the golden pussy," another man joked.

"Well motherfucker, it must be pretty damn good to Roberto because next week he is hooking me up with some new furniture," Rosa replied.

"Girl, you got a good one but just don't give it to him too often. Always keep him begging for more," Rosa's girlfriend suggested.

"I hear that!" Rosa squealed as she gave her girlfriend a high five.

Alejandro couldn't believe his ears. This bitch was making his brother seem like the biggest sucker of the year. Alejandro was so angry that he considered hurting Rosa and the four people laughing at his brother but then opted against it. Instead, Alejandro quickly circled the bar so that no one would see him and then walked towards the group like nothing happened.

"Hi Rosa, what's going on?" Alejandro calmly asked.

"Honey, how are you?" Rosa said as she opened her arms to hug him. "I was just talking about you."

"No," he answered as he pushed Rosa away. "I'm Alejandro. Can I talk to you alone for a second?"

"Sure you can." Rosa said and as if on cue her little party scattered towards the dance floor.

When the crew left, Alejandro's attitude changed completely.

"I am only going to tell you one time and one time only," Alejandro charged. "Leave my brother alone."

"Why should I?" she shot back.

"My brother is a nice guy and he don't need to be fuckin' around with some no good bitch like you," Alejandro growled.

"Why do you say that about me?" she said acting shocked.

"I'm a good girl who just got caught up in some bad luck, even your brother says that."

"Cut the bullshit. I heard all the things you said about my brother and that was really fucked up."

"We were all just joking around and exchanging crazy stories. Nobody got hurt," Rosa defended.

"Just stay away from him."

"I can't help it if your brother likes me. If he wants to take me out or buy me things, I'm sure as hell not going to stop him," Rosa said with her hands firmly planted on her hips.

"You see there is only one way to deal with people like you. So, let me break it down for you. If I catch you going out with my brother one more time, the cops are going to find your-ass in a plastic bag in some park." Alejandro's eyes were more serious than they had ever been in his life. He concluded by saying, "And I really hope you wind up having a real fucked up life."

As he walked away Rosa realized two things. One was that Alejandro was very different from his brother. The second thing was that she was going to leave Roberto the hell alone. She knew for sure that Alejandro would follow through on his threat.

*****

As Jack drove down the highway, he couldn't believe how nervous he was. Three days ago, Jack returned Cynthia's message and asked her to go out with him that coming Friday. Now here it was, the day of the date, and he was on the way to pick her up. Although he prided himself on having great composure, he was a wreck. Throughout his years with the DEA, Jack had garnered many awards for handling tough situations. Yet, he was unable to calm himself for this simple date. He couldn't stop his hands from sweating or his heart from racing. To make matters even worse, he had a severe case of dry mouth and feared that bad breath was sure to follow. He checked his pockets for some kind of gum or mint but had no luck. "My first date in six months and I'm going to have bad breath," he worried.

Jack wanted the night to turn out well and even went to the extent of buying a new suit for the occasion. Not that he didn't have any clothes, he had plenty. The problem was, all of his attire had cop written all over them. For the most part, Jack's wardrobe was pretty outdated. The few stylish pieces that he did have were either too formal or too casual for the occasion. The man at the shop helped him pick out the perfect outfit. It was dressy but didn't make him appear stuffy and it looked good on him.

Jack was only ten minutes from the house when he finally found some mints in the glove compartment. He breathed a sigh of relief and wondered why he worried so much. Somehow, he thought the date would turn out just fine.

"If he likes women who wear a lot of makeup, he can forget about it," Cynthia said as she gave herself one final look-over in the mirror. Although Cynthia did give in to having her hair done at the beauty parlor she refused to go through too much trouble. She kept her outfit really simple, especially since she didn't want to attract Jack in any way. Her reason for accepting the date was simple; she just wanted to keep her mother quiet about her not dating anybody. With Jack calling all of the time, Cynthia figured she might as well get it over with now.

It wasn't that Cynthia didn't find Jack attractive. On the contrary, she thought Jack was a real hunk, but she believed he just wasn't her type. What's more, she'd concluded that she wasn't Jack's cup of tea either. He seemed like a nice guy, but that was the problem, he was too nice. Cynthia had calmed down a lot from her old days, but knew that deep inside, she was still drawn to a man with a little wildness in him.

The sound of the doorbell meant it was time for her date to begin. Cynthia could not wait for this night to be over and was already watching the clock.

When Cynthia opened the door, she was greeted by a bouquet of flowers. At first, she thought the gesture was rather corny but she smiled and rushed to put the flowers in a vase. "That was kind of sweet," she thought.

"Well, well Cynthia you are looking very nice tonight," Jack complimented.

"So are you," Cynthia replied while looking over his suit. It sure beats the polyester get-up that she was expecting him to wear.

"Would you like something to drink?" Cynthia asked.

"No, that's okay. I don't think we have the time for that. We have a six thirty reservation at Le Détente's and it's a little after six, so we better get going."

"A French restaurant," she thought. "This is going to be interesting."

As Cynthia put on her jacket she hoped he wasn't one of those schedule freaks. Jack thought that Cynthia was looking even better than he had remembered.

During the ride, the conversation was pretty predictable and stale. Both of them tried to act the way they thought the other person expected, so neither was feeling very comfortable. Cynthia was beginning to regret her decision to come on the date.

At the restaurant, the couple was surrounded by the soft sounds of a live pianist. The seats were perfectly padded and the flower arrangements on the table were fresh as a summer's day. Jack had requested a table by the window. The cool breeze was refreshing but not strong enough to dim the flames from the candlelight. The atmosphere had all of the ingredients for a perfect evening.

Cynthia and Jack stared at their menus for several minutes, until they were interrupted by their Waiter. “May I take your order?" he asked.

“Cynthia, you order first," Jack insisted in an attempt to stall since he hadn't found anything on the menu he liked.

“No Jack, why don't you order first? Maybe I'll end up getting the same thing," Cynthia replied.

“Ladies first,” Jack awkwardly smiled fearing that this date wasn't getting off to a great start.

“Excuse me waiter, can we have a minute alone?" Cynthia asked.

“Sure, take your time. The kitchen closes in four hours," the waiter smiled. He could always tell a couple on their first date and wondered if it was even a blind date.

“Look Jack to be honest with you, there really isn't anything on this menu that I would want to eat," Cynthia admitted.

“What a relief,” I'm glad I am not the only one.” Jack laughed.

“Why don't we drive to the nearest supermarket and take some things back to my house? I make a mean spaghetti," Cynthia offered.

“Sounds great."

“There's only one thing I have to warn you about,” Cynthia said, looking serious.

“And what's that?" a worried Jack asked.

“You have to help me cut up the ingredients," Cynthia smiled.

“But of course," Jack grinned as he grabbed Cynthia’s hand to help her out of her seat. “Let's get out of here."

Back at Cynthia’s house, Jack was in the kitchen cutting up onions, garlic, green peppers and anything else Cynthia threw his way. Before they knew it, they were actually having a good time.

They found they had much more in common than they expected. They both loved the same kind of music and wrote poetry in their spare time. What's more, Cynthia and Jack were hooked on Abbott & Costello reruns with their favorite episode being the one where Abbott and Costello meet Frankenstein, the Werewolf, and Dracula.

When Cynthia laughed at some silly joke that Jack had made, he looked at her and wondered how she could have been mixed up with a slime ball like Alex Sanchez.

"Cynthia, why were you attracted to Alex Sanchez?" Jack asked. Even before he'd finished pronouncing Alex's last name, he knew he had said something wrong.

"I was wondering how long it was going to take before you started asking a million questions about that part of my life," Cynthia said defensively. "Just trying to do your job, I guess."

"I didn't mean to pry, and I certainly don't want you to think that I am trying to gather information about Alex Sanchez. Please accept my apology," Jack offered. "We were having a good time and I don't wan't to ruin it."

"Apology accepted. Now you tell me why you became involved in law enforcement?" she asked.

"Okay let's make a deal. I won't ask you questions about Alex, if I don't have to talk about my job." Jack offered. "Is that a deal?"

"It's a deal," Cynthia agreed as she extended out her hand.

As Jack shook her hand, he didn't want to let it go. It was warm and soft, yet she had a strong grip, which suggested that she possessed some type of inner strength.

After enjoying a great dinner, Jack suggested that they go bowling.

"Jack, there is no way I'm going bowling," Cynthia responded as she cleared the table.

"Why not?"

"I'm not dressed for it."

"I am not either, but at least you can go upstairs and change," Jack said convincingly.

"Okay, the truth is that I really suck at bowling and I'm not going to embarrass myself out there," she admitted.

"Cynthia, you said you love music right?"

"Well yeah," Cynthia reluctantly answered wondering what she was getting herself into.

"I know of this bowling place where tonight is Disco night. So are you game for it?"

"Why didn't you say that in the first place? I'll be ready in ten minutes," Cynthia said as she dashed upstairs.

Jack went bowling on a regular basis but he had never had so much fun. Although you were not supposed to dance in the bowling lane as you threw your ball, Cynthia changed all that. Jack really liked to bowl but he enjoyed watching Cynthia even more. To him, she had the cutest butt he'd ever seen. Unknown to Jack, Cynthia was checking his butt out as well. She'd concluded that his backside was well stacked.

On the drive back, Jack refrained from asking Cynthia when they would see each other again. Neither one of the them wanted the date to end but Jack decided not to push his luck, just in case she was just pretending to have a good time for his sake.

At the front door Cynthia considered inviting Jack in, but decided against it. She didn't want to give him the wrong impression.

He longed to hold her close to him and kiss her perfect set of lips but this was their first date and he didn't want to come on too strong.

"Well I had a good time and I hope you did too," Jack smiled. He hated the ending of first dates just as much as he hated the beginning of them and couldn't decide which was more awkward.

"Everything was great," Cynthia paused wondering if Jack had planned to plant a kiss, but apparently he hadn't. "Well, it's pretty late so I better go inside."

Before he turned to leave, a few words poured from his lips,

"You know ah, give me a call some time and maybe we can hang out again, sometime."

"Okay that sounds good," Cynthia politely responded.

One hour later, Cynthia was in her bed thinking, "he wasn't so bad after all." In fact, her new friend had turned out to be a lot of fun. Before turning off the lights Cynthia came to the conclusion that they probably would never go out again. "It's one thing to go out on a date with someone like me, but to date someone with my past on a regular basis is a different story,"
Cynthia concluded. "Especially a cop."

Jack reached home and instinctively turned on his television set with his nearby remote. The screen glared brightly but he wasn't paying attention to it. Instead, he thought about Cynthia. Although he hoped that he would see her again, he had a feeling that she would never call him back.

# Chapter 17

“Roberto there is a big difference working for Jimmy, compared to Hector,” Alejandro said.

“Yeah I know what you mean. Hector treated us great and we owe him a lot, but Jimmy really shows us around," Roberto responded as he dimmed the lights.

“I still can't believe the size of Jimmy's Miami operation, I never realized it was so huge,” Alejandro marveled.

“I don't know why he trusts us so much, but I'm not gonna fight it," Roberto said as he made himself comfortable in his bed.

“With all the money that we're making now, we could get a fuckin' dope apartment.”

“I don't want to move," Roberto mumbled. "I like it here."

“Sooner or later, we have to move," Alejandro insisted as he sat up in his bed in the darkness. “It might be too dangerous for Mama' if we stayed here. You remember what Jimmy told us. Now that we're major players, we have to watch our backs."

"I guess you're right, but what reason can we give her for moving out?"

"Don't worry bro, leave all the lying to me." Alejandro chuckled. "Telling white lies is my specialty."

"You know what I think? You want to move just so you can have all the girls you want," Roberto said as he launched his pillow at his brother.

"How can you think that of me?" Alejandro said with a high pitched voice and shocked expression pasted across his face.

"I think you sometimes forget, that I know you better that anyone else," Roberto explained. "I can tell what you're gonna do and when you're lying."

"You remember that game we used to play as kids, paper, rock scissors?" Alejandro reminded.

"Yeah, I remember. We always threw out the same signals," Roberto remembered. "Do you think we could still do that?"

"Let's try it now," Alejandro suggested. At that same moment Alejandro's beeper went off and he leaped from his bed to respond. "I guess we have to do it some other time. I got to call Jimmy first."

"Yeah, we'll do it some other time," a disappointed Roberto responded. "Business comes first."

*****

*Dear Cynthia,*

*How's everything in Baltimore? I was really glad that you called me the other day. I had a feeling from the first time we met, that no matter what happened, we would become good friends.*

*When we spoke on the phone you told me some things about your past. A lot of good things and some stuff that you were not too proud of. I guess that's why I'm writing you now. I am feeling guilty about some of the things that I am doing.*

*First of all, Alejandro and I have dropped out of school for one semester. To make matters worse, we didn't even tell our grandmother. She still believes we are taking classes. I hate lying to her but she would be too upset if we told her the truth.*

*The other thing is our new friends. They live in the fast lane. I don't like them much, but Alejandro seems to enjoy being around them. I really don't know what to do. I don't want to stop hanging out with Alejandro, but I don't feel too comfortable with this new group. There was a time when Alejandro and I were very close. We could even finish each other's sentences. Now I have no idea what he's thinking.*

*Maybe I am just getting jealous that Alejandro has met some new friends. So don't worry, we will be all right. Cynthia thanks for listening. I always feel much better after having talked with you. Please take care.*

*Sincerely yours,*
*Roberto Sanchez*

*PS: Please send me a recent picture of you. I want to put that picture next to the other violets I have in my room.*

*****

"I can't believe you talked me into going to this dance," Cynthia wined.

"Well dear, you have been here for a while now and I think it's about time you start socializing again," Betty explained.

"But this kind of thing really isn't for me," Cynthia said.

"How do you know until you try it? Besides, from what I hear, there will be a lot of eligible bachelors at this particular dance," Betty teased. "So, you never know."

"You never know what?" Cynthia asked sharply.

"Oh nothing." Betty laughed.

"This is exactly what I was complaining about before. One minute you convince me to go out with some of my old girlfriends from high school, then the next minute you're trying to marry me off."

"Well Cynthia, would that be so bad?" Betty asked.

"No, it wouldn't be mom, but I'm just not ready for any of that stuff now."

Cynthia was standing directly in front of the bathroom mirror applying her make-up when her mother came over to add some finishing touches.

"Mom what are you gonna do with that flower?" Cynthia asked.

"Since I know how much you enjoy them, I was just going to put it in your hair," Betty offered happily.

"Look Ma, I am going to a dance, not my first prom. I know you mean well, but just back off a little bit," Cynthia insisted.

"Well Cynthia you look just as beautiful without it." Betty smiled.

"See ya later, Ma." Cynthia called out as she raced out of the door. Even though she wasn't enthusiastic about attending the dance she didn't want to be late.

"Just be careful," Betty added with a worried look on her face.

As Cynthia walked to her car, she realized that she shouldn't be so hard on her mother. Betty meant well but sometimes she just came on a little too strong. As she drove, Cynthia began thinking about the old gang. How were they now? Were they married? Did any of them have any children? Since this was strictly a "girl's night out" she knew they could do a lot of catching up and even started looking forward to hanging out.

*****

As Cynthia drove up to the hall, she quickly concluded that this evening was going to be much more than she expected. "The Wagon" used to be a cheap place where any Joe Blow could hang out. Now it appeared to be a ritzy spot for all of the high society folks in Baltimore. An attendant parked her car and she got a closer look at the Mercedes-Benz collection. From the very old models to the more recent ones, they were all there. She knew she was going to be in for some evening.

As she walked into the main hall, she noticed that all eyes were on her. She wore a simple silver strapless dress revealing her well-defined back and most men wondered who was the mystery woman with the hard walk. Cynthia looked around and found the table where her old buddies were seated. She was a little annoyed that no one told her that The Wagon had changed so drastically but she tried to retain her composure.

"Look who's here!" Erica shrieked. "They told me you were back in town but I didn't believe them. Look at you. I hate you. You're probably the same size that you were back in High School."

"Erica, it is really good to see you, too. How long has it been since High School?" Cynthia asked as she made her rounds of hugs and kisses.

"Let's not talk about ages," Helen warned. "One of these men walking around may hear us talking and figure things out."

"Still the same old Helen, always worrying what somebody else is thinking," Cynthia laughed. "But I gotta give it to you, you look great."

"She better, since she's in here looking for husband number four," Chelsea remarked.

"Helen you've been married three times?" Cynthia asked.

"It's only really twice. I had my second marriage annulled, we were only married for two months," Helen defensively answered. Her initial smile was instantly transformed into an intense frown after Chelsea's comment.

"Enough about Helen, Cynthia tell us what's up with you?" Erica quizzed.

*"Well, I left home after High School because I wanted to escape a father that was emotionally abusive. I was finally old enough to realize his sexual advances were not only out of line but illegal. My first stop was in Los Angeles. Where I was immediately approached by some bogus Hollywood agents who promised to make me a big star. That was a dead-end; the only thing they really wanted to do was make me into a hooker. So, after a couple of months of bumming off of them, I had to choose between turning tricks or running away again. I chose to run away.*

*I hopped around for the next couple of years before finally settling down in Miami. As a symbol of my new beginning, I changed my name to Candice. I also began hanging around the neighborhood low lives and developed a serious drug habit. My personal relationships were as fucked up as the rest of my life and I spent my free time dating drug dealers until I ended up marrying one of them, Alex Sanchez. For a short time, we lived a crazy life together until I nearly killed myself from a drug overdose. I've just spent the last five years of my life in a mental home."*

"That would surely shock them if she told them that," Cynthia thought to herself. "No, better play it safe."

"I was married and played homemaker while my husband ran the family business," Cynthia responded.

"You see girls, you can't believe all of those wild rumors you hear," Chelsea interrupted.

"What rumors?" Cynthia asked sharply. She hoped that she wasn't invited out just to answer nosy questions about her past.

"Well Cynthia, I didn't believe any of them, but there was one that said you married a famous drug lord. Another claimed that you were in a nut house," Chelsea joked.

"Now Chelsea, why did you have to bring that up tonight?" Erica asked in a concerned voice. "Cynthia, there's been some rumors about your past, but I don't think we should bring them up."

"Listen girls, rumors don't bother me not one bit," Cynthia lied. "It just means people find me interesting."

"Girls look over there," a very enthused Helen interrupted. "It's Jonathan Miles looking in our direction. I'm sure you've all heard of him?"

"I haven't. Who is Jonathan Miles?" Cynthia asked.

"Dr. Jonathan Miles is only the hottest and most successful Doctor in this whole part of Baltimore," Erica answered.

"He can check me out anytime. I think I feel a cold coming on," Helen laughed as she cranked out fake coughs.

"You guys are too much," Cynthia smiled. She was beginning to think that hanging out with old friends wasn't such a bad idea after all.

"Guys straighten up, he's coming over to our table," Helen nervously instructed.

"Hello ladies, I hope you are having a good time tonight, my name is Jonathan Miles." After introducing himself to the group, he then looked directly into Cynthia's eyes and asked her to dance.

"No thank you," Cynthia answered gently. "Maybe later on, but thank you for asking."

After Cynthia's rejection, he said his good-byes and returned to his table. His eyes continued to remain on Cynthia.

"What is the matter?" Helen blurted out. "Are you crazy? Why would you turn down Dr. Handsome?"

“He was attractive but I don't think he is really my type,” Cynthia admitted.

“Young, handsome, and wealthy, that is everybody's type.” Helen immediately responded.

The women broke into laughter. That one-liner was the catalyst for several topics over the next two hours, which ranged from issues with men to problems on the job. Although they all thought The Wagon had become a little stuffy in the last few years, they were still having a great time.

“Girls why don't we all go to the ladies room to freshen up. That way we can get a good look at most of the guys here without appearing too desperate," Helen suggested.

“But we are desperate," Erica said playfully.

“You three can go but I'll wait for you to come back,” Cynthia offered.

“Come on Cynthia, it'll be fun, just like it was in High School," Helen insisted. “Remember, how we used to go everywhere together?”

Once inside the bathroom, there was more girl talk until Chelsea went into her bag and brought out some coke. Chelsea took the first hit and then Helen joined her. Cynthia could not believe what was happening. Even her high society High School buddies were into drugs. Her face was overcome with a look of disapproval and she remained motionless.

“Cynthia please don't look that way. We're not drug addicts we just snort a little once in a while. It's a special occasion," Erica explained. She then snorted some coke herself and motioned for Cynthia to do the same.

After Cynthia fully recovered at the Institute, she enrolled herself in a twelve-step drug program. They spent a lot of time teaching her how to refuse drugs under difficult circumstances; however, dealing with the situation face to face was much more difficult than she had imagined.

“No that's okay Erica, I'm not into that," Cynthia struggled.

“Come on Cynthia don't be such a prude. Live dangerously once in a while,” Chelsea teased.

“Leave her alone if she doesn't want to do it, that's fine,” Erica defended.

"Okay ladies we have been in here too long. I'm probably missing my chance to marry Mr. Right," Helen intervened. "Let's get out of here."

"Why do you want to marry again? You'll only wind up getting another divorce," Chelsea jabbed. "Helen, are you sure you give good head? You know that might be your problem."

Chelsea laughed loudly while everyone else remained quiet.

"I certainly know how to satisfy a man, your ex-husband included," Helen snapped.

"And what in the hell do you mean by that?" Chelsea responded.

"Hey you two, cut it out. Let's get back to our tables before people think we're a bunch of lesbians having sex in the restroom." Erica interrupted.

As Cynthia journeyed home, she was glad that her mother talked her into hanging out with her old friends. She was also proud of herself for turning down the coke that was offered to her.

"Those girls are one crazy bunch," Cynthia thought.

Cynthia knew hanging out with them on a regular basis wouldn't be possible, but she did look forward to getting together every once in while.

*****

It had been a long time since the boys visited their grandmother's church but Alejandro and Roberto promised to accompany her on this sunny Sunday. So, the twins and Mama' Sanchez climbed the church steps together.

Roberto and Alejandro looked especially handsome in their navy blue suits. Alejandro dressed his up with a rose colored silk handkerchief and matching shirt. Roberto stuck with the standard white handkerchief and shirt. Mama' Sanchez modeled her favorite pink dress and matching hat. She strutted proudly between her beloved twins.

When the twins first arrived in Miami they went to church often, but as they got older, they were no longer forced to go. First, they skipped a couple of Sundays to study for exams. Then they missed a few due to their hectic work schedules. Before they knew it, three years had passed. It was time to return.

"This place is a lot smaller than I remember," Alejandro marveled.

"It's the same size. You've just have gotten bigger," Mama' Sanchez reminded.

"Look, there is Mrs. Cruz," Roberto said as he pointed to an elderly woman. 'She always gave us mean looks if we acted up too much."

As they walked to their seats, they were greeted by Father Ramos. "Mrs. Sanchez, are these the same twins that used to attend every Sunday?"

"Yes, they are. This is Roberto and this is Alejandro," Mama' Sanchez smiled.

"You boys have really grown into fine looking young men, your grandmother must be very proud of you," he continued.

"Yes I am. They are both doing very well, working and going to school," Mama' Sanchez proudly responded.

"And boys, I know you must be very proud of your grandmother. It's not every day that the church honors someone. Your grandmother is one special woman. We are blessed to have her in this church," the Priest acknowledged.

Roberto and Alejandro grinned from ear to ear. "Yes, we also feel very lucky to have her," Roberto agreed sounding many years older than he actually was.

"It was nice seeing you again. I must get going because I have to review today's sermon," the Priest explained as he headed towards the back room. "I hope you enjoy the service."

Mama' Sanchez and the twins sat in her favorite row, right next to their nosy neighbor Mrs. Gonzalez. The service was over two hours. It was filled with spiritual songs, biblical messages, and a tribute to Mama' Sanchez.

One by one, the members spoke of Mama' Sanchez's tireless work in the church's various charity projects as well as her efforts in the community. The twins smiled and nodded their heads in agreements. Mama' Sanchez sat proud with teary-filled eyes.

The twins never really knew how much the church appreciated their grandmother. They were happy that they were able to share in their grandmother's happiness, though they concluded they probably wouldn't visit again anytime soon.

After everything was over, most of the people gathered outside to bid their congratulations. Mama' Sanchez was surrounded by a bunch of her peers while Roberto and Alejandro stood quietly by her side.

One of the ushers's at the Church approached the elderly women and asked them if they would want to attend the Church's party. They were told that the proceeds from the party would go to the Church's after school program.

"Sorry but at my age, I'm not into partying," Mama' Sanchez giggled. The other ladies agreed and also began to laugh.

"Well, what about buying raffles?" the usher asked as their ladies paused to catch their breath.

"Sure, I will buy a couple, but you don't have to worry about me winning anything. I've never won anything in my life," Mama' Sanchez laughed.

"Well, if you do finally win, it will be a large screen TV."

"I could use one of those," Mama Sanchez said smiling. "That would surely be a blessing."

Mama Sanchez reached in her purse and handed the usher two dollars.

The remaining women also purchased a few raffle tickets. Afterward, the raffle tickets were tucked safely away. Each of the ladies said their good-byes and raced towards their respective homes to finish making their Sunday dinners.

Back at the house, Mama Sanchez plopped herself down on the couch. She was a little tired. "Being the center of attention really takes a lot out of a person," she thought.

As soon as Mama Sanchez caught her breath, she called her grandsons. "Roberto, Alejandro, come here for a second."

"Yeah Mama, what is it?" Roberto asked.

"I want to thank both of you for today," she said warmly.

"Thank us for what?" Alejandro dumbfoundly asked.

"For going to Church with me and for being such good boys, too." Mama Sanchez got up from the couch and hugged both of the twins tightly. "I love you both so much."

Alejandro and Roberto, each gave their grandmother a kiss on the cheek. "There isn't anything that we wouldn't do for our Mama'," Roberto whispered. "We love you more than anything."

*****

It had been a couple of months since Cynthia had hung out with her old high school buddies. Since then, many things in her life had changed. The most important change was her relationship with Jack Lloyd.

Ever since their first date, the twosome began to see each other pretty regularly. They really enjoyed each other's company and things were getting serious.

Ironically, it took more than two weeks for Jack to breakdown and call Cynthia to find out if she really did have a good time that first night. She reassured him that she wanted to see him again and they'd been dating ever since.

On the second date, both confessed that neither one of them wanted to seem overly anxious so they both tried to play the cool role. That part of the game was over. Cynthia and Jack promised that they would try to be as real and honest as possible.

It was picnic day. Cynthia was in charge of bringing the wine, cheese, food, fruit, and a small radio. Jack's job was to bring the blanket.

Cynthia didn't mind preparing the entire meal for them. This came as a shock to her because she never saw herself as the domestic type. For Jack, Cynthia would do almost anything. She had finally found what she had been searching for her whole life. In Cynthia's eyes, Jack was good looking, had a great body, and a crazy sense of humor. He was also humble and a good listener. "What more could I have asked for?" she often thought.

There was only one thing about him that bothered her. Jack worked entirely too hard. He often worked sixty to seventy hour weeks. Cynthia thought as their relationship progressed Jack would cut down on his workload. But he didn't. Now that they were seeing each other more frequently, Jack began cutting back on important things, like sleeping. Cynthia was extremely worried about this and decided to voice her concerns at today's picnic.

"Honey, will you please help me spread the blanket?" Jack asked.

"Wow. This is really a nice blanket. It must be new," Cynthia said excitedly.

"It is new. I bought it on the way over. I stayed all night at the office and I did not have the time to go back to get one from my apartment. I would've felt too guilty if I didn't show up with the only thing that I had promised to bring," Jack said as he made himself comfortable on the crisp new blanket. He lied flat on his back and waited for Cynthia to join him.

"Jack, there is something that I want to talk to you about." Cynthia said while still standing.

"What is it?" Jack asked thinking that Cynthia was getting ready to give him the speech that he'd heard many times before. It was the one where the woman declares that things are moving a little too fast and suggests that maybe they should slow down a bit. Or worse yet, maybe they should just focus on being just friends. He wondered why women always claimed to want a serious relationship and then try to bail out when you give them one.

"I am really concerned about you working so many hours. You're gonna run yourself into the ground. I know your work is very important to you, but I can't have my man walking around looking worn down," Cynthia said as she sat down Indian style on the blanket. She then leaned over and kissed Jack passionately on the lips. "You have to slow down."

"Is that it?" Jack asked with a look of relief on his face.

"Yeah, that's it," Cynthia smiled.

"Well, lady, consider it done."

*****

Pacing the floor of his room, Hector Ramirez wondered what went wrong. It was only a couple of months ago that he was bringing in loads of money from Jimmy's operation. He had a fabulous apartment, a closet full of clothes and a bad ass car. Now he was sharing a bathroom with the other tenants that lived in the seedy rooming house that he was renting in downtown Miami.

He had already tried pleading with Jimmy for his old job but it was useless. Jimmy wouldn't hear of it. "I only give a person one chance to mess up," Jimmy barked. "Hector, you've already used yours up."

For a while, Hector was doing a great job moving drugs for Jimmy. He supervised a large number of street level dealers and provided them with their supply. He also helped collect some of the money. Hector was very meticulous and triple-checked everything for accuracy.

Hector's problems began two months ago when he got hooked on crack. He lost control and started using it in large amounts.

This was detrimental to his business because the stuff he was using was supposed to have been distributed to his dealers. What's more, Hector then began throwing wild parties with other users. Then the street level drug dealers started to cheat him out of hoards of money. By the time Hector discovered what was happening it was too late; he was down nearly a hundred thousand dollars.

When Jimmy fired him, Hector got really down on himself. Now, he continually lived on the edge and went through the money he'd saved up like it was water. Last month, Hector bunked in a crack house for two weeks. There, he received an endless supply of crack until he ran out of money, and then they threw him out. For the next several weeks, he sold anything of value that he owned. His car, clothes, watches, and anything he could get his hands on were all traded in for a few tastes of crack. Next, he borrowed or stole from nearly every person he knew. It was no longer safe for Hector to go to his old neighborhood because he had made too many enemies.

Hector blamed most of his problems on Jimmy, Alejandro and Roberto. After all the good work that he did for Jimmy, Hector reasoned that Jimmy could have given him another chance. He believed that once he kicked the drug habit, he could make Jimmy even more money than before. He blamed Roberto and Alejandro the most because he believed they didn't go to bat for him. He asked Alejandro to get him his job back but it was no use. Alejandro claimed he did all that he could but Jimmy turned down his request. Hector thought that was bullshit. Alejandro and Roberto were Jimmy's right-hand boys. Jimmy would have listened to them if they'd asked.

Now Hector was dropping crack to switch to heroin. It was a completely different high compared to when he was on crack. The feeling from crack was much better but Hector decided to settle for a little lower lift. According to his low finances, his crack addiction was becoming much too expensive.

*****

Today was a sad day for Mama' Sanchez. Alejandro and Roberto were moving out. The twins were barely twenty-one years old and she wondered if they were leaving the nest a little too prematurely.

"Mama', Roberto and I promise to continue with our education. And with the big raises we got at work, we'll have no problems keeping up with the rent," Alejandro said convincingly.

Alejandro also told Mama' Sanchez that they were lucky enough to obtain an apartment in a nice low-crime neighborhood for a really cheap price. "We really lucked out," he continued.

"Are you sure you boys don't need me to go with you to help you set up?" Mama Sanchez asked nervously. Even though she was full of pride, her hands were trembling.

"No, that's okay, but as soon as we get it together you will be our first guest," Alejandro smiled as he took the last box out of the house and into the moving van.

"You know, Roberto, this really makes me feel wonderful. This just proves that you can still raise intelligent, honest young men in these rough times," Mama' Sanchez said as she hugged Roberto tightly.

"Mama', there is something very important that I feel I must tell you," Roberto said as he pulled away from his grandmother's embrace.

"Roberto, what is it?" Mama' Sanchez asked anxiously.

"Yeah Roberto, what is it?" Alejandro asked sharply after entering the apartment to look around for last-minute items.

Roberto paused for a second when he caught a glimpse of Alejandro's evil stare. "I love you very much, Mama', and I would not ever want to disappoint you," Roberto stammered. A well of tears started to build up in his eyes.

"Don't worry," Mama' Sanchez consoled. "If you keep on the path that you are on now, I'll never be disappointed."

# Chapter 18

"After all I've done for these guys, this is how they end up treating me," Hector though. "And that Fuckin' Roberto, I asked him for some money and he turned me down flat. If it weren't for me, they would never have gotten into the business. I was the one who introduced them to Jimmy and everyone else. I was the one who taught them everything they know about drugs. If it wasn't for me, they wouldn't have the fancy clothes or that nice duplex apartment of theirs."

"Who did they run to when they had that problem with Juan? It was fuckin' me, Hector Ramirez. I got them out of that jam, and what thanks do I get? Nothing."

Hector was across the street from Mama' Sanchez's apartment building guzzling down his last bottle of wine. He had been drinking continuously for the past three days and was becoming increasingly frustrated. His appetite for heroin was increasing and alcohol just didn't satisfy his cravings.

Hector was rambling on and on about how much he had been mistreated, sometimes thinking to himself about what had happened and other times talking out loud. Sure, it was wrong of him to steal money from Jimmy, but those things were expected in this business. Hector was pretty sure that Jimmy would have stolen from him if the roles were reversed.

"For now, fuck Alejandro and Roberto, and especially fuck that little Jimmy bastard," Hector hollered in slurred speech. Hector believed a big score would provide him with enough start-up money to develop anew in another area. With his knowledge and experience, he thought he could make a killing someplace else.

He watched a van pull up in front of Mama' Sanchez's house. Two men came out and unloaded a large television set. They rang the bell and Mama' Sanchez opened the door smiling widely. The men holding the TV then disappeared inside Mama' Sanchez's apartment for several minutes. As they departed, Mama' Sanchez gave each of them two dollars and locked the door behind them.

Mama' Sanchez was thrilled. Only two days had passed since someone from the church called to tell her that she'd won the grand prize. Mama' Sanchez was so happy about her prize that she cleared off a space on a counter for it as soon as she got the news. She even took off from work to make sure that she wouldn't miss the delivery of her 36" color television.

It was now five minutes to four and Mama' Sanchez told the twins to arrive at the house around 4:30. She wanted to surprise them with her new TV. It had even looked larger than she imagined.

"Fuckin' old slick bitch," Hector complained to no one in particular. "After hiding the money all this time, she's finally starting to spend it. I always knew she had some money hidden away. I know her grandchildren didn't buy it for her.

Well this is it. It's time for Hector Ramirez to get paid." Hector raised himself off the park bench and tried to shake off his drunk stupor. He then picked up his half empty bottle of wine and stumbled his way across the street.

*****

Once again, Roberto was feeling uneasy about being caught up in Miami's drug scene. "This isn't right. I have to get out now," Roberto thought. "At first, Alejandro said that we'd only be doing this for a couple of months and that we'd be back in school full time for the next semester. Well it's been more than two months. The next semester has already started and it's almost finished. Alejandro and me have already made more money than we could have ever dreamed possible. We have enough money to pay for school and our apartment for the next two years."

Roberto looked intensely at his image in the mirror. "Sure the new clothes and the respect that I get from people are nice, but this just isn't right. All of the money that we have is blood money. Cynthia was right when she told us not to get seduced by the streets."

Roberto took the wad of money he had tucked in his pocket and tossed it on the dresser.

"Well, it's still not too late!" Roberto screamed. At that moment, he decided to get out of the drug business and move into a career that he could live with. He couldn't take it anymore. Lately, he had to worry more about the cops or some rival trying to rip him off since he and Alejandro had become pretty notorious. The other day, Jimmy even suggested that they start walking around with their own security. As far as Roberto was concerned, this whole thing was getting completely out of hand. That was why Roberto planned to get out of the business whether Alejandro agreed or not. Although he loved his brother deeply, Roberto knew that he had to help himself before he could help Alejandro or anyone else.

With this final decision being made, Roberto felt like a large weight had been lifted off his shoulders. He always did his best thinking while he was alone and was glad that Alejandro wasn't around to influence him. Roberto looked at his watch and realized that he was going to be late if he didn't get moving. He was very anxious to see his grandmother.

"Hold on, just wait one minute," Mama' Sanchez called as she walked from the bathroom to the front door. When she opened it, she was greeted by Hector Ramirez.

"Hello Mrs. Sanchez, remember me? I am Hector Ramirez," he said.

"Yes, I do remember you, and I also asked you to never visit me again," Mama' Sanchez said bluntly as she attempted to close the door.

"Well, this isn't a social visit," Hector growled as he forced his way into the apartment shoving Mama' Sanchez out of his path. "I'm here for the money."

*****

Nancy Garcia stared at herself in the freshly cleaned glass, wanting to make sure that she was perfect. She made great use of the enormous mirrors in the lobby as she carefully checked herself from top to bottom. Her long, brown, curly hair shined in the light, complimenting her hazel eyes. Although Nancy only wore a hint of makeup on her eyes and cheeks, she doused her lips in red lipstick to make them absolutely irresistible. As she continued to admire her reflection, she appreciated how nicely her skin-tight dress hugged her hips. She was glad that she'd left her bra at home and liked how seductively her V-neck showed off her small, but perky breasts. Her legs were long and shapely. And if that didn't grab her date's attention, she knew she had one of the sexiest walks in Miami and that surely would.

Nancy met Alejandro while walking down one of the busiest streets in town. As Alejandro drove down Ocean Drive, he nearly got into an accident trying to check her out. When he regained control of his vehicle, he got her attention and cruised along the side of her to make his move.

"Hey you," Alejandro called out as he scrambled for a better choice of words.

"Are you talking to me?" Nancy asked, knowing that Alejandro had been watching her for some time.

"Come on babe, what's a guy have to do to win your heart?"

Nancy laughed and Alejandro took her reaction as a green light to pour on his charm. He pulled all of his old one-liners out of the bag and before she knew it, they were on for a date. Nancy heard all of Alejandro's sly lines before, but he had a way of making tired cliches seem fresh.

Nancy was nobody's fool. She figured Alejandro had arranged the date at his apartment so that he could try something, but there was no way anything was going to happen. It wasn't that she didn't find him attractive. That wasn't the case at all. Nancy just knew that if she wanted to have a relationship with him, she couldn't just put out the first time he tried something. There was something about Alejandro that she liked, and she planned to have him for the long haul.

Nancy got off the elevator and walked to Alejandro's apartment. She gently knocked on the door.

"Come on in," Alejandro whispered. "I've been waiting for you."

Nancy slowly opened up the door and walked inside. Alejandro was nowhere to be seen. The further she walked into the apartment, the darker it got. When the front door closed behind her, it was almost pitch black. Nancy was one tough cookie and figured it was probably one of Alejandro's silly tests. She was sure she'd pass it.

"Alejandro, where are you?" Nancy called out. Suddenly, someone grabbed her from the rear. Her first reaction was to turn around and give the perpetrator a swift kick between the legs but she couldn't free herself from the grip. Nancy began to squirm wildly and was just about to scream for dear life when she heard his reassuring voice.

"Nancy, don't worry, it's me Alejandro."

"Why did you scare me like that?" she barked.

"I didn't mean to scare you so much, it was just a joke," Alejandro said while caressing her neck and shoulders. "I'm so sorry."

"Alejandro, let me go, I'm pissed at you."

In response to Nancy's complaint, Alejandro dropped his hands from around Nancy's waist. He then, spun her around to see her face. He slowly slid his hands up her waist and across her breasts. Alejandro took turns between kissing her shoulders and licking her neck. Even though Nancy tried to resist his advances, she was slowly becoming turned on.

At this point, Nancy forgot why she was originally angry with Alejandro, but she still remembered that she didn't want to go all the way with him. "As long as we stay away from the bedroom, I'm probably safe," she figured.

Alejandro began a circular massage on Nancy's breasts. Nancy then swung her head back to allow Alejandro to kiss her lips. As they leaned against the hallway wall, Alejandro ran his hands down her strapped dress until he reached her inner thighs. He then wildly darted his tongue in and out of her mouth.

Nancy didn't clearly remember the details of Alejandro's physique, but with his body pressed up against hers, his appearance didn't matter. In between kisses, Alejandro removed the straps of Nancy's dress with his teeth sending her dress sailing to the floor. Alejandro, seemingly out of nowhere, squirted some type if liquid on her back.

Before she could react, Alejandro gently rubbed the lotion all over her body sending chills up and down her spine. The more he rubbed, the hotter the lotion got. Nancy smiled to herself.

Nancy was so enthralled in her own excitement that she didn't realize that Alejandro had removed his shirt and dropped his pants. Since he wasn't wearing any underwear, he was now completely nude. Nancy stood shivering in her favorite-laced panties, she then took the excess lotion on her hands and started rubbing Alejandro's muscular chest. By this time, Nancy had reconsidered her decision to hold off on sex. She moved her hips repeatedly until her undies fell to her ankles.

Alejandro and Nancy gyrated simultaneously, swaying back and forth like the waves in a violent river. Nancy was wet with anticipation and the feeling of Alejandro's manhood pressed hard against her thigh made it impossible for her to resist Alejandro's advances. She grabbed Alejandro's manhood and stuck it forcibly inside of her. Repeatedly, she guided the head in and slowly pulled it out. By the fifth insertion, Alejandro was becoming impatient. He removed her trembling hands and powerfully thrusted his dick deep inside her. She and Alejandro both screamed in ecstasy.

Nancy was impressed. Alejandro didn't last as long as some of her other lovers, but for those wild fifteen minutes of sex, it was certainly the best.

Alejandro and Nancy were laying comfortably on his bed when they were startled by Alejandro's alarm clock.

"Oh Nancy, let's get up! I shouldn't have been here for that alarm, it's telling me that I'm running late for my visit with my grandmother.

"Sorry, but I have to run," Alejandro said apologetically. "Don't worry, I'll pick you up later tonight and we'll hang out."

"Okay Alejandro, but you first have to drive me home." Nancy insisted.

****

"Good Lord! What on earth are you looking for?" Mama' Sanchez asked Hector as he frantically threw objects around the living room. He then flipped over the end table and broke Mama' Sanchez's treasured antique lamp.

"Lady cut out the act. You know what I'm looking for," Hector demanded.

"I swear I don't know what you're talking about. Maybe, if you tell me, I can help you find it," Mama' Sanchez pleaded.

"I am trying to find out where you hid the money!" Hector yelled.

"What money? I don't have any money."

"Don't lie to me, I know Alex left you a lot of money when he died, so you can stop the bullshit," Hector ordered.

"Sorry to disappoint you, Mr. Ramirez, but there is no money. In fact I wasn't even speaking to my son when he died. He was a no good bum just like you and he wasn't allowed in my house."

"You're lying." Hector said as he raced through the bedroom.

"You must have some kind of bank books or expensive jewelry hanging around this dump," Hector said as he continued to rummage through Mama' Sanchez's belongings. He then headed for the bedroom.

"Maybe you have it hidden in here." Hector then pulled out a long knife and began to slice the mattress up. When he realized the mattress was also bare, he ran over to the closet tossing the racks of neatly hung dresses on the floor. "There must be some kind of safe in here," he moaned.

While Hector was consumed with searching the bedroom, Mama' Sanchez thought she could use the time to call the police to get this crazy man out of her house. She crept into the living room and picked up the phone.

"And what do you think you're doing!" Hector yelled as he slammed the receiver down and ripped the only phone in the house off the wall.

"Why are you doing this Mr. Ramirez? I told you that there is no money here. I only have what I have been saving in the bank all of these years, and that's only about three thousand dollars," Mama' Sanchez said as she began to cry frantically.

"Look lady, just give me Alex's money and I'm outta here," Hector offered in a calmer tone. "All I want is the cash."

"Even if my son Alex had left me money, I would not have accepted it. That money would have been drug money and I could never take it. People like you and my son are like cancer in the community."

"Look, I'm not here for a sermon, I'm only trying to make a living," Hector explained.

"But at whose expense? You sell drugs to your own people. How could people like you and Alex look at yourselves in the mirror?"

"People like me, Alex, and your beloved twins can look at ourselves in the mirror very easily," Hector said slyly.

"Why are you talking about the twins?"

"Oh, I am very sorry. I forgot that they didn't tell you," Hector laughed.

"Tell me what?" Mama' Sanchez asked, though she didn't want to hear the answer.

"Your precious Alejandro and Roberto are selling drugs for me and have been doing it for many months now," Hector boasted.

"You're lying!" Mama' Sanchez said as she slapped Hector across his face.

He felt stunned for a second and then returned her strike with a blow so hard it sent the elderly woman sprawling to the ground near the couch.

"Stupid woman! How on earth do you think they were able to move out on their own into a fancy apartment? You see how they dress. Last month, Alejandro bought his car with cold hard cash. I guess the twins also failed to tell you that they dropped out of school almost a year ago. I guess they know where they can make some real money. Don't look so sad grandma. Selling drugs is in their genes. You should be proud of yourself. Years ago you raised one drug dealer. Now you have successfully raised two more. You must be doing something right." Hector said sarcastically as he snatched a bottle of wine from Mama' Sanchez's china closet.

Mama' Sanchez sat on the floor motionless. She had wanted to believe with all of her might that Hector was lying, but she knew deep inside that he was telling the truth. Everything was beginning to make sense now. The twin's never invited her over the apartment. They claimed it was too small and they wanted to fix it up before she came over. She also called their job to give them a message but was told that they no longer worked there. Alejandro later told her that she had spoken to an employee who did not like them.

Hector continued his rampage while Mama' Sanchez sat on the floor oblivious to her surroundings.

"How could everything I worked so hard for turn out so badly? First, I lost both of my children to drugs, now Roberto and Alejandro have slipped away. I just can't take much more of this," Mama' Sanchez cried.

After searching the entire house. Hector walked back into the living room. "I'm only asking you one more time, where's the fucking money?"

# Chapter 19

"Mama' is going to kill me," Alejandro thought. "I told her I would be over here by four thirty and it's after five o'clock."
After parking his car, Alejandro jogged down the remaining half block trying to think of a good excuse for being late. "Surely, I can't tell her I was boning one of my girlfriends for the past hour he thought." "I don't think Mama' would like that excuse."

Instead of lying, he decided to just tell her he was running late. Then, he would flash his great smile. "That always gets me out of trouble," he laughed.

When he got up to the apartment, he realized that the door wasn't locked. Even though Mama' lived in the neighborhood for many years, she always kept her doors locked. But what was more disturbing was the loud noise that was coming from inside the house. Alejandro immediately pulled his Smith and Western 9mm. gun from his waistband. If anybody was messing with his Mama', they would surely have to pay the consequences.

Pointing his gun straight out, he sprinted into the house. The place was a complete mess, with chairs overturned, busted lamps, and religious paintings sprawled over the ground. Alejandro turned and saw Roberto banging his fists against the wall. Suddenly, Alejandro couldn't hear any of Roberto's outbursts nor did he focus on the overturned garbage or broken bookcases. His full attention was drawn to his Mama', outstretched on the ground behind the couch.

Alejandro instinctively ran over to her, but it was too late. When he grabbed her wrists, he knew she was already dead. The shock of seeing his Mama' lifeless on the floor still did not register in Alejandro's mind minutes later. Alejandro remained on the floor with his Mama's head laying in his lap, as he gently caressed her hair with his hands. Alejandro softly pleaded with Mama' to wake up. He promised her he would always protect her from now on, if she would just open up her eyes. He then looked up to the ceiling and asked GOD to wake her and promised to be a changed person if he would. Alejandro vowed to get out of the drug business for life. But his prayers went unanswered.

"Roberto, what happened here?" Alejandro asked as he looked up at his mirror image.

"I have no idea. I just got here a few minutes before you did," Roberto responded with tears streaming down his face.

"It looks like Mama' has been strangled," Alejandro observed. "Did you see the marks around her neck?"

"I didn't notice that. My God, who could have done this? Mama' didn't have any enemies!" Roberto cried.

"Roberto, you know there are a lot of people who are beginning to be jealous of us. It could be any one of them."

"Maybe it was just a burglary and Mama' caught them in the act."

"Maybe, maybe." Alejandro said as he looked back down on Mama' once again realizing that the terrible nightmare was very real.

"Whatever the reason it won't bring her back to us." Roberto said as he dialed 911 on his cellular phone. When the operator responded, Roberto described how the scene looked at the time of his arrival. In the meantime, Alejandro searched the room for clues. He spotted something that appeared to be familiar on the floor near the kitchen table. He picked it up and handed it to his brother who had just finished his telephone conversation.

"Are you thinking what I'm thinking?" Roberto asked as he held an almost empty pack of cigarettes in his hand.

"Yes I am. This is a brand that very few people smoke. In fact, the only person we know that smokes this is, Hector," Alejandro said angrily. "Well Roberto, what do you want to do now? This is pretty good evidence for the police and I bet it has his prints on it."

The sounds of police sirens were fast approaching, Roberto had little time to decide.

"First let's deal with Mama'. Planning the wake and the funeral is going to take a lot of work. Then after we put Mama' to rest, we'll deal with Hector Ramirez," Roberto said as he slipped the pack of cigarettes in his back pocket.

The police rushed inside the apartment discovering Roberto and Alejandro again crying alongside their precious Mama'.

The twins had the funeral at the same church where Mama', worshipped every Sunday. Alejandro and Roberto were overwhelmed by the large turnout for their beloved Mama'. It seemed like the whole neighborhood showed up to pay their respects. They decided not to send her body back to Cuba to be buried; instead they buried her body in Miami where they could visit her regularly.

In the three weeks since her death, Alejandro-who was usually talkative and outgoing-was very quiet. He kept his distance from friends, especially the ones who tried to get him to open up. He feared they'd discover that he was responsible for his grandmother's death. After all, he was the one that convinced Roberto to trust Hector.

Since Alejandro wasn't his sociable self, Roberto did all of the entertaining. With the help of nosy neighbor Mrs. Gonzalez, Roberto played host to the many people who stopped by to give their condolences. It hadn't been an easy time for him, but Roberto knew how his grandmother would have wanted him to conduct himself. For Mama' Sanchez's sake, Roberto stayed strong.

After the visits began to dwindle, the twins decided it was time to take care of Hector. Alejandro had the woman at the front desk of Hector's rooming house tell him he had company downstairs. When Hector arrived, he was surprised to see his former colleagues at the reception area.

“Hey Alejandro and Roberto, what's up?"

“Hector, don't tell me you haven't heard?" Alejandro asked excitedly.

“Heard what?"

“We're leaving Jimmy's organization and starting our own team in another part of Miami," Roberto responded. “We need your expertise.”

He was thrilled. The twins had finally realized how much they needed him. The twins escorted Hector to Alejandro’s car and started a night of partying with him. They first stopped at The Flamingo, one of Florida's finest restaurants.

“You know I have to hand it to you guys. You never forget a friend when he's down, and I admire that," Hector said smiling.

“How could we forget about you Hector, you've done so much." Roberto said.

“You know, I told the guys that you two wouldn't forget about me and here you are. This is one of my favorite restaurants."

“Hector, eat and enjoy your food,” Alejandro said trying to fight back the temptation to shoot him in the head publicly.

“Before we eat I first want to say a prayer for your grandmother. I know she must have been a wonderful woman."

“That's all right Hector. I will say something for my grandmother later,” Roberto interrupted. Even though the twins wanted to prolong Hector's eventual death, they weren't going to allow him to turn their grandmother's murder into a mockery.

Two hours passed and the twins watched Hector continue to stuff his face with food and alcohol.

“First of all fellas, how much money have you saved up?"

“Between the two of us, we have close to a hundred and fifty thousand dollars," Alejandro responded abruptly. The more Hector spoke, the more he longed to kill him.

“That's enough to get us started. Now all we have to worry about is finding a supplier," Hector stammered in between spoonfuls of rice and beans.

“We'll have no problem on that end. Alejandro has gotten pretty close with some of Jimmy's suppliers and they assured us they would help us out.”

“That’s fucking good news. But you know what, that Jimmy may be trouble. He won't like the idea of you two leaving and setting up a business with me."

"Hector, what can we do?" Roberto asked pretending to be interested in his response.

"We'll have to kill him," Hector insisted.

"Wouldn't they come looking for us?" Roberto asked.

"Hopefully we can set it up, so that nobody would know who did it. And with the fight to see who would take over for Jimmy, you could just ease out of the organization," Hector said convincingly.

"That's a good idea," Roberto said as he struggled to crack a smile.

Alejandro was getting real impatient by this point. He suggested it was time for Hector to meet their connections guy outside of Miami.

Hector and the twins got into the car and headed for the Florida Keys. Forty minutes into the drive, they stopped at a desolate Harbor called the Mantero.

"Hector, our connection should meet us here shortly."

"So fellas, like I told you before, stick with me and I will make you very rich," Hector boasted.

"How long do you think that will take?" Roberto asked nervously as the three of them sat on a bench near the water. Roberto was having second thoughts about killing Hector. What if they were wrong about the cigarette package?

"Within two years, we'll all be set. Alejandro is there any more beer in the car?" Hector asked.

"Sorry Hector we ran out of beer," Alejandro said.

"That's okay, all I need is a good smoke anyway," Hector said while removing the pack of cigarettes from his back pocket.

"You dirty motherfucker!" Alejandro yelled as he pulled out his gun from his waistband.

"Alejandro what are you doing?" Hector screamed.

"I am going to kill your ass Hector!" Alejandro yelled.

"But why, I've done nothing to you or your brother. I don't understand. I thought we were all going to be partners," Hector pleaded.

"Hector do you really think that me and my brother would ever be partners with a piece of shit like you?"

"Hector, I just want to ask you one question, why?" Roberto asked tearfully.

"Why what?" Hector said while concentrating on the gun that was pointed directly in his face by Alejandro.

"Why did you kill our grandmother?" Roberto asked as the tears came flowing freely down his cheeks.

"I don't know what you're talking about. I was no where near your house on the day your grandmother was killed. And why would I wanna hurt that nice woman?" Hector said.

"You fucking liar!" Alejandro said as he struck Hector across the face with the gun.

"Hector why are you still lying?" Roberto cried.

"But I'm not lying," Hector sobbed.

"I know you are lying because one of our neighbors saw you leaving the house earlier," Roberto said, hoping that Hector would fall into the trap. "Alejandro, shoot this lying bastard."

"Okay wait, wait a minute. I will tell you what really happened. I went over to your grandmother's house to talk to you. I was gonna beg you to let me work for you but when I entered the apartment I saw her already dead on the floor. I knew it would look funny, so I got scared and ran out of there. I was too afraid to tell anybody," Hector explained.

Roberto breathed a deep sigh of relief. Based on his response, Roberto knew that Hector was in their grandmother's apartment on the day of the murder.

"Come on, Alejandro, let's kill this no good bastard." Roberto ordered.

"Now this is what I'm talking about." Alejandro said as he grabbed Hector by the arms twisting it to his back.

"No, No," Hector yelled as the twins led him past the sand towards the water. The twins then dragged Hector about three feet into the water and submerged his face into the grimy water. Hector flung his arms and legs back and forth trying to escape his fate. For several minutes, Alejandro and Roberto repeatedly dunked Hector's head under water. When Hector appeared to start losing consciousness, Roberto took another look at him and ran back towards the sand.

Alejandro realized that he had to finish the job himself. He didn't mind, this was not really Roberto's kind of thing anyway. As he was beginning to sink the slowly dying Hector, Roberto returned pushing Alejandro away.

He took the rock that he had picked up off of the beach and began hitting Hector repeatedly over the head. There was one blow, then another, then another. In a few moments, the area where the men stood was surrounded with blood. Hector's lifeless body began to sink.

"Okay, stop Roberto, he's dead." Alejandro said as he attempted to grab Roberto, who was frantically still swinging in the water searching for Hector's body.

It was over. The only thing that was left for Alejandro and Roberto was to go back to the car to retrieve the large plastic bag that they planned to put Hector's body in. Then they would take his body where nobody would ever find it.

*****

"Sweetheart, I think you are over doing it." Betty said calmly.

"Mom, this is the best that I have ever felt in all of my life," Cynthia said excitedly.

"But look at you. The only thing you ever do when you come home from work is work in the garden or work-out down here in the basement."

"I know mom, but this really relaxes me." Cynthia defensively responded.

"I don't see how you can enjoy this lifting weight stuff. You are covered with sweat and you always say you're too tired to socialize. Cynthia what ever happened to that doctor that was calling here for a while?" Betty quizzed.

"He was a nice guy. But I really wasn't interested in him."

"Well dear, you're not getting any younger. I know from reading those Cosmopolitan magazines at the supermarket that women have their needs," Betty said grinning.

"No, kidding," Cynthia thought. It had been years since she'd had sex. She figured she was probably a virgin all over again. At least working out, sometimes took the edge off of wanting to have sex. Other times, pumping iron made her as horny as hell.

"Mom I already told you, more than once, I'm quite satisfied with my life," Cynthia insisted. Although she silently admitted that being next to a warm body at night wasn't such a bad idea.

"Well, whatever the case, I just came downstairs to give you your mail. Once you're finished flexing your muscles, I'll start dinner," Betty said sarcastically.

Cynthia looked through the mail and immediately spotted a letter from Roberto. She tore open the envelope and began reading.

*Dear Cynthia,*

*Hello, how are you? I hope everything is still going well for you in Baltimore. Cynthia, I know we recently spoke on the phone, but I want to thank you again for the floral arrangements that you sent to my grandmother's funeral. They were very beautiful, and the violets were a nice touch. If my Mama' would have known you, I believe she would have liked you a lot.*

*Alejandro is handling things pretty good on the outside, but I'm starting to get worried about him. My grandmother was the one person who kept Alejandro balanced. With her not being around, I'm afraid that he's going to get out of control. He used to share a lot of things with me. Now he walks around like nothing bothers him. As for myself, I'm doing O.K. I miss her terribly, but what can you do when a person is gone forever. I often wish I could go back to the times when she used to force us to come in from outside so she could give us lunch or dinner.*

*There are so many other things that I want to talk to you about that I wouldn't know where to begin. There are things I can't even talk about in letters or over the phone, so I have to see you in person. Right now, you're the only person that I can trust. You would understand the things that I'm going through and understanding is the one thing I need most.*

*Sincerely yours,*
*Roberto Sanchez*

*PS: Please don't worry, me and Alejandro will both be fine.*

*****

The doorman called their apartment on a secret phone because he was suspicious of the strange visitor. He was a young man dressed in expensive clothes, flanked by what appeared to be two bodyguards. The tenants in apartment #11 rarely had guests, except for the young ladies, of course.

“It's okay, you can let him up.” Roberto answered. “Alejandro wake up, Jimmy is on his way upstairs.”

Alejandro emerged from his bedroom in a silk robe and matching boxers. He stood barefoot in his doorway rubbing his eyes and scratching his head.

“Why is Jimmy coming over here?" Alejandro asked. “It's too early in the morning for this shit.”

“Alejandro, I don't know why Jimmy's here but it must be very important.”

The doorbell rang and Roberto went anxiously over to the door to open it. A bright-eyed, fully energized Jimmy was standing in the hallway with a wide grin.

“Rise and shine guys. I've got some serious stuff to talk about." Jimmy ordered.

“Couldn't it wait until later? I just got in a few hours ago." Alejandro whined.

“Alejandro, you better start to slow down or you're gonna burn yourself out, trust me I know," Jimmy laughed as he sat down comfortably on the couch.

“Jimmy, only two bodyguards? Are you starting to let your guard down?" Roberto snickered at his own use of words but quickly squashed his laughter when he caught a glimpse of Jimmy's incredibly serious expression. Apparently, this wasn't the time for silly jokes.

“The rest of the fellas are downstairs in the cars. I *never* slip up," Jimmy assured. “And don't you forget it."

“Well Jimmy since you are here, what the hell is so important? Why couldn't it wait until later?” Alejandro snapped.

“Alejandro, you're lucky that I like you because I never let anyone talk to me the way you do," Jimmy said as he walked in the living room and playfully slapped Alejandro in the head. “Just don't let it go to far."

“Jimmy you want something to drink?" Roberto offered.

"No, I'm all right." Jimmy then turned to his two attending bodyguards. "Fellas, wait outside on the terrace until I finish talking to these two gentlemen," Jimmy commanded as he waved his hand in that direction. He then made himself comfortable on the couch. Roberto and Alejandro shared the space on the loveseat.

"Now let's get down to business. You know for the past year we have widened our organization to the Northern East coast, specifically New York. We've been doing great business there until lately. It seems that someone is moving in on our crack business in the Washington Heights area."

"So why don't our guys in New York take care of the problem?" Alejandro asked impatiently.

"They tried to handle it, but they couldn't. That's why we have to go to New York and take care of things," Jimmy replied.

"Is it going to be a war?" Roberto asked.

"Hopefully not, we'll only do that as a last resort. Wars are very bad for business. You run the risk of being killed or getting busted by the cops. It's just not worth it."

"So why are we going?" Roberto asked.

"Because the organization figured that since the guys making the problems for us in New York are around our age, we would know how to deal with them. The old timers we have in New York don't know how to handle a bunch of wild Dominicans."

"When are we leaving?" Alejandro asked.

"Friday morning, and Roberto I want you to stay behind." Jimmy said.

"Why don't you want me to go?" Roberto disappointedly asked. Even though he was planning to leave the business, he still wondered why Jimmy selected Alejandro over him.

"I need somebody that I can trust to stay behind and look after things while I'm gone. Alejandro, you and I will leave Friday morning and if everything works out, we should be back in Miami sometime on Monday."

Jimmy rose from the couch and gave the signal for his guards to join him.

"So, Alejandro make sure you get a lot of rest. In a couple of days, we're going to shake things up in the Big Apple," Jimmy warned. "And you better be ready."

# Chapter 20

"Kevin where do you think you're going now?" his mother asked.

"I'm going outside for a little while to play." Kevin answered.

"Did you do your homework yet?"

"Yeah, I did it in my last period class."

"Well okay, but don't be out too late tonight. I still haven't forgot that stunt you pulled on me last weekend," she reminded. "I don't want to have to hunt you down."

"Yeah Ma, I know."

"Be careful."

"I will,' he said as he closed the door to the three-bedroom apartment that he shared with his mother, three sisters, and two brothers.

As soon as Kevin left his project building, he was greeted in the streets as some type of important person. And in his own way, he was. Kevin Thompson was only 13 ½ years old but he had been running wild in the streets for the last three years.

He was now the lookout for one of the busiest drug dealers in Brooklyn.

Kevin was the eldest boy and the third child of six. He grew up in one of the most dangerous neighborhoods in the country; Brownsville in the heart of Brooklyn. He didn't grow up with a father, and although his mother loved her kids dearly, she didn't have the slightest idea on how to be a good parent.

Kevin was short for his age, so he had to rely on his street smarts to help him survive. The neighborhood kids called him Peanut because of his size and the shape of his head.

Joyce Thompson never figured her life would turn out this way. Once, she was one of the most attractive girls in school and often dreamed of making it big. In her imagination, she would create visions of a nice house with servants. She never had any career goals and figured she would just hook up with some guy that made a lot of money, then she would be set for life.

In her senior year of high school, Joyce met a man that promised her the moon. He was a fast talker and had a 'decent' business selling pot in the hood. She saw a lot of promise in him and began spending most of her free time entertaining him. Before she knew it, she became pregnant. Shortly afterwards he went to jail for selling drugs. It was his first drug charge so they released him after six months. He was soon released and got her pregnant again. The next time he got locked up, he had some time to serve.

As an uneducated woman supporting her two kids on a minimum wage salary, Joyce felt the quality of men she had to choose from was greatly diminished. Soon, it was one loser after the next. When Joyce Thompson finally did wake up, she found herself with six kids, on welfare and wasn't very hopeful about the future.

Joyce was no fool. She did notice that Kevin always came in the house with new bikes, toys, or sneakers. When she asked him about where he got the money to pay for all the new stuff, he told her that he saved the tips he got from packing bags at the supermarkets. Joyce knew that he was lying, but what could she do? Kevin helped her buy food or clothes for his brothers and sisters. And besides, Kevin wasn't her biggest problem at the moment. Joyce recently found out that her oldest child would be having a child at the age of fifteen.

Peanut's job in the street was easy. He was responsible for spotting "the man" before he found them first. "The man," also referred to as the Police, would stop people for anything that was deemed suspicious.

Peanut knew everybody and everybody knew peanut. If Peanut saw someone that he thought may be five-0, he would either relay a hand signal or shout a warning message to his boys down the block. That would tell them to cease whatever the fuck they were doing at the time.

Peanut was pretty proud of himself. Despite the fact that he no longer attended school, he was pulling down more cash than some of his former teachers. He stashed his money in a sneaker box under his bed in the hopes that he could one day save enough money to take his mother and siblings out of the jungle. He was also up for a promotion after completing a really important project. A promotion would take him to the next level, which was a Steerer. In this position, the Steerer advised people where they could buy drugs. It was a very important and dangerous job. A good Steerer would tell someone they didn't know to get lost if they tried to make a drug buy because the police were just getting too smart and tricky in their undercover operations. Strangers couldn't be trusted since the cops often posed as crackheads to make an arrest.

"Yo Peanut, let's play some taps," Ralph said.

"Nigga you know I'm working. That stupid ass game is just going to distract me," Peanut insisted.

"Damn it's almost nine o'clock. I'm hungry," Kenny wined. Kenny was one of the kids in the bunch who didn't work for anyone. He went to school and did well. His problem was loneliness. He was an only child and his mother was never home. She partied too much to care about him. His father was a deadbeat dad and hadn't been around since Kenny was two years old.

"Look Ralph it's five of us. Take this money, go to McDonalds and go buy us lunch," Peanut directed as he handed Ralph a twenty-dollar bill.

"Good looking out Peanut," one of Kevin's companions hollered. Damien was always excited whenever anyone talked about food. Even though he claimed to be on a strict diet and exercise program, he could never resist a free meal: that probably accounted for the fifty extra pounds he carried.

Ralph and Kenny raced down the block on their way to Micky D's." Peanut watched them as they playfully tossed Ralph's basketball back and forth to each other. A proud grin emerged across his face when he thought about how much his peers admired him. He was one of the youngest cats in the business, but also one of the most respected. He had the responsibilities of guys twice his age.

Peanut didn't really remember much about his father and he didn't care for most of the men that his mother dated. He preferred when it was just him and his family and felt he was responsible for taking care of them. He hated when his mother used to worry about not having enough money for the kids. So, as soon as he started earning some extra cash, he began giving his brothers and sisters weekly allowances. Later, he was even bringing in enough loot to pay all of the bills.

Even though peanut held the purse strings, that didn't stop his family members from giving their opinion about Peanut's lifestyle. His siblings resented taking orders from an adolescent and they often argued and fought with him. But when one of his sisters needed a new pair of jeans or one of his brothers wanted the latest sneakers, they would ask Peanut for the money. And Peanut didn't mind this one bit, as long as they stayed in school and didn't run the streets like he did, there wasn't really anything that he wouldn't do for them.

Every now and then, Peanut wondered what it would be like to live in a normal family setting. He sometimes wished he had a father around with a good job who could put his family in a nice neighborhood, one like the kids on the Cosby show lived in. Playing the adult on a regular basis was pretty tiring. Sometimes Peanut longed to act his age, especially on those hot summer days when everybody played tag in the streets or raced past the open fire hydrant to cool off. Peanut never joined in on these activities because he had to maintain his image.

At times, he would get angry at his mother for not trying harder but then he would realize that she was doing the best that she knew how. After all, she was no different than the other adults in the neighborhood who spent the majority of their time drinking and drugging. Peanut vowed that he would soon put this drug business behind him so that he and his family could join the Huxtables.

"We're back," Ralph hollered. He and Kenny began passing around French fries, burgers, and shakes. The crew hung out on the corner until about midnight, then the next shift rolled in.

To outsiders, the life that Peanut and his friends lived daily seemed strange, but that was the only life they ever knew.

*****

"Look at this fuckin' room. It's pretty fly," Alejandro said excitedly. His eyes beamed as he looked around the fancy New York hotel suite.

"Jimmy, did you see the furniture in the lobby downstairs?' Alejandro rambled. "Between the fancy couches and the expensive rugs it must have cost a million bucks to fix this place up."

Alejandro was normally very cool in most situations but he couldn't hide how impressed he was with his surroundings. New York was very different from Cuba or Miami.

"The doorman downstairs was really decked out and the bellhops didn't even look like bellhops. They were dressed more like some sort of elite Marines' unit."

"Hey Alejandro, get used to it," Jimmy said calmly. "You'll be living like this forever, if you play your cards right."

Alejandro was only half listening to Jimmy's predictions he continued to admire the whole scene. "And look at the view from the window, you can see all of Time Square from here. I feel like I am some kind of rock star or something."

It was five o'clock on Friday. Jimmy, Alejandro, and Raul had just arrived in New York City from Miami. At the airport, they were met by Orlando Gomez, one of Jimmy's leaders in upper Manhattan. All of them were staying at the four star Mariott Marquis Hotel on 45th Street and Broadway. Their rooms were three hundred and seventy dollars a night and that didn't even include tax and gratuity.

Unlike Alejandro, Jimmy was not impressed. He hated the Times Square area and would have preferred the Waldorf Astoria. He never asked Raul how they ended up in the Mariott and just assumed it was a matter of availability.

"Don't get too excited about being in New York. We are going to have *some* fun while we're in town, but remember, we are here to handle some serious business," Jimmy warned.

"That's just it, Jimmy. You still haven't filled me in on the details," Alejandro responded sharply. "What business do you have here?"

Jimmy had strategically waited until the last minute to tell his young protégé the reasons for their arrival in New York. Although Jimmy was training Alejandro to be his right hand man, he still believed Alejandro was a couple of years away from handling that job. So, he often kept most of the information to himself.

During the plane ride, Jimmy considered the countless problems that could arise in the Big Apple. He figured out the answers to most of them and knew he could wing the rest of the problems even if there were some unexpected difficulties.

As far as people went, Jimmy liked Alejandro a lot but there was nobody that he fully trusted. A long time ago he learned that it was best to keep things from people until it was necessary for them to know. Jimmy believed that the fewer the people involved in your business the better off you were.

"Okay Alejandro, as you know, we have a small operation in New York. Nothing compared to what we have in Miami. We have locations in Brooklyn, Manhattan, and the Bronx. The problem is with distribution."

"Well Jimmy, why don't you just have more people sell for you?" Alejandro quizzed.

"It's not that simple. We're not able to expand right now. There are too many other drug gangs in the area," Jimmy explained. "Lately, we are having a problem with this new gang in Washington Heights, they are trying to move in on our territory."

"So what are you going to do? You didn't come here with much muscle. It's just me and Raul." Alejandro asked.

"Getting guys to go to war is not the problem. Between Orlando and my other leaders, we have plenty of men. But the last thing that I want to do is to start a war with these wild New York motherfuckers. It would be bad for business," Jimmy advised.

"Then what else do you have planned?" Alejandro said.

"Since my boss will give me an endless supply of drugs to sell, even more than I can get rid of, I think I can make some kind of deal with these New York gangs. I'm sure they don't have the same kind of hook up," Jimmy paused and then gave Alejandro a sharp look.

Alejandro you must learn that putting a cap in somebody's ass isn't always the best way of dealing with your enemy," Jimmy said as he winked his eyes. "Sometimes, your enemy can be your best money-maker."

Alejandro just sat quietly, taking mental notes.

"Ah, I say it's time to take care of our stomachs," Jimmy said shifting the conversation. "That so called food on the airplane tasted like shit. Let's check out a few of the spots around here before I die of starvation."

"I'll go next door to get Orlando and Raul," Alejandro said.

"After we eat, we're getting together with all of my leaders downtown to talk about problems and strategies," Jimmy established.

"It'll probably be some real characters there," Alejandro laughed.

"That's an understatement," Jimmy quickly replied. "So, you better watch your ass."

*****

"Uptown four men cruised around in a black Maxima with a tan interior. Angel slowly lowered the window to allow some of the smoke to escape. The smell of weed was in the air. Blocks later, the car halted at a red light in front of a church. It appeared that the members had just been released from some special service, but that didn't stop the occupants from performing their normal routine.

"Yo mommy, damn you look good. Come over here so I can talk to you for a second," Angel called out.

The two girls ignored him and continued crossing the street.

"Hey I'm talking to you. What the fuck? Are you two bitches deaf or something? If you didn't want niggas talking to ya then you shouldn't wear those short skirts showing your ass cheeks," Angel hollered as he drove off when the light turned green.

"Yo, Angel, you right. I hate bitches like that. They want you to sweat them and shit, then when you do, they act like they don't know what's up," Edwardo snickered.

"Forget them hoes. They wasn't about shit anyway," Angel said as he peeked back at the girls in his rearview mirror. "I gotta drive by the spot, to make sure that everything is cool."

Angel was a mid-level drug dealer who had people selling drugs for him in Washington Heights. Angel was a pretty big guy with an even bigger reputation on the streets. He grew up in the hood and got into some small run-ins with the law until he finally did some real time in jail. Once he came back out, he quickly reestablished the fact that he was going to be a major player in the neighborhood.

His sidekick was Edwardo. Edwardo was the typical "yes" man. He admired anything and everything about Angel. His association with Angel made him an important man in the hood too.

They first met while they were both attending a tough junior high school in the South Bronx. Back then, Angel was more interested in girls than in his schoolwork. Edwardo was too busy trying to keep away from the local school bullies.

One day after school, when Edwardo was about to get beat up again, Angel stepped in and saved Edwardo's ass. He didn't do this because he felt sorry for Edwardo or liked him, Angel only got involved because he was bored and craved a challenge. This situation just gave him the best opportunity to get in a fight.

Regardless of the reason, Edwardo was extremely grateful. He soon began hanging around Angel all of the time. Angel, who didn't have many friends, welcomed the company. Angel was pretty big for his age and the other kids were instantly afraid of him.

By the time both boys went to high school, they were best friends. Edwardo no longer was the scared little nerd that everyone picked on. Instead, he began bullying other kids. Angel was completely tired of school and believed he could make a lot of money if he quit. So, in the tenth grade he dropped out. Edwardo soon followed.

As teenagers, both boys focused on petty drug deals and basically sold weed to the neighborhood kids. They'd built up interesting reputations for themselves. Angel was considered the quiet, big guy that you didn't want to piss off. Edwardo was the little punk with the big mouth. At first, Angel got arrested a few times for either selling drugs or getting into fights. During Angel's short stints in jail, Edwardo would always revert back to the wimp he was in grade school.

"Everything is running like clock work. Motherfuckin' business is booming!" Angel shouted as he drove around 171$^{st}$ street and Broadway.

"These three main blocks that you're running are like gold mines," Edwardo said.

"And money wait until we take over from 174$^{th}$ street on up. Then we'll really be large," Angel boasted.

"But what about Orlando and his crew?" asked Edwardo.

"Fuck Orlando, and fuck his boys. They don't have the heart and soon we're just going to conquer block after block," Angel said.

"Then it's going to be a war," Edwardo said.

"It's not going to be a war. You ask motherfuckers on the street who they fear more and they'll tell you that it's me. They all know I am a crazy nigga that don't care about shit," Angel said as he slammed his fist on the steering wheel.

"You're right Angel, you're right," Edwardo nodded his head in agreement.

"Anyway, after all this shit is done and I finally got enough fuckin' money to chill with, I'm going back to the Dominican Republic to live like a fuckin' king. Right there in San Francisco de Macoris where some of my friends got bad ass houses," Angel said.

"Yo Angel, I'm gonna be chillin' right with you," Edwardo smiled.

"But look Eddie, Don't worry about Orlando. He ain't shit. I've been shot at and I've been stabbed twice," Angel pointed to the wound on his neck. "You gotta have the attitude that you're not afraid to die out here or some punk motherfucka may try to steal your heart."

"Damn right, man."

Angel's mini speech was abruptly cut short when a truly beautiful Dominican girl walking on the sidewalk grabbed their attention. She had the kind of body that filled grown women with envy, so much so, that her father was reluctant to send her to the corner store alone.

Her golden tan was spread out evenly over her entire body. Her firm breast and ass were true indicators of her youth and it was clear that gravity in no way had affected her figure. She wore a simple orange dress with matching sandals.

"Damn girl you got a nice fat ass. Can I talk to you for a second?" Angel anxiously asked.

At first, the girl appeared shocked by the rude greeting but the glitter from the sparkling Maxima quickly changed her attitude. She eyed the loud mouth and quickly determined that he looked much more handsome than he sounded. Angel was neatly dressed and intensely staring at her. The car then pulled up next to her, she stopped her stroll, and a conversation began.

*****

It was near midnight. The gang was gathered at a secret place in the East Village. This was going to be the most important meeting in Jimmy's life and he wanted everything to run smoothly. Each leader that represented a major area in the Organization's New York Region was expected to attend. They could only bring one assistant with them.

Jimmy was a little nervous and did not totally trust everyone in attendance. He knew he had not yet gained their absolute respect and loyalty. However, if everything went according to plan, he was certain he'd have their allegiance by the time he left New York.

As soon as the clock reached twelve o'clock, the men began pouring inside. Orlando Gomez was in charge of security and everyone was thoroughly searched before they were seated. Jimmy, Alejandro, and Raul sat in disguise on an elevated platform. They were positioned at a safe distance away from the crowd.

Earlier, Alejandro had inquired about the disguises and Jimmy provided him with a long winded explanation. For one, Jimmy was concerned that if any one of these New York guys got caught by the police they would immediately snitch on him. Jimmy also thought that the guys wouldn't respect him as much if they knew his real age, especially since the majority of the attendees had him by more than ten years.

Pancho, Ortiz, and Jose Martinez from the Bronx arrived first. They had a nice crack ring covering some blocks near the Grand Concourse but they were looking to expand. Pancho had been in gangs most of his life and was one of the founders of the "Spanish

Dukes." This gang had thousands of members throughout New York City.

Next entered the infamous brothers, Big Mo and Little Mo. They sold heroin and a little coke but they knew the real money was in selling crack and they wanted their share. Jimmy did a lot of research before he selected Big Mo to handle things in Harlem. He chose him because Big Mo was already established and had an army of guys ready to sell everything and anything for him. He also owned a lot of the streets from dealing heroin.

Donald Simms was brought up in the tough streets of Brooklyn and knew which areas were real gold mines. His right hand man was Russell Walker. Although, there was the occasional shoot out with rival drug dealers, Donald Simms handled his business without stepping on anyone else's toes.

Orlando Gomez was the one who had picked Jimmy up at the airport. He was anxious to solve the problems he was having in Washington Heights. An area in upper Manhattan largely populated by Dominicans. Overall, the neighborhood contained good hardworking people. But were often overshadowed by the few Dominicans whose only concern was on how to make a fast buck. This younger generation of Dominicans were about to squeeze Orlando out of his own location.

Mr. Fernandez sent Jimmy to straighten things out and to more closely observe Orlando. He wanted to determine if Orlando was strong enough to handle additional authority. Even though Jimmy was only around for a few hours, he already felt Orlando was the man for the job. He appreciated how very loyal Orlando was to the Organization and believed they never had to worry about Orlando betraying them. While he recognized that Orlando had a few weak areas, he was convinced that they wouldn't prevent him from doing a great job running New York.

Jimmy's conclusion about Orlando made him relieved. Now he would avoid two problems; finding a person he could trust to replace Orlando, and having Orlando killed.

Jimmy thoroughly evaluated each of the men in the assembly. They dressed and spoke differently but they all shared their love of the business. In addition, they all demonstrated certain distinct leadership qualities. It was easy to see how each one survived the drug business and wound up on top.

"Quiet everyone," Orlando called out. "Let the meeting begin." A sudden hush covered the room.

"As you know, I brought you here to discuss the Organization's plans to extend its holdings in New York," Jimmy explained. "We're already supplying you with the majority of the drugs that you sell now."

Jimmy paused to see if anyone would dare ask a question but nobody did.

"We want you to double your sales but I personally came here to help solve any issues that would prevent you from reaching our goals."

"So Big Mo, let's start with you. What is your major problem?" Orlando asked.

"Well, it's like this my man," Big Mo said as he stood up from his chair. "I need a supplier that can get me an endless amount of coke. It's just that simple."

"Well that's no problem," Jimmy answered. "The Organization is one of the biggest coke producers in the world. Stick with us and you'll be bigger than Nicky Barnes."

"Thanks man," Big Mo said as he began to feel comfortable with the man in the fake beard and mustache.

"How's your protection?" Jimmy asked.

"Nobody in Harlem is crazy enough to mess with Big Mo," he laughed.

"Good."

"Pancho, what about the Bronx?" Orlando asked.

"Well we're having some gang problems, but we can handle them. Recently, we're finding that the junkies are going back to heroin and we can't come close to making the same kind of money with them on that shit."

"Is that so?" Jimmy confidently said. "Don't worry, the Organization will handle that for you."

As each man got up to speak, Alejandro jotted down a series of notes for Jimmy to review later. He listed their complaints in great detail and even added his personal comments.

"Brooklyn it's your turn." Orlando ordered.

"The name is Donald Simms," a short hefty man growled. "We're having major problems with the police. Every time we get on a roll, they come in and bust a key location."

"Sounds like you have a leak, if you ask me," Jimmy suggested, knowing that his statement could cost someone their life. "We'll put some money into the right hands and the police should leave you alone for a while."

Looking to his left. Jimmy looked at his new friend Orlando.

"Now you have a big problem. It seems that some other dealers are trying to take what you have. You could go to war, but that would bring unwanted publicity down on everybody."

"You're right about that," Orlando eagerly agreed. He never wanted to go to war. In spite of his brave exterior he was afraid to die.

Jimmy silently searched for alternatives in his head. "I need more time," He admitted. Over the next couple of days, I will help you acquire the resources that you need to tackle this issue. I just need to make a couple of calls."

Jimmy was a very convincing speaker and had the ears of all the leaders in the room. He knew that if he could make good on all of his promises, they would follow him unconditionally and become permanent members of the Organization.

"Tomorrow, I want you to tell your rivals that you are being protected by the Organization. Let's see what happens next," Jimmy commanded.

"I will tell you what is going to happen next, nothing." Donald blurted out.

Orlando had to agree, Jimmy, the guys on the street would find it funny as hell if we went around bragging about protection from the Organization."

"Well, then we'll just have to deal with that."

Jimmy looked around at the puzzled faces. "Trust me on this one," Jimmy said firmly. "Now, make sure you keep Orlando posted."

Jimmy then turned to Alejandro and whispered something in his ear.

"The meeting is now officially adjourned," Alejandro informed the awaiting audience. Although most of the attendees remained seated, Jimmy and his entourage left quickly and headed back to the hotel.

It was almost four o'clock in the morning and Jimmy was curious to find out what the reaction was on the streets. They didn't get to bed until 7 a.m. but Jimmy believed that was more than enough time to spread the word about the Organization. After breakfast, Jimmy and Alejandro knocked on Orlando's door.

Hey Jimmy, what's going on?" Orlando greeted him in a rather subdued way.

"Nothing much, you tell me, what's going on?" Jimmy asked.

"Well, I just got off the phone with my people in Washington Heights. Nothing has changed. Those guys are still crossing our borders to make deals in my territory. Pancho and Jose are still having problems in the Bronx, too. And in Brooklyn, one of their street dealers was robbed," Orlando informed them.

"I figured this would happen," Jimmy said.

*****

"Now what do we do next?" Orlando asked.

"It's time to go to plan B," Jimmy stated.

"And what's that?" Orlando curiously asked.

"Sit down and I will go over everything with you," Jimmy insisted.

For the next several hours Jimmy explained his next course of action in detail. He pointed out that he wanted everything carried out exactly the way he planned it. Next, Orlando was directed to call every leader that was at the meeting and explained that Jimmy would take care of all their major problems. He then informed them that he would oversee the entire New York operations and all problems should be directed to him only. If necessary, he would forward their requests to a higher authority.

After staying up half the night, Jimmy, Orlando, Raul and Alejandro retired to their rooms before 10 o'clock. "Tomorrow is going to be a busy day," Jimmy thought. "I'll definitely need my rest."

# Chapter 21

"Isn't it some kind of sin to be gambling on Sunday?" Alejandro asked with a devilish grin on his face.

"No way," Jimmy laughed. "And even if it was, I know you would still have your ass with me in Atlantic City."

"This roulette stuff isn't that bad, " Alejandro said. "I hit on that last spin."

"Yeah, this and black jack are my favorites."

"Jimmy, this is my first time out gambling in a professional joint like this," Alejandro said happily. "It's great. I just don't understand why you picked tonight to hang out?" Alejandro asked.

"Hey Alejandro, look up and tell me what you see?"

"I see lots of mirrors, lights and some fancy bulbs."

"There are hidden cameras in those fancy bulbs. We are being filmed even as we speak. In fact, everybody in this place is being filmed and they hold on to the tapes for a certain amount of time," Jimmy explained.

"So what?"

"Well whatever goes down tonight, we'll certainly have a good alibi. There will be a visual record of us losing our money."

"Oh, I get it," Alejandro said while looking over at Jimmy. It was then, he realized that he still had a long way to go before he was in Jimmy's league.

It was late Sunday night. Angel and Edwardo was club hoping. This was their normal routine to celebrate the previous week's returns. Angel and Edwardo were drunk and feeling good. They were going to make one last stop at their neighborhood club, where they would pick up their girlfriends and dance some more before dawn.

"Angel, give me the keys to the car, I'll drive. You've been drinking too much, " Edwardo insisted.

"Motherfucker, you've been drinking the same amount of shit that I have, so what the fuck are you talking about?"

Both men staggered across the street to the car, as their argument grew more heated. Just as Angel was about to hop in the driver's seat, a dark blue van appeared. Angel became alarmed but before he had a chance to pull out his gun, five men in masks jumped out and started pouncing on him. After they felt they had gotten their first victim under control, they moved to a shaken Edwardo. After they had sufficiently beat Edwardo, they tossed the men into the van.

Once inside, additional flurries of punches were thrown. Angel and Edwardo never had a chance. They were drunk, outnumbered and overpowered. Within minutes, their eyes and mouths were covered and they were both handcuffed.

The Van drove to an unfamiliar location in Spanish Harlem. Once there, Angel and Ewardo were taken to a basement in an apartment building. The only thing that they could make out was the loud Merengue music being played from up above. They could hear the rustle and bustle of guests entering the location above them. It sounded as if someone was having a big party.

Angel and Edwardo were left in a room for an hour, although it seemed like forever. A masked man entered and snatched Edwardo out of the room. Angel left alone squirmed wildly in an attempt to free himself from the handcuffs until he realized the situation was hopeless.

Three men entered the room. "Listen up," one of them barked. "You are being held hostage. If your people cooperate, you will soon be released unharmed.

One of the men removed Angel's blindfold. It wasn't until then with a gun trained at his head, that Angel realized he was in some deep shit. The room wasn't the least bit familiar to him and he also didn't recognize any of the angry men that were standing over him. The man closest to him removed the gag around his mouth and then unlocked the handcuffs.

"Don't do anything stupid," he warned. "If you do, you're a dead man."

Angel was feeling sore from the initial beating and his wrists were bleeding from the handcuffs. He cautiously stretched his arms and legs in an attempt to get the feeling back in his limbs.

"You motherfuckers, you don't know who you are dealing with. You really fucked up now," Angel bellowed.

"Bring him over to the door," a dark-haired hefty man directed.

The remaining two men scooped Angel up and shoved him into a vacant room. The three men exited and left Angel alone in the room.

"We're over here," one of them hollered.

Angel looked through a peephole in the door and saw his assailants waving at him. Edwardo, still bound by handcuffs, was shivering next to them.

"Yo Angel, just chill out. As soon as they get what they want, they'll cut us loose!" he yelled.

"Look Eddie, don't worry about a thing. This here is light stuff!" Angel replied.

"When are we going to get out of here?" Edwardo asked.

"There's been a little change in plans," one man responded.

"What do you mean, a change in plans? Our guys will give you anything you request," a nervous Edwardo stammered.

"Shut the fuck up and just look through the peephole at your friend," he shouted back.

Angel took that last line as a warning signal, what was it that they wanted Edwardo to see? Suddenly, he heard a noise coming from the door on the opposite end of the room. It sounded like an army of footsteps. Now that the alcohol had worn off, Angel was totally aware of his surroundings and positioned himself in a defensive stance. He was prepared for anything, even two or three men.

Initially the sounds continued to draw closer, but as soon as they seemed right outside of the door they stopped. The bottom half of the door swung open and a full-grown pit bull appeared. Angel was immediately overcome with anxiety. While he was ready to fight a man, he never dreamed of combating a dog. But before he could figure out what to do next, two more agitated pit bulls entered the room.

"All right, motherfuckers you win, what do you want?" Angel cried. "Anything, just name it!"

"My man it's a little to late to talk that shit now. We warned you about the Organization. We told you that Orlando and all of his people were protected by it but you still walked around like a big shot talking a lot of shit. Now you're gonna pay."

"Fuck you and the Organization!" Angel yelled.

"Please get him outta there!" Edwardo cried. Although he was greatly concerned for his friend's life, he also knew that he would probably be next to join him.

Angel turned all of his attention towards the dogs and tried to formulate various survival strategies in his head. It seemed the dogs were already agitated and they growled fiercely as they walked towards him. Angel backed up until he was near the wall. He looked around for a weapon but only spotted the plastic milk crates beside him.

The instant he raised the milk crate over his head the dogs began to act wildly. Strangely enough, the dogs appeared to be barking but they weren't making any noise. Angel remembered that this was a normal practice by drug dealers, they would cut a dog's vocal chords so that they could surprise unexpected visitors like robbers or cops.

The first dog lunged at Angel's leg but was thrown off course when Angel struck the dog with the plastic crate across the face. The dog went flying backwards. The second canine began to attack Angel's other leg and was also sent whirling backwards after being hit with the plastic crate.

Angel was not as lucky with the third dog. While Angel was attacking the first two dogs, the third dog circled behind him and struck viciously. Angel felt the sharp teeth pierce his lower leg and fell to the ground in pain. At first, he tried to release the dog's grip by slapping the dog's mouth but it was useless. The third Pit Bull had his jaws firmly locked on Angel's flesh.

The first dog now returned with a vengeance. It leaped at Angel's chest and pushed him flat on his back. The second dog, also recuperated by now, began tearing at Angel's right arm. Angel realized that he didn't have a chance. The three dogs were chewing all over his body.

Blood was everywhere. In a last effort to save himself, Angel summoned up all of his remaining strength and grabbed one of the dogs by the neck. He blocked out the excruciating pain being inflicted on his body and squeezed the life out of the dog with his bare hands.

By now Angel's leg was a mangled mess. He threw the dead dog from his clutches and attempted to save what was left of his leg by jabbing the dog below him several times on the nose. As soon as he thought freedom was near, the first dog lunged at his throat. Finally, Angel was ready to declare defeat. He was losing his last bit of strength and his blows were powerless.

Moments later, Angel was motionless. The dogs, covered with blood, continued to jerk their heads wildly back and forth in anticipation of another battle. Their job was finished though, Angel was dead.

"Oh my God, they've killed Angel!" Edwardo screamed.

"Yes, your friend is gone. Now it's time to deal with you," one gunman uttered bravely.

"Please, I beg of you. Don't send me in there!" Edwardo pleaded.

"Oh no, we would never do that. You are more valuable to us out here."

"Whatever it is, I'll do it," Edwardo anxiously responded. "Just let me go."

"Go back and tell Angel's people what happened here tonight. Let them know they should never fuck with the Organization again."

"Okay, you got it," Edwardo responded.

Edwardo was blindfolded again and returned to the van.

"You better not go to the police Edwardo," the voice ordered.

"And another thing, don't bother looking for Angel's body."

Edwardo was taken to a desolate area and released. He decided not to report the incident to the police.

*****

"I have never in my life had a day like today," Gary sighed. "And I've been doing this for the past fifteen years."

"And from the calls on the radio, this could be going on all night," his coworker Susan advised.

As the city's paramedics went rushing from one aided case to the other, the Police Department began circulating the news that a tainted supply of heroin was out on the streets. It was responsible for the string of visits they'd been making to various locations. Neighborhoods in the Lower East Side, Harlem, and the Bronx were hardest hit by this new drug crisis.

One case after another, emergency calls involving drug overdoses rolled in. So far, seventy-two cases were reported, with eight people dead. "Tango and Cash," a new mix of heroin named after the recently released Sylvester Stallone movie, was at the bottom of all the mayhem. It was now seen as the drug of choice by thousands of addicts.

*****

Jimmy looked out of the window as the plane was leaving New York and kissed his troubles good bye. He had accomplished many things during his visit and was ready to start taking care of business back in Miami.

On the plane ride, Jimmy and Alejandro took full advantage of all of the amenities in first class. They ordered the finest wines, enjoyed a scrumptious dinner, and stretched out in their plush extra-wide seats.

"I'll never forget this trip," Alejandro marveled. "It was the best."

"Yeah, it was kind of interesting. I'm glad things worked out. My boss will be pleased when I give him an update," Jimmy said confidently.

"You had to handle a lot of issues. Are you sure that you took care of everything?" Alejandro asked.

"Don't worry. We shouldn't be having any major trouble out of New York for a while," Jimmy responded.

Meanwhile, back in Brooklyn, tragedies were still brewing. There was a knock at the door.

"Who is it?" a youngster's voice asked.

"It's the police."

"Wait a minute. I'm going to wake my mother," the boy answered.

Moments later, an alarmed mother came rushing to the door.

"Yes can I help you?"

"Yes we are looking for Ms. Joyce Thompson."

"I am Ms. Thompson.

"We would like to talk to you, please open up. It's about your son."

"That boy is always getting himself into trouble," a grumbling Ms. Thompson said as she opened the door. "But, thank GOD you found him. I've been worried sick since we haven't seen Peanut in almost two days. And this isn't the first time that he pulled something like this. So what has he done now? And when do I have to go to Juvenile Hall to get him?"

"Well Ms. Thompson, it's not that simple."

At that moment, Ms. Thompson's oldest child Theresa raced over to her after running up five flights of stairs. She was hysterical and Ms. Thompson couldn't make out anything she was saying.

"Girl, what's the matter with you?" Ms. Thompson anxiously asked. "Why are you so upset?"

"The police just found Peanut dead in the playground. His head was completely off," Theresa said crying uncontrollably.

"Oh my dear God, not my Peanut!" Ms. Thompson exclaimed. She dropped to her knees and looked at the two cops for answers. But sadly there were no answers that could ease the pain of a mother losing her child to the streets.

# Chapter 22

On the way to Miami, Cynthia's mind was racing. This was the first time that she had gone back there since her hospital stay and that seemed like a lifetime ago.

Cynthia viewed her life in distinct sections. One set of memories focused on her life in Baltimore with her abusive father. Other times, she remembered her wild period, where she hooked up with Alex and ended up overdosing. Then, there was her comatose span where she spent many years acting like a vegetable. Now, Cynthia took time out to appreciate the new stage in her life and hoped that Jack was the right guy to share good clean times with.

Even though everything in her life was going well, she still felt nervous about flying into the city that had caused her so much pain.

It had been a week since Cynthia saw Jack. He told her that he had important business in Miami, so he sent her a round trip ticket so they could spend some time together. Cynthia took off from work on Monday and was looking forward to the nice long weekend getaway. There were a lot of things Cynthia hoped to accomplish while she was in Miami, shopping was definitely high on her list since she felt she was in dire need of new clothes. She also wanted to visit a couple of friends, the first being Nurse Mitchell. Earlier in the week, they spoke on the phone and Cynthia promised to meet her for lunch as soon as she arrived.

Cynthia was looking forward to their meeting: they had a lot of catching up to do.

After checking in at the hotel, Cynthia looked at her watch and realized that she was running behind schedule. She dropped her bags, changed her shoes, and headed straight for the restaurant.

At first, there was no sign of Nurse Mitchell, so Cynthia wondered if she was also running a little late or had even forgot about their lunch date.

"Nurse Mitchell always kept herself too busy," Cynthia murmured. I'll just have a drink at the bar while I wait."

Normally, Cynthia rarely drank, but waiting for Nurse Mitchell made her nervous.

"Excuse me, are you looking for somebody?" a nearby voice asked as Cynthia ordered her drink at the bar. Cynthia turned swiftly to provide her response and was pleasantly surprised.

"Oh my God! Anita it's you." Cynthia hopped off of the stool and hugged Nurse Mitchell wildly.

"Well, well look at you Cynthia. You look like a million bucks," Anita Mitchell smiled.

"I look okay but I can't believe how much you've changed. Your hair looks great, and look at your clothes. Just how much weight have you lost?"

"Twenty two pounds and counting," Anita boasted.

"Hmmm, what's behind all of the changes?" Cynthia asked slyly. "It sounds like there is a man somewhere in this picture."

"Yes, there is."

"Okay, start from the beginning. Where did you meet him?"

"At the rehabilitation center downtown. My youngest child Janet was hit by a car, and her leg was broken in two places. She had to learn how to walk all over again," Anita sighed.

"I am so sorry to hear that. How is she now?"

"She's doing well now, and the doctors say that she could be walking without a cane by next summer."

"That's good news," Cynthia said while gently rubbing Nurse Mitchell's hand.

"I was taking Janet to therapy three times a week and that's where I met Clarence. His son was enrolled in the rehabilitation program because he had recently lost one of his fingers while playing with firecrackers. Week after week we kept bumping into each other and that's how it started," Anita's excitement was becoming contagious.

"Tell me more," Cynthia said anxiously.

"Well, let me see. He's a single parent and works as a Sanitation man. He is tall and dark, just the way I like them and loves good soul food.

"He's also a very lucky man to get a women like you," Cynthia added.

"No I'm the lucky one. But enough about me, what is going on with you? And please don't tell me that you are content with your life and you don't need a man right now."

"It's funny you should say that Anita, that's exactly the way I felt when I first left Miami. Men were the furthest thing from my mind, then I went out with Jack.

"Ooh, I loved the way you said his name, go on," Anita said.

"Well, he is really a warm sweetheart once you get to know him. He has a great sense of humor, is intelligent and has a strong personality," Cynthia said warmly.

"What about his looks?" Anita interrupted.

"He has a body that won't quit," Cynthia answered triumphantly.

"Now, I can't wait to meet this Jack."

"Anita, you've already met him. He was the DEA agent that came to see me on my last day at the hospital, remember?"

"You couldn't stand him, what happened?" Anita asked.

"He kept calling me in Baltimore, and finally I decided to go on a date with him. We hit it off big time," Cynthia smiled.

"Do you love him?" Anita asked anxiously.

"I don't know about that. But what I do know is that he's the best thing that has happened to me in a very long time," Cynthia admitted.

"Look at the two of us. Two good women with two great guys that are crazy about us. Could it get any better than this?" Anita's face was suddenly overcome by a devilish grin." How's the sex?"

"What's that?" Cynthia asked.

"The sex. How's the sex between you two?" Anita asked bluntly.

"Oh, we haven't had sex yet," Cynthia answered in a quiet voice.

"Girl, what are you waiting for?" Anita advised. "Cynthia, I know it has been a long time for you. So you better test everything down there to make sure that it is still functioning right."

"Don't worry, there are some things you never forget," Cynthia giggled.

"Well you better hurry up. If Jack is as fit as you say he is, he needs another outlet other than working out with weights."

For the next three hours, the ladies filled their stomachs with food and drinks. It was the kind of evening old friends would share, which was somewhat ironic because Anita and Cynthia hadn't built up their relationship until Cynthia emerged from her coma last June. But few friends ever experienced the intensity of this twosome and Anita promised to visit Cynthia in Baltimore on her next vacation. At the end of the evening, Anita and Cynthia got up from the table, kissed each other on the cheek, and bid their farewells.

On the second day of her stay in Miami, Cynthia was starting to feel more comfortable at her old stomping grounds. She couldn't stop thinking about the great lunch she had with her pal Anita the day before and she also enjoyed the nice romantic dinner she shared with Jack before he rushed off to work. Today she was going to see the twins, Roberto and Alejandro. "They seem like such nice kids," Cynthia thought. "It was probably best that they never met Alex. Who knows how they would have turned out if they had."

Cynthia planned to meet them for breakfast at her hotel. Then, they'd buy some CD's or catch a movie. She was really excited about spending a whole day with the twins. She had already felt close to Roberto through his letters, but she felt like she didn't know Alejandro at all.

The phone rang and Cynthia tried to guess who was calling before answering it. Roberto was on the line and he was down in the lobby waiting for her. Cynthia picked up her purse and headed for the door, sporting a T-shirt, black jeans, some open-toe sandals, and black shades. She caught a glimpse of herself on the way out and began to feel underdressed. "I'll keep it simple," she concluded. She even wore no makeup.

As soon as she got off the elevator she spotted one of the twins.

"Hello Cynthia how are you?" Roberto greeted as he kissed her lightly on her cheek.

"I'm fine," Cynthia answered wondering which twin stood in front of her. "Sorry, I can't tell the two of you apart? Which brother are you?"

"I'm sorry, I'm Roberto. Alejandro could not make it."

"That's a shame, why not?" Cynthia asked feeling a little disappointed.

"He went to New York on vacation for a few days," Roberto replied. "I'll just have to do this time."

"Of course, we'll have to enjoy ourselves without him."

Cynthia wrapped her arm around Roberto and escorted him into the waiting streets.

In Miami, a flood of beautiful people coated the sidewalks but Roberto and Cynthia just seemed to stand out. Cynthia's light brown hair crouched perfectly around her shoulders, seemed especially breathtaking on this summer day. Roberto, also quite handsome, seemed to attract the attention of many of the passing ladies. Roberto enjoyed the attention from strangers and wondered if he would ever again be lucky enough to walk the streets arm in arm with Cynthia.

As they marched down Collins Avenue, Roberto's crush on Cynthia began to intensify. Every time he glanced at her gleaming smile, she became more attractive to him.

After an hour passed, they settled on eating at this trendy little cafe by the water. They picked an outside table so they could enjoy the sunny weather. Cynthia ordered a green salad with a glass of water. Roberto ordered a cheeseburger, fries, and a large soda. When the food arrived, Cynthia eyeballed Roberto's food but knew she couldn't take a chance on the extra calories.

"Cynthia, how is everything in Baltimore?" Roberto asked.

"Great!" Cynthia exclaimed. "I'm even considering buying a flower shop downtown. The owners want to retire and are offering me first crack at the deal."

"Are you ready for that" he asked.

"I don't know. At first, I was really excited about the idea of owning something but lately my plans have changed," Cynthia answered.

"Why is that?" he asked.

"I met a really nice guy," Cynthia smiled. "Jack Lloyd has become a priority."

Roberto's heart suddenly dropped. He felt like someone hit him in the stomach with a tire. Even though he assumed Cynthia must have had a man in her life, he didn't expect to hear about it so soon. As crazy as it seemed. He couldn't understand why he was feeling jealous. Cynthia was his stepmother. This woman, as gorgeous as she was, had been married to his father.

"Oh, I am happy to hear that," Roberto struggled while putting on the best fake smile he could come up with.

"So Roberto, what about you? I know you must be driving the girls around here crazy," Cynthia winked.

"I wish that was the case. Alejandro is the ladies man I'm not. For some reason, even though we are identical twins, women just aren't attracted to me the way they are to him."

"Well is there anyone in particular, that you're interested in?" she asked.

*"Yes, and it is you. I would like nothing else, than to go back to your hotel and spend the entire day making love to you,"* he thought.

"Yes there was. Her name is Rosa. We met at a club and went out a couple of times. Suddenly, just when I thought things were going well, she began to avoid me. I called her a few times but she always said she was too busy to see me. The last time I called, I found that her number was changed. She doesn't even come to the club anymore," Roberto sadly responded.

"Well Roberto, It's hard to meet that special someone at one of those clubs. Why don't you try other places?" she said.

"Like where? You think I'm going to meet Mrs. Right hanging around on a park bench?" Roberto joked.

"You just might," Cynthia replied. "In fact, after we leave here, let's go hang out at the Botanical Gardens. You will see a lot of women there."

"A lot of good that would do me," he complained.

"Roberto what is the matter with you? Don't be so down on yourself. You have a nice body and the face of a model. You also have great conversation, I bet the only thing you need is a little more confidence. And I'm going to help you out in that category," Cynthia said as she grabbed his hand in hers. Roberto called the waiter over to pay the bill. Then the two of them walked out of the Cafe and followed the sign pointing towards the Botanical Gardens.

Even though Roberto believed that Cynthia only said those things to cheer him up, it was still nice to hear- especially coming from her.

# Chapter 23

"Da Riiing! Da Riiing!" Alejandro vowed to have the telephone changed Every time it ranged. "Who is it?" Alejandro asked.

"It's me Jimmy. I'm about fifteen minutes from your house. Me and the fellows are coming to pick you and Roberto up." He said.

"What for?"

"I gotta show you something, man. It's gonna blow your mind," Jimmy chanted.

"All right if it's that good, I definitely want to check it out."

"Don't forget to tell Roberto," Jimmy ordered. "See you downstairs in fifteen."

For the next five minutes Alejandro sat across from Roberto in the living room trying to convince him to come along. Ever since he met up with Cynthia, Roberto was becoming more reluctant about the Organization and tried to keep clear of Jimmy.

"Come on Roberto," Alejandro wined. "Jimmy says he has something he's gotta show us."

"Yeah, I know. With Jimmy, everything is an emergency."

"Look, you know he rarely drops in on us," Alejandro said as he stood up and checked for his keys in his pocket. "This must be important."

Roberto looked at the urgency on Alejandro's face. He pleaded with him, and that was rare coming from Alejandro.

"I'll be down in two minutes. But this better be good."

Lately, Roberto rarely got a chance to hang out with his brother and if it meant putting up with Jimmy for a little while, he would just have to grin and bear it.

"Hey fellas what's going' on?" Raul greeted as he stood outside the car.

"Nothing much, man. What about you?" Alejandro asked as he gently slapped Raul on the back.

"Not a damn thing."

Since Alejandro and Jimmy returned from New York, all of the fellas had more respect for Alejandro. Jimmy told them how well Alejandro handled himself up North and everyone was impressed with him. It was generally decided that maybe the twins were more valuable additions to the Organization than most of the gang previously thought.

"So Jimmy, what are we going to check out?" Alejandro asked. Roberto just stood in silence.

"Get in the car. You'll find out soon enough," Jimmy ordered.

"Should we take one of our cars?" Roberto asked.

"Nah, we already have three cars rolling with us as it is."

"Okay whatever you say," Roberto said as he and Alejandro climbed into the back of the car. "You're the boss."

As the four crowded themselves in the back of the limo, Jimmy passed around a few beers. Everyone drank freely, except for Roberto. He thought it was too early in the day for him but as far as the other guys were concerned, "Any time is Miller time."

The cars drove for a long time until they reached the outskirts of the city, near the water. The ride was long and tiresome.

"Jimmy how far in the hell are you taking us?" Alejandro impatiently quizzed.

"Just a little bit longer" Jimmy answered calmly.

"If I didn't know any better, I'd think this was some kind of contract hit going down," Roberto said laughing nervously.

No one responded. Raul looked at Jimmy for direction but Jimmy remained silent.

Jimmy held his beer close to his lips before sipping. "Maybe this is a hit."

Roberto felt a sudden cool go down his back. He knew he could never trust Jimmy, but now he felt like a cornered rat searching for a way out.

Alejandro stared directly at Jimmy. Then Jimmy, not one to back down from anyone, matched his stare and upped it one. By now, Roberto was visibly beginning to panic. Two-minutes later, Jimmy and Alejandro broke out into laughter, Raul joined in. The three men laughed so hard they began spilling their beer all over the place.

"Roberto, I can't believe for a second, you took me serious." Jimmy winked.

"No Jimmy, I knew you were joking all along. I just wanted to see how far you were going to take it." Roberto somewhat relieved, was still shaken.

"Hey guys, that project I was working on is finally finished," Jimmy voiced proudly. "Take a look at it."

The car came to a screeching halt in front of two large gates. Jimmy dialed a code on his hand-held remote and the gates swung open to display Jimmy's private botanical garden. The scene was filled with different types of colorful plants and flowers. Some of the shrubbery, including the cone shaped topiary trees of hemlock and the Japanese Hollis were imported from all over the world. It was a beauty that seemed to go on forever.

For most people, the display would have been absolutely breathtaking, but Alejandro found the array of greenery pretty uneventful. He believed that all of his meetings with Jimmy should focus on the Organization and didn't understand how a bunch of flowers were going to help him multiply his money.

"What's here that is so important?" he barked.

"This is a house that I bought almost a year ago," Jimmy answered proudly.

"You gotta be shittin' me. No fuckin' way," Alejandro said sounding a little more impressed since Jimmy explained that he actually owned the property they were admiring.

"Yeah boy, it's all mine."

"All of this land and shit is yours too?" Alejandro anxiously inquired.

"Jimmy nodded positively and cracked a wide grin.

The line of cars continued to tour the grounds of Jimmy's mansion. After passing the gardens, they came upon the recreation area, which included tennis and basketball courts as well as an Olympic sized pool.

As much as Roberto hated to admit it, he was greatly impressed. Jimmy was still young and his new living quarters were really overwhelming.

As they approached the mansion, Alejandro was amazed at how much the large structure resembled the White House, including the white columns. "Jimmy is becoming as big as the President," Alejandro thought.

For the past six months, Jimmy hired the best architects, structural engineers, flooring contractors, carpenters, and interior designers that money could buy. They all worked around the clock to complete his dream house.

Once inside, Jimmy gave the twins their own personal tour while the others waited by the cars. The three-floor mansion had eight bedrooms, ten bathrooms, and three suites containing working fireplaces. There was a full library with the latest technological equipment, two dens on the second and third floors and a conference room on the second floor. There were kitchen and dining areas located in each of the four wings. Two huge living rooms were on the second and third floors. There was also a massive weight training room containing the newest exercise equipment. The game room consisted of billiard and ping-pong tables as well as an enormous video collection.

"I've never seen any place like this in my life," Alejandro admired as they approached two large wooden doors with brass handles. "This is great."

"Go ahead Roberto, open the doors," Jimmy said.

After following Jimmy's instructions, Roberto stood back and inhaled his surroundings. They were standing in front of a large ballroom, complete with marble floors and a grand piano.

Touring the first floor seemed to take an eternity. Next, they climbed the set of winding staircases; Alejandro and Jimmy took one route while Roberto took the other.

"Roberto, over here," Jimmy called out from the other end of the hallway. Both staircases led to the second floor but at opposite ends of the hallway. As they entered each room, they were greeted by intriguing artwork and fine furniture.

"Damn, I can't believe you really own all of this," Alejandro said. "You'll live like a fuckin' king."

"Well, let me tell you the entire truth. Everything you see is in my name but I don't necessarily own it," Jimmy confessed.

"I don't get what you mean," Alejandro said.

"Fernandez gave me the money to buy this place for him. He provided the specs for the house and monitored everything from his home in Bolivia. He still can't come to this country legally, so he definitely can't own anything here," Jimmy explained.

"So why did he buy this place and fix it up?" Roberto asked.

"He slips into this country from time to time and when he does, he will stay here. That will only be twice a year. So basically, this place is mine."

Jimmy pointed to the largest doors in the middle of the third floor. "You gotta check out this room. It's the master bedroom."

It was like the expensive Fifth Avenue hotel room Alejandro visited when he was back in New York. It had everything the other bedrooms had, but was much bigger. Jimmy walked over to the large bookcase and hit a lever. The bookcase slid to the left revealing sixteen video monitors.

"Anyone for some TV?" Jimmy laughed.

"What's all this?"

"Roberto, these TV monitors are hooked up to video cameras that oversee every room in the mansion and throughout the grounds. You can see who's playing tennis or who's fucking in any of the rooms."

"Man this shit is wild. Can it really do all of that?"

"Yeah, just take a look," Jimmy said as he began changing the various channels on the monitors. "These are the rooms on the first, second, and third floors. Here are the hallways, dining rooms, and all of the other areas."

"This is one bad setup!" Alejandro exclaimed.

"I don't have time to show you everything, but you should be aware of the four major exits," Jimmy said as he pointed them out on the screen. "These don't even include the three secret ones."

"You have secret exits?" Roberto asked as he became more impressed with each new discovery.

"That's right. One leads to the garage. The other one takes you to the underground tunnel leading to the other side of the estate. The last one leads to a sealed room which has enough supplies to keep a person alive for months."

"Why are you telling us all of this?" Roberto asked.

"Because I know I can trust you guys with anything. The other guys have been with me much longer, but you two are my boys. Even though I know we don't always get along," Jimmy said as he looked directly at Roberto.

At that moment, Roberto started to feel a little guilty. "Maybe Jimmy isn't a bad guy after all," Roberto thought. "He's always treated us good and has never asked us to sell drugs directly."

"Now check this out," Jimmy continued, pointing at a TV monitor. It was directly focused on a major exit at the back of the house.

"See what?" Alejandro asked.

"Do you see those two cast brass urns on the back steps?"

Roberto and Alejandro nodded.

"Well, they contain poisonous gas that can be detonated from inside this room by pressing that button right there." Jimmy said.

"How can you buy all of this stuff without the government getting suspicious?" Roberto asked.

"That part is a little tricky, but so far we have been able to slick the Fed. I own a lot of legitimate businesses and my accountants doctor up the books so that it looks like we make a lot more money than we actually do," Jimmy said.

"Then don't you pay a lot more on taxes?" Roberto asked.

"Shit, we get killed with taxes but at least all the money is clean."

"Jimmy, I gotta give it to you, everything is all figured out," Alejandro winked. "You are definitely the man."

"Yeah, I know. Now, let's go back downstairs and have some drinks with the fellas," Jimmy directed.

Alejandro looked around the room one last time to inhale the scenery. "You know a guy could quickly get used to all of this," he confessed.

"Don't worry, you'll own something like this one day," Jimmy replied. "Just always be loyal to me and watch my ass."

The past several months had been one wild ride for Alejandro. Ever since he got back from New York, he and Jimmy had become inseparable. Every night was a party night filled with booze, drugs, and women. Alejandro recently tried coke for the first time and enjoyed it, although not as much as the people around him. To Alejandro, coke was just another way to feel good.

Roberto was busy balancing the Organization's books. He was always good with numbers and this was right up his alley. Even though, the dollar amounts that he recorded didn't seem real.

Alejandro and Roberto were making more money than they knew what to do with. Alejandro was always trading in his car for another one, buying new clothes, or hanging out at the most expensive spots in town.

Roberto remained a homebody. He rarely went out, so that meant he rarely saw Alejandro. He put most of the money that he made in the bank to prepare for a rainy day.

It was Thursday night, but Jimmy insisted that Roberto go out with him and Alejandro to bring in the weekend. In spite of his reservations, Roberto agreed to join them with the understanding that he would probably leave early. They ended up at a small club in a bad section of town. Roberto noticed that Jimmy seemed to feel more comfortable in dives like this rather than the swanky clubs Alejandro preferred.

No matter how comfortable Jimmy felt, he was no fool and never arrived with any less than eight bodyguards when he went to the local neighborhood spots. He realized his new cars and fancy clothes could easily make people jealous and cause them to lash out at him.

"Roberto, are you having a good time?" Jimmy asked as he did a line of coke.

Although the small dump, crowded with former convicts playing loud music wasn't at all appealing, Roberto wanted to stay on Jimmy's good side tonight. "It's not too bad here," Roberto reluctantly replied.

"You know guys, a person would really have to be stupid to mess up this kind of operation. I'm only twenty eight years old and can buy almost anything I want," Jimmy said.

"You know Jimmy, I always wondered how you got everything at such a young age?" Roberto inquired.

"Who cares how he got it. The man has it now, that's the important thing," Alejandro interrupted.

"Fuck it, I'll tell you. There was another guy who used to do the same things I do now. He ran the Miami part of the

Organization pretty well until he eventually got greedy and tried to muscle Fernandez out of the game. So, he was eliminated and I was next in line for the spot," Jimmy said as he shook his head.

"That fuckin' Alex Sanchez just got too greedy."

"Alex?" a startled Roberto asked.

"Yes, Alex. Why you writing a fuckin' book?" Jimmy snapped.

"Nah, it all just sounds interesting," Roberto said as he gave his brother a sharp look.

"Well let's change the subject," Jimmy suggested as he was overcome by a feeling that he was talking too much.

Roberto felt the blow as Jimmy's words replayed in his head. Now he knew exactly why his father was killed and who did it. Jimmy had never revealed his boss name before. Fernandez was responsible for his father's death and Roberto couldn't let that comment rest.

Roberto desperately attempted to conceal his emotions with a fake ass smile on his face. He felt like a traitor. Even though he'd never met his father, and his father didn't even know he had children. Roberto resented partying with the men connected to his father's murder.

Alejandro was initially stunned by the news, but seemed to take the events in stride. In Alejandro's eyes, Alex Sanchez caused his own death by being too greedy. Jimmy was just the beneficiary of the deal. Alejandro quickly tried to put the conversation out of his mind. So he could get his groove on, the night was still young.

"Alejandro what about those two girls you been checking out all night. Which one are you taking home?" Jimmy asked.

"I don't know yet, I'm still trying to decide," Alejandro laughed.

"Well fellas, I'd really love to hang out all night but I have to get up early tomorrow," Roberto said.

"Take it easy bro'," Alejandro waved to his brother with one hand and lined up another coke hit with the other.

"See ya later, Roberto." Jimmy added. "Raul have somebody drive him home, this is a pretty fucked up neighborhood, I doubt if he'll be able to catch a cab."

"That's okay Jimmy. I'll be all right. Alejandro walk me to the door, I gotta discuss something with you," Roberto said.

"Fellas I'll be right back." Alejandro tasted his powdered fingers as he got up from his chair and walked with his brother towards the exit.

"Raul keep an eye out for both of them," Jimmy ordered.

Roberto grabbed Alejandro by the arm and hurriedly pulled him outside of the club.

"Did you hear what Jimmy said?" Roberto asked as he walked towards the street lamp.

"Yeah, I heard what he said," Alejandro responded nonchalantly. "I hope you're not gonna trip."

"Well, what do you have to say about it?"

"Say about what?" Alejandro asked sharply.

"Alejandro, Jimmy knows who murdered our father," Roberto said tearfully. "In fact, he's working for the man, I mean we're working for the man that had him killed."

"Roberto, Jimmy didn't have anything to do with our father's death. The big boss had him killed. You heard the story, Fernandez had a good reason to do what he did."

"I can't believe you would say that. We really don't know why everything happened the way that it did. We only know what Jimmy told us," Roberto argued.

"Why would Jimmy lie to us? He doesn't know we're Alex Sanchez's sons."

"So you're not going to do anything about it?" Roberto challenged.

"There's nothing we could do about it anyway," Alejandro shrugged. "Besides, I think you forget that our father was no angel. Maybe he got what was coming to him."

"You know, sometimes I feel like I don't know you anymore. Ever since you been hanging out with Jimmy, you've changed."

"There's nothing wrong with having a good time every now and then. I don't like to keep myself sheltered in my apartment like you do."

"If hanging out all day and night with a bunch of gangsters and doing coke is having a good time, I would rather stay at home," Roberto defended.

"Sometimes you can be so fucking wimpy. Damn I wish you were more like Jimmy," Alejandro confessed.

"Fuck you, Alejandro. Why don't you go back in there with your boys and finish partying?" Roberto snapped.

"That's exactly what I'm gonna do. See ya!"

"Fuck you!" Roberto yelled. Without looking back, Alejandro lifted his middle finger in the air and answered Roberto appropriately.

*****

Back at the apartment, after a night of heavy partying, Alejandro finally made up his mind. It was time to hit the skins.

In a king-size bed he passionately kissed her. He held the shapely brunette's breast in his hands and pressed her full lips against his. Their tongues wagged back and forth like dogs in heat.

While he enjoyed what was happening up top, he was constantly distracted by what was happening below his waist. The curvaceous blond was now moving up his thighs. This went on for some time until the brunette joined her friend down below.

"Double your pleasure, double your fun," they moaned.

Alejandro took out a gram of coke and lightly sprinkled it on his penis. He heard an erection lasts longer with the help of cocaine. Although he still couldn't tell if the myth was true, he knew for sure that it provided a great incentive for oral pleasure.

When the coke had been licked away, both women mounted themselves on top of him. The loud music playing in the background drowned out the moans of pleasure. One gyrated on Alejandro's cock while the other slipped her vagina in and out of Alejandro's mouth.

At one point, the women began touching, holding, and kissing each other. They were feeling extra erotic and took turns hovering over Alejandro's dick.

The entire scene was wild, even for Alejandro. Throughout the escapade, he stopped his own feelings to admire the two beautiful women he had under his power. The episode ended much like it had begun, wild and furious. Alejandro had never felt so satisfied in his life. He was also pretty wet since the women had saturated him with their juices. It was clear that they had reached orgasm.

He turned toward his nightstand for another few hits of coke. With his free hand, he massaged his manhood to spark some new energy. In a parched exhausted voice, Alejandro whispered, "Just give me a couple of minutes, and I'll be ready for round two."

# Chapter 24

"I am sorry, but there is no answer at that apartment number," the doorman explained. "The boys must have passed here without me seeing them."

"Can you please try the number again?" the visitor asked anxiously.

"No problem, maybe they're resting."

Meanwhile, the twins were in the midst of another one of their disputes.

"There is no way that Janet Jackson is better than Madonna." Alejandro said.

"Look, you can just see the difference in the videos. Janet, sings and dances better than Madonna," Roberto argued.

"Bro' you gotta look at the entire picture. Madonna is much sexier than Janet. One night with her and you'd probably have to go to some kind of podiatrist to get your toes straightened out from all of that good shit," Alejandro laughed.

"Why does everything always come down to sex?"

"Because that is the way that life is. You just haven't figured that part out yet."

"You're completely wrong."

"Wait a minute, " Alejandro explained. "Why do people bust their asses in high school for good grades?"

"So they can go to a good college," Roberto answered triumphantly.

"And why do they want to go to a good college?"

"So they can get a good job," Roberto reluctantly responded. He was beginning to feel that he was being had. "Wait I know where this is headed."

"You better believe it. By having a good job, you can get a good car and house. Wham! You get good pussy for life," Alejandro said excitedly.

"There you go distorting things again, that's not the main reason guys go through all of that hard work."

"Well give me another reason?"

At that moment, the intercom from downstairs sounded.

"Who is it?" Alejandro inquired.

"Mr. Sanchez, you have a visitor."

"I said who is it?" Alejandro asked impatiently.

"Mr Sanchez, she won't give her name. She says that she is an old friend of the family," the doorman responded.

At first, Alejandro was going to deny the mystery women but then he figured it was probably an old conquest that wanted to have another go at it.

"Send her right up," Alejandro insisted.

"Who was that?"

"Some babe who wants to play mysterious. She's on her way up now. Don't forget, if I give you the signal, you gotta break out for a while."

In a few moments, there was a light knock at the door. Alejandro, trying to play it cool, waited until the person began knocking again.

"One minute," Alejandro responded calmly.

When Alejandro opened the door, he couldn't believe his eyes. He looked down at the woman standing in front of him and hugged her immediately. Tears rolled down his face as he embraced her. Roberto screeched with sounds of joy when he joined Alejandro at the door.

"Oh my god, I can't believe you are here," Roberto said as he tried to find a place to grab the woman. In a time frame that seemed like forever, the three of them stood at the doorway hugging each other, no one wanting to let go.

"My boys, my boys I have found you." Sister Catherine smiled warmly. "You are more handsome than I imagined."

"Sister Catherine, I still can't believe that you are here in Miami," Roberto marveled.

"Sister Catherine, please come in," Alejandro invited.

"Boys step back. I want to take a good look at you." Sister Catherine said with tears streaming down her face once again, After realizing all the time that had past by. "Just look at you, all grown now."

"We have certainly changed a lot through the years," Alejandro admitted.

"I don't care how much you two have changed. You and Roberto will always be my boys."

"Sister Catherine, after all this time, how can you still tell us apart?" Roberto asked.

"It's easy. A mother can always tell her children apart. It's in your eyes," Sister Catherine confessed.

"When did you arrive here in Miami?" Roberto asked.

"About three hours ago. As soon as I got settled in the hotel, I rushed right over," she said.

"How did you know where to find us?" Alejandro asked.

"The same gentlemen who helped me get you here tracked you down through his contacts."

Everyone was seated in the living room and the twins stared intensely at Sister Catherine. She had changed a lot. She was not the robust Nun with that stern voice that they remembered. Now, Sister Catherine was elderly and frail looking, but somehow she still had that same magical smile. A grin that would make you do almost anything.

"So how's everything back in Cuba?" Roberto asked.

"Everything is good. The Orphanage is twice as big as it was when you boys were around. We have more children than ever before," Sister Catherine said proudly.

"After all this time, are you tired of taking care of so many children?" Alejandro asked

"No, never. It is what I do, and it keeps me going. Unless God decides to retire me, I'll continue."

"Sister Catherine would you like to have something to drink?" Roberto offered.

"Yes, that would be nice Roberto. Boys I am so sorry to hear about your grandmother, I heard she was a very good woman.

"She was the best. You left us in good hands," Alejandro said smiling.

"Now boys tell me how it was growing up in Miami?" She asked.

"It was great. We couldn't have asked for anything more. We can never repay you for all the things that you have done for us," Alejandro said as he held her hand.

Tears began to fill her eyes. "That is so good to hear. I have been so worried about you over the years but with the Police always watching us, I couldn't contact you."

Roberto handed Sister Catherine a glass of orange juice and sat down on the couch. "Sister Catherine, that's all in the past. Today we are all going to spend the entire day together."

"I know you two have many things to do. Don't let me get in the way," she interrupted.

"We can't possibly think of anything else we would rather do than spend time with you and show you the city," Alejandro insisted. He tossed Roberto a light jacket and took his keys out of his pocket.

The twins and Sister Catherine spent the next four hours touring Miami. They ate at one of the finest restaurants. Over lunch, the twins filled Sister Catherine in on everything she'd missed since they left Cuba, except for their dealings in the Organization, of course. They visited the famous Cathedrals and even offered to take her on a shopping spree, but she declined. After all this time, Sister Catherine had remained a simple woman.

Back at the apartment, the threesome crashed on the couch. It had been one long day and Sister Catherine was tired and trying to catch her breath.

"I want to thank you boys for showing me the city. It is very nice here," she said.

"For you anything, please just ask," Alejandro said proudly. "Finally, we are in a position to pay you back for all of your support and we want you to know the sky is the limit."

"That is not necessary. Whatever I've done for you in the past was out of pure love. It's not something that has to be repaid," Sister Catherine contended.

"But we really want to help you in any way possible. Maybe we can give you money to help you out in Cuba," Roberto volunteered.

"That won't be necessary. You boys know I couldn't take any money from you, even If I wanted to."

"Why not?" Alejandro asked.

"Alejandro, I may be an old lady, but I can still figure out what is going on here."

"I don't understand. What do you mean?" Alejandro asked.

Both of you are too young to have accumulated such wealth. Not one time since I got here, have you mentioned your jobs or school. Yet you have this fancy apartment, fine clothes, and expensive cars. This could only mean one thing, that you are doing something illegal," Sister Catherine voiced angrily. "I apologize if I am wrong. But tell me, if I am?"

There was nothing that either Alejandro or Roberto could say. They couldn't think of a fabulous lie to tell her, nor could they admit to the truth. They stood silently, like two children who had brought home bad report cards.

"That's what I thought. Boys how could you do this?" Sister Catherine said in a defeated tone. "I am so disappointed in you both."

The words pierced their hearts like a sharp dagger. Why do they always seem to hurt the very people that they love so dearly? If there was a hole, they would have certainly jumped in. Anything would have been better than seeing the look of heartbreak across Sister Catherine's face.

"Sister, I know you are disappointed but it hasn't always been easy for us. It is no fun growing up and never having any money," Alejandro said in an attempt to explain.

"Alejandro, you think I don't know what it feels like to be poor?" Sister Catherine argued while shaking her wilted fists.

"We always figured that we would make a lot of money and return to Cuba. We only wanted you to be proud of us."

"Roberto, I would be proud of you if you were a garbage man or a mechanic. As long as you made an honest living and took care of your family, that would have been good enough for me."

"Sister we haven't been doing this for a very long time. So, you shouldn't be too mad at us," Alejandro pleaded.

"Even if you have been doing this for only one day, did you think of all the lives that you've destroyed?" Sister Catherine asked in a concerned tone. "And don't you dare say you're doing this for me. You know I didn't raise you like that."

Alejandro held his head down in embarrassment.

"At the home we tried to teach you children many lessons," Sister Catherine continued. "But one of the most important ones was the meaning of true wealth. It's better to be rich from within than recklessly chasing material things. I guess I must have failed in getting that point across to you."

"Sister Catherine, you did not fail," Roberto said sadly. "We chose not to listen and have failed you and the other Sisters back home. We sincerely apologize."

"I came here because I wanted to see you one last time." She then paused and took a deep breath. "I am dying of cancer and there is nothing else the doctors can do for me."

"Sister Catherine, why don't you stay here with us?" Roberto wept. "We'll take care of you."

"My child, I can not. I must go back to be with the children that need me now. I want to be buried next to the home and the people that I have cared for all of these years. They are my family," she said.

"And what about us?" Alejandro asked bravely. "We need you too."

"No matter what you do in this world, I will always love you deeply. Though I may not like the way that you live, in my heart you will always be those skinny little boys that I grew to love so much."

"We love you too. Please don't go," Roberto begged.

"But I must. Boys I have never told anyone this before, but out of all the hundreds of children that have gone through our doors, you two have always been my favorites."

She slowly got up from the couch and ordered Alejandro to call her a cab. Although they would have preffered to drive her back to the hotel, the boys knew it was no use. Once Sister Catherine made up her mind about something, it could not be changed.

"I will miss you greatly. But remember, you will always be in my heart," she said as she walked into the elevator. Before the doors quickly closed behind her, she caught one last glimpse of her twins. "Take care of yourselves," she called out. As quickly as she had arrived, Sister Catherine was gone.

Later, both Alejandro and Roberto decided to stay in for the night. This was nothing new for Roberto, who was satisfied reading a good book or watching a basketball game on TV. But for Alejandro, this was unusual. He had received several calls inviting him out for the night but he turned them all down.

Sister Catherine's visit was on both of their minds. Not only did they regret letting her down, but they were reminded of how much they had changed since they left Cuba.

Roberto often tried to justify his actions. At first, it was to save enough money for school but now he had more than enough. Next, it was to keep an eye out for his brother, but Roberto realized that each of them had their own destiny. So what was holding him back from quitting? Maybe he was enjoying their lifestyle more than he was willing to admit.

The money wasn't the main issue for Alejandro. Sure, it was nice to have, but the feeling of power and respect was what he treasured most and that was the main reason he remained a member of the Organization. Jimmy and the guys weren't really bad people. It's not like they went around shooting and killing people on a daily basis. Plus, the only people who did get hurt were those that was already in the business. Sister Catherine really left an impression on him. After much soul searching, he knew there was only one thing he could do.

Alejandro hopped out of his bed and knocked on his brother's bedroom door. "I'm glad you're still up. We've got to talk," Alejandro whispered.

"I was thinking the same thing, come on in," Roberto responded.

"I thought about this long and hard: I want us to get out of the Organization. What we're doing just isn't right," Alejandro said sternly.

"I was thinking the exact same thing," a shocked Roberto agreed. "I was going to tell you tomorrow that I'm getting out with or without you."

"Hey bro', after all we've been through, we still think a lot alike."

"How do you think Jimmy will take the news?"

"It doesn't matter, there isn't anything he can say that could change our minds," Alejandro said. "When do you want to tell him?"

"The sooner the better," Roberto insisted.

"You're on," Alejandro said. For the first time in a long while, both Alejandro and Roberto slept peacefully. It was also decided that after they get out of the Organization, they would somehow see Sister Catherine again and prove to her that they had changed their lives.

*****

***Dear Cynthia,***

*What's going on? Of course this is Roberto writing you. I am sorry that I haven't spoken to you in a long time, but things have been pretty hectic around here lately.*

*I really don't know where to begin. Alejandro and I have been involved in some pretty serious stuff for some time now. I'm not too proud of it but I think it's over now. The last time we spoke on the phone, you told me to be careful not to make the same mistakes that you have made in your life. So, I guess you had some idea of what we were doing. I just don't think you realized how deeply involved we were or who the other players were in this whole mess.*

*But Cynthia, before you get anymore upset, I have some good news. Alejandro and I have decided to get out of the business. In fact, we're leaving real soon but first we have to do it in a way that is not disrespectful to the higher-ups. Then we are going to take the money that we've made and move to another part of the country.*

*I hope you're not too disappointed in me. I knew it was wrong from the beginning but I did it anyway. So, that's the latest news with me. Now what about you? I hope your mother is okay. How's your social life. Are you still seeing that guy, Jack? If so, then he must be a pretty special guy.*

*Well, I gotta go. Alejandro just walked into the apartment making a lot of noise. He just told me to tell you that he said "hello." As soon as you get this letter, please call me.*

*Sincerely yours,*
*Roberto Sanchez*

*PS:*
*I thought putting violet petals in the letter would be a nice touch. Take care.*

Alejandro was crouched over Roberto's shoulder trying to get a glimpse at his correspondence.

"I thought *I* was a little kinky, but you got me beat bro," Alejandro smiled.

"Why do you say that?"

"Because you still got the hots for Cynthia even though she was married to our father," Alejandro giggled.

"You know, at times you can be a real asshole. I don't have some type of juvenile crush on Cynthia. We're just good friends and I enjoy writing her letters." Roberto said defensively.

"Sure you do. You're only interested in keeping the family close," Alejandro replied.

"Why am I even talking to you about this? You couldn't possibly understand this," Roberto said furiously.

"Well, whatever I just came over here to see if you wanted to go to the gym and workout. I didn't come over to start a fight with you," Alejandro said.

"No I am not going to the gym today, maybe tomorrow. I am just going to relax around here this afternoon," Roberto said.

"I hope you haven't gotten used to all of this luxury. We'll be giving this all up pretty soon. The cars, leather furniture, fancy clothes. I mean everything," Alejandro said.

"You know how I am. This stuff doesn't mean anything to me. As far as I'm concerned, the sooner we get out of it, the better."

"Well look, I'm outta here. I'll catch you later." Alejandro said as he raced to his room to get his gym equipment.

"Yeah later."

Lying down on the couch, Roberto began to think that Alejandro's observations were correct. He looked at Cynthia as more than a family friend and he might have even had a crush on her. But as far as he was concerned, he had worked all of that out of his system, or had he? He had to admit, after he found out that Cynthia was seeing Jack, he was very jealous. At times, he even fantasized about kissing her.

After re-evaluating the situation, Roberto decided he would control his feelings about her. He didn't want to jeopardize their friendship because it just meant too much to him.

# Chapter 25

"Cynthia, slow down a little bit. What are you trying to do, kill me?" Jack moaned.

"No sweetheart, I'm not trying to kill you. I'm just trying to make you sweat. Unless you wanna stop, you've got to keep up the pace. Let's keep on going," Cynthia asserted. "You know, I could do this all day long."

"I hope you can because you won't make me stop first," he huffed.

Competition was an integral part of Cynthia and Jack's relationship. After jogging five miles at a rather fast pace, neither Jack nor Cynthia wanted to be the first one to give up.

"Okay Cynthia, on the count of three we'll both stop," Jack suggested.

"All right, on the count of three."

"One, two, three, stop."

Jack stopped short as Cynthia continued her stride.

"I won, I am the best!" Cynthia cheered as she jumped triumphantly in the air.

"That's not fair, you cheated," Jack argued in a friendly tone.

"No I didn't, I just wore you out," Cynthia boasted.

"You wore me out, did you?" Jack took the last of his energy and began charging at Cynthia full speed ahead.

"Jack what are you doing?" she asked as she began to back up.

"You'll soon find out," he said. When Cynthia realized Jack was planning a game of run, catch, and kiss, she strategically out-maneuvered his advances. Jack chased Cynthia fiercely for two blocks before he finally caught up with her and playfully tackled her to the grass. He then smothered her with kisses. At first she pushed him away wildly with her hands. Then she began to melt in his clutches.

Later, back at Jack's apartment, the couple planned the rest of their day in Washington.

"What time are we meeting Bobby and Virginia for dinner?" Cynthia asked.

"Seven o'clock," Jack replied.

"I really like being around Bobby and Virginia. They are a pretty cool couple and so down to earth. I hope that they like me," Cynthia added.

"Don't worry about that. They both think you are the greatest thing since milk," Jack laughed.

"Jack, is Bobby's leg ever going to be all right. It's been a long time since the explosion and he still walks around with a bad limp."

"No it's doubtful that he'll get much better but he still goes to rehab for it, three times a week."

"Why doesn't he put in his papers to retire?" Cynthia asked.

"And do what? He's been a cop his whole life. Even though he's no longer out in the field, he enjoys working around the office."

"Why don't **you** just work inside?" Cynthia asked.

"Cynthia, you know that's not me, it would drive me crazy."

After dining with Bobby and his wife, Jack and Cynthia returned to the apartment. Cynthia showered first. While Jack showered, Cynthia set up a movie in the living room. When Jack emerged, the two cuddled closely and shared popcorn.

"This time Jack, I won't take no for an answer. I will sleep out here in the living room and you will take the bedroom," Cynthia demanded.

"No that's okay, you can have the bedroom," Jack offered.

"No I won't. And if you don't sleep in there, it will be a long time before I come over and visit again," Cynthia threatened. "I mean it."

"You win. No more arguments from me. Here are your blankets," Jack said as he tossed the linen on the couch. "Goodnight."

Jack bent down and kissed Cynthia on the forehead. Cynthia smiled widely. A couple of hours went by, and they both had the same problem, neither of them could fall asleep. The sexual tension between them was too strong.

She had known Jack now for nearly a year but she was afraid of knocking down that last wall in their relationship. What if they had sex and everything between them changed? She loved the way that things were now and didn't want to ruin their friendship.

Jack hadn't dated much. He was always preoccupied with other things. While he was growing up, Jack focused on his studies and sports. Not that the women weren't attracted to him, it's just that they weren't his priority.

When he graduated high school, he went straight to the DEA. His first few years were spent trying to learn as much about his job as he could. His dates were few and far in between. Most of the time, he was set up on blind dates by friends of his, who thought that he would be a great catch.

Janice was one of the girls that he really liked. She was smart, attractive, and loved sports. The sex was great, but something was still missing. After six months, Janice finally confessed that she was in love with her female roommate. Although she admitted to caring for Jack more than any of the other men she'd dated, she still chose to end the relationship. Jack was crushed. Instead of sharing this experience with any of his friends, he poured himself back into his work to deaden the pain.

Other women would get fed up with Jack's busy work schedule and would look for companionship elsewhere. The script was always the same. In the beginning, the women would find Jack challenging. His work ethic was something the women believed they could change, but in the end, they realized that Jack was pretty set in his ways. Finally, they'd give him the standard speech, "You're a great guy and someday you'll make some woman very happy, but I just can't deal with this stuff."

Cynthia was different. She was the breath of fresh air he longed for and he wanted her in the worst way. But he knew, even in the beginning of their relationship, that he would have to be patient when it came to sex and he was prepared to wait.

He didn't want to scare her away but he also couldn't stop thinking about how sexy she looked in those jogging clothes.

"Jack are you asleep?" Cynthia whispered as she stood huddled near his door.

"No I'm not, come on in," Jack said. Cynthia sat on the edge of the bed.

"Look, I know we've been seeing each other for a while. You've been very patient with me and I really appreciate that," Cynthia said nervously. "I don't want you to think that I'm acting childish but I don't know if I am ready to have a sexual relationship yet. It's been such a long time and..."

"Cynthia, I'm not with you for sex," Jack interrupted. "I'm with you because I love being around you and if it takes five years until you are ready, I'll wait. Cynthia, I don't know if you know this, but I'm in love with you and have been for some time now." Jack gently held Cynthia's hands in his and massaged them tenderly as he waited for her response.

That was all Cynthia needed to know. She also loved him and wanted to spend the night together in his bed more than anything.

She slowly released his hands and began leaning him back on his bed. Their lips, then tongues were softly introduced. It was as magical as their first kiss.

After their first night of passion, Cynthia woke up early the next morning. Being in Jack's arms was startling at first, but then she relaxed as she recalled the previous night. Cynthia had never felt so secure in her life and she went back to a peaceful sleep.

Moments later, Jack awoke and found Cynthia in his arms. He was also caught off guard because he thought his memories of their intimacy was all a beautiful dream, much like the ones he had been having about her recently. However, the memories of Cynthia's pleasing fragrance was too strong and he knew their time together was very real. As Jack laid in bed with his woman by his side, he tried to recall his life before he'd met Cynthia. Nothing stood out, so he drifted back to sleep.

*****

"I still don't understand why you have to go back to the States. What business do you have there? I am sure somebody can take care of it for you," Mrs. Fernandez insisted.

"It was rare for Sergio Fernandez's wife to question him on any of his decisions. But lately, she has been extremely worried about him and their relationship. When Sergio first returned home from prison, he spent most of his time with his family. But lately, he spent the majority of his time managing his business.

"I have important things to take care of in the States and I need to handle it myself," Fernandez responded firmly.

"But Sergio, you don't understand. Whenever you go away on business, it's very hard on the children. They are afraid that you will never come back," she cried.

"But that's ridiculous, our children know how much I love them."

"They know that you love them, but remember, you were gone for five years and they missed you a great deal."

"When I return, we will all go on a family vacation. Don't worry, I'll make it up to them," Fernandez offered.

"So, you're still going?" she asked fiercely.

"Yes I'm still going, I have no choice," he said defensively.

Mrs. Fernandez walked out of the living room and raced upstairs crying hysterically. "I was the one who waited for you all of these years!" she screamed.

Sergio considered going after her but decided that would have been futile. "What good would that do?" he thought. "I'm going to Miami, and that is that."

Now that Fernandez sat alone in the living room, he began to question himself. Why was it so urgent for him to go? There really wasn't anything important happening in Miami yet, he felt compelled to go anyway. He had everything that a man could want. A beautiful devoted wife and kids and more money than he could spend in a lifetime. He also controlled vast regions of the world through his drug activities but it just wasn't enough.

Lately there were only two major things in his life that he thought about. The first was his Organization. He often marveled at how successful it was and concentrated on making it even more powerful. His other constant thought was Eva. He came to the conclusion that it was no coincidence that he was happier when she was around. What he thought was just respect for an employee was now becoming something else. That secure feeling that he felt when she was around, was not only because she was his bodyguard. To Fernandez, she was his soul mate.

Eva knew things about his life that his wife couldn't even comprehend. Eva had been in his corner for many years. She helped him carry out his affairs discreetly behind his wife's back and was one of the few people he requested to visit him while he was in prison. Eva Santos was the sophisticated, complicated, and extremely sexy lady that Fernandez craved, everything his wife was not.

"Maybe it's time to see how she feels about me," Sergio thought. "Over the years she hasn't given me any clues about her feelings for me but if I turn on the old charm, anything is possible."

*****

"Mom, dinner was great. Let me help you wash the dishes," Cynthia offered.

"You dry and I'll wash," Betty suggested.

"When are you going to buy a dishwasher? It's so much easier."

"Cynthia, I have a lot of time on my hands and I really enjoy doing little things like washing dishes around the house."

"Here's the Dawn liquid," Cynthia said as she handed her mother the bright green bottle. "Suit yourself."

"Thank you my darling daughter," Betty smiled. "Now, I'd like to take a moment to change the subject."

Cynthia knew her mom had spotted an opportunity to question her about her relationship with Jack. Her heart beat quickly in anticipation of where this conversation was going to lead.

"Cynthia, it seems like things are getting pretty serious between you and Jack."

"Yeah, everything is going pretty smoothly. I'm going to visit him again in Miami in about two and a half weeks."

"You're going to Miami again?" a concerned Betty asked. "You know what they say."

"Yeah ma, I know. Why buy the cow if you can get the milk for free. Well I'm no cow and Jack doesn't like milk anyway."

"Hmmph," Betty answered not knowing what else to say.

"Jack has a lot of business that he has to take care of in Miami and I miss him a lot. This is the longest time we've been apart since we started dating," Cynthia admitted. "Anyway, I had such a good time the last time I went, I don't mind going back."

"Honey it's really good to see you this happy. I can tell just by looking at you that you're in love," Betty teased.

"I don't know, maybe you can call it that," Cynthia reluctantly admitted. "But whatever it is, this feeling feels pretty good."

"You deserve all the happiness you have coming your way," Betty said excitedly.

"Mom, I want to ask you something," Cynthia said in a serious tone.

"Go ahead honey, what is it?"

"Did you know what was going on?"

Immediately Betty Hancock placed the dirty dish back into the sudsy water and closed her eyes. Only seconds ago she was so overwhelmingly happy, now she was forced to think about the past. "Why is my daughter spoiling the moment? She wondered. "We don't have too many pleasant conversations like the one we've just shared."

Betty opened her eyes and looked sympathetically at the young woman standing next to her. "Cynthia, let's not bring up things that happened so long ago. You're happy now and that's what counts."

"Maybe it's easy for you to try to forget everything that happened but I can't. I'm the one who has to deal with the shame and guilt," Cynthia confessed as she tried to remain composed.

The abuse Cynthia suffered caused her so much pain that she often wished she could substitute her childhood memories for someone else's. At sixteen, Cynthia decided she was better off in the streets than at the hands of her father. She ran away to Los Angeles, California and didn't contact her parents until years later. When Betty heard Cynthia's voice on the other end of the telephone, she begged her to come home until Cynthia finally broke down and told her of her father's sexual abuse. Betty was caught completely by surprise and her first reaction was to defend her husband. She called Cynthia a liar.

In Betty Hancock's mind, those allegations were too painful to face. It was easier to believe that Cynthia was just a rebellious teenager than to label her husband a child molester.

The topic was never discussed again, even after Cynthia's father died several years ago. Cynthia and her mother avoided revisiting the past and appreciated that they were getting along better than they ever had. Neither wanted things to change between them.

"Mom, I love you, but I need to know the truth. You owe me at least that! Cynthia demanded.

"Honey, what do you want to know?" Betty asked calmly.

"Did you know that he was abusing me?"

"Cynthia, of course not. At least, I didn't suspect anything in the beginning."

"In the beginning? Cynthia questioned. "You mean you never noticed how he always wanted me around him or how touchy-feely he was with me?'

"No, I thought that you two were just close. It seemed pretty normal. How was I to know?" Betty cried.

"I gave you little hints, Mom. But you chose to ignore them," Cynthia charged.

"Honey, I didn't ignore them. By that point, I felt there was nothing I could do."

"You could have left him," Cynthia argued.

"Cynthia, it just wasn't that simple," Betty paused wondering if she should open another can of worms. "I know I shouldn't tell you this, but for a long time, I was jealous of you. I was his wife but he gave you all of the attention. At first, I really didn't know what was going on but by the time I did suspect something, I was too afraid to say anything."

"Afraid of what?" Cynthia trembled.

"Afraid of losing you both," Betty answered bravely.

"But I was your child, you were supposed to protect me," Cynthia wept. "You left me to fend for myself."

"Honey, when I finally tried to help, you had totally blocked me out of your life."

"Can you blame me? I thought you knew what was going on all along and refused to do anything about it."

"Well soon after that, you ran away from home. So, I guess I took the easy way out," Betty said.

"Did you ever confront Dad about it?" Cynthia anxiously asked.

"Yes, I did but he said that you made it all up to get our attention," Betty said.

"How could he say that? He knew the things he made me do!" Cynthia cried out. "Do you believe me now?"

"Honey, of course I believe you. Will you ever forgive me for not protecting you in the past?" Betty said as she wiped her trickling teardrops from her face with her sudsy hands.

The two women hugged in the middle of the kitchen. Neither said a word. They realized that while they could not change the past, they could definitely build a new future-together.

# Chapter 26

Roberto was hanging out in his brother's room. It was early afternoon, and neither of them had any appointments scheduled. Over the past week, Alejandro had been trying to distance himself from Jimmy and his boys. A part of him missed hanging out with them, but he knew he couldn't continue down the same path.

Jimmy sensed that something was wrong with his two star employees. So, he decided to drop by for a surprise visit.

"Hey Jimmy, come on in. What's going on?" Alejandro said nervously. He knew something was definitely up if Jimmy took time out of his busy schedule to pay him and Roberto a visit.

"Hey guys, how's it going? Alejandro, I haven't bumped into you in a couple of days and I wanted to make sure that everything was still cool," Jimmy explained.

"Yep, everything is fine. I was just getting ready to call you," Alejandro lied.

"Roberto, why are you so quiet?" Jimmy asked.

"I just have a lot of things on my mind, Jimmy."

"Well if I can help with anything let me know," Jimmy said.

"Well there is something real important that me and Roberto want to talk to you about," Alejandro interjected.

"Wait a minute, have I got some news for you," Jimmy uttered anxiously.

"What is it?" Alejandro quizzed.

"Fernandez, the man himself, is coming to Miami. He will be visiting here in about two weeks," Jimmy said.

"Why is he coming? What's the special occasion?"

"As far as I know, there is no special occasion. Maybe he just wants to check out his new crib. Anyway, I'm in charge of the festivities," Jimmy announced.

"What festivities?" the twins asked simultaneously.

"I'm planning to throw a bad ass party in Fernandez's honor."

"In only two weeks, we're going to throw a big party?' Alejandro asked, a question that he'd already answered for himself.

"You've got that right. We'll handle all the shit like the invites, the food, booze, and entertainment. Money is no object; I really want to blow his mind with this party.

"By the way, what did you want to tell me?"

"Oh it was nothing, it can wait until later," Roberto blurted out before Alejandro had a chance to respond.

"Okay fellas, I'm outta here. Give me a call in three hours. I'll tell you where I am and we can hook up to talk about the details," Jimmy offered.

"You got it, see ya later," Alejandro said smiling as he closed the door behind Jimmy and his men. He then turned around to confront his brother, "why didn't you tell him that we're quitting?"

"Because we're not quitting now," Roberto insisted.

"What the hell are you talking about?" Alejandro asked looking confused.

"Like I said, we're not quitting or at least not until the party's over," Roberto declared.

"Why not? What does Fernandez's party have to do with us?" By now, Alejandro was becoming extremely annoyed with his brother. Roberto you was the one who wanted to get out of the organization in the first place, why the sudden change of heart?

"We're going to kill Fernandez for murdering our father," Roberto commanded. "And we're going to do it at the party. Do you understand now?"

*****

As she laid comatose in the hospital, she could not see or feel anything. Candice was in a trance. In fact, the only thing she could do was hear that the surrounding voice sounded like Alex.

*"Candice I am so fuckin sorry," Alex Sanchez cried.*

*"This is all my fault." As he patted her forehead with a wet cloth he continued to cry out, "You were like my little angel and I did nothing to protect you from all the bullshit."*

*Candice remained still as Alex began stroking her hair. She knew she was in some type of hospital room but had no idea how she got there or why she was brought there in the first place. As she listened to the confessions of the man kneeling at her bedside, she actually felt sorry for him. Even though she felt a strong connection to Alex she also felt like she was being called to someplace else. Was she ready to die yet? Not as far as she knew, so she focused on her lover's words and made a silent commitment to continue living.*

*"I know that you haven't been perfect, but it wasn't your fault. You've been through so much, dealing with fuckin' people like me all the time. You deserve a much better life than the shit I've given you."*

*Alex tried fiercely to hold back his tears but they soon erupted and came streaming down his face. He then looked up to the ceiling and closed his eyes.*

*"God if you let Candice survive this shit, sorry for cursing but it's been a long time since I've spoken to you, I promise to stay out of her life for good. I will let her go, so she can enjoy the kind of life that someone like her deserves," Alex pleaded. "I swear it."*

*After ending his prayer, Alex began to bawl uncontrollably. He realized that if by some miracle she did make it, he still*

***would be forced to give her up. He then clutched her hand as if it was for the last time and bid her farewell.***

Cynthia suddenly woke up. She was in her bed in Baltimore not in some intensive care unit. She wondered if it all was just a dream or some distant memory. Although Cynthia wasn't a spiritual person, she did realize that what happened to her could not be easily explained through some scientific theory. It all seemed so real and she could still feel Alex's presence.

To most outsiders, Cynthia's marriage to Alex must have looked like a complete disaster. They were two people who appeared to have nothing in common and they fought constantly. On the other hand, there were moments where the two of them did click. In some strange sort of a way, they had a mutual respect for each other and genuinely enjoyed swapping adventure stories.

Cynthia was one tough cookie, she knew how to handle herself and Alex appreciated that quality. It was her cool exterior and inner toughness that Alex found irresistible in the first place. He knew that he could never be attracted to any woman that would let him push her around.

As far as Cynthia was concerned, she knew that Alex loved her deeply and at the time that was enough. She realized he was incapable of showing love in a typical way, just as she was unable to receive love without putting up her defenses. She also realized their relationship was destructive. The truth of the matter was, each of them needed someone who could apply the brakes in their fast and wild lifestyles. As long as they remained a couple, disaster was sure to follow.

For a long time, Cynthia felt guilty thinking about Alex. His outlandish behavior reminded her of a turbulent time in her life. Although Alex was definitely one of the most memorable characters in her life, she still didn't think that was a good enough reason to spend a large portion of her time thinking about him. The past was the past and in her opinion it was time to move on.

Now, Cynthia was totally in love with Jack. Until recently, she didn't realize how much she cared for him. Her love for Jack was far greater than her love for Alex. Her relationship with Jack was based on honesty and trust, they left the drama for the real actors and actresses. She loved everything about him.

Somehow Cynthia believed her recent dream was a sign from Alex telling her it was okay to go on with her life and put the memories they shared behind her. Just as Alex had bid her farewell, it was time for her to set him free as well. Now, Cynthia felt she could give herself totally to Jack with no more reservations. As she laid her head back on the pillow, a single teardrop streamed down her face. She didn't know this for sure, but she had a strong feeling that Alex would no longer be appearing in her dreams.

*****

After a Council meeting in Downtown Bolivia, Fernandez invited Eva to a private meeting in his office.

"I think that the Council has complete faith in you. Last quarters numbers were really good," Eva complimented.

"That has a lot to do with what's going on in New York. Our guy Jimmy did a helluva job for us. New York is now our fastest growing market," Fernandez proudly responded.

"Initially, the Council followed you because they feared you, but now they have complete trust in your abilities," Eva assured.

"I knew it would be just a matter of time before I bounced back, but enough about business. Let's talk about us," Fernandez said while looking at Eva directly.

"What about us?"

"Do you know how hard it is for me to concentrate on things when you're so close to me?" Fernandez whispered as he grabbed Eva by the waist and pulled her closer to him.

"Hmmm, now you have an idea of how I have been feeling all of these years." At that moment, they both looked at each other and broke into wide smiles.

It was only days ago that Fernandez approached Eva and told her of his feelings. It was a big surprise to him, when he found out that she was in love with him too. At that time, Eva then revealed the depth of her feelings for Fernandez. She confessed that she was in love with him from the first moment they met. Each time they spoke about business, her longing for him intensified. When Fernandez was sentenced to jail, Eva became somewhat of a recluse as she patiently waited for his release.

When Fernandez was finally freed, Eva had lost the courage to confront him with her feelings. She expected him to return to his wife and pick up where he left off. She settled for just being around him and did not want to jeopardize their friendship or lose her job by revealing her true feelings. But now that she knew the feelings were mutual, everything was different.

"Eva my dear, why don't we take the rest of the afternoon off and go somewhere alone. I know a nice Chateau a few miles from here. We would have complete privacy," Fernandez suggested.

"I thought we both agreed that we would begin our relationship in Miami," Eva reminded. "I want us to have a fresh start.

"But I don't know how much longer I can wait. I want you like I've never wanted anyone else," Fernandez said as he gently kissed her on the lips.

"I know, I know. I've felt that same way about you for years. But if we've waited all these years, what's two more weeks?"

"It seems like a lifetime away," Fernandez disappointedly responded.

"No, look at it as the beginning of our new lifetime together," Eva smiled. "I promise you it's worth waiting for."

The side door opened swiftly and Victor entered. Fernandez and Eva stood in the center of the room in a tight embrace. It didn't faze Victor one bit. In fact, very few things in life did.

"Mr. Fernandez it's time for us to leave," Victor announced.

"Okay Victor, we'll meet you outside shortly." Fernandez replied.

Victor exited the room as quickly as he entered it. He was on his way to inspect the cars to ensure Fernandez's safety.

"I've known Victor for years now and I still don't know if he likes me," Eva commented as Victor departed.

"Don't worry about whether Victor likes you or not. He respects you and that's much more important," Fernandez answered.

"Victor is so serious," Eva complained as she ran her fingers through Fernandez's hair. "Doesn't he ever let his guard down?"

"I hope not," Fernandez laughed. "That's probably why I'm still alive today. That's what I love about him. For as long as I've known him, and that's close to twenty years, he's always taken care of business."

Fernandez was right about that. Victor Castillo always focused on business because he had but no other choice. He grew up in La Paz, the capital of Bolivia. There, he lived with his parents and watched them struggle to pay the bills.

Victor's father, Domingo, worked odd jobs throughout the years. He did everything from working in the fields to working on cars. When Domingo wasn't working, his main hobby was beating up on Victor's mother Maria Castillo.

Maria was a small woman. She was known for her cooking and dancing. Victor still remembered when she took him by the arm and danced with him around the house. Even though they were very poor, Maria always found ways to entertain her only child.

Domingo's entrance often put a damper on Maria's delightful mood. Although she tried her best to ensure that everything in the small, cramped apartment was in its place, Domingo managed to find faults. It would often start with a minor complaint that would escalate into a full-blown fight. Domingo's angry screams would be followed by solid hits to Maria's face and body.

The chaotic household was taking a big toll on Victor, and he responded by refusing to speak. A couple of times Maria saved up enough money to take Victor to a doctor to have him evaluated and they concluded that he was probably grossly retarded and would never talk. Maria knew the doctors were wrong. She figured that her son was reacting to all of the abuse in the household.

To save her son, Maria often considered taking Victor and running away, but at that time, abandoning a husband was unheard of. Maria married Domingo at a very early age and he was the only man that she knew. Despite the beatings, she chose to stay by her husband's side because she didn't know how she'd ever live without him.

As Victor got older, the beatings became more frequent and severe. Not only did Domingo continue hitting Maria, he also beat up on Victor who he blamed because Maria couldn't have anymore children. He never realized that her infertility was a result of his abuse. Domingo was also ashamed of his son, who was still not talking. Maria often intervened on Victor's behalf but would then become the target of Domingo's rage. He would beat her up until he passed out from one of his drunken stupor.

One day Domingo came home drunk from work and began to throw Maria around the house. Usually Maria wept silently when Domingo beat her, but this time she cried out in pain. Victor ran into their bedroom and yelled for his father to stop beating her. This was the very first time his parents had ever heard his voice and they turned around in shock. In response, Domingo did the only thing that he knew how, he raced outside to the nearest bar and drank some more. Maria grabbed Victor and pulled him closer to her with tears running down her swollen face. "Thank you for coming to my rescue," she cried.

Now that Domingo knew that Victor would try to come to Maria's defense he became even more agitated. Domingo would often drag Victor and his mother into the living room and threaten them both with his shotgun. Every time Domingo struck, he vowed to seek revenge.

When Victor was fourteen, he obtained a job working in the fields. When he got paid, he was forced to give his entire paycheck to his father. Maria had to scrape up the money she had saved for grocery shopping, just to give Victor money for bus fare and lunch. One day after returning from a hard day at work, Victor walked into the apartment to find his mother putting ice on yet another black eye and swollen lip.

"Enough is enough!" Victor called out as he walked into his parent's bedroom to find his father knocked out from the alcohol. Victor went into the closet and snatched his father's shotgun. He then went over to his father and placed the barrel right to his father's head. Tears streamed down his face as he contemplated whether he should blast his father's head off.

The cold metal that was placed by his father's forehead immediately awoke Domingo from his deep sleep. He wasn't positive, but he believed that his son was standing over him with a gun.

"Boy have you lost your God damn mind?" his father yelled.

"What the hell are you doing?"

"Please Victor don't do it," his mother pleaded after rushing in the midst of this wild scene. "That man is your father."

"But we'll be better off without him!" Victor yelled back.

"No my son, this would be wrong!" She continued to plead.

"He is my husband and your father."

"Maria, don't let the kid fool you," Domingo said confidently. "He'd never do it."

"Get up you drunk bastard!" Victor ordered.

"Didn't I tell you to never touch that shotgun. I'm going to beat your ass good for this one," Domingo growled as he rose from his bed.

"No, you're not!" Victor screamed as he raised the shotgun once again in Domingo's direction. "I am sorry Mama, please forgive me."

"Son no! Please don't!" Maria screamed.

But it was too late. The blast hit Domingo directly in the face, killing him instantly. The kick from the shotgun sent Victor whirling to the ground. Victor got up and took his mother by the hand and escorted her out of the room. Later, they told the authorities that a bandit had come in and killed Domingo. The police did not believe their story but since they had no witnesses the case was not investigated any further.

When Victor realized his father was out of their lives for good he felt relieved. He only wished that he had killed his father a lot sooner. Now that his father was gone, he immediately assumed the role as man of the house and promised to provide his mother with the life that he thought she deserved.

The morning after the funeral, Victor decided to surprise his mother with breakfast in bed. But she surprised him. When he entered her bedroom, he found his mother hanging from a rope. In a suicide note, she explained how guilty she felt because she failed to save Victor from the abuse. She also described how she had failed as a good wife. Although, she didn't blame Victor for shooting his father, she did wish things could've turned out differently. While she admitted that Domingo was a terrible husband and father, he was her life. From as early as she could remember, she was groomed to be a good wife and mother. Now with Domingo gone and Victor almost grown there was nothing else left for her to live for. She told him that he was smart enough now to make it on his own. She ended the letter by saying that she was very sorry and loved him deeply.

"But I don't want to make it on my own," Victor wept as he tried to focus on the crumbled page. "I want to make it with you around."

For the next two days, Victor stayed with his dead mother in her bedroom. He then finally buried her himself and left La Paz for another city in Bolivia.

At the age of fifteen he joined the Bolivian underworld and quickly made a name for himself. He was a freelance killer until he met Fernandez and became a member of the Organization.

After working for Fernandez for many years, he was called the Assassin. A sawed off shotgun and dark shades became his trademark. Anyone who double-crossed Fernandez had to deal with him.

From their very first encounter together, there was an instant bond between the two men. Fernandez understood Victor and never tried to change him or invade his privacy. Over time, Victor viewed Fernandez as the only true friend that he had and the Organization was the closest thing to family that he knew of.

Victor dated women from time to time, but as soon as he felt they were getting too close to him he dropped them. He never drank, smoke, or even uttered a curse word. His only bad habit aside from murdering of course, was gambling. Although he wasn't addicted to it, it was the only thing he could think of to do with all the money that Fernandez paid him.

Most people thought that Victor the Assassin was invincible, but he knew better. Victor believed his days were numbered and was waiting patiently for the day when he would die of a violent death like so many of the people that he had killed. In spite of this, he had no regrets for the killings and felt that each of them were evil men who had it coming to them.

Victor was an excellent marksman, who enjoyed shooting people. Every time he had a target, it was like killing his father all over again. Nothing could stop him.

# Chapter 27

"Well in two more days this whole thing will finally be over," Roberto said.

"Be quiet, I'm trying to watch the end of this movie," Alejandro snapped. His body was turned in the direction of the TV but he couldn't tell you what it was about if you asked him. In all honesty, he had been too consumed in his thoughts about dealing with Fernandez on Saturday night.

"You know this reminds me of when we were younger and living with Mama'," Roberto recalled. "We would stay up all night watching TV

"You mean I would be trying to watch the TV and you'd be too busy talking through the show," Alejandro responded.

"Alejandro, do you think we are doing the right thing?"

"What kind of question is that? Hell yeah. Remember this is the same guy who had our father killed," Alejandro reminded.

"I know you don't like to hear this, but our father was no saint. Maybe he had it coming to him," Roberto suggested.

"Roberto, are you trying to flip the script or what? This whole thing was your idea, remember?"

"Yeah, I know, but..."

"But what?" Alejandro interrupted. "Look, our father was no saint but nobody deserves to die the way he did. Anyway, after all of the lives Fernandez destroyed, he deserves to be taken out too."

"Do you think that we can pull it off?" Roberto asked nervously.

"Of course, just follow our plan carefully," Alejandro insisted. "There are only a few people who know that mansion as well as we do. We've been back there three times since Jimmy first showed it to us.

"But you know how much security that's going to be around."

"They're going to be guarding the grounds and all around the house. Few guards will actually be placed inside the house. That's why we have to try to be alone with Fernandez on the third floor. By the time people discover his body, we will be back in the crowd or outta there."

"Don't forget to go to the bank tomorrow morning to withdraw everything that you have," Roberto reminded. "We might have to leave the city that night.

"Roberto do you think that our father would have liked us if he was still alive?" Alejandro asked.

From all the things that Cynthia told me about him, he was dying to have kids. Yeah I think that he would have liked us. But the real question is, would we have liked him?"

"Of course, he's our father," Alejandro answered, not sounding too sure himself. "We're his blood."

A deep silence covered the room.

"Since we're talking about a whole lot of past stuff, Roberto I must admit that there were times when I was jealous of you. I mean between the two of us, you were always smarter," Alejandro admitted.

"I was never smarter than you Alejandro, I just took school a little bit more serious."

"Well, I eventually got over that and realized that it wouldn't have been fair to be the best looking and smartest one too," Alejandro said as he launched his pillow at Roberto.

"Better looking one? Bro' I suggest you look in the mirror. We are exactly alike. From our hair to our banged up pinkie toes."

"I guess you forgot about the tattoo," Alejandro reminded. Roberto stood up and looked at his right shoulder in the mirror. "You know I wish I never would have gotten this damn thing."

"I bet you still blame me, after all of these years," Alejandro laughed.

"Why are you laughing?" Roberto asked.

"Because back then, you were really gullible but don't worry, you've come a long way," Alejandro said.

Roberto suddenly looked very serious at his brother.

"Alejandro, what if we don't make it?"

"Don't worry, I'm not going to let anything happen to you. We just have to watch each other's back when the shit starts to hit the fan," Alejandro said.

"Well, just in case we don't make it. I want to tell you that I'm sorry for some of the terrible things that I said to you a few weeks ago. I guess I was jealous of how close you were getting with Jimmy," Roberto admitted.

"No sweat, I knew you didn't mean those things, I was surprised that you thought anybody could come between us,"

"For a while, you and Jimmy were pretty tight. Plus, you do have a lot of things in common. After all, both of you have that wild streak in you," Roberto winked.

"Yeah all of that may be true. Me and Jimmy are still really cool with each other, but you're my twin, my other half. There isn't anything in this world that I wouldn't do for you and I know you would do anything for me," Alejandro smiled. "So please Roberto, don't ever forget that I love you."

"Alejandro you are a great brother and I love you too," Roberto said as he gave his brother a tight hug.

"Okay now cut out the mushy stuff and let's get to bed. We both have to wake up early in the morning," Alejandro directed.

And just like they used to do when they were younger, they brought blankets into the living room and camped out on the floor. Each prayed silently, that everything was going to turn out okay.

"Alejandro, you asleep yet?" Roberto whispered.

"Almost, why?" Alejandro asked.

"I just thought. What if Jimmy gets in the way of us killing Fernandez?"

After briefly thinking about the possibilities, Alejandro blurted out, "I guess we'd have to take him out too."

*****

“Hello, Kate?”

“Yes?”

“What’s going on? This is Jack.”

“Oh my god, do they really have phones in DC?”

“Stop kidding. It hasn’t been that long,” Jack laughed.

“I haven’t spoken to you in three months and I’ve left messages all over town for you. If it weren’t for my phone conversations with Bobby’s wife Virginia, I wouldn’t know how you were doing.” Kate complained.

“Sis, I’ve been really busy. In fact most of the time, I’ve been working in Miami,” Jack explained.

“You know I don’t like it when you are out there. You remember all of the mess that you got into before.”

“I remember Sis, but this time we are real close to hitting it big. I can just feel it.”

“You and your instincts. Well what else have you been up to?” she asked.

“Virginia probably already told you, but I’ll say it again. Cynthia and I are getting pretty serious.”

“Do you think she’s the one?” she asked.

“Kate, I know she’s the one for me,” Jack said confidently.

So, when are we going to finally meet her?”

“As soon as I get some free time, we’ll come out to the coast and check you out in San Diego. I know the kids must be really big now.”

“Jack they are so big that you probably wouldn’t even recognize them.”

“Kate, I really miss you and the kids and can’t wait to see you. It’ll be good hanging out with family and I know you’re gonna love Cynthia. She’s a sweetheart,” Jack said.

“Well she better be a real winner, if she’s gonna be with my brother,” she said.

“I gotta go now, but I’ll see you real soon,” Jack promised.

Telephone talks with big brother Jack always made Kate feel good. She worried about him because he spent so much time by himself. Growing up it was different. Jack was their parents’ favorite and in their eyes, he could do no wrong. He was an excellent student, good looking, and had tons of friends. He also had a great sense of humor and that's what Kate loved most about her brother.

There was never a problem of jealousy because Kate admired Jack as much as everyone else did. Besides, Kate was the only girl in the family so she got more than her share of attention.

Things changed dramatically when both of their parents died over a three-year span. Although they were both grown at the time, they were devastated. Jack was hit the hardest but often tried to hide it. Kate thought she could put everything behind her after she got married and started a family of her own.

Kate was successful, but Jack became a recluse. He distanced himself from most of his childhood friends and eventually moved away. He claimed it was because of his work, but Kate knew he wanted to get away from many of his childhood memories. Jack even avoided her because she resembled their mother so much.

Now, Kate believed that Jack had finally found someone to bring him alive again. If Jack's new girlfriend already had this affect on her brother, Kate concluded that Cynthia had to be pretty special. She couldn't wait for Jack to get married and start a family of his own. She thought that was exactly what he needed to return to the old Jack that she grew up with.

*****

"Jack, this restaurant is lovely."

"I drove pass it one day and thought that you might like it."

"This place is so romantic. The music, the atmosphere, everything is perfect here."

"You know Cynthia, there is nothing in the world that I wouldn't do for you," Jack said as he smiled widely. "And I really appreciate every time you fly down to Miami to spend the weekend with me. It would be extremely lonely without you."

"I'm not just doing it for you. There is no other person that I would rather be with on a Saturday night," Cynthia said as she kissed Jack's hand. "You mustn't forget that."

"As they sipped their wine, Jack and Cynthia looked into each other's eyes.

"Cynthia I know I haven't been giving you the attention that you deserve lately, but I promise you, once all of this stuff in Miami is wrapped up –it's going to be all about us."

"Jack, don't worry. I know you love me, just like I hope you know I love you," Cynthia said as she planted a soft kiss on Jack's lips.

"Now tomorrow, I am going to be busy most of the day," Jack admitted. "But I will find some time to be with you, I promise."

"There you go again. I am a big girl. There's plenty of things that I can do tomorrow," Cynthia insisted. "I'll be fine."

After all the time that Cynthia spent with Jack, she had never told him the full story surrounding the twins. All Jack knew was that they were the children of one of Cynthia's old friends. She felt guilty about keeping this secret from him, but knew it would only cause him to become alarmed.

For some strange reason, she couldn't get her mind off of them. She had just spoken to Roberto and he filled her in on everything, including their plans to kill Fernandez. Although she tried to talk him out of taking revenge on Fernandez, it was no use. The boys had made up their minds and there was nothing more that she could say or do over the phone. That's why on this trip she planned to personally talk them out of attacking Fernandez because she knew they wouldn't stand a chance. She'd ran with men like Fernandez most of her life and they ate young guys like Roberto and Alejandro for breakfast.

"Cynthia, there is something very important that I must tell you, " Jack nervously stuttered.

"What's wrong, you look upset?" She said.

"I was going to wait until after dinner but I can hear my own heartbeat pounding in my ears."

"What is it?" Cynthia asked anxiously.

"Cynthia, you know I love you," Jack began as he looked deeply into his woman's eyes.

"Yes, and I love you too," Cynthia replied.

"We both get along great and when we're not together it drives me crazy," Jack confessed.

"Yes I know," Cynthia said smiling, until the moment was interrupted by a beeping sound. "Honey wait a minute, my pager went off."

Cynthia that can wait," Jack said as he took the microphone from the maitre d', I guess what I'm really trying to tell you is that I love you and I want to spend the rest of my life with you."

"Cynthia looked up from her pager and watched Jack stoop down on one knee in the middle of the crowded restaurant.

"Jack, what are you doing?" Cynthia said nervously.

Jack went into his pocket and removed a velvet box. When he opened it, an exquisite diamond ring peaked out. "Cynthia Hancock will you marry me?"

The surrounding patrons began clapping and cheering, "Say yes! Say yes!"

Cynthia was trembling with wild excitement, "Jack, of course I will marry you. I've been waiting for someone like you my entire life."

The newly engage couple spent the next hour holding hands over dinner. They ate and chatted about their future lives together.

Towards the end of their meal, the waiter came over to the table and told Jack about an urgent telephone call. He figured that it had to be someone from work since they were the only ones he'd told about dinner. In an effort to create a perfect evening, Jack left his cellular phone at the hotel.

While Jack was gone, Cynthia was beeped again. She raced to the pay phone to call the number, it was Roberto. He and his brother had decided to continue their plans to kill Fernandez that night during the party at the mansion. Although Cynthia tried to convince him from doing it once again, Roberto told her that their decision was final.

"Listen Roberto, you can't be serious. You are going to get yourselves killed," Cynthia cried. She quickly lowered her voice after realizing that she was talking too loud. "Please don't do this."

"It's just the chance we're going to take."

With an exasperated look on her face, Cynthia tried to dissuade Roberto one last time, "You don't have to do anything. You can just walk away from it all."

"Cynthia you don't understand. This man killed our father, we must do something to avenge that," Roberto insisted.

"Roberto you didn't even know your father," she said. "He's really not worth it."

"Maybe we would have gotten to know him if he wasn't murdered. Who knows? Maybe we all could've been tight right now had my father still been alive," Roberto said sadly.

"You gotta give up these fantasies about your father. I was married to the man and while I did love him and sometimes miss him, the bottom line was that he was a drug dealer. He hurt a lot of people selling the stuff. Try and remember that," Cynthia strongly suggested.

Roberto was beginning to regret calling Cynthia. "I already know all of the stuff that you're saying, and I've thought about it a lot. But it still doesn't change the fact that Fernandez is the guy that had my father killed- and that's the bottom line."

"Roberto, lets say that you do kill Fernandez, then what? Do you think that his men will let you just walk out of there without doing anything about it?" she asked.

"Don't worry we have a game plan. We'll be fine."

"It sounds like you're determined to do this," Cynthia sighed.

"Yes we are. We want to see Fernandez dead," Roberto responded back.

"Well let's do this another day when we can all sit down and discuss this to make sure that it will work," Cynthia boldly suggested in hopes of delaying their plans. She was prepared to say just about anything.

"Sorry, but we can't do that. We have no idea when Fernandez will return to the United States. So, we need to take advantage of this opportunity, now."

Speaking loudly again into the phone. "An opportunity to get you killed. Roberto I thought you were smarter than this, you and Alejandro. What about the dreams you told me you had? What about the letters you wrote to me? Was that somebody else? You spoke of finding true happiness, please don't do this," Cynthia begged.

"Cynthia no matter what you say, this is something that we must do. I just wanted to thank you for everything that you've done for me and I wanted to tell you something that I never had the courage to tell you before," there was long pause on the phone. "I love you very much," he said.

"Roberto I love you too. You've become a part of my family," Cynthia wept.

"Cynthia, promise me that if me and Alejandro don't make it back, you'll contact Sister Catherine and tell her that we tried to get out, but we were not successful," Roberto added.

"Roberto stay right where you are, I am coming right over there to talk with you," Cynthia said desperately.

With a sudden calm in his voice, Roberto whispered, "Be happy Cynthia. Good bye."

"Roberto you don't have to do this! It's not too late to change your mind!" In the middle of Cynthia's frantic pleas, she heard the phone go dead. Roberto had hung up.

Cynthia got off the phone feeling very helpless. She knew the twins didn't stand a chance against Fernandez and all of his men and decided there was only one thing that she could do. She returned to the table and spotted Jack on the way back from his phone call.

"Honey something just came up, I must leave right now." Jack said hurriedly. "I am so sorry."

"That's okay. There is something that I have to take care of now too," she replied.

"Honey do you mind catching a cab back to the hotel?" Jack reluctantly asked.

"No it's not a problem," she said.

"Well look, I have a feeling that all of this work is going to be all over real soon. So just hang in there with me."

"Jack no matter what, I also want you to know that I love you dearly and don't you ever forget that," Cynthia said tearfully.

Jack paid the bill and hugged Cynthia tightly. Although, the couple had hugged numerous times in the past, this embrace was different. Without saying it in words, they both clung tightly to the other like it would be their last time in each other's arms.

"Love you," Cynthia whispered.

"Love you too!" Jack shouted as he ran across the street to his car.

After hopping in a cab, Cynthia quickly made up a list of things that she had to do on a napkin from the restaurant.

*****

Jack raced through the streets of Miami towards DEA Headquarters. He had just been told that Fernandez was back in town and Jack wanted to be sure that he wouldn't miss the opportunity to get him this time. When he arrived at his office, he found an address taped to his computer monitor. The source told his office that there was going to be a large party tonight that was in Fernandez's honor.

Jack knew he had to act fast so he ordered a layout of the property from his car. He also asked his chief to send him twenty-five of the best men they had available.

"So, Fernandez is having a party," Jack thought. "I guess since I wasn't invited, I'm just going to have to crash it."

# Chapter 28

Roberto nervously paced up and down the hallway in the apartment as he repeatedly glanced at his watch. He wondered what was taking Alejandro so long and then began to suspect the worse. Did Fernandez or Jimmy somehow find out about their plot to kill Fernandez? Or was Alejandro at some Police Station being questioned about the deaths of Juan or Hector?

The only person that he'd told about their plot to kill Fernandez was Cynthia and he trusted her with his life. Of course he had no way of knowing whether Alejandro opened his mouth to anyone.

"Worrying now is not going to do any good," he thought.

As much as he tried to maintain his composure, Roberto could not relax. He picked up the telephone to tell Jimmy that they might be running a little late when he suddenly heard the keys jingling in the front door.

"Where in the hell have you been?" Roberto shouted.

"I had to take care of some business," Alejandro said as he laid his duffel bag on the floor.

"Business?" Roberto asked as he slammed the phone receiver back down on the table. "What was her name?"

"I wasn't out there getting laid," Alejandro said proudly.

"Anyway, I gotta show you something."

Roberto looked down at Alejandro's rather large duffel bag and decided it was not the time to exchange gifts. "Whatever you have to show me can wait for later," Roberto advised. "We gotta go over the plans one more time before we leave."

"Are you sure, you're really gonna like this one?" Alejandro said while displaying a devilish grin.

"Do you wanna back out at the last minute?" Roberto questioned.

"Of course I don't, Fernandez's ass is going down tonight!"

"Then, we better leave right now. I don't want us to get there late, it might cause them to get suspicious," a nervous Roberto stammered.

"Roberto, you're right, we better leave now. We can go over the plans one last time in the car."

*****

"Jimmy you've done a fine job with the house. All of my little details have been carried out and I'm quite pleased," Fernandez complimented. "This party also shows that you can handle anything, even on such short notice."

"Thank you Mr. Fernandez, but I had a lot of help in getting it all together," Jimmy admitted.

"Jimmy don't be so modest," Eva said clung closely to Fernandez "Are we having any more problems in New York?" Fernandez interjected even though he had promised not to discuss business during the evening.

"No, everything is under control. But once again, I can't take all of the credit for that either. You see those twins over there? They've helped me tremendously," Jimmy said as he tried to get their attention from across the room.

Roberto and Alejandro walked across the grounds towards Jimmy, Fernandez, and Eva.

"Mr. Fernandez, I want you to meet my right hand guys, Roberto and Alejandro," Jimmy said proudly.

"Hello guys. I've heard a lot of good things about you," Fernandez said as he gripped each of their hands for a handshake.

"These guys right here help me handle most of my problems. Alejandro was the one who went with me to New York," Jimmy boasted.

"Well look, keep up the good work. And who knows, soon you will be able to buy a house like this one," Fernandez smiled.

"Nice to meet you, Mr. Fernandez." Roberto said as he and his brother began walking away.

"They seem awfully young, Jimmy." Eva commented.

"They are young but they act like men twice their age. I would trust them with my life," Jimmy confessed.

As Roberto and Alejandro walked away, Fernandez stared intensely in their direction. Not only were they strikingly handsome, but there was something very familiar about them. The way that they walked and even the little subtle gestures. Fernandez could not put his finger on it yet, but with his excellent memory, he would soon figure it out.

The twins trembled in Fernandez's presence. If only talking to the man made them that nervous they wondered how they were ever going to kill him. There was something about Fernandez that intimidated most people. His eyes gave you the impression that he knew exactly what you were thinking, and sometimes he did.

Back at DEA Headquarters, Jack and his team began to suit up. They planned to raid the mansion in four hours and were reviewing all of the possibilities. Hours earlier, a scouting team was sent to check out the mansion and gather information. They found out how many guests were expected to show up, how much security was in place, and how accessible Fernandez would be.

"Jack are you sure that twenty five guys will be enough to bring a guy like Fernandez down?" Bobby Coleman inquired in a concerned voice.

"You heard what the scouting team said, they only have ten to twelve security personnel on site. We can certainly handle that," Jack said confidently.

"What about the attendees?" Bobby asked. "They might be armed too."

"That's why we are going to wait until the party is almost over before we attack."

"Look Jack, I just don't want anything to go wrong," Bobby said.

"Bobby, I didn't know that you cared," Jack teased.

"Jack this is a very dangerous guy and this may be the last time that we ever have a chance to track him down," Bobby said.

"That's why we have to go in with a small team," Jack responded. "Anything larger than twenty five men might tip him off. Besides, Fernandez doesn't have his regular team with him anyway. He's just planning to drop into Miami, party his ass off, and rush back to Bolivia- just like he did last time."

"Well look let's go over the plans one more time," Bobby ordered. He raised his voice to get the attention of the other agents in the room. "Remember these are not the exact plans to the mansion, we couldn't get them on such short notice. There have been some recent renovations but we're hoping that they couldn't have made too many changes in the past six months."

*****

It was now ten o'clock at night and the party was in high gear. Jimmy promised Fernandez that he would keep the festivities nice and simple. By eight o'clock, about a hundred people arrived just as Jimmy had planned. By midnight, he hoped the party would be winding down. Although Jimmy believed that four hours was a short time for a major blast, he also knew the guests would leave satisfied. After all, they would receive as much shrimp, lobster and steak they could eat. The champagne was plentiful too.

In a room adjacent to the ballroom, there was the best coke that Miami had to offer. Jimmy invited some of his friends from the old neighborhood as well as his employees. A few of the beautiful people from Disco Inferno came as well as a few of the folks from the other clubs he frequented. If it was up to Jimmy, he would have started the party at midnight and continued until dawn, but Fernandez called the shots. After midnight, Fernandez knew he would be feeling bored and restless. He also wanted to reserve that time for his close friends.

Jimmy put Raul Martinez in complete charge of security. It was his job to make sure that Mr. Fernandez and his people were well protected. He and his crew ensured that no one ventured off to the second or third floors of the mansion, because they were off limits to all guests. Also, the party was by invitation only. The guards were at each of the entrances to ensure there were no surprise visitors.

"Raul, Jimmy sure knows how to throw a good party," Carlos said smiling. "Look at all of the nice looking babes."

"Yeah things are looking pretty good. But remember you're here to work. Make sure everybody is checked out because I don't want any problems tonight," Raul ordered. "I mean it."

"Raul chatted with the guards at the main entrance when he noticed a mysterious man entering from a side door. He quickly tried to blend in with the crowd, even though he didn't say a word or make eye contact with anyone.

"Are you sure he's okay? He gives me the creeps." Carlos admitted.

"Jimmy told me that he's one of Fernandez's guys from Bolivia. From what I heard, he has complete run of the place. Shit, he can go places in the mansion that I can't," Raul confessed. "I think his name is Victor but I've heard most people call him the Assassin."

"Excuse me lady, what was your name again?" the guard asked.

"It's Cindy," she said firmly.

"Well I don't see your name on the list. Who invited you?"

"One of Jimmy's friends. He told me it would be all right with Jimmy," she said.

"Believe me, I'm clean."

"What was the guy's name?" the guard asked in an interrogating tone. Now, Cynthia found herself in a very uncomfortable situation. She didn't think security would be as tight as it was and didn't have enough information to come up with another lie. She hoped her sexy blond wig and revealing outfit would be enough to get her inside but it was clear that this guard wouldn't budge. Should she press her luck? One thing was for sure, if the guard decided to search her. He would easily find the automatic handgun in her purse.

"I heard the commotion over here, what seems to be the problem?" Alejandro inquired.

"This lady is not on the guest list even though she insists that someone invited her," the guard said sharply.

"Well, she's right about that. She's a guest of mine," Alejandro said convincingly. "She's cool."

"If you say you invited her, then that's fine with me, Alejandro. Sorry about that," the guard apologized as he extended his hand towards her for a handshake. "By the way, what was your name again?"

"It's Cindy," Cynthia smiled as she shook the guard's hand firmly.

"Come on Cindy, I want to introduce you to some people," Alejandro said as he grabbed her by the arm.

They slowly strolled towards the pool area where the guests were at their networking best.

"What in the hell are you doing?" Alejandro asked.

"That's the same thing that I wanted to ask you!"

"Cynthia, I know what I am doing here. You're the one that doesn't belong here. If I hadn't come along to save your butt, who knows what kind of trouble you would be in now."

"Do you really know what you're doing?" Cynthia snapped.

"I don't think so. There is no way in the world that you and Roberto really believe you can get away with killing Fernandez. Just look around you, there are guards everywhere. Even if you get lucky enough to kill him, you would never get out of here alive."

"You don't know that for sure. Why don't you just go back to Baltimore and stay the hell out of our business," Alejandro demanded.

"Alejandro, I know more about this business than you do. This is not some game you are playing, these guys are for real," Cynthia argued.

"Don't you think that I know that? I'm not some little kid playing cops and robbers out here. I know that I may not make it outta here alive."

"What about Roberto? Are you both willing to sacrifice your lives for a drug dealer?"

"Cynthia look don't try and change our minds. We thought about this long and hard. We're not about to change our minds now. So please, just get out of here before things get started," Alejandro advised.

"I came here because of you two and I am not going to leave without you," Cynthia insisted.

Just then, the two of them heard a familiar voice. “Oh my God, Cynthia what are you doing here?” Roberto asked urgently.

“You shouldn’t have come here.”

“I was trying to talk some sense into your brother. Maybe I will have better luck with you.”

“Forget about it Cynthia, we’re not changing our minds,” Roberto responded.

“That’s the same thing that I told her.”

“Now why don’t you go home, you might get hurt! Roberto prodded.

“Look, I love you guys too much to see you get hurt. If I can’t stop you, let me at least help you?” Cynthia desperately asked.

“Cynthia no disrespect, but what could you do?” Alejandro inquired.

“I have a fully loaded .45 caliber automatic weapon in my pocketbook with two fully loaded mags,” Cynthia said.

“So what does that mean?” Alejandro quickly interjected.

“Alejandro have you ever killed anyone with a gun before?” Cynthia asked.

“No.”

“I have,” Cynthia admitted.

“Roberto, I guess she’s in,” Alejandro conceded.

“Not until you boys make me a promise,” Cynthia insisted.

“What’s that?” Roberto asked.

“You gotta promise me that after everything is over, you two are out for good. There will be no more drugs or any of this stuff in your lives,” she said.

“I promise you that,” Roberto swore. “We are definitely leaving after this”.

“Yeah Cynthia you don’t have to worry,” Alejandro added. “We’re definitely out after this one.”

“I hate drugs so much, especially after it messed up my life in the past. I promise myself that after I left the hospital I would never be caught up in this stuff again. But, if it means saving your lives, I’ll do it one more time. But guys don’t ever go back on your words,” Cynthia said sternly. “Because if you do, you won’t ever have to worry about Fernandez’s guys coming after you, you’ll have to answer to me.”

“Where is Fernandez now?” Alejandro asked.

"He's inside the house, dancing in the ballroom," Roberto answered in a hushed tone.

"How many people are always around him?" Cynthia asked.

"Only three that I can tell, his date for the evening Eva Santos, his bodyguard Dominic Quinones, and Jimmy, who sticks to him like white on rice," Roberto replied.

"I figure there's nothing we can do about Eva and his bodyguard? But I think I can find a way to get rid of Jimmy for a little while," Alejandro offered.

"When do you want to go afterFernandez?" Cynthia asked.

"It has to be soon. The party is ending in another hour and we might need the guests here as a cover to escape," Alejandro said.

Back at DEA Headquarters the men were ready for almost anything that could be thrown at them. Bobby finally convinced Jack to take another ten guys with him. That brought the total to thirty-five.

"Okay guys, quiet down. Everyone knows their assignment and where they're supposed to be?" Jack asked. The men nodded in response.

"I hope he comes along peacefully, but in the event that he doesn't, I want everyone to be extremely careful. Remember, we all have loved ones that we want to go back home to tonight." Jack took on the role of a general about to lead his men into battle.

"All right guys, it's time to rock and roll!"

Outside the men piled into various transports. The DEA even had a tank on standby as a precaution.

"Damn Jack, I wish I could go with you." Bobby said.

"Bobby you've already helped me a lot by designing the master plan to help us take Fernandez down. You've done all that you can do, so let me take it from here," Jack winked as he gave his friend a high five.

"Jack, if the shit really hits the fan, call for backup. Don't try none of that John Wayne shit."

*****

"Did I ever tell you that you were a great dancer?" Eva whispered in a seductive tone.

Fernandez looked into her eyes holding her close to him. "No, you never have."

"Well you are, just look at all of those women admiring your style. I'm almost starting to get jealous," Eva whispered.

"There's no need for that. Eva, you know you're the most beautiful woman here. Tonight I want to prove that dancing is not the only thing that I'm real good at." Fernandez took two steps backwards and began gyrating wildly. Eva laughed so hard that she thought she would nearly pass out.

"You're too much, Sergio," Eva chanted.

"You better believe it," he answered back.

The game plan was simple. Alejandro was responsible for getting Jimmy out of the way. Roberto needed to get Fernandez and his date upstairs, preferably the third floor in the left wing of the mansion. This point was furthest from where the festivities were being held. Cynthia's job was to sneak up to the second floor and take out anyone leaving from upstairs.

"Jimmy what's going on?" Alejandro asked.

"Nothing much, I'm just trying to make sure that everything is running smoothly," Jimmy replied.

"Look you threw this party and you're not even having a good time. There are honeys all over the place and you're just standing here baby-sitting Fernandez."

"They'll be plenty of time for honeys later," Jimmy responded sharply.

"Well Jimmy, the truth of the matter is that I got to talk to you and it's important," Alejandro said anxiously.

"Go ahead man. What is it?" Jimmy said in a very concerned tone.

"I can't tell you here, it's pretty private," Alejandro commented.

"Alejandro, can it wait. I really don't want to leave Fernandez," Jimmy responded.

Fernandez and Eva walking were over to them when they overheard the last bit of conversation. "Go ahead Jimmy. We'll be okay for a while," Fernandez advised. He was hoping Jimmy would leave so that he could have some privacy with his Eva.

"Okay but I'll be back shortly," Jimmy replied.

"Take your time, Eva and I are going outside for a breath of fresh air."

"But only after one more dance," Eva insisted as she escorted Fernandez back into the middle of the dance floor.

"But only after one more dance," Eva insisted as she escorted Fernandez back into the middle of the dance floor.

After feeling confident that Fernandez was in good hands, Jimmy directed Alejandro to one of the rooms upstairs. He figured he could focus all of his attention on his friend's problems. Jimmy began talking to Alejandro in the hallway on the third floor. "I must admit, lately I was starting to feel like we weren't as close as we used to be."

"Nah Jimmy, me and you are still tight," Alejandro smiled.

"That's good because you're like the brother I never had," Jimmy said sincerely. "Now, which room would you like to hang out in?"

"This one is cool."

"Now what's so urgent?" Jimmy asked.

Alejandro, who had his back to Jimmy, slowly turned around and took out his 9mm. Glock hand gun. "Jimmy, please hand me your gun," Alejandro directed.

"Alejandro stop kidding and put that gun away," Jimmy laughed.

"I'm not kidding. Just do what I told you."

"Jimmy, now in a state of disbelief, slowly removed the gun he kept tucked away in his back holster. Then he knelt down and placed it in front of him.

"Alejandro I can't believe you're doing this to me. After everything that I've done for you, this is how you repay me?" Jimmy said as the tears swelled in his eyes. "We're supposed to be boys."

"Jimmy man, you don't understand. This has nothing to do with you. I'm sorry that I'm even doing this to you. You treated Roberto and me real cool. But this is about Fernandez and I need you out of the way for a bit," Alejandro explained.

"What about Fernandez?" Jimmy cried.

"Years ago he had Alex Sanchez killed," Alejandro said sternly.

"Yeah I know, I'm the one that told you the story," Jimmy replied.

"Well, Alex Sanchez was our father and tonight Fernandez will pay with his life!" Alejandro demanded.

"Alejandro, please don't do it. Fernandez is too powerful. Anyway, you and your brother aren't killers, Jimmy warned. "You'll never get away with it."

"Well tonight, we're sure as hell gonna find out if we're killers and I say Fernandez is going down," Alejandro responded.

"Alejandro, just put down the gun and forget about it. I won't tell a soul about this and if you want to quit the biz, it's no problem. You probably already have a nice stash of cash, you're pretty set," Jimmy added.

"Sorry Jimmy, I can't do it. This isn't about money.

"So what are you going to do with me, shoot me?" Jimmy asked humbly.

"Now Jimmy, you know I can't do that. Just go over to that wall and hit that secret panel. Wait in there until everything is finished," Alejandro advised.

"Alejandro please don't do it. You'll never make it out alive."

"You're probably right, but what would you do if you were in my shoes? I bet the exact same thing," Alejandro looked at Jimmy as if it was for the final time. "Take care my friend."

"Alejandro closed the door behind Jimmy and could hear him desperately yelling for him to change his mind. Alejandro locked the door to prevent Jimmy from escaping but he did leave the panel open so that someone would eventually find him.

"This air feels wonderful Sergio," Eva said as she inhaled the fresh breeze.

"Yes it does, but having you near me feels even better. "Fernandez gently kissed Eva on the back of her neck.

"You know I could dance all night," Eva said enthusiastically. "I feel great!"

"Save your energy," Fernandez advised with a special twinkle in his eye.

"Roberto approached the embracing pair, "Excuse me, Mr. Fernandez. I just left Jimmy upstairs and he told me to come and get you."

"What does he want?" Fernandez asked impatiently. He hated being interrupted while he and Eva were sharing one of their special moments.

"I don't know, I think he has something that he wants to show you," Roberto suggested.

"Okay then lead the way my boy," Fernandez directed. "Eva why don't you wait for me right here."

"Not on your life, I'm not leaving your side tonight," Eva responded.

Roberto led Fernandez and Eva up the winding staircase near the ballroom entrance. Fernandez's bodyguard Dominic joined them. As they made their way passed the second floor, Roberto winked at Cynthia giving her the signal that everything was going smoothly. It was now up to her to make sure that they would not be disturbed. Alejandro was scheduled to meet them shortly.

*****

The door was suddenly unlocked and opened.

"What happened here?" Victor said as he looked down at a very nervous Jimmy standing in a small area in the room.

"Nothing, I made a mistake and locked myself in there," Jimmy responded.

Victor knew Jimmy was lying because the surveillance cameras showed one of the twins taking Jimmy into the dining room. Victor became suspicious when he noticed that Jimmy hadn't returned with him.

"Are you sure that everything is all right?" Victor replied.

"Yes I'm sure. I wish you would stop asking me that," Jimmy snapped.

By now, Victor knew that something was terribly wrong and believed Fernandez might be in some kind of danger. The last place that Victor saw Fernandez was outside by the pool, so he quickly left Jimmy awkwardly standing in front of the secret panel while he darted downstairs.

Jimmy was anxious to get to Fernandez because he knew that wherever Fernandez was, the twins soon would be. He dashed down the smaller staircase that led directly to the pool area.

As he rushed downstairs, he prayed he wasn't too late. Jimmy was facing a tough situation. While he knew he had to stop Alejandro and Roberto from killing Fernandez, he wondered what he would do with the twins then. Alejandro was right, if Fernandez had murdered his father he probably would have done the same thing. On the other hand, he couldn't allow the twins to murder his boss.

# Chapter 29

"We just got word from the scout team that the party is almost over and the majority of the guests have already left," DEA Reynolds told Jack.

"How many people are still around?" Jack asked.

"It's still a little hard to tell, but I would say around forty. Most of them are members of the Cartel," Reynolds responded.

"What about Fernandez?" Jack asked.

"There was a positive ID on Fernandez about ten minutes ago," Reynolds answered. "He was hanging out by the pool, but I'm not sure where he is now."

Jack sat back in one of the DEA super vans. It was equipped with the latest gadgets in surveillance and combat. It even had a couple of rockets that Jack could utilize if necessary.

Jack quickly reviewed all of the options that were at his disposal.

"So Jack what do you want to do now?" Reynolds asked.

Jack did not want to unnecessarily risk the life of his men but there was no guarantee that Fernandez would leave the house peacefully either. So, he decided that they should head towards the mansion.

"Reynolds, we're going in," Jack advised. "Relay the message to the others." Whatever the outcome, he just had to live with it. The cars, trucks, and vans headed towards the mansion which was now only a mile away. Jack hoped he wasn't letting his personal hatred for the Fernandez Cartel cloud his mind and prayed he was making the right decision. In any case, the agents were moving full speed ahead.

*****

Victor sensed major trouble in the air. Before he started on his mission to locate Fernandez, he ducked in a nearby room to get himself ready for battle. His body was filled with adrenaline because it was times like this that made Victor feel alive again. He grabbed his pair of dark sunglasses from his jacket pocket and grabbed his trusted sawed off gun that he had hidden earlier in the closet. As he emerged from the desolate room, he was transformed from Victor Castillo to the Assassin and was ready to face any challenge that came his way.

Five minutes had passed and Fernandez wondered why there was still no sign of Jimmy. They were waiting in the master bedroom and Fernandez's patience was wearing thin.

"Mr. Fernandez, I don't know what is taking Jimmy so long," Roberto explained, even though he believed Alejandro had locked him away somewhere. By now, Roberto was also becoming anxious and wondering why Alejandro hadn't made his grand entrance yet.

Sergio Fernandez had been in this business for a long time and he could spot a trap a mile away. This scenario was beginning to look like a set-up and it was becoming clear that Jimmy would probably never arrive.

As a smoke screen, Fernandez offered to make everyone a drink. Roberto, Eva and Dominic stayed in the living room, while Fernandez dipped into his private den to check out the 12" surveillance monitors. He carefully examined each screen, and at first, everything seemed normal. Then he noticed Jimmy walking around the pool area.

"Hey people, how's everybody doing?" Alejandro said as he entered the suite.

"The boss is starting to get upset. We've been waiting fifteen minutes for Jimmy," Dominic said.

"Well knowing Jimmy, if he said to meet him here, he'll be here," Alejandro replied. "He's a man of his word."

Now with all of the players in place; Alejandro and Roberto tried to position themselves so that they could drop all three of them at once.

"Maybe, we won't have to shoot Eva," Roberto thought.

"Why should she get hurt? She's only Fernandez's date for the evening."

Alejandro stood near the front door, while Roberto tried to make small conversation with Dominic at the opposite end of the room where Fernandez exited to make the drinks. As soon as Fernandez walked through the door, the ambush would begin.

By now, Fernandez had figured out the plan. While he wasn't really worried about himself, he was concerned about Eva being in the room with a couple of junior killers. He proceeded to walk back into the living room but first he grabbed a nearby remote control and gently touched his own weapon to reassure himself.

Eva was beginning to feel increasingly uncomfortable. She noticed how the twins had strategically placed themselves on the opposite ends of the room so that she and Dominic were in the middle. Eva now was calculating how fast she would have to draw her gun to smoke both of these young punks.

"Sweetheart, can you please come here?" Fernandez called as he stood near the doorway leading into the living room. At that moment, Alejandro knew they were on to them. "It's now or never," Alejandro called out.

Alejandro reached behind his back and quickly pulled his 9mm. Gun. At the same time, Fernandez with a push of a button cut off all the lights in the suite. The twins were totally thrown off. Fernandez and Eva retreated backwards into the bar area.

Alejandro fired several shots at the door where Fernandez and Eva previously stood. Roberto had his gun out by now and had released several shots in Dominic's direction. One shot hit him in the stomach and the other in the chest. Dominic died instantly.

Throughout all of the gunplay and darkness, Alejandro and Roberto failed to realize their new set of circumstances. From within the den, Fernandez pushed assorted buttons to seal the twins off from them. This new scenario also prevented the twins from escaping.

*****

"Where the hell is everybody?" Jimmy wondered. He searched all over the grounds and saw no sign of Fernandez or the twins.

"Wait a minute," he thought, "There's no way the twins would try to kill Fernandez out here, that would be foolish. They must've some how taken him back in the house."

Jimmy started jogging back towards the house when all of a sudden it seemed he was greeted by a host of bright lights.

"This is the DEA. We want everyone to exit the mansion with their hands up," a voice from a bullhorn commanded. "You are completely surrounded and there is no way you can escape."

Jimmy then spotted the men dressed in black army fatigue outfits. They were all armed with automatic Guns. Grouped in columns of three, they surged towards the front gate.

Jimmy grabbed the U.K. 47 assault rifle from one of his armed guards and fired at the approaching agents. He hit two of them and brought them down. The war was now on.

*****

Cynthia waited nervously by the stairs on the second level. Her heart raced fiercely when she heard the shots fired from upstairs. Nevertheless, she maintained her composure as she struggled to stay calm. Moments later, she was overcome by bright lights that were coming in from outside. Cynthia peaked over the balcony to try to get a handle on the situation and saw a swarm of cops flooding the estate.

"What luck?" she thought. The cops planned a raid in the middle of the twin's plan to kill Fernandez. Surely, they couldn't have prepared themselves for this."

Cynthia decided she couldn't wait any longer. She planned to rush upstairs to get the twins the hell out of this mess. As she raced up to the third floor with her .45 automatic in hand, she heard the exchange of gunshots outside. This caused her to run even faster. As soon as she approached the last stairwell leading up to the third floor, a man with black shades and a sawed off shotgun by his side greeted her.

"Oh shit!" Cynthia exclaimed.

The Assassin raised the shotgun under his arm and fired. On pure instinct, Cynthia ducked before the first shot was released. She then dived to the floor and quickly crawled to a nearby dining room. The door slammed behind her and Cynthia found a comfortable spot under the large table.

Kaboom! A large crashing sound filled the air. The Assassin kicked in the door, almost knocking it off its hinges. At that moment, Cynthia wondered if the mahogany table was sufficient cover but realized it was her only alternative at the time. Cynthia fixed her gun on the floor as she waited for the opportunity to take a shot at her predator. The Assassin never entered. He stood silent and the only noises Cynthia heard were from outside.

Cynthia eyeballed her surroundings. Like most of the rooms in the mansion, it was huge. She sprung from under the table like a blossoming flower thinking that the Assassin had spared her life. Then it hit her, the main dining area had several entrances and her attacker was probably behind one of the other doors.

"He's only repositioning himself," Cynthia thought. "Which door will he choose?"

*****

"That was a silly thing to do. Fernandez's voice sounded loudly through a speaker into the twin's area. "Tell me, who sent you?"

"Nobody sent us," Roberto answered bravely.

"Fuckin' liars! There's no way two little punks like you would have enough balls to want to take me out alone."

Alejandro and Roberto scanned the room for a way out but they were trapped. Although they heard Fernandez's voice loud and clear, they could not see him. Roberto continued talking to Fernandez so that Alejandro, who was very familiar with the mansion, could focus on finding a way out. "There has to be a way for us to escape," Alejandro thought. "I just have to remember."

"Fernandez, It's about time that a bastard like you is finally taken out," Roberto said bravely. "Your days are numbered."

"Such bold words coming from a little nobody like you. I guess you have no idea how powerful I am," Fernandez said.

"Fuck power," Alejandro interrupted. "Before this night is over, we will have our revenge!"

"Revenge, what could I possibly have done to you two?" Fernandez found himself wondering about their motives.

"Do you remember Alex Sanchez?" Alejandro yelled.

"Ah yes, I remember that fuckin' lowlife."

"You had him killed!" Roberto said.

"I might have, but what does that have to do with you?"

"Fucking bastard, that was our father! You will pay for his death!" Alejandro screamed.

Fernandez covered the microphone. "I knew those twins reminded me of something or somebody I knew," he whispered to Eva. "It's that God damn Alex Sanchez. Fuck!"

He removed his hand from the microphone and directed his words at the twins.

"Well, it looks like history is going to repeat itself," Fernandez laughed. "But this time, instead of killing one Sanchez, I'll get to kill two."

"I wish that you would come out of that room, you little pussy," Alejandro shouted as he fired several shots at the door.

"Be careful for what you wish for because you just might get it," Fernandez warned.

After a couple of minutes passed, the door between the twins and Fernandez slid open.

*****

Jack was well respected by all of the men that worked for him because he led by example. Tonight was no exception. The army of agents followed Jack past the front gates. There was rapid gunfire and smoke erupting from the battlefield. Jack had his men cover all of the exits as he slowly headed towards the mansion.

The unorganized thugs didn't have a chance against well-trained officers of the DEA. One-by-one, members of the Fernandez Cartel were being taken out. Even though the weaponry on both sides was pretty evenly matched, the cops were more skilled and got better results.

Jimmy realized that the Cartel was fighting a losing battle, so he quickly summoned Raul and several other guys to knock out the lights throughout the estate. "My men won't be such easy targets in the dark," Jimmy thought.

Like trained dogs, Raul and his crew carried out Jimmy's orders to perfection. While Jack Lloyd and some of his men converged near the pool, the lights that were once shining so brightly on the estate began to vanish. Each bulb was shot out until the estate was nearly blackened. The only lights that remained were the ones by the poolside. Now Jack and his men were sitting ducks.

First, a man to Jack's right was gunned down. Then another one of his agents that was twenty feet behind him was hit. As Jack glanced over near the garage, he noticed Fernandez's men setting up two fully loaded M240 machine guns. With that type of armory he knew that he and his men didn't have a prayer. He wanted to retreat but was confused as to what he should do next. In the meantime, he and a couple of his men sought cover behind a bar that was set up by the pool.

It was now just a matter of time before the bar would give way to all of the firepower that was being thrust upon it. Jack only hoped that his other men were having better luck than he was.

"Jack I'm fucking hit!" An agent next to him yelled out.

"Hang in there buddy. I'll get you out of this alive," Jack said as he lifted the man by the shoulders and planned to make a run for it. He knew that once he made it passed the front gates, the guys manning that area would protect him. The problem was getting over there in one piece. As soon as he was about to go for it, he heard several large explosions. The last explosion was by the garage; the men firing Fernandez's's machine guns were now dead.

Jack looked back over his head and saw Bobby hobbling across the grass with another fifty men by his side.

"Hey buddy, I kinda thought you might need my help," Bobby called out as he threw another grenade at Jimmy's men.

"What are you doing here?" Jack asked.

"I wouldn't have missed this for the world."

“Jack wiped the sweat off of his forehead and was suddenly feeling re-energized. “What took you so long? You should’ve known that you would have to save my ass,” Jack said as he let out a sign of relief.

“Okay I’m here now, so let’s go kick some butt,” Bobby ordered. With Jack and Bobby leading the way, the new team advanced towards the mansion firing fiercely. It was the bloodiest battle that Jack had ever seen.

After realizing they were outnumbered and outgunned, Fernandez’s men finally began to surrender. The weapons were tossed outside and the men came out of their hiding places with their hands in the air.

“Would you look at that?” Bobby laughed as he directed his agents to confiscate their weapons and take the men into custody.

“This feels pretty good.”

“It’s still not over yet,” Jack reminded as he pointed at the mansion. Fernandez is still somewhere in there.”

“But not for long,” Bobby replied.

Suddenly one of Fernandez’s men came charging at the cops.

“Fuck all of you!” a voice called out. It was Jimmy. He had been hiding behind a large tree during the exchange of gunfire. He appeared with two automatic weapons blaring in each hand.

“Everybody get down!” Jack yelled. But it was too late. Several of the agents were already caught by Jimmy’s fury. Bobby hit the ground hard and remained motionless

# Chapter 30

Cynthia refused to go down without a fight. If her enemy wasn't coming to her, she was determined to find him. She chose to go through a door next to a small balcony that led to a kitchen. As she carefully made her way across the marble floors, she saw movement. Cynthia quickly fired several shots in that direction but the only thing she hit was a few pots that were hanging from cabinets and a not too happy refrigerator.

Although she was relieved by the false alarm, she knew the noise definitely revealed her whereabouts to the Assassin. Even worse, she still didn't know what had become of Alejandro and Roberto on the third floor. Cynthia darted through a door that she thought would lead her to the main hallway. As soon as she entered, she immediately knew that she had made the wrong move. The room was completely dark and the only thing she could make out was a large pool table. "Maybe this is some sort of recreation room," Cynthia figured. "I'm really in no mood to play games."

Cynthia began to search for the light switch by dragging her hands against the wall. "No luck," she whispered.

Cynthia couldn't locate the switch against the wall and prayed that her eyes would eventually adjust to the darkness.

She took a deep breath and raced towards the center of the room in hopes of grabbing the hanging light switch. Cynthia stepped on something that caused her to fall to the ground. She didn't see the white cue ball that someone had shot off the table hours earlier. As Cynthia hit the floor, she badly twisted her ankle.

More importantly, Cynthia's sudden fall saved her life. At the same time Cynthia tripped, the Assassin had fired a string of shots in Cynthia's direction. Large sounds echoed around her. By falling over the cue ball, Cynthia narrowly missed being hit by one of the shotgun's many pellets. Her life was spared.

Impulsively, Cynthia fired back at the Assassin. He scrambled towards the open door quite puzzled by the return shots since he assumed that Cynthia was dead.

*****

Jack returned fire as Jimmy raced to the mansion.

"Bobby, my man, say something to me!" he yelled as he huddled over to his friend. At first, Bobby barely moved. Then he attempted to sit up.

"Oh shit, this really hurts!" Bobby said as he grabbed at his leg.

Jack smiled widely, now that he realized his friend was going to be all right. "Motherfucker shot me in my bad leg," Bobby grumbled. "Get him."

They both watched Jimmy run towards the front door. Raul trailed closely behind him. It suddenly occurred to Jack that this was the same guy that he was running after a while ago when he and his men busted one of Fernandez's safe houses.

"Bobby I know it's that same guy that got away from us before!"

"Well Jack, you better do something now," Bobby instructed.

Jimmy knew he'd be saved if he could just make it inside. He knew that place better than anyone. Once inside, he could plan his escape. Jimmy and Raul reached the steps of the mansion when they were suddenly blinded by the shining lights, from the circling helicopter. Two men aimed their guns directly at them. Raul

Raul took it upon himself to act. He shielded his eyes with one hand and began firing his automatic weapon into the sky with his other hand. After blasting five or six shots, he was hit several times in the chest by return fire. He fell quickly to his death.

When Jimmy realized his companion's fate, he stood frozen. He glanced over at a bloody Raul and had no reaction. The men in the helicopter continued to hover over him.

"This is the DEA, don't move another inch!" Jack called out as he pointed his gun at Jimmy.

"Put down your weapon and drop to the ground!" Jack ordered.

"Jimmy heard those words but knew that he couldn't comply. In that brief moment, Jimmy reviewed the events of his life. "Maybe things would have turned out differently if my father had stuck around," Jimmy thought. "What a fucked up way to end it all."

He regretted that he would never marry or have kids. Who would really care about him once he was gone? Alejandro and Roberto were his only true friends. He forgave them for what they had done and believed they had a right to seek their revenge on Fernandez. Jimmy always knew that the twins were really good guys and wished they had never gotten caught up in this whole ordeal.

Jimmy glanced back down at Raul and wondered how long it would be before the cops would shoot him dead.

"Jimmy don't do it! It doesn't have to end this way. Just drop your weapon!" Jack yelled.

As he concentrated on the front door, Jimmy closed his eyes for a second and attempted to visualize how his death would feel because he knew he would soon find out.

Jimmy inhaled his last sweet bits of life and spun around with both weapons. "I'll die fighting motherfuckers!"

"He didn't even have a chance to fire a single shot. He was hit several times immediately in the middle of his chest and died instantly.

Jack walked over to Jimmy and looked him squarely in the face. He wanted to be sure that Jimmy Acosta was now dead.

*****

Fernandez escorted Eva quietly down the secret tiny staircases. He believed they had successfully averted the twins unharmed. As far as Fernandez knew, the chaos of the guns, drugs, and slew of dead bodies were far behind them.

As Fernandez walked ahead of Eva, he believed he could be content as he planned a future with the woman that he deeply loved.

"Come on Eva, we must hurry, "Fernandez said hurriedly.

"I am coming Sergio." Eva said as she labored down the steps.

"Once we go down underneath the house it will connect us to the drainage system. That will take us to the other side of the estate. "We're home free then," Fernandez cheered.

"Sergio, I don't think I can make it," Eva moaned. "Maybe you better go without me."

Fernandez walked back up some steps where he found Eva doubled over in pain.

"Eva what are you talking about? We're almost there."

"I'm so tired. I don't think I can do it," Eva sadly responded.

"What is the matter with you Eva? You are in great shape. Even better shape than I am," Fernandez laughed.

"Just go on Sergio! The twins may be coming soon."

"Those boys are still running around upstairs looking for us. They'll never find their way out," Fernandez said confidently. He then reached out and grabbed at Eva's hand in an attempt to pull her up.

"Darling I can't," Eva sighed.

"Well, if you're too tired to walk then get on my back. I'll carry you out of this hellhole."

She placed her arms over his shoulder and allowed herself to be lifted up. They made it down the remaining stairs but then Eva realized there was another long tunnel that remained.

"Sergio, please put me down," Eva whispered.

"Eva, but why? We have made it under the house. Now all we have to do is travel through the rest of the tunnel."

"Sergio please," she softly said.

When Fernandez laid Eva gently on the ground he was able to see her pale complexion shimmering in the light. Her eyes were weak and sickly looking. This did not resemble the woman that danced with him only a few hours earlier.

weak and sickly looking. This did not resemble the woman that danced with him only a few hours earlier.

"My dear, please listen to me. I can't go any further. You must make it without me," Eva said as she coughed up blood.

"Oh my God! Eva, what happened to you?" A very concerned Fernandez asked.

"Back at the house, I was hit by one of the bullets," she explained.

"But where?" as he frantically searched her body for the wound. Finally he discovered that her back was drenched with blood.

"I don't have much time left. So I just want to tell you that the past several weeks have been the happiest times of my life. Pretending to be your woman was a dream come true," she spoke softly as more blood poured from her lips.

"Eva, you are my woman. It just took me too long to realize how much you mean to me," Fernandez said as he kissed his dying woman on her forehead.

"I will take your words with me," Eva said weakly.

"Eva, please don't go. I feel like I've just found you."

"My love, kiss me one last time. Then promise me you will go," Eva demanded. "You still have so much life to live."

"Eva I will kiss you, but we will leave here together, somehow.

Fernandez leaned over and kissed Eva longingly on her lips. He pulled back to see her reaction, but there was none. Eva Santos was gone.

"No!" Fernandez cried out. "Not my Eva."

Fernandez looked up towards the sky and damned the Gods. He took off his jacket and placed it over Eva's face. Then he headed furiously back upstairs towards the twins.

"Nobody is going to take away my Eva and get away with it!"

When Fernandez reached the top of the stairs he entered the dark room like a mad man. Now he was determined to seek his revenge and nothing would stand in his way.

# Chapter 31

Cynthia was now alone in the dark room breathing heavily from her twisted ankle. Although Cynthia realized she was very fortunate this time, she knew she had to think of a plan to bring her assailant down before her luck ran out.

Cynthia changed her strategy and began thinking like a hunter, instead of the hunted. She quickly doubled back to where the action began. She found a side room near the main stairs and hid inside. "Why should I go to him?" Cynthia pondered. "He'll eventually come to me."

Now, Cynthia felt like she was in control of her own destiny. She scanned the hallway as she peaked through an opening in the slightly cracked door. From her location, she could see both ends of the hallway. She could also see the top of the staircase.

Her heart began to race when she realized the Assassin was headed towards her direction. "There he is," she whispered to herself.

"Just a little bit closer," she quietly whispered. In just a few steps she would be able to get a good, clean shot but suddenly he stopped in his tracks as if he sensed danger. As he stood in front of the main staircases, he was thinking about going downstairs.

Cynthia knew this might be her last chance to take him out, so as soon as he turned his back, she bolted from behind the door pulling the trigger. To Cynthia's surprise, no shots were fired. Her gun had jammed on her. When the Assassin saw the helpless look on Cynthia's face he understood what had occurred and attempted to aim his shotgun in her direction. Cynthia knew her only alternative was to try and knock the Assassin's gun from him.

She winced in pain as she tackled the Assassin to the ground before he shot off his shotgun. The two tumbled down the staircase. As they fell, Cynthia struggled to take possession of the shotgun but the Assassin refused to release his grip. Halfway down the stairs, the gun flew out of both of their grasps.

When they finally hit the bottom, they both laid still. Cynthia suffered a bruised eye and cut lip. The Assassin appeared to have a badly dislocated shoulder. She also noticed that his glasses flew off during the scuffle and his neck was contorted in a very unusual position. Cynthia concluded that it was probably broken. Determined to rise triumphantly, Cynthia used the banister to pull herself up as she looked at the injured Assassin.

Now that Cynthia believed she was free of the Assassin, she decided to go up to the third floor to rescue the twins. Like a bear on a mission to protect her young, Cynthia was deeply committed to bringing Roberto and Alejandro back alive.

"You bitch!" The Assassin uttered as he grabbed Cynthia's leg in an attempt to pull her down to the floor as she passed him."Get the hell off of me!" She yelled as she kicked at him furiously. With his remaining strength, the Assassin flung Cynthia to the bottom step. Simultaneously, the two warriors stood up and prepared for battle. The Assassin punched Cynthia in the face, sending her reeling towards the main entrance of the ballroom. He then raced over to her and began to drag her by her hair. Cynthia fought him with her arms and legs until he was forced to release his grip. She then grabbed a falling vase from a nearby table and smashed it over his head. Cynthia tried to run towards the stairs, but the Assassin, who had recovered quick grabbed her by the end of her dress. He threw her into a wall and was prepared to blast her with full-blown punches until he winced in pain. His right shoulder was throbbing. Cynthia used this pause as an opportunity to throw a blow of her own. The Assassin responded with a left hook so powerful that it sent her crashing to the floor. The Assassin was becoming impatient and wanted to end this fiasco. He extended both of his arms in an attempt to choke Cynthia to death when she quickly took hold of his right arm with both hands and began to twist it. He screamed in pain but Cynthia continued to apply pressure until she heard it snap. The Assassin fell to his knees as Cynthia released the dangling limb. She then shoved him to the ground and once again made a run for the stairs.

Cynthia could hear the Assassin cursing behind her. She looked back and saw him get up, his face spelled outraged. Cynthia grabbed the banister and began to pull herself up the steps faster than she ever had before.

"It's no use, I'm going to kill you!" The Assassin growled as he limped behind her. The Assassin quickened his pace in anticipation of Cynthia's imminent death. However, he suddenly noticed that his victim seemed to regain a new confidence. She was no longer scrambling for her life but planning to snuff him out. Although he originally thought she was running from him, he now realized that she was actually running towards something. Victor's displaced shotgun.

The Assassin accelerated his stride in an effort to obtain the shotgun before Cynthia did but that was impossible. When Cynthia finally reached her destination, she collapsed on the steps with the shotgun now beside her. She grabbed the gun and lifted it swiftly in the air. The Assassin, now only arms length away from her, attempted to snatch the weapon out of Cynthia's hands but it was too late. The shotgun went off in his face at point blank range. The Assassin went tumbling down the remaining stairs to his death.

*****

"Damn, we looked all over," Alejandro remarked in a frustrated tone. "It's as if he just disappeared."

"He's not even showing up on the TV monitors," Roberto observed.

"Now wait a minute. He's no ghost he has to be here somewhere. There are only two ways that he could have left,"

Alejandro explained. "Let's separate. I'll take one door and you take the other one."

"Alejandro, what if we still can't find him?" Roberto asked anxiously.

"If we still can't find him, we'll meet back here in two minutes and get the hell out of here."

"Sounds like a plan," Roberto agreed.

"Roberto, please be careful. Fernandez probably has something up his sleeve, we want to get out of this alive," Alejandro cautioned.

"Hey bro', you watch your back too. See ya in a little while.

The twins headed towards their assigned doors. Simultaneously, they turned around and wished each other well. They both let out a nervous laugh. As soon as they were out of each other's sight, they became extremely nervous.

Minutes later, a crazed Fernandez entered the empty room. There was a secret panel that the twins knew nothing about. Once inside, Fernandez began to pour himself a glass of his favorite liquor and downed it in one gulp. Then he poured himself another one as he checked out the TV monitors. Most of his men were dead while the others had been arrested.

"Sergio Fernandez, come out with your hands up," a voice called out on a bullhorn. "If you don't come out, we're coming in.

On the monitors, Fernandez noticed the DEA agents were gearing up to storm the house. With the flick of a few switches, he calmly detonated the urns on the back steps. The agents immediately retreated as they gasped for air.

"That should buy me enough time to find the twins," he thought.

Fernandez didn't have to look far for Alejandro and Roberto because the two minutes were up. Both were heading back to their meeting place as they had earlier agreed.

Fernandez took his last drink then threw the bottle crashing to the ground. Roberto heard the bottle breaking inside the room and stood outside quietly.

"Roberto, is that you?" Alejandro asked nervously from the opposite door. "Are you okay?"

Fernandez heard his voice and began firing shots in that direction. Alejandro dove for cover.

"Yeah Alejandro I'm here and I'm okay," Roberto yelled from the other side of the room. Fernandez then fired several shots in his direction.

"I am glad you're both here," Fernandez laughed. "Now you can die together!"

"Motherfucker it's you that's gonna die!" Alejandro screamed.

"Strange thing, that's exactly what your father told me."

"Fernandez, you should've died a long time ago," Roberto called out. "You're an evil man."

"Maybe that's true but it will surely take bigger men than you two to bring me down!"

Fernandez began to map out his strategy. He would take out one brother then the next. Fernandez walked slowly towards the first door.

"Roberto, what do you want to do now?" Alejandro asked helplessly.

"Alejandro, remember what we used to do when we played Cowboys and Indians back in Cuba?"

"Yes, I remember!" Alejandro responded with a new confidence.

"Well, lets do the same thing here!" Roberto suggested.

"Sounds good to me!" Alejandro agreed.

In the next few moments, the boys were completely silent. Fernandez began to ask himself. He wondered if the boys decided to avoid a confrontation and had moved to other areas in the house. And what was this Cowboy and Indian shit? Fernandez pondered over which door he should open first.

Alejandro and Roberto stood perfectly still as each tried to sense when the other one would strike. This was the tactic they used when they were smaller to defend themselves against neighborhood kids. It worked then but that was a game. This was for real.

With guns drawn, Alejandro and Roberto each shouted, "Now!" Only a microsecond difference from the other. The doors flung open and Fernandez suddenly found himself in the center of two armed men. He couldn't decide which twin to strike first and that delay proved to be costly. Alejandro shot Fernandez twice, hitting him on his right leg and left shoulder. Roberto shot Fernandez three times, twice in the chest and once in the abdomen.

In his final moments, Fernandez fired two shots from his gun. He hit one twin in the shoulder, then spun around and shot the other in the neck. The badly injured twin collapsed immediately and Fernandez intended to use his last bit of energy to finish him off. As Fernandez took aim, he was shot in the head, the bullet then exited from his forehead. The gun-battle was now over, Sergio Fernandez was dead.

"Come on, get up! Fernandez is dead and we have to get out of here," he cried as he rushed over to his brother. "Oh no!" What happened?"

One of the twins bent down to tend to his injured brother. He was covered with blood and twitching on the ground from the bullet to his neck.

"Don't worry. I will take care of you!" he said as he sobbed.

"Once we get out of here, it will be just like the good old days. Just you and me. We don't need anybody else. We just need each other."

The wounded twin's movement became less violent as he began to fade away. In his final breath, he tried to talk to his brother but he began choking in his own blood. Soon he just remained silent and just communicated to his brother through his eyes.

"I know, you don't have to say it. I love you too but you better not leave me," the twin said as he ripped off his shirt and placed it under his brother's head.

He didn't know whether to leave his brother to get help or remain by his brother's side. He decided to stay. He knelt down and placed his brother's head in his lap. As he looked down at his mirror image, he struggled to hold back the tears in his eyes.

"Come on, keep fighting. You're going to be the best man at my wedding and me in yours. If you leave me, I'll never be an uncle or anything. Come on damn it! Don't die on me, you're all I got left!" he cried.

"After all we've been through, I know you are not gonna leave me now. You remember when we were younger back in Cuba?" We used to get into all kinds of trouble. What about the races? I would always beat you, and you would get real mad," Trying desperately to block the opening that allowed the blood to gush out of his brother's neck, he continued to ramble on.

"You thought that you wouldn't like it in this country but you got used to it pretty fast. Look, when all of this is over, we are gonna take off and just relax someplace. The only thing you gotta do is get better. I will take care of everything else," he said while his fingers trembled through his brother's hair.

The dying brother tried to speak once again but gargled on his words. He struggled to keep his eyes open despite the blood that blinded him. After softly squeezing his brother's hand, a peaceful look emerged across his face. He looked up at his brother one last time and then closed his eyes forever.

"No!!"

Cynthia heard the initial gun shots now she heard the screams. She dragged herself down the long hallway in the direction of the noise. When she first entered the suite she was overcome by the smell of blood. As she continued further, she spotted Fernandez's corpse. Then she saw one twin lying dead on the floor and the other twin sitting motionless in an overstuffed chair.

"What happened in here?" Cynthia cried.

"We went after Fernandez and shot him, but before he died, he hit my brother," he said in an emotionless tone. "Now he's dead."

"I'm so sorry," Cynthia sobbed. Although she knew that this was the probable outcome, somehow an "I told you so" didn't seem appropriate.

Cynthia began to cry uncontrollably. She had grown very attached to the Sanchez boys. The lifeless body on the floor was more than she could take. In spite of her grief, Cynthia began to wonder about which twin had died. She didn't want to ask but she remembered that Roberto had a tattoo of a half heart on the back of his right shoulder. Alejandro did not.

Cynthia slowly walked over to console the twin sitting in the chair. His shirt was off, so it would be very easy to tell which one he was. She wanted to know, but she was also afraid to find out the truth. If it turned out that Roberto had died, she would be crushed because she was closer to him than his brother. On the other hand, Alejandro meant everything to Roberto. If Alejandro had died, where would that leave Roberto?

While the twin sat in his own little world, Cynthia circled to his back. When she spotted the half heart shaped tattoo, she knew this was Roberto. Alejandro was dead.

"Stand up Roberto, let me just hug you."

As the two stood hugging, ten agents stormed in the room brandishing heavy weapons. Jack Lloyd stood across from them in disbelief. His fiancé was standing before him in a blond wig, battered and beaten in the midst of dead men.

"Jack, please don't ask me any questions. Just get us the hell out of this place," Cynthia pleaded

# Chapter 32

TWO MONTHS LATER....................

Cynthia was in her garden tending to her flowers and plants. Cynthia and Jack just bought a new house and were getting married in just two months. Betty Hancock entered the garden for an afternoon visit.

"Cynthia the mailman just came by, here's your mail. After you finish reading it, please come inside. I have made you over a terrific lunch," her mom said smiling.

"Just a minute," Cynthia said as she removed her soiled gloves and anxiously opened the letter from Miami. This was the first letter she'd receive from Roberto since the incident at the mansion.

"Thank God, that's all over," Cynthia thought. "Now that Jack is retiring, maybe we can start leading a normal life."

What a stark contrast to all the violence Cynthia faced just a couple of months ago. But for the few physical scars that were still healing, Cynthia had found an inner peace that she had been searching for her entire life.

She had called Roberto several times, but he was always too busy to talk. He said it was because he was trying to relocate so that he could start a new life.
Although, Cynthia missed Roberto's friendship, she was glad that he was using his time wisely. She was also glad that Roberto had kept his promise to get out of the business.

*Dear Cynthia,*

*How are you? I am sorry that it has taken this long for me to write you, but I've been really busy. I am going to stay in Miami just a little bit longer than I originally planned. I am currently taking real estate courses and will be enrolled back in college soon. I'm also working at the local gym. They allow me to use the facility for my new exercise program. It's pretty cool.*

*I hope everything is going well for you in Baltimore. I miss you very much. Please thank Jack again for everything. I still think about Alejandro all the time but hopefully the pain will eventually subside.*

*Sincerely yours,*
*Roberto Sanchez*

*PS*

*Let's stay in touch because you're the only family that I have left now.*

After reading the letter, she immediately knew that something was very wrong. She stood up from where she had been seated and began to read it over again, but this time more slowly. It was as if someone had turned on a light in a dark cave, everything had become very clear to her.

Over the past two months, Cynthia had been very worried about Roberto. She had even considered going back soon to visit him to make sure that he was all right. The two times that she had gotten a hold of him, he had seemed very different, distant and cold. Cynthia thought this was due to the loss of his brother but she now realized that wasn't the case at all.

Now, everything made sense. This letter was very different from the other letters she'd receive from Roberto. This one had a completely different rhythm to it. The words didn't sound like Roberto at all. But the biggest concern she had was the omission of any reference to flowers and most notable violets. Roberto always joked that she would know his writings because of this. So if this was not Roberto writing her, it had to be Alejandro. And if that was the case, Roberto was dead. But why would Alejandro pretend to be his dead twin brother, it didn't make any sense.

At Fernandez's mansion, Cynthia made sure that she looked for Roberto's tattoo and had found it. Now she reasoned that Alejandro could have easily gotten the same tattoo. The real Roberto would have left Miami soon after his brother's death.

Cynthia wondered why Alejandro was still around when he knew what they had promised her. A feeling of betrayal suddenly overwhelmed her as she began to examine Alejandro's motives. The answer was clear. Now that Fernandez and Jimmy were dead, Alejandro could easily inherit the top spot in the drug scene.

"But that couldn't be. He knows how I feel about drugs and he knows I put my life on the line to save his butt. I warned them that if they ever went back on their words, they would have to deal with me and I meant it!"

There was only one thing she could do now.

Upstairs in her room, Cynthia shoved some clothes in a suitcase. A surprised Betty walked into the bedroom. "Cynthia where are you going?"

"Mom, I'm going back to Miami to take care of some unfinished business."

"I thought you took care of everything the last time you were there?" Betty asked nervously.

"I thought so too, but I was wrong. A friend made me a promise. He said he would get out of the drug business but he hasn't. Now, I have to do what I said I would do if they didn't get out," Cynthia responded.

"And what do I tell Jack when he comes home?" Betty asked.

"Tell him that I will be back in a couple of days and not to worry."

Cynthia grabbed her suitcase off of the bed and headed to the airport to catch the next flight to Miami.